I0583408

A Deadly Calm in Cedar Key

a novel by

Edward Braddy

Praise for <u>A Deadly Calm in Cedar Key</u>

"A gripping crime thriller with literary depth. The storm-torn Florida setting jumps off the page, while the fraught father-son relationship at its heart adds genuine emotional weight to the twists and turns. Thought-provoking, chilling, and impossible to put down—this is the kind of story that sticks with you long after the final page!"

Kristin McTiernan, author of *The Twitter Crush*

"It is hard to believe that this is Mr. Braddy's first novel. He grabbed my attention from the first paragraph and held it through the last. The author takes you on an exciting look at the flawed yet sympathetic character of a disgraced, aging lawman in the small village of Cedar Key on Florida's Gulf Coast, who returns from forced retirement to solve the murder of his best friend. This is a story that will take your breath, and your heart, and be well worth the investment of your time to read. I am already looking forward to his next book!"

Nick West, author of *Storm of the Century*

A DEADLY CALM IN CEDAR KEY
Copyright © 2026 Edward Braddy
All rights reserved. Printed in the United States of America.

ISBN (paperback): 979-8-9946724-6-4
ISBN (eBook): 979-8-9946724-0-2

This book is a work of fiction. People, places, events, and situations in this story are the product of the author's imagination, and any resemblances to actual persons, living or dead, or historical events, are entirely coincidental.

Cover designed by Juan Padrón at jcovers.com

No part of this book may be used or reproduced in any manner whatsoever without written permission by the author except in the case of brief quotations embodied in critical articles and reviews.

Acknowledgments

Although the idea for this book is uniquely mine, it came together with the help of many people. I want to first express my appreciation to my parents and children for their constant encouragement, and especially to my wife, Pauline, who endured many revisions, plot-tinkering, and talk-throughs with a gentle smile and loving patience. Gratitude is owed to Lindsey Lander, Jen Lynn Smith, and Gayle Jones, whose constructive feedback strengthened the story in numerous ways. A heartfelt thanks goes to Kristin McTiernan for her skilled editing and to Juan Padrón for the exceptional graphics and cover design. Finally, to you, the reader: Thank you for giving these characters a chance to find a place in your imagination.

Now, welcome to the story …

For Pauline

and our family

STAGE ONE — DISTURBANCE

A clustering of thunderstorms with slight but increasing wind circulation

Gliding above the sapphire water of the Caribbean Sea, a squadron of pelicans flew toward the sinking sun in a loose V-formation, twelve on the right and nine on the left. The Trade Winds pushed them along a westerly course beneath clear skies.

The Captain, old and weary, lifted his eyes from the undulating waves where only a few white caps crested. He couldn't see his island home, but he wasn't worried. He knew this route. He had flown it many times.

They had been in the air for almost an hour, and it would take at least that long to return to their colony. The Captain felt a pang of hunger. Soon it would be time for Last Feeding.

Shortly after sunrise, he had led his squadron east and then south, flying seventy feet above water until he spotted a large school of sailfin mollies. The pelicans dive-bombed the hapless prey again and again. Most of his fellows had eaten well, but a few fared poorly as the terrified fish scattered. Then the pelicans drifted in the current for a half-hour before he led them south to a sandbar where they rested. That had been First Feeding.

A grunt from behind, sharp and rattling, disrupted his peace, and the Captain lifted his eyes expecting to see land in the distance. Instead, he saw thunderheads, rounded and dark and wide on the horizon, and he noticed larger swells on the water and more frequent white caps.

Another grunt from the squadron, and it irritated him in the same way the treble hook caught in the pouch of his bill did. As with the hook, he could not do much about the rivals in his colony. The memory of an earlier meal would not satisfy their anticipation of the next one, and he was their captain for only as long as they had confidence that he could lead them to the ever-shifting feeding pools of the Caribbean.

It was the natural order of things. Beneath his gray-brown plumage were scars he had earned when he had toppled his colony's leader many years before. Since then he had gained other scars and even suffered an eye injury from challengers, but he had endured. He always endured.

The Captain issued a grunt of his own, one that said, "Forward." The course he was on would bring his squadron back to the southern tip of Cayo Avalos in time to hunt for shoaling mullet before sunset. Any delay, and they would miss Last Feeding.

Another half-hour and he felt the wind shift. He smelled rain. Lightning flashed. The wind coaxed the waves even higher, and the sea darkened as it rolled beneath white breakers. He had flown through storms before, and he knew the bad ones could be disorienting and send a squadron wildly off course. Other storms were so bad they had killed some of his fellows.

More lightning flashed, and he felt a vibration in the air as thunder roared its warning. The Captain sensed another disturbance, a new wind pushing in from the south. He hoped it was an errant gust, but after a few minutes, he knew that it, too, would not diminish. He looked again to the thunderheads. One mass was more distant than the other, but the gap between them was closing. He faced the threat of not one storm, but two.

Irritation gave way to worry. His desire to eat vanished before his will to survive. As a dozen lightning strikes singed the blackening sky, the Captain accelerated the beat of his wings and turned his squadron forty-five degrees north. He would lead them around the storm. Far around the storm. The moonrise would be his guide to bring his squadron safely back to the mangroves of Cayo Avalos.

They would miss Last Feeding, but they would live. As a chorus of thunder roared in the distance, his rivals hissed their displeasure.

— *Chapter 1* —

Jerry coasted the golf cart to a stop beside The Wayward Breeze, where a skinny man sat on a bench with a bag of ice on his ankle and a cigarette in his mouth.

"Are you alright, young man?"

The skinny man stared ahead.

"Looks like you might have hurt yourself," Jerry said pleasantly.

"No kidding."

Jerry got out of the golf cart. It was yellow with attractive cursive lettering that read, 'Cedar Key Hospitality'. A few cars were parallel-parked nearby, and he saw approaching headlights down by the pier. Most people had turned in for the night or were inside one of the half-dozen restaurants and bars along Dock Street. A middle-aged couple strolled arm-in-arm on the opposite sidewalk, and a stargazer leaned against the aluminum railing above water that gently lapped against the seawall.

Jerry grimaced at the broken sidewalk outside the restaurant—the likely cause of the young man's misfortune. He pulled a small notepad from his shirt pocket where he recorded various 'hazards to pedestrians', which is what he called them in his frequent updates to the Cedar Key Town Council. This one was already on his list.

"I've got compression wrap in my first aid kit that I'd be more than happy to give you. Let me have a look at that ankle."

The skinny man pulled his foot back and blew a stream of smoke in Jerry's direction. Unfazed, Jerry stooped for a closer look.

"There's quite a bit of swelling. Looks pretty bad."

"Well, it is." A woman holding a Styrofoam cup appeared at the door of the open-air restaurant and approached the two men. "But he just wanted to ice it."

Jerry smiled. "Good evening, Charlene."

Charlene handed the skinny stranger the drink. "Here, hon. Iced tea. On us."

"I hope business has been good tonight," Jerry said.

"'Bout the same," Charlene answered as she pulled a cigarette out of what he could only guess was thin air since the tight cut-off jeans and skimpy tank top did not leave room to conceal a pack of cigarettes. "Can I get a light?" she asked the stranger.

The skinny man pulled a lighter from his shirt pocket.

"I didn't get your name, fella," Jerry said.

"I didn't give it."

"Look, mister, I don't mean to be brash. I was going to suggest you ride with me over to the fire department. The health clinic is closed, but those boys over there can give your ankle a good look."

"Like I told the lady, I just want to rest it a bit, and then I'll be on my way."

Charlene arched an eyebrow. "On your way where, hon?"

The stranger looked left and right down the sidewalk, as if making sure no one else would hear him say something he wasn't supposed to reveal. He gave the waitress a hopeful look. It was the first time he had made eye contact with either of them. "Mermaid's Cove," he said.

Charlene's voice took on a sultry quality. "Oh, those are some cute cottages. I thought they were closed."

"They had been closed," Jerry said. "Guess not anymore." He turned back to the stranger. "That's quite a walk for someone with a bad ankle. Anyone picking you up?"

"No. I was just grabbing some dinner and taking it back to my room." He nodded at the containers stacked in a plastic bag at his side, then winked at Charlene. "One of the back units by the water."

"You must be awful lonely back there by yourself," she purred.

Jerry cleared his throat. He knew Charlene flirted sometimes just to prove to herself that she was still desirable, but her insecurity had no justification since plenty of men constantly pursued the twenty-nine-year-old waitress.

"I hope you got the grouper," he said, changing subjects.

Charlene answered for the stranger. "Cheeseburgers."

Jerry chuckled. "My grandchildren are the same way when they visit. A town with the freshest seafood, and what do those young'uns order? Cheeseburgers or chicken fingers." To his satisfaction, he saw the skinny man smile. So, Jerry made his pitch. "I can run you over to your cottage. Be more than happy to."

"I told you already. Not interested."

"Okay, friend. Have a nice evening."

Jerry got back in his golf cart and puttered down the road, disappointed less in the skinny man's rudeness than in the lingering stink of the cigarettes. He couldn't help but smile, however, when he heard Charlene say just before he got out of earshot, "He only wanted to help, you jackass."

Jerry circled the marina and paused to chat with the middle-aged folks he had seen earlier. A nice couple from up north, they were staying in one of the hotels for a couple of days while checking out some condominiums as a potential investment. He then drove to the pier and got out, pausing to appreciate the salty breeze. A few anglers were trying their luck on the outgoing tide, and he wasn't surprised to see Kemper McRae settled into a folding chair, line in the water, and Julep at his side.

"Got a good moon tonight," Jerry observed as he scratched the dog's head.

"It's decent."

"Caught anything?"

"Trout."

"Any keepers?"

"Nah."

Kemper had a deep, gravelly voice, but he didn't use it much.

The dog leaned into Jerry's leg, appreciating the scratches. Part Labrador and part hound, he sported a blue and white ticked coat.

"How's the Twice the Ice business?" Jerry asked, referring to the vending machines Kemper owned along Florida's Big Bend coast.

Kemper tipped a can of beer underneath his thick gray mustache. "Cold. Ice is cold."

Jerry gazed beyond the pier. The silhouettes of Seahorse and Snake Keys floated atop calm waters. A lone sandhill crane flew toward its roost on Atsena-Otie Key. He never tired of this place.

They talked for a few more minutes, mostly about trucks that had pulled through town and the boats they towed. Jerry had a Chevy and Kemper drove a Ford, so their rivalry was both friendly and serious.

"Well, I'll make one more round before calling it a night. Anything you need?"

Kemper lifted a plastic cup and spat a stream of tobacco juice in it. "I'm good."

Jerry scratched Julep once more and returned to his golf cart.

He and his wife had retired to this quaint town on Florida's Gulf Coast and lived a comfortable life until Betsy got the cancer. First, it took their savings, then it took their home, and finally, it took Betsy. That was seven years ago.

The widower had withdrawn from the community and lived in an unkempt single-wide trailer when the police chief showed up for a wellness check, along with the pastor of the church that he and his wife had attended back in better days. They convinced him he could honor his wife's memory by re-committing himself to the town she so dearly loved. So, Jerry joined the Citizens Auxiliary Patrol, established by the Cedar Key Police Department and the local Chamber of Commerce. He took to it with passion.

Now the seventy-four-year-old widower was a reliable fixture around town, his snowy white hair and wrinkled face in the bright yellow golf cart, offering directions, information, or just friendly conversation to tourists and locals alike.

He was about to return to the Chamber parking lot when he thought about the injured man who would be hobbling back to Mermaid's Cove by now, and that is why the yellow golf cart puttered past the parking lot and onto the main road heading out of town.

A quarter mile later, he saw the man limping on the side of the road with a plastic bag in one hand and a Styrofoam cup in the other. With no vehicles coming or going, Jerry coasted alongside the stranger. "Now I insist you ride with me," he said firmly.

Skinny Man stopped, his breathing labored. Without saying a word, he stepped into the golf cart. A few minutes later, Jerry pulled up to the partially lit sign for Mermaid's Cove.

"I'd recommend you put some more ice on that ankle first thing in the morning," Jerry said as he shooed away a swarm of mosquitoes.

"Yeah, I will." Skinny Man got out of the golf cart. He reached into his front pocket and pulled out some crumpled dollar bills.

"Don't even think about it," Jerry said with a broad smile. "Happy to help."

Skinny Man grabbed the drink and plastic bag. "Okay, thanks."

Jerry added a nod. "And if you're in town tomorrow, try the grouper."

"Sure," Skinny Man said as he walked away, tossing a 'take care' over his shoulder.

Some clouds had moved in front of the moon, and Jerry watched the man limp past the office building and into the darkness of a property covered by a thick tree canopy. He started back to town but braked after a hundred yards, turned the golf cart around and sped back to the cottages. He parked next to the sign, sprayed mosquito repellent on his neck and arms, and retrieved a roll of compression tape from his first aid kit. Jerry took pride in going that extra mile.

He stepped gingerly onto the uneven ground where the paved path ended at the manager's office and walked to the back of the property where two cottages stood near the water's edge.

Skinny Man stood in front of one of the cottages. A big bearded man stood in the doorway, the light from inside spilling out around him. He held a crowbar in one hand and furiously scratched the side of his face with the other.

"I told you it wasn't my fault," Jerry heard Skinny Man say.

Bearded Man's voice was quick and agitated. "I figured you'd done got picked up, man. I was, like, getting ready to bail."

"Like I said, I hurt my foot and had to rest it for a while. No big deal." Skinny Man held up the plastic bag. "Look, I got us some food."

Bearded Man reared back with the crowbar before realizing the bag did not pose a threat. "Don't want it, man. I done got my fix for the night." He resumed scratching.

Jerry instantly felt queasy and light headed. He did not want to be in this situation, so he turned to walk back to his golf cart but stumbled on the uneven ground, lost his balance, and fell with a grunt. Dizzy and winded, he lay on the grass for a moment and did a quick self-assessment. No sharp pains to indicate injury. He began pushing himself off the ground when a cold, blunt object pressed hard into his shoulder. Jerry rolled over on his back.

Bearded Man towered over him pointing the crowbar in his face. Skinny Man limped up beside him, still holding his drink and bag of food.

"Who the hell are you?" Bearded Man said. Jerry stared at him, unable to find his voice.

"That's the dude who drove me here," Skinny Man said.

"Drove you here?" Bearded Man sounded nervous, and he spoke rapidly. "Why would he do that? Is he your friend now? He must be police."

"No, he's not."

"You're going to get us busted, man."

"I hurt my ankle. He gave me a ride, that's all."

The skinny man's words reminded Jerry why he was there. This was just a misunderstanding. He would show them he had not meant to intrude, so he forced a smile and held up the compression tape.

There was no time to react as Bearded Man wheeled the crowbar and slammed it down on Jerry's forearm. Skin split and bone broke, but the pain did not arrive for another moment. Then it seared through his arm, and Jerry stared in horror at his shattered forearm that dangled below the elbow. His mouth stretched open, but no sound came. Just a silent scream.

"No!" Skinny Man protested, but it was too late.

"Why's he here, P? Why's he here?"

Skinny Man reached down and picked up the compression tape. "He just wanted to help."

"Help? No way, man. No way."

Jerry rolled on the ground, holding his arm to his chest. His voice returned, and he released a deep, guttural wail.

Skinny Man's voice quailed with panic. "Oh, this is bad. What do we do?"

"We get out of here. And we don't bring no help."

Bearded Man lifted the crowbar again and slammed it on Jerry's head. The already agonizing pain Jerry felt exploded as his cranium cracked. The crowbar fell again. And again. Blood sheeted his face. His whole body shuddered, the disorienting pain increasing and spreading with each blow. But when Bearded Man brought down the crowbar a final time, Jerry felt nothing. The pain had fled, replaced with a warming numbness that quickened from his face to his chest, down his arms and legs to his fingers and toes. Although his eyes were open, the two strangers faded away and were replaced with darkness. Blessed darkness.

Then Jerry saw a light, small at first but larger as it came near, and in the light, he saw the joyous face of his dear wife Betsy. She was as beautiful as he had ever seen her.

— *Chapter 2* —

The body lay on the dock by the Channel Number Four boat ramp, a yellow rain poncho covering its head and torso.

The poncho belonged to Jeff Hammond. He and his brother, Randy, had launched their Carolina Skiff at first light to stalk the redfish around the oyster bars. They had just cleared the bridge when they spotted the body and an overturned golf cart partially submerged in the muck.

With reddened eyes on a hangdog face and clothes covered in mud, Jeff knelt beside the body. Randy took slow draws from his thermos and stared vacantly to where the sun peeked above a distant tree line like a reluctant witness to an unspeakable horror.

Doyle McKinney approached the dock. The blue lights of his patrol car pulsated behind him. "Got the call. Appreciate it," he said awkwardly.

"It's Jerry," Randy said, no further identifier necessary.

The police officer pulled back the poncho to perform a visual check. The head was swollen and distorted, the skull broken, and the eyes had been violated by a hungry crab or some other aquatic creature, but there was no mistaking the face. It was Jerry.

Doyle removed his hat and ran a hand through thinning hair as he considered his next steps. He needed to secure the crime scene, but it was in the channel on the other side of the bridge. Even with a rising tide, it would be difficult to access the site and collect any useful evidence.

"Probably should have left the body where you found it," he said to the brothers.

"Didn't seem right," Jeff said.

"No, I reckon it didn't."

Two other anglers walked up, their truck and trailered boat parked where the access road curved downward off the main road.

"Anything we can do, Doyle?" one asked. They all knew each other and preferred first names over titles like Officer or Lieutenant—such is the way in small towns.

"No," Doyle said before changing his mind. "On second thought, can you keep other folks from pulling in here? It's going to get crowded with official business pretty soon."

As if on cue, a siren signaled the arrival of Cedar Key's only fire engine. The volunteer firefighters were the town's first responders and had to visit the site even though there was no one to rescue.

The Chief of Police arrived a few minutes later. The insignia on the side of the Ford F-150 Police Responder matched the insignia on his Cedar Key Police Department baseball cap—the only indicator that Rylan McCrae belonged to law enforcement. He had been drinking coffee on his back porch and watching the clam boats launch when the call came in, and he rushed to the scene wearing blue jeans, boots, and a long-sleeved fishing shirt.

"What have we got?" he said.

"It's Jerry," Doyle replied. He pointed under the bridge. "That's where they found him."

Rylan paused to absorb the shock of learning the victim was a beloved member of the community. He looked at the two brothers who stared back at him with the hopeful trust people in traumatic situations instinctively give to authority figures. The police chief turned away.

A morning breeze pushed across the muddy marsh, bringing with it a dewy cleanliness that seemed strangely out of place. A splash drew his attention, and he turned to see a ripple by the nearby mangroves where a Great White Egret paused from its morning hunt to observe the commotion. Another splash showed where baitfish were being chased, and it reminded Rylan that death was common in Cedar Key just below the water's surface.

He took a deep breath and put on a stoic mask. "Any ideas?"

"Too soon to say," Doyle said. "If I had to guess, I'd say hit-and-run."

Rylan looked up at the bridge as he talked through the theory. "Golf cart on bridge…poor lighting…collision with vehicle…impact launches golf cart and victim over railing into the channel. Driver, too scared or drunk to notice, keeps going." He scratched the stubble on his chin. "It's possible."

He squatted by the body and lifted the poncho. "Dead on impact. Doubt he felt a thing," he said loud enough for the Hammond brothers to hear. He straightened up and faced Doyle. "Did you get statements from them?"

"Not yet." Doyle swore under his breath. He should have begun that already.

"And we need to close off the bridge and gather evidence."

Doyle swore again. The bridge connected Cedar Key with the mainland on the only road in and out, State Road 24. They were about to upset a lot of people.

"The county folks will be here soon," Rylan added, referring to the Levy County Sheriff's Office. Cedar Key was too small for a full-service law enforcement agency, so the county provided additional support as needed. "I'm going to look for the point of impact on the bridge, see if there's any evidence lying around."

Rylan asked the first responders to stay with the body and started up the access road. He resisted the urge to pull a cigarette from his shirt pocket as he walked up the incline. He was trying to quit or at least cut back. Plus, it was not the image he wanted to project, and he had been increasingly concerned about his image.

"How 'bout one of you run down to the Quik Stop and get us some biscuits," Rylan said as he approached the two anglers waving off traffic. "Folks will be arriving on empty stomachs. A dozen'll do. Sausage and egg. Some plain."

"Sure thing."

Rylan reached into an empty back pocket for a wallet he had left at home. "Tell Mama Thighs I'll come by this afternoon and pay up."

He continued toward the bridge, thinking about procedures and protocols. Rylan had not seen many hit-and-runs in his three years as Cedar Key's police chief, and none of those had resulted in death. In fact, unnatural deaths were extremely rare in this quiet town of seven hundred.

Despite the situation, Rylan felt confident. His police department was small but well-trained. He would get to the bottom of this tragedy. He looked up, and another feeling—a feeling of pride—swept over him as he saw his own face on a campaign sign planted on the other side of the road. The sign read, 'Rylan McRae for Levy County Sheriff'.

A low, gurgling growl came from the island side of the bridge, and he knew a big truck would soon come into view. The police chief swore and turned around to head back to the dock. He was not about to let his investigation go off the rails before it even began.

The truck slowed and turned onto the access road. It belonged to Kemper McRae, Rylan's father, and the morning was about to go from bad to worse.

Kemper stepped off the running board on his Ford F-350 Super Duty Platinum. Tall and lanky with a square jaw under a cowboy hat, he wore enough muscle on his frame to hold his own in a fight, not that he got into many. In fact, the last one was six years ago, and it was not much of a fight even though it had ended his career as Cedar Key Police Chief—the position his son now held.

He strode over to the dock. One of the volunteer firefighters pulled back the poncho. Kemper stared at Jerry's lifeless face and mangled eyes for more than a minute. His mind turned to that day when he and the preacher had dropped in on Jerry alone in his trailer, despondent over the loss of his wife and talking about not wanting to live anymore. Kemper thought of Jerry's remarkable turnaround, becoming a pillar of the community even as his own pillar crumbled.

"Figured you'd be in the creeks this morning," Rylan said as he approached the dock.

"You figured wrong."

"I planned to call you once I got this going. It'll get busy, you know. How'd you hear about it?"

Kemper didn't answer. Instead, he looked back at the body.

"Kemp, this here's a crime scene." That's how Rylan addressed him. Not Dad or Pops or even Father with all its built-in tension. Just Kemp. "We can't let just anyone on site."

"I ain't just anyone."

"Look, I don't want a scene."

"Then don't cause one."

Rylan swore and stepped away. He saw Doyle leaning into his cruiser and talking on the CAD radio, probably coordinating with the marine unit to get a boat up the channel.

Kemper stared at the water. Channel Number Four. Some places had cute or clever names for their landmarks and natural features, but the town fathers of long ago were not so pretentious here. So, the fourth channel that cut through the small islands collectively known as Cedar Key was simply called Channel Number Four.

He saw the golf cart in the muck on the other side of the bridge. The tide would peak soon and begin its slow retreat, but much of the vehicle was already exposed. The Hammond brothers were still on the dock and seemed to be looking at the same thing.

"Did you boys find Jerry?" Kemper asked.

"Yes, sir," Randy answered.

"That's something no one should have to face, but it looks like you two handled it right."

"Thank you, sir."

"We'll figure this out. I promise."

"Yes, sir."

"How's your mom and dad?"

"They're doing good."

"I saw where your daddy won that flats tournament up in Steinhatchee."

"Yes, sir, he did."

"Tell them I said hey."

"I will."

Rylan scowled. The police chief did not wear jealousy well. He figured Kemper would soon strike up a chat about hunting or fishing or some other such nonsense while they had a dead body lying between them. That was Kemper's style, or rather, that had been his style back when he had been the police chief—the simple but sincere conversation. That personal touch had made him a popular figure for many years.

Rylan adjusted the brim of his baseball cap and spat on the ground. Sure enough, the brothers did seem a little more at ease now, and what they had experienced was pretty awful. He should have offered words of comfort when he first arrived. He should have assured them the way his father had, even though his father had no damn right to be offering assurances of anything.

Rylan turned and barked orders to Doyle about staging the area for the county vehicles soon to arrive. With a sigh, he turned back to his father.

"—a six-point at fifty yards," a firefighter was saying in mid-conversation.

Kemper stroked his mustache. "Is that a fact? Thick cover in there."

"Yes, sir."

Kemper nodded. "Well, son, that takes some serious skill."

Rylan had had enough. "Listen, Kemp, you're a civilian. If you still had the badge, you wouldn't let friends of the deceased wander onto a crime scene. So, I'm asking you to leave. As soon as I learn more, I'll have Doyle call you."

"Why's the body here?" Kemper asked.

The question stumped Rylan. He knew it was a tactic to get under his skin. "Because he was killed right up there on that bridge."

"You sure about that?"

Rylan considered ignoring his father, but others were paying attention. He tried to project a cool demeanor. "I'm still piecing this together, but Doyle thinks it might have been a hit-and-run."

"You can rule that out," Kemper said.

"Just like that, huh?" Rylan shot back, his irritation rising.

"Jerry never came this far out. Never."

"We're just starting the investigation. We'll learn more once we pull that golf cart out of the water. And I want to get up on that bridge and look for evidence."

"Look at Jerry's head. If that's the result of a collision, then that golf cart would not be in one piece. Ain't no way."

Rylan chewed his lip before conceding the point. "I was beginning to think that, but for Christ's sake I just got here myself. I'm going to look at all possibilities before ruling things out. It's called being thorough."

"Did you rule out suicide?" Kemper's sarcasm was thick.

"What's your point?"

"It's as likely to be a suicide as it was a hit-and-run, which means it was neither. He was dumped here, but killed somewhere else."

"You got it all figured out, don't you?"

"No, but I got more of it figured out than you do. What you're doing now is wasting time."

"No, Kemp, me talking to you is wasting time."

Another stare-down followed before Doyle intervened. "Update for you, boss. Medical examiner and CID are on the way." He sighed. "The sheriff's coming too. She'll be here within the hour."

"She don't need to be here," Rylan said, almost spitting out the words.

"I know."

Rylan turned back to his father. "This place is about to get crowded. I'm asking you to let me do my job."

"Before you hand it over to the sheriff," Kemper said with a smirk.

"That ain't going to happen."

Kemper turned to the volunteer firefighters standing over Jerry's body. "I appreciate you fellas."

"Thank you, sir," they said as Kemper turned and headed back to his truck.

Rylan's shoulders slumped and he exhaled pent-up frustration as his father walked away from the scene. His relief was checked, however, by a twist in his stomach that questioned whether Kemper would actually walk away from the crime.

— *Chapter 3* —

Some people meditate or pray as a way of coping with unsettling events. Kemper McRae liked to drive his troubles away.

He turned his F-350 Super Duty off County Road 347 and entered a trail just wide enough for his truck. The tires bit deep into the sugar sand, and his body pressed into the leather seat as the vehicle gained traction and surged into the Florida scrub. His hands gripped a steering wheel that shuddered as the truck rumbled over uneven ground. This was the first sensation of escape.

The gurgling growl of the V8 Turbo Diesel engine reverberated off dense flora and created a dissonance that echoed inside the cab. Burning fuel mingled with salty air and pungent pine. These were the other sensations.

No other combination of smells, sounds, and vibrations could create this experience. The truck rolled down the trail, mauling small plants, sweeping against sago palms and saw palmetto, and chewing up turf in the Cedar Key Scrub State Reserve. Kemper did not give a damn.

Truck therapy is what Jerry had called it, but to Kemper, it was simply The Zone. Worries and regrets faded away in The Zone. Problems seemed smaller and burdens more manageable.

He stepped on the accelerator as he entered a hammock of oak, cypress, and slash pine. Shards of sunlight pierced the dense canopy and flashed inside the cab as he swept through the stand of trees. An opening a hundred yards ahead marked the end of his journey. He glanced at the dashboard long enough to see the speedometer reach fifty. With hardwood trunks inches away on either side, Kemper closed his eyes and began to count.

"One Suwannee one, two Suwannee two, three Suwannee three…"

When he reached five, he stood hard on the brakes and stiffened his arms to keep from being thrown into the steering column. Seventy-four hundred pounds of truck lurched violently to a halt. He waited a few moments before opening his eyes.

Dust enveloped everything. He let the engine gurgle its satisfaction until a quick wind snatched the dust away. Over the dash, he saw nothing but water. The truck perched on the edge of a sandy bluff overlooking a small bay that was impossible to access by boat.

Kemper got out of the truck and stepped off to see how far his front tires were from the sharp drop into the water. Eighteen inches. He should have counted slower. A half-dozen small creeks fed the bay. In the distance, an oyster bed broke through the waterline as the tide receded. The water was smooth. No tails broke the surface to show where redfish rummaged. A screech of gulls flew overhead.

Being alone in the clearing usually cleared his mind. This is where he came to terms with his troubles, where he made sense of the messy, complicated, and tragic world on the other side of The Zone.

Not this time.

Words formed in his mind, but he did not feel like speaking them aloud. *What the hell happened, Jerry?*

He replayed the previous evening in his head, including the brief conversation with his friend on the pier. Nothing stood out. He knew Jerry would have chatted with at least a dozen people, and a few of them might know of any unusual interactions.

His mind turned to Charlene. Jerry had a fatherly affection for the waitress whereas Kemper's feelings tracked in a different direction. Surely, Jerry would have talked to Charlene last night.

Then reality set in. There was not a damn thing he could do about it. He was on the outside looking in because he no longer wore the badge.

A feeling of helplessness swept over him, a sensation he rarely had and one he detested. It stirred a memory of a high school football game—Cedar Key's only playoff appearance. His team inches away from the winning touchdown with a few seconds left on the clock. A whistle blown. The star quarterback forced to the sidelines after his helmet was knocked off on the previous play. Watching as a nervous second-stringer fumbled the snap. Watching a different color jersey fall on the ball. Watching as time ran out before Kemper McRae could return to the field and save the day.

He spat in the dirt.

There was at least one thing he could do. He could tell Charlene before Rylan or Doyle showed up and shocked her with the news of Jerry's death.

He ran a finger under his lip and flicked the snuff tobacco into the water. Back at his truck, he pulled a half-empty pint of Jim Beam from under the seat and retrieved his handgun from the magnetic holster mounted under the steering wheel. He walked to the top of the bluff. The sun climbed in the late morning sky as barrels of clouds rolled in.

Kemper gulped down most of the bourbon but left one swallow. He held up the bottle and looked at the sun through the amber liquid. "Last one's yours, Jerry." He flung the bottle high and shattered it into a thousand pieces with a crack shot from his Smith & Wesson Magnum .44.

He looked out over the bay—a perfect blend of land, sky, and water. Kemper aimed at the oyster bed and unloaded the rest of the cylinder. Five shots, reckless and wasteful, yet it was the only substitute for his rage.

And Kemper had a problem with rage.

Twenty minutes later, he pulled his truck onto a lime rock road and drove it through a stand of pines a few miles east of Cedar Key. The road opened into an upland pasture where three manufactured homes sat in no particular pattern. Kemper veered his truck toward the one on the right. A yawning Charlene stepped out onto the redwood deck as Kemper pulled up next to her faded black Monte Carlo.

"I thought I heard you coming through the woods," she said as he exited the vehicle. Kemper's truck had an acoustic signature unlike any other.

"I need to tell you something," Kemper said as he joined her on the deck.

Suppressing another yawn, Charlene misread his expression. "You know I'm still with Tommy." A snug T-shirt revealed the generous contours of her ample bosom. Kemper stroked his mustache as he searched for the right words. His silence allowed her thoughts to continue in the wrong direction. She pulled at the ends of her hair. "I, uh, could be agreeable to a different arrangement."

Kemper sighed. *Just get it over with.* "Sit down there," he said, pointing to an aluminum chair rusty around the joints. "What I'm about to tell you is gonna hurt."

"Oh my." She remained standing.

"Jerry died last night."

Her eyes widened, and she quickly turned away. Her head dropped and her shoulders drooped. A few sniffles, a hand raised to wipe her nose, and then the crying began. Kemper moved closer and put a hand on her shoulder. She slammed a fist against the deck railing, turned, and fell into his arms, her head against his chest.

The next few minutes passed with nothing more than cries of 'no' and 'not Jerry' as she clung to Kemper for support.

"Did you see him last night?" he asked after Charlene composed herself enough to step back. But the tears continued to fall from her hazel eyes.

"Yes, of course. He stopped by to check on me like he always does."

"About what time?"

"I don't know. Ten, ten-thirty, maybe. He looked fine. He looked, you know, healthy. What was it? His heart?"

"No. He was killed."

"Killed?" Those words brought a second shock. She pulled a cigarette from a pack on the deck railing and sat on the chair that faced the open field. "Killed," she said again, taking a long drag.

Kemper sat in the matching chair with identical rust stains. "You want me to call your brother? See if he can come over? I know Jerry was—"

"Like a father to me. Hell, he was kinder to me and Wes than our daddy ever was, that's for sure. I loved that old man."

"He cared a lot about you, Charlene."

"He cared about you too, Kemp. Cared about all of us."

Kemper didn't acknowledge the comment. His mind was fixed on the face of his dead friend. The damage to his head could not have come from a single devastating blow, but multiple ones. Kemper hadn't done police work in a long time, but he was sure of this—it wasn't an accident.

"Somebody killed him. He was found this morning in the channel by the bridge. Rylan thinks it may have been a hit-and-run, but it wasn't. He was murdered."

Charlene took another long drag as she processed that bit of information. She exhaled the smoke and turned her eyes on Kemper. No more tears.

"I bet it was that weirdo I seen last night."

"What weirdo?"

Charlene then told Kemper all about the skinny man with the injured ankle.

— *Chapter 4* —

Paulie's ankle was still swollen. His head hurt, too. He had been thinking about everything that happened the night before, and that gave him a headache. The skinny man wasn't accustomed to thinking much, at least not the '*what if*' kind of thinking.

Chilling was more on his level. Chilling meant living without worry or hurry. He knew how to chill. Smoke a bowl and chill. Bang the burn into his veins and chill.

Work came before chilling, but he was okay with that because it wasn't difficult work. Driving down from Atlanta, obeying the speed limit—his boss insisted on that—and transferring product from the trunk of his vehicle to the blue rain barrels behind the meth house. That was work. After that, he could chill.

It was different this time.

Tank had gone along for the ride, and he had gotten messed up, so Paulie had to improvise and make decisions. And everything had gone to hell.

Paulie stood in front of the wide window of the meth house. He tried, again, to replay the events as if he could change the results if he could just figure out what he should have done differently. His focus failed. He looked out to where the worn path disappeared into the woods, expecting to see flashing lights and police vehicles, but all he saw was the sun baking the grass in the field that stretched between the house and the tree line.

The open field bothered him, clear and bright under the sun. Patches of purple and yellow wildflowers rippled in the breeze. It was beautiful while everything else around him was ugly and messy. His world was ugly and messy. It's what he preferred.

Thick oak boughs covered in lichens and draped with Spanish moss hung over the house, casting a dank shadow over the building. A rusted aluminum awning stretched unevenly to the rear. The cinder block house needed a pressure wash and fresh coat of paint, and it was as filthy on the inside as it was dirty on the outside. Dusty rooms. Carpet smeared with dirt and dried mud from people who had tracked it in from the grassless perimeter around the house. Empty cereal boxes, soda bottles, cigarette cartons, used needles, and zip bags were strewn all around. Dirty T-shirts, shorts, and jeans covered the floor and couches and tables. The toe-end of a sock fluttered on a rotating fan.

Upkeep was a low priority for the meth heads in the meth house.

And it wasn't really a meth house because no one there cooked methamphetamine. Mexico produced a better and cheaper product than anything coming out of a backwoods meth kitchen in Florida. Mexican Ice worked its way into big cities like Atlanta, where it was controlled and distributed by gangs. Those gangs had territories that stretched beyond city limits and even beyond state lines.

One of those territories for one of those gangs was the Big Bend region on Florida's Gulf Coast.

The operation was simple. Every week, Paulie drove a nondescript, recently serviced automobile, minding all traffic laws, down Interstate 75 from Atlanta to Gainesville, where he took State Road 24 to the meth house located a little east of Cedar Key and just off Federal Highway 98. Bags of Mexican Ice were taken from the vehicle and stored in rain barrels under the awning until local dealers came by to collect their cut. They turned over the cash from the previous week's run, and Paulie returned it to his boss, Full Stop Sylvia, while the dealers traveled north and south along Highway 98, selling meth to fritterheads and puddle junkies.

The Ninety-Eight was Sylvia King's most profitable territory and the only one with the potential for growth. Her gang was in decline, and she knew it. She controlled six corners in Atlanta, three hick towns on the Florida-Georgia line, and the Ninety-Eight. In the last year, she had lost two suburban territories outside Atlanta and been completely pushed out of the Macon and Tallahassee markets. A half-dozen of her slingers had been killed or disappeared, and a dozen more had switched to rival gangs. Tank, on Full Stop's orders, had made an example out of two of them for their betrayal.

Tank was an enforcer. Paulie hated him because Tank was paranoid and erratic and had a disturbing ease with violence. Enforcers were necessary in their line of work, but he wished it were otherwise. He wished everyone would just get high, relax, and chill.

That had not happened on this run.

Full Stop Sylvia had sent Tank on this trip with Paulie mostly to get him away from the double homicide, but she also wanted them to scout out a few sites along the Ninety-Eight to assess their potential as a home base in case her gang got pushed out of Atlanta.

Tank had other plans when he arrived at the meth house.

He had taken a bump from an old woman they all called Sweetie. She had been a nurse, and the meth house was her home until her dealer realized it was the perfect tucked-away place for regional distribution.

Sweetie handled the needles because she could reliably prick a vein, even a sunken one. This time, however, she missed. It wasn't her fault. Just as she pushed the plunger, Tank twitched in reaction to the screen door opening as two dealers walked in.

The spark that made the needle worth the sting failed to reach his brain. Instead, a searing burn shot through his arm. Tank flew out of the chair, punched Sweetie in the chest, and kicked her in the stomach. Then he punched and kicked Dewey—one of the dealers who was there to get his package and who had come to Sweetie's aid. After that, Tank picked up one of the broken televisions and hefted it against the wall.

The two dealers, whose sudden entrance had caused the errant injection, turned and fled through the door. Paulie, in the kitchen, pleaded for calm as the enforcer approached him, face reddened, eyes on a hammer that rested on the kitchen counter next to the burner phone. That's when the phone rang.

Tank paused, and they all stared at the phone, except for Sweetie and Dewey, who were unconscious. The phone connected Paulie to the dealers of the Ninety-Eight. He called them, not the other way around. The only other person who had the number was Full Stop Sylvia.

Paulie answered it. "Hey, what's up?"

"Making sure my boys got there alright."

"Yeah, we got here. We were, you know, doing some re-ups. They're coming in now. I was gonna call you in a few but, you know, we got busy."

"Lemme speak with T."

Paulie looked at Tank, grinding his teeth and scratching his beard. "Uh, he can't talk right now."

"What do you mean he can't talk right now? You better put his sorry ass on the phone."

"He ain't gonna make no sense."

"Ain't gonna make no sense? What the hell is going on, P?"

Paulie told her, and then he endured a string of expletives before Sylvia finally said, "Just get him out of there before he tears the place down. Or kills somebody."

So Paulie called Danny, a dealer who lived a few miles away. Paulie sometimes got high with Danny after work ended. Danny had not yet been by for his re-up, so Paulie offered to bring the package to him if Tank could crash at his place.

Danny said no.

"C'mon, D," Paulie pleaded. "Just for a few hours. Not even the whole night."

"Not a chance. You told me about this guy before."

Paulie remembered that Danny did part-time grounds work for a local inn. "What about them cottages? Them Mermaid cottages?"

"I don't have the keys."

"But you can get the keys. Remember, we chilled in one of them cottages a couple of months ago."

Danny paused as he tried to think of another excuse but came up blank. "Okay, fine. But he's gotta be quiet. Ain't nobody supposed to be there."

Paulie crinkled his nose as the pungent smell of cat shit brought him back to the present. He turned and looked for it, thinking it was probably behind one of the filthy couches or maybe under the coffee table. Wasn't his cat. Wasn't his problem.

He lit another cigarette and considered Sylvia's words. *Just get him out of there.* A simple order. Nothing about putting Tank in the cottages. Nothing about going into town for food and leaving him alone to get even higher on Danny's cut.

Paulie looked at his cigarette and wished it were a menthol like the ones the pretty waitress smoked. It might cover up the odor. Or maybe Full Stop would call and tell the meth heads to clean up the cat shit.

A snore drew his attention to a ratty couch against the wall where Tank slumbered, the fingers of one hand clawed into his beard. Small numbers were tattooed on the insides of his fingers. Paulie had once asked Tank what they represented. "Kills for the queen," Tank had said. Paulie could see flecks of blood in the beard and a dark brown blotch right in the middle of his T-shirt where Tank had pressed the old man's head when he dragged the body to the golf cart.

What disgusted Paulie the most was Tank's peaceful repose, as if some inner craving had been satiated by the killing. The drug runner wished he could smother him, or shoot him, or slit his throat. But Tank was the killer, not Paulie, so he would stand there and resent Full Stop's enforcer and all the chaos he had caused since yesterday.

Just get him out of there.

Paulie wanted to get himself out of there, but he needed to call his boss and tell her what had happened.

— *Chapter 5* —

Two full days had passed since Jerry's death, and Kemper had not heard anything from the Cedar Key Police Department despite Rylan's promise to send an officer over with an update. He looked at his phone. No missed calls. No calls at all, in fact.

He wanted to blame Rylan for his frustration, but he knew that was unfair. Kemper had left Charlene's place, gone home, and gotten drunk. The next morning, he had taken out his boat and did not return until well after sunset. Putting miles of water between him and his son was the only way Kemper could assure himself he would not interfere, so he did the same the following day, leaving early and returning late. The conditions had been favorable. He and Julep had fished the flats and the creeks and even some deep holes around fifteen miles offshore.

Kemper had hoped the itch to get involved in the investigation would go away, but it had not. Since being forced out as Cedar Key's police chief, he had worked hard to convince himself he didn't care. But he did, and now he had an intense desire to find Jerry's killer and bring him to justice.

He spent the morning cleaning his boats. In the afternoon, he worked on a fence line needing repair, yet his mind kept drifting back to the murder and Charlene's suspicions about the strange man with the injured ankle. Rylan or Doyle would have interviewed her by now. Maybe she hadn't told them all that she shared with him. Unlikely, but it was a way in, and that was all Kemper wanted.

His jaw tightened, and his pulse quickened. Kemper poured some Jim Beam on ice to take the edge off and listened to some Hank Williams Jr. as he got ready. He finished a second glass before heading into town, bottle in hand.

He drove first to Mermaid's Cove to check out a hunch. Charlene had told him the weirdo had stayed there the night Jerry was killed, but those cottages had been closed for several years. Next door was another inn, Pirate's Bay, with a similar layout. It was open for business. Maybe the stranger had been confused.

Kemper swigged from the bottle and took a pinch of tobacco before he exited the truck, then walked past the vacant manager's office to the back of the property. Dirty windows, cobwebs on door frames, and other signs of neglect convinced him that no one had stayed in these cottages in a long time. Overgrown hedges, clumps of tall grass, and fallen leaves scattered across the yard reinforced his belief.

He stopped before reaching the rear cottages. There was no crime tape on either door. *But what if there had been?* He had no authority to enter or do anything else. A pin-prick sting on his neck provided a reality check, and Kemper shooed away a mosquito. Disgusted, he spat on the ground and stared at the tobacco juice on the leaves, then he kicked some leaves to cover the spittle.

His eyes narrowed as he looked around. More leaves were gathered here than elsewhere even though he stood on one of the few spots that wasn't directly under a tree limb.

Kemper kicked more leaves, then stroked his mustache. "I'll be damned."

Ten minutes later, he pulled into the gravel lot behind City Hall and parked between a police golf cart and Rylan's truck. Nearby was another vehicle—a green and white Chevy Tahoe with 'Sheriff' emblazoned on its side in big bold letters.

City Hall faced Second Street and was surrounded by antique stores, restaurants, and an art gallery. Pedestrians—both tourists and locals alike—moved about in a casual, unhurried manner, befitting a small town like Cedar Key. Kemper entered through the back of the building, where the police department was located.

"Well, as I live and breathe!" A dainty little lady with a high, gray bun bounced out of her chair like she was starting a race. She crossed the room and threw her arms around Kemper before the door closed behind him. "It is so good to see you."

"Thanks for the call the other day."

Gladys lowered her chin as the happiness drained from her face. "I knew you would want to know about it right away. What a tragedy!"

"Now don't tell me Rylan makes you come in that early," Kemper said, lowering his voice to match hers.

"Of course not. I picked up the dispatch from my scanner at home, the one you got for me back when you were my chief." She looked at the police chief's door and then back at Kemper. "Your son is a good boss, I must say."

Kemper did not reply. He started toward the door.

"He's in a meeting," Gladys said. "I should let him know you're here."

"He'll know soon enough," Kemper said as he opened the door and went inside.

"Kemp—*jeez!*—can't you wait outside?"

"I've got a lead you need to know about."

Kemper turned to Angela Lane, who stood to greet him. "Sheriff," he said with a nod.

"I heard you were down by the dock," she said. "Sorry you had to get involved."

"He's not involved," Rylan snapped. "Kemp, I can speak with you once we wrap up, but as you can see, I'm meeting with the sheriff right now."

"About jurisdictional matters, I reckon."

"Your son seems to disagree with the interlocal agreement he signed just last year."

The interlocal agreement was a contract between local governments that enabled smaller agencies to utilize the resources of the county. Angela's countenance was confident. Rylan seemed on edge.

"It's not that simple," Rylan said. "I remain the chief law enforcement officer on any crime within city limits. No agreement changes that."

"Unless the county is contributing more than fifty percent in resources, as the agreement clearly states. Then I have operational control."

"But that hasn't been determined yet."

"Oh, c'mon!" Angela showed a flash of impatience but quickly caught herself. Two terms in office had taught her how to keep her cool in a confrontation, whether with a criminal or a colleague. She looked up at the clock on the wall. "If you're talking as of 4:47 p.m., then perhaps you've got a point. But, with what we're putting in, by this time tomorrow, the investigation will belong to the Sheriff's Office."

"I see what's going on," Kemper said, inserting himself into the discussion. "We don't get killings much in these parts, so you each see yourself slapping the cuffs on the perpetrator right before the good people of Levy County step into the voting booth."

Rylan looked offended. Angela's eyes narrowed.

Kemper continued. "This ain't about who's in charge of the investigation or which of you wins the sheriff's race. It's about finding Jerry's killer and bringing him to justice. You two seem more worried about the politics of it and who gets credit."

"No one's worried about who gets credit," the sheriff said firmly. "The chief's team and my team have been working together in good faith."

"And doing a damn fine job of it," Rylan added.

"The heads of two agencies meeting to discuss areas where there is a lack of clarity is exactly what we're supposed to do." She looked at Rylan. "But in this case, there is no lack of clarity."

Rylan started to object, but the sheriff lifted a hand to stop him as she turned her attention to his father. "I'm struggling to see how this concerns the guy whose job it is to keep our coolers filled with ice." Angela stood and approached him. Though a foot shorter than Kemper, her steely glare seemed to shrink him to a more manageable size. She sniffed. "You smell like whiskey."

Kemper replied with a smirk. "Bourbon."

"Bourbon. Pathetic. Just as it's pathetic for you to accuse me of playing politics because you know better. At least you used to know better. I do things by the book and with integrity." She poked him in the chest with a finger. "Always. Our interlocal agreement is like the one you used to sign, and we're going to follow that agreement to the letter."

"That's just process," Kemper said.

"But that will give us the best chance to find the person who killed Jerry and hold him accountable. That's how our system works." Her eyes softened, as they often did on the subject of Kemper McRae. She raised a hand to his shoulder. "I'm sorry about your friend."

She turned and faced Rylan. "I think we're done here, Chief. I'll leave you to your little family reunion."

"We're not done, Sheriff," Rylan said.

She reached the door, but turned and looked at Kemper. "What was that you said about a lead?"

It took a moment for Kemper to process the question. "I know where Jerry was killed."

"As in some place other than the bridge?"

"That's right."

"So it's not a hit-and-run like your police chief says?"

"I never said it was," Rylan objected. "I said it's possible."

"It ain't possible," Kemper said. "He was killed at Mermaid's Cove, and his body was moved to the bridge."

"How do you know?"

"Because I was the goddamn police chief here for twenty-four years, and I know a thing or two about police work!"

The sharp reaction showed the sheriff that Kemper still brooded over the earlier insult. "Both you boys take a breather," she ordered. This was the first bit of interesting information she had heard since the case opened. She chewed on a fingernail and looked down. "Tell me more."

"Charlene saw a guy. Some not-from-here acting strange the night Jerry was killed. He was staying at Mermaid's Cove, and earlier, Jerry had been talking to him, trying to give him a ride because the boy had hurt his foot."

"We've already interviewed Charlene," Rylan said. "Got a complete statement. And those cottages are empty. Closed down. They got a new owner, but they haven't reopened yet."

"The grounds," Kemper growled. "Did you search the grounds?"

Uncertainty shaded Rylan's face. "I'm not sure."

Angela fixed a withering glare on him. "This is exactly why we have the interlocal. Why didn't you tell me about this Charlene and those cottages?"

"Because my folks are on it."

"Your folks are still chasing down DUI leads, which was the point of this meeting until you got distracted on this jurisdictional issue. This is beginning to look like a misallocation of time and resources." Angela audibly exhaled. "Let's back up. Who is Charlene?"

"Just a waitress at the Breeze," Rylan said.

"She's like a daughter to Jerry," Kemper added.

"And what's she to you?" Rylan snapped.

Angela's eyes widened. "Whoa! I don't know what that's about, but—"

"We've got her statement," Rylan said, recovering his composure. "We can move on from her."

"Let's cut to the chase," Kemper said. "Jerry was killed at Mermaid's Cove. I went there and found the spot. Lot of leaves on the ground, but the blood is still in the soil."

Rylan shot out of his chair. "You went there? You can't just insert yourself into an investigation."

Kemper's moment had arrived. He squared his shoulders to his son. "I can if I'm part of it. I want in. You can give me a badge."

Rylan's eyes darted from Angela and back to Kemper. "We don't need your help, and I don't think your plea deal with the FDLE—"

"I want in," Kemper repeated. "This is important to me. I don't care how you do it, but let me be part of this."

A smug smile stretched across Rylan's face. "No."

While the two men stared at each other, Angela considered her options. Kemper was right about political calculation playing a role, but wrong about it being necessarily bad. Elections determined the people's interest, and voters had to choose between Angela and Rylan. The sheriff was proud of her record. Appointed by the governor to complete the last ten months of her boss's term after he had suffered a fatal heart attack, she won a narrow victory the following year and a resounding victory four years later.

Angela had confidence in her ability to do good police work, and she usually asserted her authority over crimes in the smaller municipalities to see them through. This simple hit-and-run case, however, was beginning to look more complicated.

She had been dealt a poor hand, for the odds of solving a crime worsened when the offender had a forty-eight-hour head start. Although she had an ace with the interlocal agreement, she no longer wanted to play that card. Not until she learned a little more.

"I'll contact CID and send my forensics guy over to the cottages," the sheriff said. "And I'll instruct them to work at your direction, Chief. For now."

Rylan's face showed more confusion than appreciation. He managed a 'thank you' as Angela left the room.

The police chief turned to his father, intending to declare the meeting over, but Kemper spoke first. "Dammit, son, I'm just angry at what's happened. I need to be a part of this."

"Well, you can't."

Rylan planned to rub more salt into the wound, but he paused. Kemper's eyes did not reflect anger, but pain. Although he did not have much sympathy for his father, Rylan had just received a good turn from the sheriff. Maybe a little kindness was in order. "You have every right to be angry, Kemp. And hurt. Jerry was a good friend to you and to this town. But let me do my job, and we'll get there. I promise."

Kemper sighed. "So there's nothing I can do on this?"

Rylan thought for a moment. "As a matter of fact, there is. I never got by the Quik Stop to pay for the biscuits the other day when we were on the dock. If you're going by—"

Kemper cut him off with a raised hand. "I'll take care of it."

— *Chapter 6* —

Kemper drove back to Mermaid's Cove and idled there until he saw the CID investigator arrive with a trio of technicians. He resisted the urge to get out and tell them what to do.

Truck in gear, Kemper pulled onto the road. When he reached the Quik Stop, he kept going, driving down Dock Street to the boat ramps where anglers put in and took out their vessels, rounding the marina and following the road as condos and apartments gave way to single-family homes. During this time, he pulled steadily from the bottle of bourbon he had brought from his house.

Kemper drank often but rarely got drunk. He did not like the loss of focus and lack of control that came with it. Getting drunk after learning of Jerry's death was an exception, not the rule, to his drinking habit. Beer on the boat, bourbon at home, and just enough to take him right up to the edge. Then he would ease off with a dip of snuff tobacco.

He could sense he was close to going over the edge, but he did not think he was there yet. Kemper figured he could make it home, feed his dog, and then let whatever happened happen. Maybe fish off the dock or stare at the ceiling or throw rocks at the moon.

Kemper was tempted to call Charlene and ask her to stop by when she got off work. That was another reason he hated getting drunk. It turned him into a selfish ass.

He had almost finished the bottle when he finally pulled into the Quik Stop. As soon as his unsteady legs hit the pavement, he knew he had slipped over the edge. His head felt like a bobber on the water. He considered getting back in his truck and going home, but it did not seem too difficult a task to go inside and pay for the biscuits, as Rylan had requested.

The Quik Stop stood on a small hill where State Road 24 curved toward the marina and became D Street. Its location and proximity to the channel gave it a unique feature—a steady breeze always welcomed the customers, no matter the conditions elsewhere.

Kemper closed his eyes and lingered by his truck to enjoy the refreshing wind in his face. Then he walked to the store and was met with a cool blast of air conditioning that hit him as he entered. A young woman at the front register greeted him with a toothy smile.

Also greeting him was a savory aroma, reminding him that he hadn't eaten anything since breakfast. He nodded at the cashier and walked to a part of the store with laminate wood flooring, four diner booths, and a sign hanging from the drop ceiling that read 'Mama Thighs's Kitchen'.

Cedar Key had several award-winning restaurants, but local folks hungry for Southern-style comfort food needed only to go to Mama Thighs's Kitchen. It was a hidden treasure, not that anyone tried to hide it from the out-of-towners. Tourists shopping for art or antiques simply wouldn't think to satisfy their appetites in a place that sold cigarettes, double A batteries, and other conveniences.

Mama Thighs sat on a round stool, fanning herself as she monitored a batch of chicken in the fryer. Something seemed different in her appearance, and it took a few moments for Kemper's brain to register it. Little red welts covered her neck and arms, and her cheeks seemed redder than usual.

"What happened to you?" he asked.

"Just some skeeter bites," she replied.

"You don't get skeeter bites around here. Not with this breeze." He smiled. "Were you out frolicking in the marsh again?"

The question was meant to be ironic. For as long as Kemper could remember, the extent of her travel was between the Quik Stop and her small block house about a hundred feet away.

"Just got bit," she said tersely. "Kept scratching them, and some got infected. Now what can I get you, Mr. McRae?"

"Couple drumsticks and some tater wedges. Oh, make that double wedges for my dog."

She rose and waddled to the table pans under the heat lamps. The same age as Rylan, Mama Thighs had lived in the community her entire life. She had given birth to her only child during her senior year of high school. It caused a mini-scandal not only because of her age but also because she was white and the father was black, and that kind of thing unnerved some people back then.

The father soon lost interest in her, and she lost interest in her figure. Instead of dropping postpartum weight, she packed more on. Most of it seemed to settle below her waist. When her son turned eight, a boy at his birthday party tried to get her attention but could not remember her name, only that she was the birthday boy's mother and that her legs were the biggest he had ever seen. He shouted, "Mama Thighs."

That got everyone's attention. She looked at the boy and then at her son and saw the hurt on his face, and that upset her far more than the insult. So, she laughed. Then the other boys laughed, and, finally, her son started laughing along with them. That made everything okay.

Then she did what picked-on people sometimes do when given cruel nicknames: She adopted the insult. That was fourteen years ago.

"You want anything else?" Mama Thighs asked Kemper.

"Yeah, I wanna pay Rylan's bill."

She moved unsteadily toward the counter with his order. "What bill?"

"The bill for the biscuits that morning they found Jerry."

The box slipped from her hand and fell face down on the floor. She stared at the spilled contents.

"That's alright," Kemper said, trying to lighten the mood. "I like a little dust and dirt seasoning."

"Lemme get you another box," she said, but she did not move. Mama Thighs stood there, slouched, face hanging low. Kemper could not tell if she murmured to herself or had difficulty breathing. A couple in a booth looked up but promptly resumed their dinner. Almost a minute passed before she returned to the food pans and prepared another box.

"That bill got paid," Mama Thighs said with a shaky voice as she handed Kemper his order. She seemed on the verge of tears. "Andy took care of it when he ordered the biscuits that morning."

Kemper understood her sadness. Jerry had been especially kind to her, refusing to use her nickname and always trying to lift her spirits. "I didn't mean to catch you off guard," he said. "Are you okay?"

"I'll be fine," she said.

She turned and headed toward the corner of the kitchen to retrieve a mop. Kemper returned to the front of the store.

"Is that all?" the cashier asked as she punched buttons on the register and smacked her bubblegum.

"Get me a can of Copenhagen." This bought Kemper a moment to focus his thoughts. Something was off, but his thinking was too foggy to put a finger on it. The cashier returned. Kemper dropped a twenty on the counter. "Mama Thighs sure got torn up by those mosquitoes. Did a swarm pass through here?"

"No, sir. No skeeters bit me, and I'm working the same shift as her." She provided change. "Poor thing won't stop scratching them either. Should've gone away by now, but she won't stop scratching and they keep festering up. Just makes them worse."

"She doing okay?"

"She ain't got a good system, you know, on account of her size. So little things get a lot worse for her. She was so sick from them bites, she went home right after she got the breakfasts made. We didn't have any dinners that evening."

"When? Last night?"

"No, sir. It was the day they found Jerry."

— *Chapter 7* —

Curiosity made Kemper return to the police department a few days later. In all his years as Chief of Police, he had never done what Rylan was set to do: host a press conference.

Kemper had issued press releases. The dozen hurricanes that made landfall in or around Cedar Key during his tenure warranted such notices of evacuation orders and safety protocols. But he had never held a press conference. The media market was too small. There were a few weekly print newspapers for the entire Big Bend region, and radio stations offered news updates but not news programming. The only daily newspaper and television stations were in Gainesville, sixty miles away, but the problems in small, rural towns were rarely their focus.

He wasn't sure that anyone would show other than the publisher of the *Cedar Key Beacon*, but to his surprise, he saw a crowd in the roped-off parking lot behind City Hall. The journalists were assigned chairs while a dozen or more people—a few of whom he recognized—stood around chatting with one another. They all stopped and stared as the F-350 Super Duty rolled by with its distinctive gurgling growl and vanity plate on the front bumper featuring the silhouette of a redfish with a cursive 'Kemper' stenciled inside.

Kemper parked at Pinner's Tackle & Gear Store at the corner of B Street and First Avenue. He popped in to let the owner know what he was doing.

"I thought I heard you pull up," Tommy said when he saw Kemper.

"Got to check on something around the corner."

"Rylan's news conference?"

"You heard?"

"Everyone has. Doyle dropped off a flyer this morning. Said Rylan wanted a big turnout."

"Seems off."

"You'd know, I reckon." Tommy started to come around the counter. "You got a minute?"

"Not really, but I can stop by after Rylan's show."

"Do that. I've got something for you."

Seeing the fishing merchandise inside the store made Kemper wish he were out on the water. A clear sky, light wind, and mild temperature conspired to deepen the desire. For a moment, he had second thoughts about going to the event, but he remembered Gladys's phone call earlier and her insistence that he attend.

He walked up as the press conference began. The lectern from City Hall had been positioned in front of the steps leading to the rear of the building, and Rylan's entire team of four sworn officers stood to one side looking sharp and somber in their uniforms. Gladys wore a dark blue dress that would pass for Sunday best, and she held a stack of papers. On the other side stood three of the town council's five members—the mayor, who owned a restaurant by the museum; a councilwoman, who worked as a pharmacist; and a councilman, who was a retired clam farmer.

The police chief came out of the building and walked to the lectern. Rylan was accompanied by four others whom Kemper recognized, having seen them in the pictures Jerry would show from his cell phone—pictures of a happy, smiling family. They were not smiling now.

Rylan cleared his throat and began. "About a week ago our community lost a dear friend, Jerry Whitmore. Jerry was a man everyone knew and loved, a man whose volunteer work helped hundreds and gave our town a reputation of friendliness. Standing beside me here are Jerry's daughter, her husband, and their two children, who have traveled down from Ohio to attend the Celebration of Life service tomorrow. They will return to Ohio with Jerry so that he may be laid to rest next to his beloved wife Betsy, who also enriched our community for many years."

He turned and looked at the family. "Jerry Whitmore was the heart and soul of the Cedar Key community." The police chief then offered a few anecdotes of Jerry's work with the Citizens Auxiliary Patrol.

Kemper shifted on his feet and looked around, uneasy with what he observed. Rylan's words were true enough, but the staging of the press conference seemed inappropriate. He wondered why his son would make such an effort, then he noticed that neither the sheriff nor anyone from her office was present.

"And he was taken from us in a senseless act of violence," Rylan said with a raised voice. "What was first thought to be a tragic, hit-and-run accident, we now know was something more sinister. Jerry was killed in an act of cold, calculated murder."

Amid a few gasps from the crowd, Kemper could see that Jerry's daughter was losing the battle to maintain her composure. Her husband placed a comforting arm around her shoulders. The two kids looked like they would rather be anywhere but here. Kemper felt the same way.

"I am committed to securing justice for the Whitmore family," Rylan said. "We have a sketch artist's rendering of the man we believe is responsible for this horrific crime."

Gladys took a step forward but stopped as Rylan continued.

"Cedar Key is a peaceful town of good and decent people, as are all the folks of Levy County. Someone came into our community and took one of our own from us, and until that"—Rylan paused as if the words had caught in his throat—"until that evildoer is brought to justice, I will not rest."

The elected officials and police officers began clapping, and soon everyone else joined in.

Except Kemper.

"Son of a bitch," he said softly. As he turned and walked away, he muttered another thought. "Ange is going to be pissed."

Kemper remembered that Tommy had something to give him, so he stepped back into the store. Tommy walked out of the back storage room holding a large three-by-four-foot picture frame. He set it down and leaned it against the checkout counter. "Well, Kemp, how was the press conference?"

"Over the top."

"You remember this?" Tommy said, changing subjects. He had served a few terms on the town council, including one stint as mayor. It left him with a feeling of disinterest that bordered on disgust anytime politics intruded on his sphere of influence.

He pointed to the frame, which held a detailed map of the coastline from Cedar Key to the Suwannee River. Hundreds of creeks marked the jagged coast, and dozens of red, white, and blue pushpins were scattered across the canvas. The script across the top read, 'Fishing For Justice With Chief McRae'. At the bottom was one more revealing: 'The Cedar Key Mystery Fishing Tournament'.

"We're making room for new inventory, and I found this collecting dust," Tommy said. "Thought you might like a memento."

"You can keep it," Kemper replied.

"You sure? There's a lot of good memories tied up in this map. And good works, too."

"Maybe. But I don't think I have any place to put it."

"In that big damn house of yours? You've got to be kidding me. Hell, hang it in your boathouse. It'd look great there."

Kemper stared at it without saying anything more.

"Well, I'm putting it in the back of your truck anyway. You can get rid of it if you want, but I hope you don't. It meant something to a lot of people, Kemp, and you should be proud of it."

Kemper didn't stop Tommy from placing the framed map in his truck bed, and he didn't thank him either. He got in his truck and drove away.

Julep leaped off the porch and trotted over to greet Kemper when he pulled onto the driveway. The dog wagged his tail excitedly when Kemper started walking toward the boathouse because that usually meant a fishing trip. Julep swiftly covered the length of the wooden dock, turned, and snapped a bark at Kemper.

"Not today, old boy," Kemper said when he caught up with him.

He entered the boathouse and leaned the picture frame against a live well. 'Fishing For Justice With Chief McRae'. He winced. Kemper had always hated the title. But it was his fault—at least that's what Tommy used to say. The mystery fishing tournament never would have happened had Kemper McRae not been both a good angler and an honest man.

Many locals considered Kemper and Tommy to be the two best fishermen in the Big Bend region. Consequently, both men fielded lots of questions about their tricks and tactics and, more importantly, the locations of their honey holes that produced so many trophy fish. While Tommy had no problem abiding by the fisherman's code of lying through his teeth to avoid revealing his top spots, Kemper felt uncomfortable deceiving the people he served, even if they should know better than to ask.

His solution was to tell the truth but in a cryptic manner. He began using law enforcement terms like *Trooper*, *Undercover*, and *Probable Cause* to designate his best spots. Evasive, to be sure, but not a lie.

When a local pointed to a picture hanging in Tommy's store and asked, "Where'd you catch that tarpon?", Kemper could honestly answer, "At the *Bomb Squad*," so named because the hookset had led to a massive blow-up on the water.

A curving creek where schools of redfish always seemed to hold was the *Academy*. *Interrogation* was where his baitcaster had a noisy conversation with a gator trout. The bait shops and bars buzzed with speculation. Where was *Duty?* Where was Kemper's *Hunch?*

Tommy saw an opportunity. His term as mayor was ending, and he wanted to leave his mark as a public official, so he started The Cedar Key Mystery Fishing Tournament, the mystery being Kemper's single best fishing spot of the season. The winner would be whoever came closest to guessing its location, as indicated by the pushpins on the canvas map. The grand prize was not just a trophy and name on a plaque, but also a half-day fishing trip with Chief McRae. Off-duty, of course.

"What do you want to call your top spot?" Tommy had asked.

Kemper thought about it and concluded that all the terms he used led inescapably to one thing: *Justice.*

It was quirky enough to work. The annual tournament became one of the most popular events in the Big Bend. Every year, the location of *Justice* changed because tides, currents, and winds changed the underwater contours of the flats and creeks, which affected fish behavior. Kemper studied a myriad of factors the way a high-roller studies racing forms, and he spent countless hours navigating the coastline.

Anyone stopping by Pinner's Tackle & Gear Store could purchase red, white, and blue pushpins for $5, $10, and $20 to stick on the map where they hoped Kemper's *Justice* might be found. Prizes were added for the biggest fish, the most fish, and for the elusive grand slam of catching four different species of game fish. Additional awards were available for women and junior anglers. Entry fees and sponsorships added to the fundraising totals, which would then go to local food banks and other charities.

Pleasant memories flooded back. The tournament had been a huge success and gave Kemper years of satisfaction. He had been at the height of his popularity, and he loved the tournament almost as much as he loved wearing the badge. It ended abruptly with his fall from grace. A brutal assault on a visitor, a plea deal following an investigation by the Florida Department of Law Enforcement, and it was all over.

Julep's whimpering brought Kemper back to the present. The dog rested with his head on his paws, eyes shifting from Kemper to the flats boat hanging in its harness.

"Why not?" Kemper said. He looked at the tide clock above his workstation. "A little fishing might do me a world of good."

— *Chapter 8* —

Paulie was driving back to the meth house, and he was not happy about it.

He should be in hiding, or at least back in Atlanta, chilling and gaming on his computer. Instead, he was on Interstate 75, cruise control set at sixty-nine, using the blinker whenever he changed lanes, and maintaining a safe distance from the car in front of him. He was a few miles north of his exit, and his anxiety was rising.

After what had happened last week with Tank and the old man, Paulie figured Full Stop Sylvia would be more cautious. That was the reputation she enjoyed, and that was why he was driving a boring Toyota Corolla and obeying all traffic laws.

"We got to keep it real on the Ninety-Eight," she had said when Paulie suggested they lay low for a few weeks. "We miss a run, someone else moves in."

"Let me switch territories," Paulie said. "Chris can do mine, and I'll—"

"No, P. The Ninety-Eight is you. The slingers all know you. I send down someone new, half the slingers get skittish."

"They get skittish when they see Tank."

"Tank ain't going. It's just you, P. Do the run, stay at the crib, and bring back the money. I need you on this."

That conversation had stayed in his head for most of the trip. He had tried to forget about it as he drove the four and a half hours from

Atlanta, but it was back on his mind as he took the Gainesville exit to State Road 24 that would lead him to Cedar Key.

Paulie pulled into the second gas station from the off-ramp. Even this part of the trip followed a plan to minimize risk. He paid at the pump with a prepaid Visa card purchased with cash from Walmart. This gas station had outside bathrooms, so surveillance cameras would not record his visit.

He used the restroom and came back to refill the gas tank. As he stood at the pump, Paulie closed his eyes and leaned his head back to enjoy the warm sun on his face. His conversation with Full Stop played out again, and this time he understood what bothered him.

I need you on this.

Sylvia King did not use words like *need*. She gave orders, not explanations, and she never pleaded with anyone to do anything. Coming from the gang's leader, *I need you* sounded strange. Like weakness.

A new model Mustang pulled up to the opposite gas pump, music spilling from the windows, and a young man got out of the driver's side and began to fill up. He was about Paulie's height and size and looked similar in age. A young woman, blond and thin, exited the passenger side. "Go Gators," she said with a giggle before heading into the store.

That's right, Paulie thought, this is Gainesville, home to the University of Florida, where the Gators play. College town. College students. Pretty boy with a pretty girlfriend, probably driving the car his daddy got him. A rich lawyer or rich doctor's son, no doubt.

Paulie had no rich daddy. He had a grandmother who had raised him in Cliftondale outside of Atlanta. She still lived there. He didn't visit much, but he sent her $1,000 every few weeks to help cover the cost of her meds. She once asked him what kind of job he had that paid so well. "Computers," he had said. "I design programs for computers."

He smiled. *And if Grams ever asks again, I'll tell her I learned computer programming at the University of Florida.*

The college girl returned with a twelve-pack of Miller Lite while Daddy's Boy finished filling up.

"How 'bout them Gators?" Paulie said.

She smiled and got in the Mustang.

Gas tank full, Paulie got in his Corolla. His mind turned back to the job. To the gang.

The gang did not have a mascot, nor did it have team meetings or strategic planning retreats. No whiteboards with weekly goals, no Zoom pep talks, and no slinger-of-the-month bonuses. He ran drugs, other people did other things, and Sylvia called the shots. That's how it worked. Follow the rules and stay cautious.

Yet going back to the Ninety-Eight so soon after a murder was not cautious. It was reckless or desperate, or both. He pulled the seatbelt across his body and heard the click as it locked. And something else clicked: the realization that he was expendable. If he got caught, he faced more than just trafficking charges. He would be held responsible for that old man's death.

Paulie braked and looked for oncoming traffic. Under the interstate overpass stood a college town full of young people his age, a whole other world where he could blend in and break free.

The drug runner idled on the side of the overpass where urban development gave way to rural Florida, to small towns where the vast majority of folks were decent, hard-working, and God-fearing. But the weaker ones had needs that Paulie satisfied with his weekly runs.

Paulie looked again under the overpass, tempted to turn in that direction. Then he thought about Sylvia. *I need you on this.* Maybe she would need him for more than just running drugs one day.

He pulled onto the road and drove to the meth house.

— *Chapter 9* —

Julep heard footsteps approaching the boathouse before Kemper did. He raised his ears and softly growled a warning. Kemper looked over the rim of his reading glasses.

"Be patient," he said.

The fishing trip after Rylan's press conference had been good for his soul. Determined to go again, Kemper checked the tide clock. Another hour of rising water was needed before he could float his boat.

"Be patient," he repeated, this time to himself.

Kemper sat at his workstation with fluorocarbon fishing line in one hand and braided line in the other, and he bit his bottom lip as he concentrated and joined the two lines with a uni-knot. A woman's voice startled him.

"Are you in there, Kemper?"

"Yes, I'm here," he replied, uncertain whether it was who he thought it was.

Sheriff Lane entered the boathouse. "I've been standing on your front porch for the last ten minutes, thinking you were a late riser."

Julep stood at attention, ears forward, eyes fixed on the unfamiliar face.

"It's alright, boy," Kemper said, lowering a hand to scratch his dog's head. "She's one of the good guys."

"My word, Kemper! And I thought your main house was impressive."

The boathouse was larger than it looked and more modern than its cedar shake exterior conveyed. Electric lifts held a twenty-six-foot bay boat and seventeen-foot flats boat above dual slips enclosed by retractable aluminum doors. A kitchenette had a sink, refrigerator, and two-burner stove, and a pump and generator station were in the corner next to a lean-to lavatory. Wicker chairs and a patio couch sat around a cypress coffee table in the center of the room. A decorative cast net stretched across the ceiling, and nautical artwork adorned the walls along with vintage fishing rods. The most startling feature, however, was the four-poster bed, neatly made and covered with a silky mosquito net. It was centered against a wide window overlooking the bay.

"If PJ ever kicks me out," Angela said, "I'm moving in here. This is quite the escape."

"How is your old man?" Kemper asked.

"Still driving that rig and fussing about it every chance he gets. Never turns down a job, though."

"He's a good man."

"That he is."

Between mounted speakers hung a framed map of the coastline, pushpins stuck all over its canvas. Angela squinted for a better look. "Is that from the fishing tournament you used to do?"

"It is."

"'Fishing for Justice with Chief McRae.' PJ loved that tournament."

"Runner-up one year, if I recall. Weight category."

"He was proud of that. Never found your mystery spot, though."

"Few ever did."

She raised a skeptical eyebrow. "Was there really a place called *Justice*, or did you make that up? And I'm a constitutional officer, so you better tell me the truth."

"I never lie about fishing."

"Never got into it myself. But real justice—that's my thing. It's an ideal, of course, and one we pursue imperfectly, but I wanted you to know we are pursuing justice for your friend. I hope you can see that."

"That's not my world anymore, now, is it? So you keep the concept. I'll fish the place. If you want to see what I call justice, grab a rod and get in the boat. I'll take you there."

Angela looked at the boats hanging above the slips. She didn't need to be an angler to know they each cost close to a hundred grand. "Are you worried a hurricane will destroy this place?"

"I set the pilings myself. They're steel and run deep. The frame is steel, too."

"Storm surge?"

Kemper leaned back and stroked his mustache. His prideful tone was as thick as his Southern accent. "Floaters will handle rising water. Might lose some of the dock, but she'll hold."

"When did you have time to do all this?"

His jaw hardened. "When I was no longer allowed to pursue your kind of justice."

He stood and set the fluorocarbon fishing spool in a cabinet. Other tools of the trade hung on pegboard behind his messy workstation, a stark contrast with the rest of the boathouse.

"I don't want you to take this the wrong way," Angela said, "but this has quite the woman's touch. Did Bee Bee do the decorations?"

A sullen expression washed over his face, and Angela knew she had broached a sensitive subject. Bee Bee stood for Brenda Belinda, who was either Kemper's ex-wife or estranged wife. Her departure from Cedar Key had coincided with Kemper's departure from the police department. A lot had happened then, blurring the befores and afters.

The dock extended another fifteen feet past the boathouse and ended in a perpendicular T. A large umbrella shaded a wooden rocker. "You like to fish off the dock?" she asked.

"Only when they're biting." Kemper wiped his hands with a rag and tossed it on the table. "Now, Sheriff, do you mind telling me what you're doing here?"

She bit her bottom lip and avoided eye contact. "I could use a cup of coffee."

He stood. "Let's go to the main house."

As they walked down the dock, Julep moped behind them. Fishing trip canceled.

"I reckon this is about Rylan's little stunt the other day," Kemper said.

"I'll admit I stewed on it over the weekend."

"Makes it harder to assert control without looking—"

"Petty? Yeah."

"Sheriff, this is a problem between the two of you. I don't have a badge anymore. My only concern is that this political bullshit is going to get in the way of—"

"Justice for Jerry."

"Are you going to finish all my sentences?" Kemper said, irritated.

They reached the shore and crossed the backyard in silence. After climbing the steps to the wraparound porch, they entered his house through the back.

"Politics is part of it," Angela said as Kemper poured water into the coffee pot. "But it's more than that. It's about who's best for the job and who's best for this case. I have more confidence in my ability than in Rylan's. Think about that DUI rabbit hole. That's bad decision-making. That's tunnel vision at the outset of an investigation."

"Fair point."

"You're damn right it's a fair point," Angela said, her voice rising. "And a big setback. Solving this crime is going to be a hell of a lot harder now that the police chief gave the perp a big head start."

"Look, Sheriff, I know how this works. You've got the authority with the interlocal agreement to put Rylan on the bench. Hell, you don't even need the agreement because you're a constitutional officer."

"It's a good tool to foster cooperation with intergovernmental agencies."

Kemper smirked. "Did you pull that out of some bureaucratic manual?"

"I do things by the book, Kemper. You know that."

The coffee machine belched. Kemper filled a mug and handed it to the sheriff. "Enforce the agreement. End the distraction."

She sighed. "After Friday's press conference, it's a little more complicated than that."

Kemper shook his head in disgust. "Damn shame Jerry chose to get murdered in the middle of an election."

"You know I'm going to beat your son."

"You know I don't care."

"What is it between you two?"

Kemper didn't reply. Instead, he poured himself a mug of coffee.

Angela didn't press him. She had arrived with a purpose, but a twist in her stomach and a tingling down her spine gave her pause.

Kemper's big house provided enough visual distractions to delay her decision. Knotty pine walls, leather furniture, high ceilings, a chandelier made from antlers. He had acquired this waterfront property in unusual circumstances around the time of the violent assault that cost him his badge. A plea deal with no admission of wrongdoing followed, along with a forced retirement and no more questions asked. That was the Big Bend way of letting an old cowboy ride off into the sunset.

"This is an amazing piece of property," she said while taking in an exquisite view of the Gulf through wide floor-to-ceiling windows. "I didn't know the ice business was so profitable."

"It ain't, but it throws off enough to fuel my boats and get my truck up and down the road."

"But not enough to pay for all this. Waterfront property. Boathouse. Two boats. A big truck with all the bells and whistles. Did you really need the vanity plate?"

"Where is this going, Sheriff?"

"You know I never thanked you for helping me get my start. I was talking to my staff attorney about you last night. You remember Bill Rogers? He reminded me that you had written a letter to the governor recommending my appointment."

"Quite a few folks did, as I recall."

"But not everyone took the governor fishing like you did back then."

"Back then," Kemper repeated with a smirk. "So is that why you're here? To say thanks?"

"I'm curious why you recommended an inexperienced young woman over some of those good ol' boys who were next in line."

"Seemed right."

She smiled at the lie. "No, it didn't."

Angela held the coffee mug beneath her chin, savoring the aroma. She was making Kemper uncomfortable, and she savored that too. "And a few years ago, you came out of hiding to attend my mother's funeral. I saw you in the back pew. That's another thing I never thanked you for."

"Just showing support for fellow law enforcement."

She smiled. "You knew my mother, didn't you?"

"Okay, Ange. My Southern hospitality has reached its end. I'd much rather be on the water with my dog than standing here playing whatever the hell game this is."

"It's not a game."

"Then what is it?"

"There are questions about you, Kemper—how things ended, what's happened since."

"From Bill Rogers?"

"More like FDLE."

Anger flashed in his eyes. "Some folks wanted my head, and I reckon they're pissed they didn't get it."

"But they got you out of law enforcement."

"They did."

"Do you miss it? I mean, you've done very well since. Running ice vending machines and living a high-dollar lifestyle. You care to tell me about it?"

"Don't see why I should."

Angela knew he would not elaborate, but she wanted something more—cashed out his pension, won a jackpot in Biloxi, inherited a bundle from a long-lost uncle. Anything to make sense of the personal fortune that coincided with his professional misfortune.

She began to doubt the decision she had made at church yesterday, which had brought her to Kemper's house this morning. The sermon had stirred in her a memory of her mother's last days in hospice, when she had pulled Angela close and whispered a secret that cast Kemper in a whole new light.

That her mother knew Kemper from high school was not shocking in itself. They were similar in age. She had been a cheerleader, and he had made a name for himself for his gridiron heroics. More shocking was hearing her mother speak of sneaking out of her house one night while her parents were asleep. Religion ran deep in Angela's family. Even as a teenager, her mother had earned a virtuous reputation for walking in faith, just as Angela had a generation later.

"I just wanted to break a rule," her mother had said from that hospice bed. "It was always so strict growing up. I wanted to do something crazy before I graduated. My friend convinced me to go with her to this place on the river where all the cool kids hung out. She wanted to meet a boy there, and I wanted to do something I wasn't allowed to do. So, I crawled out the window and ran down the block and got in her car. It was thrilling!"

The rest of the night had not been thrilling, but rather harrowing. Her friend abandoned her to ride off with the boy, leaving the naïve and nervous cheerleader alone. Well, not completely alone. Three men—dropouts with bad reputations—were there, and they were deep in the whiskey. From the way they gazed at her dark skin glistening in the moonlight and how they egged each other on, she didn't have to guess their intentions, only how long it would take before they acted on them.

But her mother's rule-breaking adventure ended more pleasantly with Kemper McRae returning her safely home in the early morning hours.

"I never forgot that night or what followed after," she had told Angela. "I thought about it a lot over the years, especially when times were bad. We had a hard life, your father and me. I hope returning to those memories didn't make me unfaithful to him in the eyes of the Lord."

Sitting in the pew with that conversation in mind, an idea had popped into Angela's head. An epiphany, she concluded, since it originated on church grounds. By early evening, she had worked out its logic, and she kept her staff attorney on the phone until he agreed that she could do what she wanted—even though he advised against it.

Now the sheriff felt a twist again in her stomach and knew it was her better judgment, born of instinct and experience, telling her to walk away. Her by-the-book approach to the job and the reputation she jealously guarded were at risk. Kemper was a wildcard, especially when his rage returned. It was not too late to thank him for the coffee and leave.

Stubbornness, however, prevailed.

"I know you want justice for your friend," Angela said, "but there's a right way and a wrong way to pursue it. I've dedicated myself to the right way."

"I'm not in the mood for lectures, Sheriff."

"I'm just checking boxes. Making sure nothing comes out that we don't already know in case someone was to take a closer look at you."

Kemper slammed his mug on the counter, coffee spilling over its rim. "Why the hell would someone want to take a closer look at me? Now, I've had enough of this. It's beginning to sound like I'm the goddamn suspect."

"You're not a suspect, Kemper," Angela said as she approached him. "Far from it."

"Then what's this about?"

"In Rylan's office, you said you wanted in. To be part of the investigation."

"That's right."

Sheriff Lane set her coffee down and fixed her steely eyes on his. She raised her right hand, palm out. "With the power vested in me, I hereby appoint you a Reserve Deputy of the Levy County Sheriff's Office."

"Y—you what?"

"Reserve Deputy."

"You're serious?"

"You're damn right, I'm serious. Effective as soon as you get to headquarters and complete the paperwork, so I can swear you in properly."

STAGE TWO — DEPRESSION

Disorganized winds circulate and intensify within the center of a cluster of thunderstorms

The attack came in early dawn. Piercing pain jarred him awake. The Captain caught a glimpse of a long bill thrusting at his body as he fell from his roost. He tried to flap his wings but could not extend them in the tangle of mangrove branches. Twisting to get his feet underneath him, the pelican flopped face-first into shallow water.

As he surfaced, a pair of webbed feet came down on top of him, kicking and clawing. He went under, rolled, and kicked with his own feet, the effort separating him from the assailant. The Captain scrambled out from under the mangroves to a clearing on the beach.

Where two more pelicans attacked him.

The Captain extended his wings and arched his neck, a menacing posture he hoped would give them pause. It didn't. They were on him, jabbing their bills. The first assailant—the largest of the three—joined the fray, using his weight to knock the Captain over.

The old bird rolled in the wet sand and felt the blows of hard bills on his back, under his wings, and on his belly. He tried to regain his footing but was knocked over again into the foamy uprush of a spilling breaker.

Other pelicans awoke to witness the fight. Some flushed out of the mangroves to get a closer look while others remained in nests or roosts. They clacked their approval or annoyance. None clacked their objection.

The Captain fought back. Another breaking wave separated him from the attackers. He stood and balanced himself and extended his wings. Lowering his head, he hissed an angry challenge. Pain shot through his shoulder, but with a triplet of flaps he lifted off the ground and came down hard on the largest bird. The first blow of his bill bounced off his rival's chest, but the second one found solid flesh.

The challenger squawked in agony and retreated a few feet, and the two smaller pelicans paused and grunted at each other. The Captain ignored them and jabbed at the leader of this attempted coup. He opened his bill to parry a thrust, which glanced off his lower mandible and scraped the treble hook that was caught in his pouch.

The Captain jabbed his bill directly at his rival's head, determined to bring this challenge to an end. He missed and was not prepared for the counterblow. The curved tip of his rival's bill slammed into his head just above his eye. He fell into the swash and looked up to see a blurry swirling sky. The other two pelicans rejoined the fight.

Though conscious, he felt himself slipping away under repeated blows. Desperation took over. He rolled onto his belly and pushed his wings and webbed feet against the mushy sand to get away, but dizziness unbalanced him when he tried to stand, and he fell into a spilling breaker.

Another wave crashed over him, and with it came the realization that it was over. He allowed the retreating swash to pull him into the surf.

The clacking from the beach was loud. The Captain saw a blurred image of the large pelican—wings stretched wide, head arched back—uttering short triumphant grunts. His two lieutenants began jabbing at each other.

The Captain looked at his mangrove colony. Another blurred image. He turned away and did not look back.

A desire to fly overcame him. He flapped his wings and felt a shaft of pain stretch from his right shoulder to his left side. After resting for a few moments, he beat his wings again. The pain intensified and dizziness returned, but he soon felt the sensation of lift. He beat his wings harder to stay airborne.

The sea was calm with slight swells. He dropped to within three feet of the water, stretched his wings wide, and caught the updraft, and the weary and wounded pelican glided on a cushion of air between his wings and the ocean's surface.

A rising sun edged over the horizon. He knew he should be leading his squadron toward First Feeding, yet he felt no hunger. Only pain.

Hours later, before the sun reached its peak, the Captain had covered more than a hundred miles, and the pain in his shoulder had lessened to a tolerable constant. Without knowing it, he had crossed the Yucatán Channel into the Gulf.

The updraft began to weaken as rougher seas greeted him. He smelled rain. Vibrations in the atmosphere confirmed that he neared a storm. Yesterday's storm.

The Captain beat his wings and climbed higher in the sky, for he would not turn around or alter his course. He would ignore the pain and soar over the storm.

— *Chapter 10* —

Kemper completed the necessary paperwork in less than an hour and spent another twenty minutes catching up with familiar faces before leaving the Levy County Sheriff's Office as an official reserve deputy.

The reserve deputy program was popular in Florida and especially useful in places that were budget-tight and personnel-light. Sheriff Lane had brought on reserve deputies for events like homecoming parades, Fourth of July celebrations, and the annual Suwannee River Youth Livestock Show in Fanning Springs. With sufficient training and certification, reserve deputies could serve in any capacity warranted by the sheriff.

Kemper was sworn in as a Reserve Deputy One, authorized to collect evidence, make arrests, and carry a sidearm. The sheriff allowed him to holster his Magnum .44 instead of the standard-issue 9 mm handgun. He also was issued a uniform, but Angela gave him permission to work in plainclothes as long as he clipped his badge to his belt. He rubbed his thumb back and forth over the badge absentmindedly as he left the Sheriff's Office.

Since Angela wanted to provide Rylan with formal notification of the appointment, Kemper had the rest of the day off to clear his calendar. He owned five Twice the Ice vending machines covering seventy-eight miles of coastline between Crystal River and Steinhatchee. The two machines in those two towns purred like kittens, but the other three required frequent attention to keep them spitting out ice in ten- and twenty-pound increments. Even at peak performance, each vending machine needed routine visits to empty coin boxes and stock ice bags.

Kemper started in Crystal River and needed only a few minutes to clear the machine near Pete's Pier Marina. He took another five minutes to go inside and check on the local fish bite. Some habits could not be set aside.

He drove north to Otter Creek, then to Cedar Key, where he cleared the machine near Dock Street. Then, he drove to his house to get Julep for the rest of the journey. He dumped a roll of chain link fence, a shovel, and post hole diggers from his truck bed. Yard repairs would have to wait.

"Get in, boy," he said. Julep raced over and leaped through the open door.

Kemper paused at the end of his driveway and put a pinch of tobacco between his bottom lip and gum. He held the open can for his dog to sniff and laughed when Julep turned his head in disgust. This was their normal routine. He caught the glint of his badge on the console, and he wondered if this would be the last day of anything resembling normal.

"Okay, boy, let's go check on our empire."

Kemper drove back to Highway 19 and headed north. Julep whimpered as they neared the Golden Arches in Chiefland. "You know you're pathetic," Kemper said, giving him a friendly shove. Nevertheless, he pulled in and ordered Julep a McDouble.

The F-350 Super Duty burned a lot of diesel covering this territory, but it was an acceptable tradeoff for the pleasure of cruising down the road with his dog at his side. Windows down, music up. Lynyrd Skynyrd blasted from speakers that played in sync with the deep burbling sound of the crankshaft firing at irregular intervals. Kemper sang along to "Simple Man" as he crossed the Suwannee River into Dixie County.

Clearing the ice machine in the town of Suwannee did not take long, but the one in Horseshoe Beach was his least profitable and most error-prone box. Sometimes a spotty thermostat caused the ice to clump, sometimes the stainless-steel drum stopped spinning, sometimes the tipping plate didn't tip. He had received a 'Vend Cycle Jam' text warning earlier in the day.

Kemper did a manual vend, and the ice bag did not billow out when the blower activated, leaving twenty pounds of ice on the concrete slab. He reshuffled the stack and did another vend. This time, it functioned correctly.

Julep was not in a hurry. He splashed in the water that gently lapped onto the spit of sand next to the boat ramp. A boy whose dad was pulling his boat out of the water came over and shared his beef jerky with the dog, then joined in the splashing. Kemper cycled the machine again, emptied the coin box, and hollered for Julep to get back in the truck.

Steinhatchee was the last destination. Everything worked fine as expected, so he headed over to the Salty Dreams Marina to get a fishing report. Bobbie Jean stood behind the counter. Her eyes widened and her breath caught when she saw Kemper walk in.

"Aren't you a sight for sore eyes," she said.

"Good to see you too, darlin'."

"Did you need Jimbo? He's working the lift out back unless he's grabbing an early dinner at Pauline's. Today's special is meatloaf."

"Maybe I came in to see your pretty face," Kemper said with a wink, "and to pick up your fishing report."

Bobbie Jean co-owned the marina with her ex-husband Jimbo. They had divorced several years earlier, but could not settle on who kept the business, so they continued working together. It was awkward at first. Backtalk and sarcasm spilled over the counter, but the taste of declining receipts made them both agree to set their bitterness aside. Now they ran the marina like two no-nonsense professionals, which was what they were.

Kemper had caught Bobbie Jean on the rebound, and they spent most of a year sharing outdoor fun and indoor passion. Jimbo, for his part, showed no jealousy. He stayed busy chasing women half his age.

Then the relationship ended. One Friday, Kemper told her he was going back to Cedar Key and would not stay for the weekend as he sometimes did. He did not invite her to join him as she sometimes did. For the next few months, he avoided the marina when checking on his ice machine. When he resumed collecting fishing reports, she didn't press the matter.

Bobbie Jean walked around the counter and handed him the two-page report. "Think you'll do some fishing up here this week?"

"No, but I like to keep my eye on things."

She read more into the comment than she should have. "Why don't you stick around? Austin Rivers and the Regrets are playing at Slipper Dee's tonight."

"Is that a fact?"

"It is, and it's another fact that you and I would make a mighty fine-looking couple walking in together. Sure would turn a lot of heads."

"I reckon that means Jimbo's going there with a date?"

"Oh, just some silly little thing who doesn't know a two-stroke engine from a four-stroke."

Kemper smiled, and Bobbie Jean pressed her advantage by putting her arms around his neck. "What do you say, cowboy? You and me tonight and whatever else comes our way?"

"I'm afraid I can't."

Kemper felt her weight on his shoulders deflate, and he cursed himself for creating such an awkward moment.

"I wish you'd talk to me sometime," she said. "About us. We had a good thing, didn't we?"

"We did. We sure did." Kemper kissed her on the forehead. She sighed heavily, pushing away with a soft punch to his shoulder before retreating behind the counter.

Kemper watched her sort some popping corks. He wanted to say something to repair the damage, but the best he could do was change the subject. "I'm back in law enforcement. Reserve deputy working on Jerry's case."

Bobbie Jean stopped sorting and flashed a fragile smile. "Great. Kemper's got a badge."

It would have been better had he not said anything. Better still had he not even walked inside.

Kemper returned to his truck but braked before he left the parking lot. His interaction with Bobbie Jean reminded him of an appointment he needed to cancel. He retrieved a Tracfone from the center console and punched in a privacy code. The phone stored only one number, saved as 'Professor.' He tapped the number and sighed with relief when it went straight to voicemail.

"We can't meet tomorrow," he said. "In fact, it might be a while before we get together."

He dropped the phone back in the compartment. Out of sight, out of mind.

Kemper took the county road out of Steinhatchee back to Nineteen and drove south for a dozen miles. A local road led to a subdivision between the Cross City Correctional Institution and the Little League ballfield. Five rows of manufactured homes were spread across an upland field. Kemper pulled up to the middle house in the second row, where a group of men gathered behind a truck.

Ben Matthews wore his prison guard uniform, which meant he had been observing a training exercise. He had worked in Corrections for as long as Kemper had been in law enforcement. Ben liked to say he could see his retirement just over the horizon. Last year, he reached that horizon. He returned to the facility in uniform every three months to observe use-of-force training exercises, for which he received a small stipend.

They had been friends since the days when Kemper's fishing tournament had been popular. Their friendship took on a new dimension after Kemper got into the ice vending business. Handy with a wrench, Ben never let his friend down whenever Kemper called him about a mechanical problem. He seemed to genuinely enjoy the challenge.

His son, Drew, sat on the tailgate next to a large cutting board on which were several small mason jars, a sleeve of saltine crackers, and a carton of milk. Two other men—one uniformed, one not—stood nearby along with a teenager about the same age as Drew. They were all smiling and in good spirits.

Julep burst from the truck and raced up to the boys, who patted his head and play-shoved him. Kemper approached more leisurely.

"How 'bout it?" Ben said with a nod. The phrase was not a question in need of an answer. It was Southern shorthand for, *Good to see you, old friend. I'm glad you stopped by.*

"Y'all tasting?"

"Yes, sir," Drew answered. He pointed at the jars. "This one's Dad's, this one's from Uncle Billy."

"And my granddaddy made that one," said the other teenager, Shane, who stopped playing with Julep to point at the last jar. Julep nipped at his boots before giving up and trotting over to Kemper's side.

Tasting hot sauces was one of Ben's favorite pastimes. He kept a cabinet full of homemade sauces and prided himself on his high tolerance for heat. This naturally invited competition. He grinned at Kemper. "You in?"

"Hell no. Wouldn't want to embarrass you in front of your boy."

"Shoot, he does that at my ball games," Drew said with affection. He pulled water bottles from a cooler in the truck bed and set them by the cutting board.

They started with Uncle Billy's hot sauce. The three men poured a dab on a finger and sucked it off. Drew looked at his watch and called out the time in fifteen-second increments. "Cracker," he said when he reached one minute.

Each man ate a cracker to deaden the heat and washed it down with a swig of water. They moved on to Ben's sauce. His competitors grew visibly agitated before reaching a half-minute, and both were guzzling water well before sixty seconds.

"Reigning world champ," Ben boasted as he popped a cracker in his mouth. He grinned at Shane. "Now let's see what your granddaddy'as put together."

Ben poured a generous amount on his finger, some of which dripped to the ground. Julep sniffed at it and backed away with a whimper. Ben sucked his finger clean and stood with a smirk that said, *I've got this*. After twenty seconds, he mustered 'mighty good' through pursed lips. His face reddened, and he grabbed the milk carton just before he reached the finish line. He gulped deeply, some milk spilling down his chin.

Everyone burst into laughter. Even Julep snapped a happy bark. Shane let out a holler and punched Drew in the arm.

"I told you, by God. I told you this would get him."

"Oh, it got me alright," Ben said after he recovered. "Tell your granddaddy it's going in the cabinet."

The party broke up, and the neighbors headed back to their homes. Julep received one more head scratch before the teenagers climbed into Drew's truck and drove off. Ben balanced the jars, crackers, and milk on the cutting board and grinned at Kemper. "Let's go inside and say hi to the wife."

Julep trotted up to the familiar porch.

"Smells good, Martha," Kemper said as he entered the house.

"Then you'll eat dinner with us," she replied.

"I appreciate it, but I can't. Got to get back to Cedar Key."

She turned, fist on hip, and nodded at the dinner table. "You'll sit right there."

"Yes'm."

Family pride adorned the walls of their modest home. A dual picture frame hung on one wall in the living room opposite a large family portrait. It showed Ben and Martha as high school sweethearts on the left side—she sporting the big hair of the '80s— while the right held a more recent version, both a little thicker across the midsection. Pictures of children and grandchildren were captured in statement frames with bible verses or messages like *Live, Laugh, Love*.

After changing his shirt, Ben joined Kemper at the table as Martha took pork chops out of the cast-iron skillet. Collard greens, mashed potatoes, and cornbread rounded out the meal.

"Is Drew coming back for dinner?" Kemper asked.

Ben grinned. "Shiftless young'un. He and Shane are going to the volleyball game, scouting for prom dates."

"Christy won't be joining us either," Martha added, referring to their daughter. "She's at a friend's house. You eat as much as you want, Kemper."

"How's John?" Kemper asked.

"Doing good," Ben said. "Real good. Getting lots of hours at the sawmill. Looking to put down on some property near the river. How's Rylan?"

Kemper's forehead creased, and he shifted in his chair. "He's still police chief, and he still thinks he can beat Ange for sheriff. We don't talk much."

Martha frowned. "Well, Ben, you better bless this food before it gets cold."

They kept the conversation on the food until the men reached for seconds, then Kemper got into the reason for his visit. Ben and Martha already knew about Jerry, so Kemper explained the reserve deputy appointment and how that would make it hard for him to check on his Twice the Ice vending machines.

"I'd like to turn them over to you while I work on this case," Kemper said as he sopped up collard green juices with a wedge of cornbread. "You'd clear 'em when they need clearing, fix 'em when they need fixing. Profits go to you for the duration of my appointment, and I'll even pay for your gas."

Ben looked at his wife. "Hear that, honey? Looks like I'm getting the keys to the kingdom!"

"Oh, you'll be as happy as a clam."

Ben leaned back. "I'm happy to do it, Kemp, but not if I'm taking money from your pocket."

"Now this ain't charity."

"I know it ain't, but I still don't want your money."

"Okay, Ben. I get it."

"I don't think you do, friend." Ben leaned forward. "See, me and Martha've been praying for something good to come from this awful thing that happened to Jerry. You see where I'm going with this?"

Kemper had a sense but stayed silent.

"What happened to Jerry is a tragedy. But from that tragedy, you're back where you belong, doing what you're meant to do. And this pity party you've been on for the last few years has been your time in the wilderness. Don't you see that?"

"Like Elijah, huh? I think you're reading too much—"

"I'm talking about redemption," Ben said sharply. "Another chance."

Ben had reached the point in his life where he talked openly about his faith and often looked for biblical relevance in everyday life. Kemper, however, did not want to contemplate a grand design behind the death of his friend, especially since the one thing driving his desire to get involved was unholy rage.

Ben continued. "I'm happy to help because you're meant to do this. That's why I won't take your money."

"Will you at least let me cover the mileage?"

"Fine. I'll send you my gas bill."

Martha gathered the dinner plates and took them to the kitchen. "Truth is, Ben would probably pay you to let him work on those machines."

"I wouldn't go that far," Ben said.

Martha finished her thought. "I reckon I should thank you, too, because if he ain't out there tinkering on them, he's back here trying to tinker on me."

Ben winked at Kemper. "Retirement's been good."

Kemper held up his hands. "I'll take that as my cue to leave."

As he passed through the living room, the messages on the walls drew his attention. The one that stuck with him on the drive back to Cedar Key held a simple phrase on a plain wooden block: The Good Life.

— *Chapter 11* —

She what?"

"Reserve deputy."

"You're kidding?"

"No, I'm not. She made him a reserve deputy."

"Damn her hide," Rylan fumed. "She can't do that!"

"Paperwork just came in by courier," Gladys said, "and watch your language."

"Get her on the phone. I'm not putting up with this." Rylan punched the button on his phone to end the conversation. He looked across the desk at Doyle. "Did you get that?"

"Yeah."

"She can't do that. He agreed to retire, and the FDLE agreed to close the case. That was the deal. You reckon the city attorney has a copy of the settlement?"

"He should. Or you could ask Kemper for his copy when he reports for work," Doyle said, suppressing a smile.

Rylan picked up the phone receiver, punched some numbers, and waited a few seconds before getting an answer. "Steve? This is Rylan. I need to see a copy of Kemper's settlement agreement with the FDLE... Need it now... No, just curious about something... That'd be great. Can you email it or fax it to Gladys?... 'Preciate it."

Rylan hung up and reached into his desk drawer for a toothpick. "Reserve deputy, my ass."

The door to his office cracked open, and Gladys stuck her head inside. "Sheriff Lane is in a meeting but will call you as soon as she's finished."

"Okay, thanks. And be looking for a fax or email from Steve Avery. Bring it to me as soon as you get it."

"Got it."

Rylan looked at two short stacks of papers on his desk. "Let's get back to this."

Doyle pointed to one of the stacks. "These people I talked to before Charlene gave us that intel about the guy with the injured foot, and they all say some version of nothing unusual. These other folks I interviewed after talking to Charlene, so I specifically asked if they saw a skinny guy in a hoodie and black stonewashed jeans who had a limp or injured foot. Also, a negatory on the responses."

Rylan shook his head. "No one saw this person except Charlene and Jerry. It's like he wandered into town just to grab a burger and kill the old man. Makes no sense."

"Yeah, the burgers at the Breeze ain't all that anyway."

Rylan frowned. "Except no one just wanders into Cedar Key. The out-of-towners always have a reason—fishing, shopping, you know. Eat a nice dinner, watch the sunset."

"What do you want me to do, boss? I can go back and show the suspect rendering to the first group. See if that jogs anything."

Rylan shook his head. "Not just the befores. Gotta do all of them. Even if someone thinks they didn't see him, looking at his face might ring a bell."

The lieutenant got up to leave. Rylan flicked the toothpick in the wastebasket. "I know it's a lot, Doyle, but we're behind the eight ball on this. That's on me."

"You went with what made sense at the time," Doyle said. "Can't fault you for that."

"One more thing," the police chief added, thumbing through one of the stacks. He found the paper and held it up. "This one on the

Quik Stop. So you interviewed Rachel. Why didn't you talk to Mama Thighs?"

"She wasn't in," Doyle replied. "Rachel said she had gone home sick."

"You didn't go back?"

"I figured if the cashier at the entrance didn't see a man fitting the description, then Mama Thighs wouldn't have seen him from the kitchen."

"You're probably right, but I still want you to go back and show both of them the rendering." Rylan knew this meant more work. Unfair, to be sure, but this whole damn thing was unfair. Maybe he could lighten the load. "Doyle, is that pretty wife of yours fixing you dinner tonight?"

Doyle turned. "Yeah. I imagine so. You want to eat with us?"

"No, but I was thinking, I'm stopping by Mama Thighs's Kitchen anyway, so why don't I handle the Quik Stop? You work Dock Street and then get on home."

"Thanks, Chief. I can do that."

"And how about we get Kimmy to help with the other visits?"

"Can she?"

Kim Rountree was one of Rylan's best officers. Thorough and dogged, she also was pregnant and about to give birth to her second child. Rylan pressed the intercom button. "Gladys, how far along is Kimmy with that baby?"

"Thirty-six weeks," came the response without hesitation.

"Translate that for men."

"She's got about a month to go, Chief."

"Good. Call her up and see if she can do some interviews with Doyle."

Doyle left the room. Rylan tried to think through all the moving parts. He felt the urge to smoke, so he rummaged through the drawer and found a lighter and a half-empty pack of cigarettes. After lighting up, he leaned back in his chair, hoping the nicotine would focus his thoughts. He had some choice words for the sheriff about her appointment of Kemper.

The phone buzzed after a few drags, but Rylan was ready. He thumped the speaker button. "You've got a lot of goddamn nerve!"

The voice on the other end responded with feigned shock. "Well, I never! That better have been intended for someone else, or you'll have my resignation."

"Jesus Christ, Gladys, I thought you were Angela."

"I am neither her nor the Savior, and I've warned you about taking the Lord's name in vain."

"I know. I'm sorry. So what is it? Did you hear from Avery?"

"No, but we received a bulletin from the National Weather Service. They're watching a tropical depression in the Gulf."

"Why not?" Rylan said in surrender. "When it rains, it pours."

"It will do more than that if it turns into a hurricane. It likely won't come our way, but—"

"But it might, so you know the drill. Let's get started with the preliminaries. That's—"

"Officer Rountree's responsibility, who you've now assigned to a murder investigation when she should be taking it easy and getting ready for her baby." Gladys's tone was just shy of a scold.

"Point taken. Alright, let me think about it. We've got time." Rylan ended the conversation and took a final drag on the cigarette. He checked his email but had nothing from the attorney on Kemper's plea deal.

The phone buzzed again. He cursed and punched the button. "What is it now, Gladys?"

But it wasn't Gladys who responded.

"This is Sheriff Lane, and I hear you have a problem with one of my deputies."

— *Chapter 12* —

Charlene stepped on the gas until the faded black Monte Carlo topped eighty as it raced down the two-lane road toward Cedar Key. She wasn't in a hurry. She just liked to drive fast.

A stubborn turkey buzzard stood in the road, trying to peel the remains of an armadillo from the asphalt. Charlene swerved into the oncoming lane to avoid the bird. She moved a hand from the steering wheel to steady a Tupperware bowl in the passenger seat. It had an aluminum foil lid, and Charlene did not want its contents sloshing out.

Tommy had called Charlene as she readied herself for work and told her that his friend Dan, a charter boat captain who lived in Otter Creek, had made a big batch of swamp cabbage and that Tommy was welcome to come get his share. This made Charlene the middleman for the Swamp Cabbage Run. That seemed to define their relationship. Tommy needed something; Charlene went and got it for him. This way, Tommy could stay in his store making small talk with the anglers or drinking beer at the bar. He could also enjoy the bewildered and envious looks on the faces of other men when the leggy and busty twenty-nine-year-old brought her older overweight boyfriend whatever he had requested, topped with a kiss.

Sexiest damn middleman in Cedar Key, she thought.

She moved the Tupperware from the seat to the floorboard, where it should have been all along, then blindly dug through her purse until she found a Jolly Rancher and popped it in her mouth. "Eye candy too," she said aloud.

Charlene had started seeing Tommy soon after her relationship with Kemper ended. She had hoped a fling would create some jealousy that would draw Kemper back to her, but he seemed either indifferent or slightly bemused by the whole thing. Tommy was likable and fun to be around when they were out on the town, so she stayed with him. She imagined he liked how it made his friends jealous, believing that Charlene was the one keeping his bed warm at night.

Except she wasn't. At least not anymore. Especially not when his twin daughters were in town, which was every other weekend and extended times during the summer. Then Charlene was just the middleman—not even eye candy.

She accepted that. The young waitress would rather stroke Tommy's ego than satisfy his sexual appetite, which, at his age and weight, was a fading pleasure anyway. Plus, she liked to think she kept her romantic passion bottled up for the day when Kemper would call her back.

Her phone, fixed to a holder mounted on the dash, chimed. She tapped the screen with a painted nail, and Tommy's voice came through the speaker.

"Did you get it?"

"I got it."

"Okay, I was just checking. I'm about to close and head home to get dinner ready for the girls. How far away are you?"

"I still got to stop by the Quik Stop."

"Can't you come here first so I don't have to wait around?"

Charlene smiled. When his husky voice shifted to a higher pitch, she knew she had gotten under his skin.

"I got to get my cigs and see my girl," she said.

"You don't have time for that," Tommy said, meaning *he* did not have time for that. "You're going to be late to work."

"Now you know better than that, Thumper. Work starts when I get there."

"Dang it, Charlene. I've got to get home. I've got the girls tonight."

"Then you'll have to bring your sorry ass to the Quik Stop 'cause that's where your swamp cabbage will be."

Charlene hung up and laughed. She didn't need cigarettes. The waitress had enough to cover her smoking breaks. The real reason for stopping was to friend-flirt with Mama Thighs.

Several years ago, Jerry had asked Charlene to drop in on Mama Thighs from time to time and try to boost her self-esteem. The nickname offended him, and he was appalled that she seemed to embrace it. It didn't bother Charlene, but she wanted to honor Jerry's memory and restart his special mission.

"Hey, Rache," she said to the cashier as she entered the store. "Get me a pack of minties and a scratch-off. I'm gonna go talk to my girl."

Mama Thighs fanned herself on the stool.

"Hey girl, whatcha doin'?" Charlene said.

"Oh, I'm just getting dinners ready for tonight."

"What'd you cook?"

"Chicken and chops. Got some fried okra too. You want some?"

Hand on hip, Charlene half-turned to accentuate her hourglass figure. "Honeychile, you know I can't be eating that and looking like this."

A couple eating dinner took notice. Or, rather, the man did.

"Hey, Stewy," Charlene said. "You coming by the Breeze tonight? Live music and oysters on the half-shell."

The woman sitting with him looked at Charlene, then back at Stewart. She was not amused.

Charlene turned back to Mama Thighs. "How's that handsome boy of yours doin'?" She was charitable. Mama Thighs's son was scrawny and grungy with nervous eyes, bad teeth, and wiry facial hair.

"He's doing good."

"I seen him in town, and oh my! Lotta girls got their eyes on him, I bet."

"He's a good boy. Always looking in on me."

"Now, when are you going to get your hair done with me? I got an appointment next week, and I think we should go together. Get you all gussied up."

Mama Thighs smiled. "I don't think I'll be getting me any fancy hair style."

"Sure you will, girl. We'll tease up that hair and put some bling on you. Men will be crawling over the counter to get at you. Maybe even ol' Stewy there!"

"Oh, stop it," Mama Thighs said with a wave of the hand.

"Hell yeah! Get you some uh-huh to go with your unh-unh!"

Mama Thighs began chuckling so hard, her whole body shook.

Charlene smiled, knowing that Jerry would be proud of her effort. "You know, Jerry always said we was like daughters to him. That makes us sorta-sisters, right?"

The chuckling stopped, the smile disappeared, and the mood darkened. They stared at each other before Mama Thighs looked away.

Charlene cursed herself for mentioning Jerry. She tried to think of comforting words but had none. "Well, shit."

Rylan pulled his F-150 Police Responder up to the Quik Stop, not noticing Charlene's vehicle. His mind was still on his conversation with the sheriff. He had been cursing her and cursing himself ever since he had stormed out of the office.

The police chief knew how to argue. He knew how to stand his ground and punch back twice as hard. Rules of debate: set the tone, stay on offense, rattle your opponent. He knew all these tactics when he took Angela's call.

And he blew it.

She had anchored the discussion on Rylan's false start to the investigation and his lack of thoroughness at Mermaid's Cove. Then she got to the heart of the matter and read from Kemper's plea agreement. Rylan didn't have a copy and felt unarmed. She repeated her staff attorney's opinion that the substitution of 'may' and 'may not' for 'shall' and 'shall not' in the final draft gave her enough wiggle room to give Kemper a badge.

Rylan could only counter with, "I don't think so."

Then she dropped the hammer. "By all means, Chief, call up FDLE for their interpretation. Have your little temper tantrum and get them involved, and I'll make sure every voter in Levy County knows you're impeding a murder investigation over unresolved daddy issues."

Rylan mustered a feeble, "This isn't over, Sheriff."

But it was over. When two alphas clash, the loser doesn't get a do-over the next day. Kemper would be on the case.

Rylan was still flustered, but he needed to show the suspect rendering to Rachel and Mama Thighs. Maybe they would recognize him, and Rylan would finally get a break. He gathered the papers and fixed them to a clipboard, which he carelessly dropped as he exited the vehicle. He picked them up and shuffled them as he approached the entrance, so he didn't see the door swing open just as he reached for it.

And grabbed a handful of Charlene's ample bosom.

Charlene had been looking over her shoulder, saying goodbye to Rachel, when she walked straight into Rylan's outstretched hand. The startled police chief looked up and quickly pulled his hand back. Too late.

"What the hell, Rylan? Did you lose all your damn manners?"

"I'm sorry. I wasn't paying attention—"

"No shit, Sherlock."

"I was going over some papers—"

"You can do that without feeling people up!"

"Jesus, Charlene, I said I was sorry. What else do you want?"

She curled her lip. "Nothing from you."

The words cut deep. He blinked. "Sorry, my mind was—"

"Like I give a shit," she snapped and pushed past him.

Rylan watched her get in her car and peel out of the parking lot. "Love you, too," he whispered, wishing he had only meant it ironically.

The car passed a truck that hastily made an illegal U-turn to follow her, and he recognized the vehicle as Tommy's. Rylan shook his head at the thought of all the men who had chased after Charlene over the years, himself included, only to watch her fall for the one man who did not give a damn about her.

Refocus, he told himself. He entered the store and headed toward Mama Thighs's Kitchen. "Need you back here," he said to Rachel.

Mama Thighs pushed herself up from the stool as Rylan approached. "You wantin' some dinner?"

"Only your very best. But we need to clear up some business first. I've got a sketch of the suspect in Jerry's death based on a description from Charlene who evidently saw him the night of the murder. I want you and Rachel to take a look to see if he may have come in here at some point."

The two women studied the flyer while Rylan walked over to the couple eating dinner. "How y'all doing?"

"Doing fine, Chief," Stewart replied, a forkful of fried okra halfway to his mouth.

"Hope I have your support."

"Support for what?"

"For sheriff."

The couple looked at each other and then back at Rylan. "That's right," the wife said. "I've seen your signs."

"Good luck to you, Chief," Stewart said. "I didn't know Angela was retiring."

Rylan thumbed the belt loops on his pants and glanced down at his feet. "She's not. I just think it's time to bring some fresh ideas to the position."

The couple exchanged another look. "That's a laudable goal," the lady said. "I'm sure your father is very proud of you."

Rylan shifted awkwardly, then sighed in relief when Rachel cleared her throat.

"Don't go anywhere," he said, stepping away. "I want you two to look at this facial composite before you leave."

"I ain't seen no one like that," Rachel said when the police chief joined her at the counter.

"What about you?" he asked Mama Thighs.

She didn't answer, just slowly shook her head as she stared at the flyer, seemingly on the verge of tears.

"I didn't think so," Rylan said. He half-turned and raised his voice for the benefit of the diners. "I'm just doing my due diligence. I won't get into the weeds, but there are new developments that I think are going to turn this thing in our direction."

"That's great," Rachel said. "I hope you get whoever done that to Jerry."

"Oh, I will. You can bet that no one's getting away with murder in my community."

And the floodgates opened. Mama Thighs heaved and sobbed. Rachel reached across the counter and squeezed her hand.

"Hey girl, you just let it all out. Ain't no good keeping all that sadness bottled up inside."

The crying was loud, a mix of snotty inhalations and staggered exhalations. Rylan looked around uncomfortably. The diners stared at him and Mama Thighs. A family of three approached the counter but paused at the sight of the shaking, sobbing woman. Rylan offered them a weak smile. He turned and handed Rachel another flyer.

"Why don't you tape this up by the entrance and let me know if anyone recognizes him? And don't worry about my dinner. I think I have leftovers at home."

Rylan returned to his vehicle and flung the clipboard to the floor. He tried to push his mind away from the immediate disaster and found himself revisiting the earlier ones—the call from Angela and the accidental encounter with Charlene. One had bruised his ego, the other his heart.

It had been years since Rylan had touched Charlene, and then he had touched almost all of her, and it had been accidental only because she had been a little drunk and he had been a little engaged to someone else. Charlene was the most stunningly beautiful woman he had ever met. Their intimate encounter that hot summer night had given him hope he would be able to touch her and hold her every day for the rest of his life. Just as soon as he broke up with his betrothed.

Ending the engagement wasn't easy, and it took weeks to navigate through the tears, anger, and heartbreak before he separated from his jilted lover. But when he returned to Charlene, he discovered she had—abruptly and cruelly—chosen a different McRae.

"Get back to police work," he said aloud. His mind returned to the scene he had just witnessed. Of course, Mama Thighs was upset over Jerry's death, as most people were, but her extremely emotional reaction was disturbing. Something about it bothered him. Then Charlene, with all her sass and beauty, interrupted the thought and dragged him back to his misery.

"To hell with it all," he said as he drove to his empty house. "I should've been a clam farmer."

— *Chapter 13* —

To hell with it all," Paulie said as he stared out the wide window of the meth house. "I should've been a computer tech."

His hand held a flyer with 'Wanted' written across the top. An unlit cigarette dangled from his mouth.

"It doesn't really look like you much," Danny said.

"It's close enough!" Paulie snapped. He held the flyer at arm's length. The nose, chin, and ears—not exact, but close enough. A late afternoon rain darkened the sky, but enough light shone on the facial composite to make Paulie's heart palpitate. He lit the cigarette. "This ain't right, man. This ain't fair."

"You just gotta lay low for a while."

"They want me for murder! I didn't kill the old man. It was Tank. Why ain't Tank on this paper?"

"No one saw him, I guess."

It was the waitress, Paulie thought. She was the only one who could have described him. He knew what would happen to her after he told Full Stop Sylvia about the flyer because he knew what she would tell Tank to do.

"I gotta get out of here," he said. "I gotta get out of this business."

"What do you mean?"

"I ain't cut out for this. I'm not a killer, and I don't help people get killed either." He shook the paper. "This ain't me, yo!"

Danny sighed. "Just lay low, dog."

Paulie shook his head. "They're going to fry me for this. Do they still do the chair here?"

"I dunno."

"And more people are going to get hurt. That's how this works."

Danny handed him a roll of cash. "Here's my score for the week. Let me get my package so you can get back to Atlanta. Is that cool?"

Paulie didn't respond. He took a drag and stared out the window. The rain lessened to a drizzle.

"Unless you want to chill," Danny added. "We could smoke a bowl. Might make you feel better."

A minute passed before Paulie responded. "No. I'm getting out of here."

They made for the blue rain barrels under the rusted awning, passing three ratty couches, two broken televisions, and a functioning one connected to a PlayStation. Sweetie slept on one of the couches, curled up under a filthy blanket. Another junkie lay on the floor. Paulie hoped it would be the last time he laid eyes on the place.

He drove across the open field to the tree line where the worn path transitioned to lime rock. When he reached State Road 24, he slammed on the brakes as a faded black Monte Carlo came dangerously close to clipping the front of his car. He watched it speed away.

Paulie wanted to drive fast, too, but he knew the rules. He probably couldn't top eighty anyway in the nondescript Toyota Corolla, so he pulled onto the asphalt and set the cruise control just below the posted speed limit.

When he reached the interstate, he saw the buildings under the overpass. His plan had been to scout out some student apartments to get a sense for where he might live after he left the gang. And he fully intended to leave.

He could blend in with the students, connect with a local supplier, and sell marijuana to the college crowd. Maybe he would enroll in the nearby community college and take computer classes.

Then he could get out of the drug business altogether. But with his face on the 'Wanted' flyer, Gainesville—so close to Cedar Key—was no longer an option.

Paulie took the northbound ramp on Interstate 75 and reset the cruise control. Rethinking his plan, he knew there were community and technical colleges near Atlanta. He could still take computer classes that would help him land a legit job. Plus, he would be closer to his grandmother. He could even stay at his grandmother's. And dope smokers lived everywhere, so he could sell dime bags independently to make ends meet.

A chill ran up his spine. How would Sylvia handle his departure? Would she accuse him of disloyalty? Would Tank then do to him what he had done to others whom Sylvia believed had betrayed her?

Paulie began rehearsing what he would say. Sylvia had always been direct with her crew, so maybe she would appreciate him being direct with her. He would show her the flyer and tell her he's out, that he can no longer show his face anywhere along the Ninety-Eight.

"I'm out," he said aloud. It sounded good. It felt good. Paulie said it a few more times with each iteration more forceful and confident. He added an emotional appeal. "My Grams is really sick. I'm all she's got, and I need to take care of her." Then, absently, he muttered, "Why don't you come away with me and get out of this dangerous business?"

Paulie cocked his head and laughed after those words slipped from his mouth. It was absurd to think Full Stop Sylvia would leave the drug life to run off with her tepid, wimpy driver. He lit a cigarette and burned away the thought. Just keep it simple.

"I'm out!"

His phone vibrated. He looked at it and furrowed his brow. Well, here goes.

"We out!" The voice was frantic, anguished, and unmistakably Sylvia's.

"What?"

"You hear me, P. We out! We coming to you!"

"I already left. I'm on the interstate now."

"Fuck that! Get back to the crib. We coming!"

"Wh—what's going on?"

"Here, T, talk some sense to this fool."

Tank spoke next, loud and firm. "We got hit. They got Bones and C-Dog."

"C-Dog? Wait, what?"

"They got got. *Comprende?*"

"Oh, shit. Is Full Stop okay?"

"They came hard at the queen but missed. I got her out and dropped one of the motherfuckers. But we gotta leave Atlanta 'til we can bring in more muscle."

Paulie heard a half-sob, half-scream in the background. He could feel her pain through the phone. Tank, by contrast, sounded clear-headed.

"I'm almost in Georgia," Paulie said.

"Then turn your ass around. We're going to hole up in the stash house, you dig? And then we'll catch those fuckers napping and take back what's ours."

Paulie looked at his face on the flyer. "Look, there's something you need to know."

"You've done good on the Ninety-Eight. That's why we're coming. It's safe territory. The queen is counting on you."

Paulie heard Sylvia's teary voice. "The Ninety-Eight is you, P. It's you!"

"You've got a job to do," Tank said. "That shitty house ain't fit for the queen, so you get those junkies out of there. I don't want no meth rats around when we arrive. You understand?"

Paulie saw an exit coming up and put on his blinker. "Yeah, I understand."

"Hear me closely," Tank said, his tone menacing. "Get them out now or they ain't ever leaving. You feel me?"

"What about the old lady, Sweetie? It's her house, you know."

A brief pause before, "Alright, as long as she stays away from Full Stop. And you need to get some bed sheets and pillows, and one of them floor fans, okay? Get a bunch of air fresheners for that big bedroom, and if that old lady says it's hers, you kick her ass out, you dig? We'll get the queen a better place soon, but for now, you need to make that room look good."

Paulie took the off-ramp. His stomach bubbled and turned. He pulled into a gas station and idled his car. Minutes earlier, he had worked up the courage to leave, and now he was in deeper than ever before.

Unless he ran.

A few miles away, the interstate intersected with another one that stretched west all the way to the Pacific Ocean, with many places in between where he could disappear—New Orleans, Houston, Tucson, and others. He had eighteen thousand dollars in cash from his weekly collections.

Drop the phone in the trash and drive west, Paulie told himself. *It's only going to get worse if you stay.*

He thought of Full Stop Sylvia and how it would likely get worse for her, too. Tank's words came to mind. *The queen is counting on you.* Paulie would be under the same roof now, and maybe....

He broke off the thought. A Walmart off the next exit was far enough from Cedar Key that he doubted anyone would recognize his face. He put the car in gear as the nausea began to rise.

— *Chapter 14* —

Kemper smelled the sunrise before he saw it as panicked baitfish stirred in a thousand different places, intensifying the briny fragrance that wafted off the water. His non-visual senses were enhanced. Soft splashes. Rippling water. Buzzing insects.

He lifted his coffee mug from the dock railing and savored the hot steam in the damp air. A cool breeze—strong enough to prevent gnats and mosquitoes from alighting on his arms— shifted his hair. An overnight overcast had blocked the moon and stars, but gray soon entered the black. Kemper saw a hazy, thin line of orange appear over the distant scrub. The silhouettes of his surroundings became sandbars, oyster bars, and islands.

Julep stirred beside him. The morning sunrise was one of his favorite treats, too. Kemper reached down and stroked his neck. "What do you think?"

The dog cocked his head, his attention on an oyster bar coming into view. He would alert his master should a redfish tail break the water's surface.

Kemper wasn't looking for fish. He wasn't sure what he was looking for. Ben's talk of redemption swirled around in his head. He had fished that hole before.

He recalled arriving late to the Oath of Office ceremony to watch Rylan become the new police chief of Cedar Key. More than just a point of pride, he wanted to bear witness to his son restoring the McRae name to a place of honor. He stood in the back of the room as Rylan raised his hand, but after the oath, his son added something more. "I am not my father. I will not bring shame and scandal to our community."

Kemper thought of the lies he had lived with since that clarifying moment—the lie that it did not matter, the lie that he did not care. In a few hours, he would return to the police department wearing a badge for the first time since his departure six years earlier, and he began to see his reserve deputy status as more than just a chance to pursue justice for Jerry. It was an opportunity to reclaim the honor and respect he once had. A chance not to restart his career, but to end it the right way.

Julep whimpered. Kemper looked at his dog and then out to the oyster bar where water rippled and swirled. He sipped the coffee and rested his hand on Julep's head. He still had time to witness the majesty of the Cedar Key sunrise.

An hour later, the F-350 Super Duty pulled in front of Mermaid's Cove. He wasn't sure why he stopped, other than to reset his bearings on what mattered. The police tape around the patch of ground where Jerry had been beaten to death had been removed, which made sense. Two weeks had passed since the murder.

The dense tree canopy cast shadows over the property. Overgrown grass and weeds covered the yard. Untrimmed hedges lined the perimeter and extended back to the two rear cottages.

Kemper had enjoyed the cool breeze while driving with the windows down, but with no breeze here, mosquitoes flooded into the truck. He turned the air conditioning on high to blast them out of the cab. One landed on his arm, and he smacked it. He stared at the smear of blood. More pin-prick bites stung his neck and arms as a dozen more alighted. He put his truck in drive, pulled back on the main road, and drove to the Cedar Key Police Department.

Rylan's truck was in the parking lot. Kemper grimaced. He had hoped to get there before the police chief arrived. Rylan and Gladys were moving a desk against a wall when he entered the building. They turned and faced him.

"You can work from here," Rylan said gruffly.

Gladys suppressed a smile. "Glad to have you back, Ch—" She caught herself. "Um, glad to have you back, Kemper."

Rylan turned his back to Kemper and headed to his office. "Set your things down and join me in here so I can update you on the investigation."

Kemper walked over to the desk and set his thermos down. He remembered that Gladys had a particular talent for making undrinkable coffee, so he had brought his own.

Gladys pointed to a short stack of manila folders on the desk. "Copies of the reports, autopsy, and everything else related to the case," she said. "I knew you'd ask for them."

Rylan leaned back in his chair, staring out the window, when Kemper entered the office. "First off, I think it's a bad call, your appointment as reserve deputy. I think it violates your agreement with FDLE, but I frankly don't have the time or resources to tease that out. Plus, the way FDLE works, they'd likely slow us down and pull us off the scent. So screw 'em. You're on and it's Ange's ass, not mine, if this thing blows up."

The police chief turned to face him. "I woke up this morning thinking it was a joke. That Ange was testing me to see how I'd react. But here you are. As far as I'm concerned, this is more proof that Levy County needs a new sheriff."

"She thinks I can help."

"Maybe you can, but you work at my direction. You're her deputy, but it's my case. Is that understood?"

Kemper nodded his agreement.

"Gladys has copies of everything we've got, but that's not your immediate task. You'll do what I assign you. First up is a letter in one of the folders out there from the absentee landlord of Mermaid's Cove. Some holding company up in Colorado. We called them after CID did their initial inspection, but all we got was bounced around in their voicemail system. A few days later, we got a letter, written by one of their lawyers, no doubt, denying any and all liability but pledging their full cooperation and granting us access to their property. Told us to contact Vacay Realty if we need to get into the cottages or the manager's office. Well, we knew that already because that's who let us in the cottages the morning after the murder. Anyway, this is going nowhere, but we still need to close it out. I want you to call the company and stay on it until you get a real person willing to make an official statement for the file."

"You want me to play phone tag with a company in Colorado?"

"That's correct," Rylan said. "After that, you can work on the statements Doyle and Kimmy put together. Lots of missing blanks, you know—addresses, emails, and other contact information that needs to be filled in."

Kemper's temperature rose. "That's clerical work."

"Tedious clerical work," Rylan added with a smirk. "Ange's notice of appointment said you're to work at my direction, so this is my direction. And since we're behind the eight ball, I'd suggest you better get started."

"Is that it?" Kemper said calmly despite seething on the inside.

"For now. Doyle and Kimmy will be in this afternoon. You can join us then."

Kemper hooked his thumbs in the waist of his jeans, and his fingers brushed the badge clipped to his belt. It lowered his temperature. "I know it wasn't your choice, but I appreciate this. I really do."

For the first time in the conversation, Rylan's voice softened. "Well, here's something else you'll appreciate. We have a Keurig machine if you want a decent cup of coffee. I fired Gladys from that job two years ago."

Kemper noted the shift in mood. "Well, Chief, if we can agree on the coffee, you reckon there's other common ground we can find?"

Rylan's sharp tone returned. "The only thing I want to find is the killer, and I don't want you or the sheriff getting in the way."

Kemper turned and left, disappointed less in his assignment than in the hope he had briefly felt that working with his son might lead to reconciliation.

— *Chapter 15* —

Kemper had spent two days on phone calls and reports, along with any other redundant task Rylan could conceive. At least he contributed to the investigation, he told himself. Yet his enthusiasm began to dampen, and he had second thoughts about how much of a team player he could be. Going along to get along was getting him nowhere.

He started the morning sifting through a list of violent felons who had been released into surrounding counties over the last few years. It wasn't a long list, but it had the potential to develop suspects. He made phone calls and left messages, documenting his efforts.

Rylan left mid-morning to attend a Lions Club breakfast, and Kemper found himself staring through the open door into his son's office. His old office.

Gladys noticed. "I'm so glad you're here," she said with a motherly touch. "It may not be the way it once was, but it's the way it's supposed to be."

Kemper looked at her. A simple 'thank you' would do, but he nodded instead. He got up and walked over to the Keurig machine. His frustration played out when he lifted the handle. A crack sounded across the room as the hinge broke. Gladys watched him staring at the machine.

"You know what? I can get the old dripper out of the closet and have a fresh pot ready in about ten minutes or so."

"Don't bother," Kemper said. "I need to get out and stretch my legs. Who's the contact at Vacay Realty for Mermaid's Cove?"

"I believe it's Pidge Davis. Should be in one of those folders."

"Probably is," he said as he exited the building.

He didn't make it to Vacay Realty. He didn't need to. The short walk from C Street to Second and over to D was interrupted when the very woman he sought called his name.

"Kemper McRae! Well, I'll be!" Pidge pushed herself up from a patio chair on the elevated deck at the Holey Moley Cafe. "You just get on over here and give me a hug. I haven't seen you in ages."

The top of her teased-up hair came level with his chest. He stooped enough for her to kiss him on one cheek, then the other. The kiss-kiss was Pidge's signature move, as much a part of her professional routine as handing out business cards.

Kemper had known Pidge since the first year she had served as chairwoman of the Chamber of Commerce when he had been the police chief. She had since spearheaded numerous community events along with her husband, Evan, a vice president at the local bank. They were what passed for a power couple in Cedar Key.

"Now you tell me what you've been up to while I clean you up." She dabbed a napkin in her water glass as Kemper sat and, like an affectionate aunt, rubbed the lipstick from his cheeks. "I'm meeting a client in about fifteen minutes, but they may have to wait." Pidge took a bite of her bagel and steeped a tea bag in her mug.

"I'm back in law enforcement," Kemper said. "Reserve deputy working with Sheriff Lane. She asked me to help with the investigation into Jerry's death."

Pidge looked him up and down. Her eyes widened as they fixed on his midsection, and she audibly gasped in what could have been mistaken for naughty gawking. Kemper looked around uncomfortably.

"That's a badge on your belt!" she blurted. "Well, this is good news! And it may be the only bit of good news out of this whole sad affair. Poor Jerry. I miss seeing him around town."

"We all do."

"I remember—"

"Can I get you something, sir?" a waiter interrupted.

Kemper's aggression was instant. He snatched the waiter's wrist. "How 'bout you get some goddamn manners?" he snarled. The waiter shook his arm free and looked to Pidge for guidance.

"It's okay," she said to Kemper. "He's just doing his job." She waved the server away and waited until he left the patio. "Are you okay?"

Kemper did not respond. His outburst had been just as surprising to him as it had been to the real estate agent. A few pedestrians walked by and entered an art shop. A few cars rolled down the street. A few pelicans flew overhead on their way to the flats.

"So you're wearing the badge again," she said, attempting to restart the conversation.

"I was on my way to see you."

"Well, that makes me one lucky woman."

"I've been trying to get a hold of the owners of Mermaid's Cove, but they don't like to answer the phone or return messages."

"Tell me about it! You know we manage the property for them. They were all friendly and responsive when they thought they could open up easy-peasy, but after the inspection report and the estimates, well, they just dropped off the radar."

"So they're not opening anytime soon?"

"Oh mercy no! Mermaid's Cove is a long way from opening. Now we don't mind the buzz around town because we want to keep the competition on their toes. You saw where Sunsational Lodges put on a new roof, right? Everyone's upping their game, and that's a good thing. But between me and you and this bagel, Mermaid's Cove ain't getting a Certificate of Occupancy anytime soon."

Kemper leaned back and stroked his mustache. "Is that a fact?"

"They keep the property on the books as a tax write-off, which is a shame because it's a beautiful property."

"Was a beautiful property," Kemper said. "Looks rundown now."

"The grounds have been neglected, that's all. A little mowing and trimming would go a long way. I have a guy who's supposed to do that weekly, but I don't think he's been there since Jerry's death, and he was barely getting it done before." She sighed. "I need to give him a call. I'm juggling three listings now. Picked up a new one on Friday. Just been so busy."

"Who's your grounds guy?"

"Danny Miles."

Kemper raised an eyebrow. He knew the name. "He works for Vacay Realty?"

"Oh heavens no! He's an independent contractor, if you can call him that."

"You don't sound too impressed."

"I'm not. Lazy, shiftless man-boy."

"What is he…eighteen, nineteen now?"

"Twenty-two."

"What are his responsibilities?"

"Mows, trims, whacks weeds…smokes weed."

"Drugs?"

"Oh yes. I found some of his, um, residue a few months ago when I did a walk-through. He denied it, as you might expect, but I'm sure he sees that property as a safe place to get high."

"Why'd you hire him?"

"It was a favor."

"A favor to who?"

Pidge took a moment to sip her tea and savor the sharing of unknown information, but Kemper guessed the answer before she could reveal it. "Rylan?"

"Yes. It was a favor to your son." Pidge set the cup down. She chewed on another bite of bagel while Kemper chewed on her words. He fixed his eyes on a point somewhere in the distance. She waited until they settled back on her. "Rylan came to me about a year and a half ago and asked if there was any work we could give Danny. Nothing big. Just enough to keep him busy. Keep him out of trouble, is how he phrased it."

"Is that a fact?"

"We gave him four properties around town, and all he had to do was basic yard maintenance. Mow, trim, pick up any debris. That sort of thing. Couldn't even do that, so we canceled his work on our active sites and now we pay him to keep the Cove and a few other dormant properties looking halfway decent. I've been meaning to talk to Rylan about this."

Kemper had more questions forming in his mind, but none of them were for Pidge. He stood, thanked her for the information, and told her to give his regards to Evan.

After returning to the police department, he left in his truck for the marina, where Gladys told him he would find Rylan. Though only a few blocks away, Kemper preferred to drive.

A low rattle in the center console signaled that the Tracfone had started vibrating. He listened to the voicemail message from the professor. "You cannot do this to me," said a delicate feminine voice, each word pronounced with crisp consonants. "Do not cancel our rendezvous, damn you, or I will come to you and that cursed house."

Kemper hovered his thumb over the call back button but decided against it. She wouldn't come. She never did, and he had more important things to consider.

He found Rylan chewing on a toothpick and sitting on the gunwale of Marine One. Twin 250-horsepower, four-stroke engines were mounted on the twenty-four-foot vessel. Sheldon Baker, who captained the boat, had previously put twenty years into the United States Coast Guard and never tired of telling people about it. He pressed gauges on the helm, and the exasperated expression on his face suggested something wasn't working properly.

"Need to talk to you," Kemper said to Rylan's back.

"No time," Rylan replied. "Got to get this boat out before the tide runs."

"I'm sure Shelly can handle it."

Sheldon nodded his approval at the remark.

"I still don't have time to talk to you," Rylan said.

Kemper pulled a can of Copenhagen from his back pocket and put a pinch of snuff between his gum and bottom lip. "Make time, Chief. You wanted me to report to you. I'm reporting."

Rylan turned to face him. "I'll be back in the office around four. You can brief me then, along with Doyle and Kimmy."

Kemper spat in the water. "Fine. You sit here with the boat. I'm going to bring Danny Miles in for questioning. I'll brief you later."

"What the hell are you talking about?"

"Danny Miles. He does grounds work at Mermaid's Cove, but you knew that already."

"He had nothing to do with Jerry's death."

"Did you talk to him?"

"Jerry was killed in the middle of the night, and Danny doesn't mow the grass at night."

"Damn, son, you sure got the blinders on."

Rylan looked at Sheldon, who pretended to focus on the instrument panel. "I reckon we'll have to get Mac to look at these electronics," he said to Sheldon, "if he's not wallowing in one of his stupid funks."

"Sure, Chief, I'll give him a call."

Rylan stepped onto the dock. "Alright, Kemp. Let's talk."

They walked to the parking lot and stood between the Police Responder and the F-350 Super Duty. Rylan pointed at the vanity plate on the front of the truck with 'Kemper' scripted inside a redfish silhouette. "You know how ridiculous it is for a man your age to have one of those. Like you're a goddamn teenager."

"That's not what I came to talk about."

"I know, but I wanted to tell you it looks stupid."

"What I came for—"

"And don't talk to me like that in front of a subordinate. Not while you're wearing that badge. You understand?"

Kemper accepted the rebuke. "You're right. That's my bad. But you do have blinders on."

"No, I don't. Have you seen the rendering of the suspect? Looks nothing like Danny."

"Doesn't have to. He could know something about someone else."

"He doesn't. Look, I talked to his mom. She's all busted up about Jerry. But Danny wasn't even in town that night. Got a girlfriend over in Williston, and he's been staying with her."

"You confirmed that?"

Rylan pulled the toothpick from his mouth and examined it. "There's no way he would have done that to Jerry. His mom's had a pretty shitty life, but she raised him better than what you're thinking."

"Dammit, son, I'm not suggesting he did anything wrong, but he works on that property. He may have seen something. Maybe he saw someone loitering there and ran him off. That's why we've got to talk to him."

Rylan knew Kemper was right, but he didn't want to acknowledge it. He recalled his last encounter with Danny's mother, when she broke down and sobbed in the Quik Stop after seeing the suspect rendering.

"I need to follow up on something anyway," he said, looking down as he pushed some gravel with the toe of his boot. "Just haven't had time."

"Now's the time, son. I can call Pidge to get his number."

"Don't bother," Rylan said. "Danny looks in on his mother, and that's who I want to talk to. So, let's start there. Let's go see Mama Thighs."

— *Chapter 16* —

ama Thighs woke up and instinctively grabbed the remote control on her lap. She pointed it at the television and pressed the button to bring up the time display. It was mid-afternoon.

The convenience store cook had an hour before she was needed back at work to prepare dinners. She grabbed a packet of Lance crackers from the folding dinner tray next to her chair. One of the perks of working at the Quik Stop was the bountiful supply of Lance crackers she took home every week, with her manager's permission, of course. Mama Thighs preferred Captain's Wafers with peanut butter but ate Malts and Toast Chees just as readily, between six and eight packets per day.

She kept them by her chair, on the kitchen countertop, and in her bathroom, but she didn't keep them in her bedroom because she didn't sleep on her bed. Her excessive weight and sleep apnea made lying on her back a dangerous practice.

Mama Thighs slept in a chair in front of a fifty-five-inch Smart TV, a gift from Danny. The chair was a push-button recliner, velvet red—also a gift from her son.

She adjusted the chair to an upright position and ate the crackers as she watched Dr. Phil dispense his folksy, one-liner therapy to an applauding audience. Mama Thighs watched all the daytime talk shows, recording the ones that aired when she worked so she could watch them at night. Dr. Phil wasn't her favorite, but she always learned something from him.

She found little to like about today's lesson.

A woman in tears opened up to Dr. Phil about a dark secret she had kept hidden and how it had ruined her health and marriage. Mama Thighs had no marriage to ruin and cared little for her health, but she, too, had a dark secret eating her up inside. She reached for another cracker.

The knock at the door surprised her. She rarely had visitors except for her son, and he never knocked when he came over.

"C'mon in," she said. "Door's unlocked."

Rylan and Kemper stepped inside. Their presence—one in uniform, both with badges—unsettled her.

"Sorry to bother you at home," Rylan said. "We looked for you in the Quik Stop. Rachel said you'd be here."

"Just watching my programs. Is everything alright?"

Rylan stepped between her chair and the television. Kemper stood by the door. Mama Thighs ate a cracker.

"We need to talk to Danny," Rylan said.

Mama Thighs's face warmed. "I ain't seen him. Been like a week since he called or stopped by."

"Which is it?" Kemper asked.

"Which is what?"

"Did he call or stop by?"

Her eyes flicked from man to man. "He called to say hi. You know, checking in on me. He—he's not in any trouble, is he?"

"We need to ask him a few questions," Rylan said. "Can you help us get a hold of him?"

Mama Thighs fiddled with the packet for another cracker and knocked it off the dinner tray. She gathered her hands in her lap and looked down.

Kemper raised an eyebrow. "You know Jerry was killed where Danny works, right?"

Her face reddened, and her bottom lip quivered.

Rylan smiled reassuringly. "All we want is to see if he knows anything about people being on that property late at night. Trespassers, you know. Maybe he noticed something odd."

"So, he's not in any tr—trouble?"

"We go way back, you and me," Rylan said. "Friends since high school. I've helped your son out of trouble before, and I'm willing to do it again. But we can't help him if we can't find him."

"I don't have his number. He calls from his girlfriend's phone."

"Then we'll be happy to call his girlfriend."

"I don't think he's with her anymore. I think they broke up."

Rylan's smile vanished. "Look, we can get this information without your help. We can get the girlfriend's phone records. We can get yours. Heck, I can issue an arrest warrant if that's what it takes. But I don't want to do that. I just want your cooperation."

"But you said he's not in any trouble."

Kemper leaned against the door frame, as irritated at being Rylan's backup as he was by Mama Thighs's evasiveness. Her reddening face raised red flags. He recalled his visit to the Quik Stop after Jerry's death, when little red welts from mosquito bites had covered her face and neck, and he remembered the bites he had gotten when he stopped at Mermaid's Cove on his first day of work.

His welts had faded away, but a new itch blanketed his skin as something came into focus. Mosquitoes were everywhere this time of year, especially in areas with dense foliage like Mermaid's Cove. The next best hope to repellent spray was a stiff wind to push them away, like the persistent breeze around the Quik Stop. Kemper opened the door and looked up the hill. Vertical banners in front of the store whipped crisply in the wind.

The open door drew Rylan's attention. "You got some place you need to go?" he snapped.

Kemper wasn't going anywhere, for in that moment the itch got scratched.

"Goddamn skeeter bites!" Kemper growled. He pointed a finger at Mama Thighs. "You got those skeeter bites at Mermaid's Cove, didn't you?"

Mama Thighs and Rylan stared at Kemper, jaws dropped. "Kemper?" said one. "Dad?" said the other.

"Moe-skee-toes!" Kemper shouted, as if the word alone were explanation enough. He stepped closer to her chair, his voice rising. "You were there, weren't you? You went to them cottages."

"I—I wasn't." She turned to the police chief. "Rylan?"

"Back off, Kemp!" Rylan shouted. "What the hell is wrong with you?" He reached for his father's shoulder, but Kemper swatted his hand away.

"No, sir, I ain't done." Kemper's police instincts, long dormant, had come alive. Certain interrogation tactics came to mind. He needed to attack her vulnerabilities. Her insecurities. The easiest and fastest way was to be mean and cruel. He leaned forward, hands on his knees, his face inches from hers.

"You took your fat, bloated body on those fat, flabby thighs to Mermaid's Cove because your son did something to Jerry there, didn't he?"

"Don't you talk to me like that, Kemper McRae!"

"He knows what happened to Jerry!"

"No!"

Kemper pointed in the direction of the Quik Stop. "You ain't been but from here to there for ten years, but, by God, you went to Mermaid's Cove that night, didn't you?"

"No, I—"

"But you couldn't outrun the mosquitoes. You're so goddamn huge, they ate you up like Thanksgiving turkey."

Her eyes welled up with tears. "You stop it right now! Rylan, make him stop!"

The pain on her face was crushing, but Rylan understood Kemper's strategy. He did not intervene.

"You're the most pathetic, worthless woman I ever seen," Kemper snarled. "All thighs and neck. All blubber."

She began rocking back and forth in her chair, mumbling, "No, no, no."

"Screwed a half-blind, half-wit who dumped you as soon as you squirted out his son."

"You shut up about my boy!" A flurry of spittle joined the tears as she shook her head side to side, her face redder than the velvet chair.

"And he did something to Jerry, and you got bit up trying to help him!"

"Not my boy."

Kemper's face had also reddened, his eyes wide with the whites fully surrounding the irises. He spat out his words. "Damn you, blubber, when I find out what happened—"

"Not my boy—"

"You ain't never seeing him again."

"Not my boy—"

"I will put his ass in the dirt!"

At that moment, Kemper McRae broke Mama Thighs.

"I keel you!" she snarled through clenched teeth. Mama Thighs heaved herself up with tremendous effort, clawed fingers aimed at Kemper's face.

She missed, of course.

Kemper stepped back and watched as she pitched forward, lost her balance, and crashed hard on the floor. She rolled to one side, sobbing and slobbering and sweating profusely. Then, she wailed hysterically.

Rylan shook away the shock and stepped between the adversaries. "Everyone, calm down!" he said, almost shouting. He pulled his phone from his pocket. "I'm calling paramedics."

But before he hit the call button, the wailing stopped.

"It wasn't Danny," Mama Thighs said through snot and tears. "It was them other boys."

Rylan knelt beside her and rested a hand on her shoulder. "I believe you, Maggie. Just tell me what you know."

"Mama, I'm in trouble."

Those words had broken her sleep on that terrible night. Danny had stood by her chair, shaking her shoulder. "I'm in trouble," he repeated.

"What's wrong?" she said groggily. Mama Thighs pressed the button on the side of her chair and raised it to an upright position.

"Some of my friends that I hang out with sometimes, like Paulie from Atlanta—I told you about him. Well, I was letting him and this other guy hang out at the Cove 'cause, you know, no one's there. And they were a little messed up, you know."

"I thought you weren't hanging around those types anymore."

"I'm not, Mama. I was just helping Paulie. Giving him a place to chill. Anyway, one of them got in a fight with this other guy."

"Oh my gosh, son. You okay?"

"I wasn't there. I promise you, Mama, I wasn't there when it happened. But this one guy got hurt real bad."

"How bad?"

"Real bad." Danny turned away. "B—but, I think he'll be alright. They, uh, took him to a doctor. But there's blood."

"In the cottage?"

"No. Maybe some. It's mostly outside. But the cottage is messed up from them guys trashing the place." He turned to face her. "I tried to clean it up, but it ain't no good, and if that Pidge lady comes by to look at the place, she'll blame me and I'll get fired."

That was all Mama Thighs needed to hear. Her boy was in trouble, and he needed her help. She tilted the chair forward and pushed herself up. "Give me a few minutes, and we'll go clean up that cottage."

Mama Thighs rode with Danny to Mermaid's Cove. Breathing heavily, her knees and hips aching, she followed Danny to the back. Mosquitoes swarmed all over the slow-moving target. She could not swat them away while carrying a bucket of cleaning supplies in each hand.

The room reeked. In addition to cigarette smoke, the smell of burning plastic and rotten eggs lingered. She didn't know it was the odor of smoked methamphetamine, but she knew it did not belong. So the windows and doors stayed open as she cleaned. And the mosquitoes flooded in. Mama Thighs accepted the pin-prick stings as the test of a mother's love.

After two hours, the cottage was clean. The look of relief on Danny's face made all her suffering worthwhile. She treated some of the bites with Cortisone after she reported to work for her breakfast shift, but there were too many in places she couldn't reach.

Mama Thighs began cooking breakfasts. By the time Andy the angler came in with the police chief's biscuit order, the blisters on her face and neck had broken, and she was feverish. When Andy shared the news that a body had been found by the bridge and that someone said it was Jerry, she got nauseous and almost vomited.

She completed his order and put the other breakfast items under the heat lamp. Then she rode her Compact Mobility Scooter through the stiff wind to her house. The scooter, like the chair and TV, had been a gift from her son.

Mama Thighs settled into her red velvet chair and put on one of her programs. She ate two packets of Captain's Wafers and turned up the volume, hoping the noise would distract her from the sickening feeling that her son had something to do with Jerry's death.

— *Chapter 17* —

Blubber."

"What?"

"You called her blubber," Rylan said.

"I don't remember," Kemper replied.

"That's what worries me. You were angry. Like, out-of-control angry."

Kemper ran a thumbnail around a new can of Copenhagen, opened it, and took a pinch. He looked out over Daughtry Bayou from the window of the Police Responder. The water was as smooth as glass.

"Can you keep it under control?" Rylan said.

"Keep what under control?"

"Your temper. We can't have you—"

"Yes, of course I can," Kemper snapped.

Rylan had spent a restless night unable to rid himself of the image of Mama Thighs sprawled out on the floor, heaving sobs of bottled-up pain while Kemper stood over her, teeth and fists clenched, eyes filled with rage.

It seemed Kemper had released a little of his own bottled-up pain, and the bitterness Rylan had toward his father slipped away when he picked him up just before first light. Wanting to address old wounds, he tried to think of the right words to open the conversation. All he came up with was 'blubber'.

Kemper grabbed a pair of binoculars on the dash and searched for shimmering ripples indicating fish activity. An osprey circled high in the sky, scouting for the same thing but for different reasons. Shimmering water meant mullet on the move.

A rising tide pushed across the flats and into the maze of muddy creeks around Cedar Key, flushing out snails, insects, and other aquatic critters that mullet and baitfish fed on. Fishermen threw cast nets from a small bridge spanning the creek in front of Daughtry Bayou while others waded into the shallow water around the creek's mouth.

Danny Miles was supposed to be one of those fishermen. He often netted mullet by the bridge and sold them to restaurants and bait shops. At least, that's what Mama Thighs had told Rylan and Kemper after she confessed her dark secret to them.

Rylan grabbed the CAD radio. "How's your end, Doyle?"

"Nothing yet."

"Okay. Let me know."

"Roger that."

Rylan chewed on a toothpick. Kemper spat in his dip cup. A half-circle of sun peered from the horizon, and scattered clouds dotted the sky. A refreshing breeze made it a pleasant morning for doing unpleasant things.

They were parked where the road curved behind a palm tree crowded with Spanish bayonet fifty yards north of the bridge. Rylan grabbed the binoculars and looked through a gap in the sword-shaped leaves before setting them back on the dashboard. He chewed on his bottom lip, debating whether to try breaking the tension between him and his father.

"You look good in green," Rylan said, referring to the deputy uniform Kemper wore.

"Rather be in blue," Kemper replied.

"That was good work with MT."

Kemper looked at Rylan. "Let me ask you something: You told Mama Thighs you had done a favor for her son. Was that the groundskeeper job, or was there something else?"

Rylan sighed. Not the conversation he wanted, but it was a start. "Couple years ago, Danny was passed out in the backseat of a car we pulled over for erratic driving. The driver was acting sketchy, so we had him come out of the vehicle. A meth baggie dropped out of his pocket. We searched the vehicle and found more meth and some drug paraphernalia. We hauled them in except for Danny. I took him over to his mama's and dropped him off."

"So he's a meth head."

"We don't know that. I mean, maybe now, but not then. He said he'd just drank some beers and passed out."

"And you gave him a pass."

"Yeah, Kemp, I gave him a pass. Don't act like you never looked the other way when you were police chief. I heard about some of your decision-making. And don't get me started on—"

"You're drifting off the flats, boy."

Rylan smirked. "Not something you want to get into, huh?"

"We're talking about Danny."

"Fine. I talked to him the next few days and figured he was just young and dumb. So I got him work with Vacay Realty. Pidge was happy to help."

"You sure about that?"

"It's about second chances, Kemp. Kinda like what you're getting with that badge."

"You're drifting again."

Rylan reached in the console for a cigarette. He lit it and took a deep drag. Kemper spat in his dip cup. A few minutes later, a car drove by and Rylan lowered the cigarette to his lap until the vehicle had traveled further down the road.

Kemper smirked. "Smart strategy making sure the voters don't see you smoking those lung darts."

"I shouldn't be smoking anyway."

"I think it's good to take tobacco from time to time."

Rylan shook his head. "You are such a relic."

They sat quietly in the truck, enjoying their tobacco, with only Kemper not feeling guilty about it. Rylan shifted in his seat. He had not had a one-on-one conversation with his father in years. Now he desperately wanted one. He had been fine with the wall that stood between them, one he had helped build. Now he had an urge to tear it down.

"There's some things I've been wanting us to talk about," Rylan said.

Kemper shrugged. "Have at it."

"I can see this means a lot to you," Rylan said. "Wearing that badge. Being involved."

"Don't read more into it than necessary, son. I want to see Jerry's killers brought to justice. That's all."

"And you don't think I can do it?" Rylan snapped.

"That's not what I said."

"You don't think the sheriff can?"

"You're missing the point."

"No, Kemp. That is the point. That's the only point. I saw it yesterday, and I see it now. It ain't just about Jerry. It's about you, and that's okay. That's what I'm trying to say. I didn't want you involved at first, but I'm good with it now. Maybe helping us find who did this will do something good for you."

Kemper turned his head and looked over the water. A pod of pelicans flew low toward Piney Point. Rylan relaxed in his seat, glad to have gotten that off his chest. He took a drag on his cigarette. "Anything you want to say to me?"

"About Danny?"

"No, dammit. Not about Danny or Mama Thighs or any of this police business. I'm talking about the things that happened before this. The things that made me glad you got run out of this job."

Kemper shifted uncomfortably. "I reckon there's some things that need to be said."

But nothing was said. Silence grew between them. Rylan flicked the cigarette butt out the window and sighed in frustration. Another minute passed before Kemper turned to face him.

"You want to talk about your mother or Charlene?" he said.

"I thought you were a jerk for causing Mom to leave, but I reckon I can't be too critical of you after the way I went and screwed up my engagement with Mandy. No, the real divide between us is Charlene."

Silence filled the cab again. Rylan lit another cigarette. "I hated you for Charlene."

Kemper sighed. "I didn't plan it."

Rylan's tone sharpened. "And that's why I hated you. I moved heaven and earth to get Charlene, and she went to you instead. My own dad. You know how I found out? The morning of my swearing in. I called her. Told her I wanted her to attend the ceremony. Told her about the future I wanted. Restoring honor to the family name as police chief and spending the rest of my days with her." He took another drag. "Then she tells me she doesn't want to see me. That our fling or half-fling or whatever the hell it was had been a giant mistake. She tells me to go beg my fiancée for forgiveness and get her back. I tell her it's too late for that and she's the only woman I want." Rylan paused. "That's when she tells me she's seeing you."

Kemper looked down. "I don't know how it started, son. We saw each other one day when we both were lonely—"

"Not helping, Dad!" Rylan snapped. "Do you know how goddamn humiliating it is to see the woman you love taking up with your own father?" He paused, mindful of his anger. He took off his CKPD baseball cap and knuckle-scratched his head.

He continued. "Anyway, that's the frame of mind I was in when I got to my swearing in ceremony. I had intended to say I was proud to be following in my father's footsteps. That you had been good for our community. That I was a continuation of your fine work and that a single mistake shouldn't erase a twenty-plus year career. Then I spotted you in the back, and I thought of Charlene choosing you and not me, and that's why I said those hurtful things about you being an embarrassment. I want you to know I've regretted saying that."

Kemper spat in his dip cup. "I reckon I can't blame you."

"Do you love Charlene?"

"We're not involved now. She's with—"

"Would you love her, though?"

"I'm not looking to get involved again, if that's what you mean."

"Good." Rylan suppressed a smile and changed direction. "I wouldn't be a good son if I didn't want you and Mom to reconcile. Have you thought about that?"

"Only about twenty times a day."

"Why don't you try? She's not seeing anyone that I know of. Or are you still involved with this other woman?"

Kemper looked surprised.

"Oh c'mon, Dad, I'm a cop. I know you're seeing some professor at UF and that she had something to do with you getting that house. Were you involved with her before Mom left?"

Kemper looked out the window, mouthing words like he was practicing what he wanted to say. The silence aggravated Rylan, but he knew it was not his place to break it. Kemper cleared his throat and turned back to his son.

Just then, the CAD radio buzzed, and Doyle's voice came on. "Got a car matching the description. Female driver, male passenger. I think it's him."

"Of course," Rylan said, shaking his head at the timing. He grabbed the receiver. "We're on it."

He took one last drag on the cigarette and flicked it away. Time to catch their quarry.

A blue Kia Rio with a dented front fender came into view as it crossed the bridge. It stopped on the shoulder of the road, and a young man with dark hair and a scraggly beard exited the passenger side, wearing cargo shorts, a pullover hoodie, and white rubber boots. He retrieved a five-gallon bucket from the backseat, then stretched his arms and lit a cigarette.

"Got a positive ID on Danny Miles," Rylan said into the CAD receiver.

"You want me to move in?" replied Doyle's voice.

"Negative," Rylan said. "Let's wait until he's away from the vehicle. I'll signal when."

"Roger that."

Danny said something to the woman behind the wheel. He took another drag and handed her the cigarette. She got out, bone skinny, and stretched her arms. After exchanging friendly banter with a couple fishing from the bridge, she pushed herself up on the hood of the car, then pulled her brown hair back and tied it into a ponytail.

Danny sidestepped down the rocky bank to the mouth of the creek. His rubber boots sloshed over the slippery and jagged hard-shell bottom as he cautiously waded in. He set the bucket on some exposed oyster shell, then he pulled out a cast net, cinched the wristband on his left wrist, and coiled the rope into two-foot loops.

Rylan started the engine and shifted it into drive. "Be ready," he said into the receiver.

Twenty feet off the bank, Danny widened his stance. Water rose halfway up his boots. He gripped the plastic horn at the base of the rope and draped the top half of the net over the coiled rope in his left hand. The bottom half dangled inches above the water. He clutched it in the middle with his crowded left hand and lifted a lead weight from the skirt to his teeth. Then he tossed part of the skirt over his right shoulder and repeated it four times before bunching up the remaining skirt in his right hand. Finally, he pulled his elbows to his sides.

Rylan hit the siren and punched the accelerator. The F-150 Police Responder kicked up gravel as it sped toward the bridge.

Danny had twisted his hips in preparation for the cast, but panicked when he heard the siren and saw the truck. He took a running step toward the bank. His boot dragged in the water. He short-stepped to regain balance, but his other boot slipped on the hard-shell bottom, and he pitched forward with his hands still entangled in the net and fell face-first into the shallow water.

Submerged oyster shell sliced into his chin, cheeks, and forehead, and lacerated his knees and arms. Danny lifted his face out of the water and screamed. He rolled over to free his hands from the net and splashed water on his bleeding face.

His girlfriend had jumped off the car and made it halfway down the bank. "Oh, baby, are you okay?"

Rylan and Kemper exited the truck and stood at the top of the bank, hands on their sidearms.

"Good morning, young lady," Rylan said. "You must be Tonya. I'm Chief McRae, and I'm going to ask you to keep your hands where we can see them." Danny tried to staunch the wounds on his face with his hoodie sleeve. Rylan chuckled. "Danny, that's the worst casting technique I've ever seen."

"I know how to throw a net, damn you."

"I'm sure you do. Now, why don't you come on out of there? We need to ask you some questions."

"I ain't done nothing," Danny said as he stood. "These cuts sting, man."

"You look like you're hurt bad, baby," Tonya said. "I'm going to get you a towel from the car."

Kemper stepped in front of her. "You stay right there."

"But he's hurt."

"Shut up, Tonya," Danny snapped.

Doyle had parked his vehicle on the opposite side of the bridge. He joined Rylan and Kemper. "Hey, boss, you think he was making a run for it?"

"No, this is how the boy catches mullet. Go ahead and search the vehicle. I'm sure there's some goodies in there for us."

"No, you don't!" Tonya took a running step up the bank but slipped on the loose rocks. Kemper grabbed her arm to keep her from falling and tightened his grip when she tried to pull away.

Rylan smiled. "We're all going to be good little boys and girls, okay? We're going to see what's in that vehicle and get you bandaged up. And then we're going to ask you a few questions."

"I ain't done nothing," Danny repeated.

"It ain't what you done, son. It's what you know."

A splash drew Kemper's attention to an old timer pulling up his haul from the bridge. Seven or eight silver fish twitched in the dripping net.

It was a good day for fishing.

— *Chapter 18* —

Kemper and Rylan sat across from Angela Lane, a stately mahogany desk between them. Her steely gray glare fixed on Rylan, her mouth a terse line that barely moved when she spoke. "Why is his face messed up?"

Rylan looked like a schoolboy sitting in the principal's office. He shifted uncomfortably in his chair. "He slipped and fell."

The office reflected the sheriff's competence and integrity. A bronze eagle perched on the corner of her desk. An American flag stood in one corner of the room, the State of Florida flag in the other. Diplomas for advanced degrees adorned the wall, along with accreditation certificates for the county jail and emergency call center. Other plaques recognized numerous honors, mostly for ethical leadership.

Kemper was more annoyed than impressed. He had called the sheriff to let her know they were transporting Danny to the county jail and that he had information about Jerry's murder. She redirected them to headquarters so she could participate in the interrogation. When she saw the lacerations on Danny's face, however, she sent him to the infirmary and ordered Kemper and Rylan to her office, along with her staff attorney.

"Let's try again," she said. "Why is his face all messed up?"

Rylan shook his head in disbelief. "He hurt himself as we were apprehending him. And you're welcome, Ange. This—"

"It's Sheriff in here," she snapped. "And don't try that 'you're welcome' crap with me. We're still making up for lost time."

"I'm just saying, it seems like we're getting a little sidetracked."

"We are not sidetracked, Chief. When I took this job you so desperately want, one of the first things I did was change the culture of the jail. We had corrections officers who sounded like you when it came to prisoners under their charge. Slipped and fell. Hurt themselves. Prisoners with broken teeth or broken arms, not to mention the sexual misconduct. I fired those officers. Even had one arrested. Do you understand? I will not tolerate the abuse of anyone under arrest or detention."

Kemper cut in. "It's slick, jagged, and razor sharp at the mouth of the creek, and that's why he's cut up. I've seen experienced netters slip and hurt themselves pretty bad."

Rylan slumped in his chair. "If you think I smashed his face into oyster shell, just say so."

Bill Rogers, the sheriff's staff attorney, sighed and shook his head.

Kemper stood. "Rylan did the right thing. Waiting until Danny was in the water effectively immobilized him. And if he'd had a weapon, he couldn't draw it because his hands were all wrapped up in the net. Minimal risk to officers, minimal risk to bystanders, maximum opportunity for apprehension. That's a good collar."

"That better be in the report."

"Wasted opportunity is going to be in the report if we don't get in there and interrogate him," Kemper said, his voice rising. "He talked on the drive over here, so we got a little info. But now he's getting patched up and no doubt rethinking things while we're sitting here twiddling our thumbs."

Angela's voice rose to match his. "Watch your tone with me, Deputy, or you won't be a deputy much longer. We do things by the book because it serves everyone's interests. Just like we don't hurt people in our custody. Now, was he Mirandized?"

"Oh for Christ's sake!"

Rylan interrupted. "I read him his rights when I put him in the truck. He started talking right away. He's scared. According to him, two people—both from Atlanta—were involved in Jerry's death. They supply meth to this area. Danny is both a user and a dealer and has access to those cottages where Jerry was killed."

"Why did they kill him?

"That's why we need to interrogate him while he's rattled," Kemper said.

"Danny saw it?"

"Danny wasn't there," Rylan said.

"According to Danny," Kemper added.

"Right. According to Danny, Danny wasn't there. They called him after the fact."

Kemper's anger rose again. "We got a rough idea of what happened, but we need specifics. The more he sits, the more likely he's going to clam up."

"We're waiting for the infirmary to clear him," Angela said. "Some of those cuts look like they need stitches." She pushed a button on the phone. "Is the suspect ready to be interviewed?"

"Not yet, ma'am," came the response. "We need a few more minutes and then we'll take him to Interrogation Room Two."

Angela looked at Bill. "Can you ask Rick Delaney to join us?"

Bill exited the room, and Angela turned to Rylan. "Chief, you'll take the lead on questioning. I want to know for certain if Danny is a dealer and not just a user, and, if so, the when and where of the drops." She looked at Kemper. "Deputy, you're with me in the observation room."

Rylan smiled at the assignment even though the sheriff had fully asserted control over the investigation. Bill returned with Rick Delaney, a short, stout man with a polished bald head over a neatly trimmed beard. He nodded at both Rylan and Kemper.

Angela wasted no time. "Rick, we have some suspects in the killing of Jerry Whitmore. We think they're in the Atlanta drug trade. Do you still have contacts in the DEA?"

Kemper interrupted. "Sheriff, we don't know if this is about drugs, but we do know it's about murder. That should be our focus."

"That is my focus," Angela snapped. She looked at Rylan. "Did you send us the facial composite of the main suspect?"

"I did."

"If these suspects are traffickers," she said to Kemper, "there's a good chance the DEA has a file on them already, which means we might be able to identify them." She turned to Rick. "I assume you know what we're talking about now. Can you help us?"

Delaney puffed out his chest. "I've maintained communication with several agents after completing my twelve-week training program at Quantico. If the drugs are coming out of Atlanta, there are four main—"

"That's all," Angela said, cutting him off. "Just send that rendering to Atlanta and see if they recognize our guy."

"Understood."

"Excuse me, Sheriff," Kemper said, "I don't think you want that agency involved in this."

Rick cleared his throat. "It's Administration, not Agency. Drug Enforcement Administration."

Kemper ignored him. "This is about murder, plain and simple. Getting them involved is only going to complicate our investigation."

"It's my investigation, Deputy," Angela said, "and your role in it comes at my discretion. Do you understand?"

"Perfectly."

"Can you make this a soft inquiry?" she asked Rick. "We just want to know if anyone up there recognizes our suspect. We are not, I repeat, not making a formal request for assistance."

"Yes, ma'am. I can keep it quiet."

"Soft inquiry only," she repeated, pointing a finger at him. Angela stood after he left the room. "Now, gentlemen, I think it's time we talk to Danny Miles."

Danny didn't talk.

After eight stitches on his right cheek and four on his chin, the formal interrogation lasted about five minutes. Instead of anxious and scared like he had been during the drive, Danny was surly and sarcastic. And he asked for a lawyer.

In the observation room, Kemper slammed a fist on the table. "Dammit, Sheriff, we gave him too much time to think."

"That's enough, Deputy."

"I'll talk to him, by God, and I'll get what we need."

"No, you won't, Deputy."

"You don't have to give him his phone call right away. We can sweat him."

"I'm aware of what I can and cannot do," the sheriff said. "Now will you shut up so I can think?"

Rylan joined them in the room. Bill lifted his head from a stack of papers he pretended to skim while sitting in a corner chair. "What was in the girl's vehicle?" he asked.

"Three marijuana cigarettes in an Altoids canister," Rylan said, "and there was a baggie under the passenger seat that had some drug residue. Probably meth."

"Did you get her permission to search the vehicle?"

"We got his."

"But isn't the vehicle in her name?"

Rylan turned to the staff attorney. "That'll pass court muster, won't it?"

"Maybe," Bill replied. "Depends on the judge we draw. Might get tossed on a technicality, and then where are we?"

Angela sighed. "This is a problem, gentlemen, and this is why we do things by the book. It serves our interests, not the criminals. Look, meth use is out of control, and most of our tools to fight it are ineffective, but we can't go breaking or bending rules and—"

"See, Sheriff," Kemper said, his voice rising again. "You've already moved past murder and made this about drugs."

The sheriff, police chief, and staff attorney spent the next quarter-hour weighing the strengths and weaknesses of the investigation, concluding that it currently tipped in the wrong direction and that detaining Danny might do more harm than good. Kemper brooded in silence.

Angela shook her head, disappointed. "I think we let them go and surveil them."

"Oh, hell no!" Kemper erupted. "He's an accessory, and he's covered up information about the murder. You need to charge that little bastard and stick him in a cell."

Angela glared at Kemper. "Running him through the system with his mugshot will likely scare off the ones we want. They'll go back to Atlanta, and we're back to square one."

"You think meth heads are searching the web for mugshots?" Kemper said.

The staff attorney weighed in. "We're talking about traffickers. They tend to be on the sober side of the business. They're probably watching this area carefully because of what they're implicated in with Jerry's death. Holding Danny with just partial information risks this Atlanta connection. The sheriff is right."

Kemper turned away, disgusted.

"Release him but keep our eyes on him," Rylan said, warming to the idea. "And catch the killers when they come back for the next distribution."

Angela nodded. "That's the best play with the cards we've been dealt."

"Just like that," Kemper said, snapping his fingers, "you've turned this into a drug sting."

Angela's eyes flashed with anger. "That's enough, deputy! I've had it with your backtalk and second-guessing. I'm this close to—"

"Taking my badge?" Kemper slammed his hand on the table, turned, and stormed out of the room.

Angela didn't watch him leave. Her eyes remained fixed on the table where Kemper's badge glinted under the lamp light.

— *Chapter 19* —

Kemper drove home and changed out of his uniform. He had half a mind to burn it in the firepit out back. He cursed himself for losing his temper and for surrendering his badge. For so easily giving up what he had so desperately wanted back.

A bottle of whiskey stood on the kitchen counter, but drinking alone did not appeal to him. Neither did isolating himself in The Zone. His short time with the badge had rekindled his interest in being part of the community, so before sunset, Kemper found himself climbing the wooden stairs to The Clam Shack on Dock Street.

"I'm gonna sit at the bar," he said to the hostess as he entered the upper-level restaurant.

"Yes, sir. Go right ahead."

The bar sat mostly empty, so he took a spot facing the Gulf. The sun cast a burnt orange scar across the sky. He had a clear view of Atsena-Otie and Seahorse Keys.

Two men sat at the end of the bar, locked in conversation. He knew them but didn't bother to greet them. A ballgame played on the television overhead. He asked for a beer. The bartender, a young man, offered Kemper a menu when he brought him the frothy mug.

"Don't waste your time," came a growl from the end of the bar. The speaker had a grizzled face, and his gray hair ran long and unruly under a faded Chicago Cubs baseball cap. Kemper recognized him as Willie Quinn, the owner of the establishment.

"Now you're a young pup, only been here a year or so," Willie said to the bartender as he walked over and rested his hands on Kemper's shoulders. "And this man you're serving is the one and only Kemper McRae, finest fisherman in all the Seven Seas, slayer of wicked ocean monsters and tangle-footed jaywalkers, lover and leaver of pearl-clutching mermaids, and purveyor of secret code names for boney fide honey holes."

"Oh, I've heard of you," the bartender said with a smile. He extended a hand across the bar. "The name's Al."

"And I said you're wasting your time with a menu because this old angler believes there's only one thing worthy of his delectable taste buds." He strutted over to a pair of swinging doors and pushed one open. "Hey, Scotty, get me an order of Clay Pot Clams, the McRae McStyle McMasterpiece. The hermit crab has returned!"

Kemper smiled as the tightness in his muscles and stomach eased.

Willie shouted again, "And fix up an order of clam strips pronto. The man might starve to death if we don't fill his belly with fried clams!"

"I take it you like our clams," Al said to Kemper.

"Don't tell Quintus, but the other restaurants do a good job, too."

"Quintus?"

Kemper pointed at Willie and raised his voice. "That crazy bastard might sign your paycheck as Willie Quinn, but to us old timers, ever since that *Gladiator* movie came out, he is William Quintus Maximus Elaboratus Expectorant or whatever other Roman-sounding superlative you can think of."

"I prefer Biggus Dickus, thank you very much."

Kemper lifted his mug. "To Quintus."

Quintus, or Willie, looked around with deep satisfaction. Everyone in his restaurant smiled—the hostess and bartender, the couples in the dining area, and now his friend Kemper. The dinner crowd would soon shuffle in. More people to please.

He held the door open for a waitress hefting a tray of food, then shouted into the kitchen like he had just remembered a vital detail. "And no bruised taters in that gor-met pot. Only the best for our Kemper. If you see any bruised taters, I want you to set them aside for Tommy Pinner. That fat bastard gets the bruised taters, by God!"

He strutted back to the end of the bar and drank deeply from his mug. "I haven't seen you in a long time, Kemp. I was beginning to think you didn't like us anymore."

"I'm back now, Quintus Aurelius Magnanimous."

"I hear you're working with the sheriff. I'm glad for that."

Kemper didn't reply. He didn't feel like telling his friend how short-lived it had been.

"I hope you find the prick who hurt our pal Jerry," Willie said. Kemper noted that Willie had used the word 'hurt' rather than 'killed'. Despite his rough exterior, Willie was a big softie.

Kemper held up two fingers. "Pricks, plural."

Willie didn't hear Kemper's reply amid the surrounding noises, but he saw the gesture. He flashed a peace sign. "Yeah, peace to you too, Brother Kemp."

The man sitting next to Willie smirked. "No, you deaf bastard. He said, 'pricks plural.' As in more than one." He held up his index finger on each hand. "Two pricks, you know, the way your mother likes it."

"Oof!" Willie gasped in faux shock.

"Whoa now!" said the bartender. "That's gonna leave a mark!"

For the next few minutes, the two men exchanged loud, obnoxious, face-reddening 'your mama' jokes, punctuated by an occasional 'Whoa now!' from Al.

Kemper surveyed the room and spotted a couple nearest the bar laughing along with the vulgar banter. A waitress lingered by the kitchen door listening to how it played out. She noticed Kemper looking at her and ducked into the kitchen, returning soon after with his order of fried clam strips. "I'm sorry, sir. I didn't mean to keep you waiting."

"I wasn't trying to rush you," Kemper said. "I was just taking it all in."

"I won your contest," she said with a note of pride.

Kemper raised an eyebrow.

"Back when I was twelve. I won the junior category for your fishing tournament. I caught a cobia."

"You pulled in a cobia all by yourself?"

"I did. Well, Daddy helped me some."

"What's your name?"

"Kay. It's Kayla Cody on the certificate. I still got it, along with my picture with you."

"You're Stingray Cody's girl."

"My daddy says you were the best police chief we ever had." She stepped away when his face darkened.

The hostess escorted a family of five to a booth within earshot of the bar. Willie, noticing the young kids, waved his hand in surrender. "Alright, Mac, time to shut your filthy yapper. If assaulting the virtue of my saintly, sanctified mother gets you out of your funk, then she'll gladly make the sacrifice."

"What's he in a funk about?" Kemper asked as he dipped his appetizer in tartar sauce.

"Fanny. Who else?"

"Two weeks to go," Al said cheerfully.

"Twelve days," Mac said, a dour expression returning to his face.

Kemper knew the story well. Francesca Aminta Moravia O'Malley—Fanny to her friends—was one-half of the oddest couple in Cedar Key, whenever she was in Cedar Key. Chatty and buoyant, her bronzed skin and petite body contrasted sharply with Mac's perpetually sunburnt face, sagging jowls, and gangly physique. A traveling nurse, Fanny took jobs in high-demand places in exchange for higher-than-normal wages. Eight weeks on, four weeks off, and the longer she was away, the more miserable Mac became.

"Where is she this time?" Kemper asked.

"Fricking Iowa," Mac said, chugging half his beer.

"She'll be back soon," Willie said, "and you'll be a happy camper."

"Happy boater," Al added. "You and Fanny will disappear on that liveaboard trawler, right?"

Mac smiled.

More people entered the restaurant. The hostess escorted another party to the dining area while two ladies perched themselves at the bar. They complimented Al on his arm tattoos as he served them white wine. He muted the television and turned up the music. Kenny Chesney crooned a country song.

Kemper's dinner arrived, steam lifting off the clay pot where fifty little neck clams marinated in a garlic sauce, along with potatoes and herbs.

"You need anything else?" Kay asked.

Kemper looked around the room. The light mood and friendly faces. The small-town sincerity. This was his Cedar Key. "I got everything I need."

Bits of conversation wafted by as he ate his dinner and drank another beer. Mac bragged about the improvements he had made to his liveaboard. An out-of-towner pledged to tell all her friends about this perfect little restaurant in this perfect little town. One of the wine-sippers escalated her flirting with Al.

Willie suddenly sat up straight. "Quick, Albert, hide the devil sauce! We're being raided by a gubmint agent!"

Kemper turned to see Rylan, still in uniform, approaching the bar. He took a seat next to Kemper. Al set a cocktail napkin in front of him. "What'll it be?"

"Diet Coke with a squeeze of lime."

"How'd you know I was here?" Kemper asked.

"Your truck. It sticks out."

Kemper lifted his mug. "Damn straight."

"No, I mean it literally sticks out. You're a foot over the parking stripe. I came in to write you a ticket." Rylan kept a straight face for a few seconds before smiling. He noticed a tall redhead with an appraising eye and winked at her, then turned his attention back to Kemper. "You shouldn't have stormed out."

"I don't do bullshit, son."

Rylan sipped his drink. "It ain't bullshit. We went back in and did the good cop, bad cop thing. Told Danny we're letting him go as a courtesy to his mother, and Ange added that she would charge his mother with withholding information about the killing unless Danny got his shit together."

"She used that word."

"No, that's my word. But it got his attention."

"You really think he bought it?"

"I do. He ain't that bright. Neither is his girlfriend."

"And you think he'll lead you to Jerry's killers? I bet he's on the phone right now telling those people he got picked up and that they need to stay away."

"I'll say again, he's an idiot. And he's an addict. So's the girl. Did you see her meth mouth? They'll need a fix in a day or two, and we'll have our eyes on them."

Kemper spooned a clam out of its shell. "So justice for Jerry depends on finding drug traffickers from Atlanta. Thanks for the report, sport."

"I came for another reason. I wanted to tell you I'm sorry for what happened today, storming out and leaving your badge behind. You really lost your cool."

"I'm not in the mood for a lecture, son." Kemper held up his empty mug to draw Al's attention. "Things are going good right now. Don't ruin it."

Rylan ate one of Kemper's clam strips. Then, as if struck by an epiphany, he straightened and shouted across the bar. "Hey, Willie, any chance you'd hang my campaign sign outside this fine establishment?"

"Of course," Willie said. "Be honored to. And bring some extras so I can pass them out to all my friends."

"You'll need maybe three," Mac snarked.

"Never mind the freckled Irish ape. Gimme twenty signs and I'll get them out. But only in exchange for a highly corrupt quid pro quo."

"I'm listening," Rylan said.

"That storm brewing in the Gulf—you gotta keep it from coming our way. We don't need no stinkin' hurricane this year, Chief. The last one put me out of business for two months. That's the scratch on my back, you hear?"

Rylan tipped his glass. "You got it. I'll use my special powers and point it somewhere else." He then turned his attention to Willie's sidekick. "Got work for you, Mac. The electronics on the marine unit need your attention."

Mac was a damn fine boat mechanic and under contract with the CKPD, but utterly worthless in the waning days before Fanny's return. "I don't feel like it," he muttered and dipped his bulbous nose into his near-empty mug.

Rylan turned to his father. "I'll try this again. I'm glad you were on the investigation. Wasn't at first, but I can see it was important to you. Which is why you shouldn't have given your badge back."

Kemper's eyes narrowed. "Well, there's not a damn thing I can do about it now."

Rylan smiled and pulled Kemper's badge from his shirt pocket. He set it on the counter. "Welcome back, Dad."

Kemper stared down at the shiny object, his mouth parted slightly.

"I talked to Ange after you left," Rylan said. "Let's just say I finally won an argument with her."

Kemper lifted eyes that glistened in a way they had not in a long time, and the word 'Dad'—also absent for years—stayed in his head as competing emotions of admiration, gratitude, and shame fought for attention.

"Don't get me wrong, she's still pissed at you," Rylan said. "But she's willing to keep you on. I reckon she's got a soft spot for you."

Kemper stayed silent, unable to find the right words. Or any words. He noticed anew his square jaw on Rylan's face and other similarities. His cheeks burned at the thought of his son making a greater effort—a fatherly effort—to build a bridge between them.

"We're putting together surveillance teams," Rylan said. "You'll work with Doyle. You start tomorrow."

Kemper nodded.

The tall redhead drew Rylan's attention again, her casual stare having lingered a little too long before she averted her eyes with a shy smile. "Now if you'll excuse me," the police chief said, "I think it's time for a little one-on-one politicking."

— *Chapter 20* —

The sheriff had put together a simple two-on-one surveillance plan with three teams working rotating shifts. Kemper partnered with Doyle, who worked the daytime shift in his wife's minivan. Bushnell PowerView Binoculars and a Vortex Viper Scope from Kemper's hunting rifle comprised the tools in their arsenal.

Their target, Danny, stayed at his girlfriend's house near Williston, a small town in the northeast section of the county. For the first forty-eight hours, Danny didn't leave the dwelling, although Tonya ventured out a few times to the local Dollar General. On the third day, Danny left with Tonya, driving west to Chiefland, where they parked at the far end of a Walmart parking lot. Kemper and Doyle pulled into an adjacent gas station and idled near the air pump machine. They had a clear view of the blue Kia Rio when the windows rolled down, showing Tonya on her phone and Danny smoking a cigarette.

A badly used Buick with badass rims pulled up next to Tonya's car, passenger side to passenger side with two feet between them. Its window rolled down, and a white paper bag flew out, bounced off the Kia Rio's side mirror, and fell to the ground.

"Is that a McDonald's bag?" Doyle asked.

"Could be."

Doyle grinned. "You think he ordered a Big Mac with a side of meth?"

Kemper smiled reluctantly.

Tonya got out from the driver's side and walked around to retrieve the bag. After she returned to her car, the Buick pulled away and gave Kemper a clear view of the license tag. He read it off to Doyle who radioed it to Dispatch. Before they got back on the main road, they knew the name of the flunky who couldn't toss a bag a few feet through an open window. Dewey Sullivan also had a criminal record that included domestic battery, dealing in stolen goods, and possession of methamphetamine.

Sheriff Lane added two more teams to surveillance, ensuring a close watch of both Dewey and Danny. Dewey drove around the countryside, disappearing down long dirt roads for short periods of time. Doyle and Kemper kept a safe distance, never getting in a situation where they crossed paths. The binoculars and rifle scope made a quarter-mile buffer workable, and the minivan was indistinct to the point of being inconspicuous.

Chiefland was Dewey's base of operations. When he wasn't making rural deliveries, he passed packages in the parking lots of Walmart, the Circle K, and McDonald's. Dewey was a careless drug dealer. Doyle began referring to him as Dewey Dipshit, which earned a less reluctant smile from Kemper.

The following day, Doyle peered through the binoculars and observed Dewey engaged in another drug sale in an empty lot near the high school football field. Doyle looked at the suspect rendering taped to the center panel of the minivan, then peered back through the binoculars. "That's a big ole negatory," he said, mostly to himself.

Kemper slipped a pinch of tobacco between his bottom lip and gum. "Surprised this grand plan hasn't served up our suspects on a silver platter," he said sarcastically.

"Dewey Dipshit will have to restock his supply soon. That's when we'll get him."

"We're assuming his supplier is the guy we're looking for. Did we get anything back from the DEA on that sketch or is that a big ole negatory too?"

Doyle didn't like the mockery in Kemper's tone. "It's a better plan than no plan at all. Maybe our guy just ain't on the DEA's radar. Maybe he's just a two-bit player."

"Or we're just a two-bit town," Kemper said before noticing he had offended his partner. "Look, Doyle, you've been a mighty fine police officer. I appreciate the time we served together, and I'm glad you're working with my son."

Doyle nodded. "It's an easy job when the name of your boss doesn't change, Chief McRae."

"We'll either get a break in the case or change tactics soon. I doubt we'll be doing stake-out duty much longer."

"That's good to hear," Doyle said, "because the missus is missing her minivan."

Kemper woke the next morning still bothered by his attitude toward the current situation. He knew better than to expect instant success, and he wondered why he couldn't appreciate being part of the investigation when he had been shut out entirely just a short time ago.

It was his day off, so he decided to go fishing, hoping it would improve his outlook.

He took a thermos full of coffee out to the boathouse. Julep raced ahead of him. Inside, Kemper read the numbers on the tide clock and barometric pressure gauge, and he checked a few websites on his laptop for wind, current, and water temperature. He walked over to the framed map of the coastline.

Kemper ran a finger over the canvas as the variables worked through a formula in his head. He leaned closer. Hundreds of creeks and coves to choose from. After a minute of careful study, he dropped a hand and scratched his dog's head.

"Alright, let's go catch some fish."

He flipped a switch on the support beam by the slips, and the electronic winch lowered his flats boat into the water. Julep barked his approval.

The live well was empty, and Kemper considered driving to Tommy's store for shrimp or mud minnows, but decided against it. Plenty of jigs and soft plastics filled his tackle box. He stepped into the kitchenette and pulled a bag of ice from the freezer. Behind it, he found a Ziploc bag of quartered blue crab. He grinned at Julep.

"I think it's going to be a good morning."

Twenty minutes later, he pushed into a creek north of Rattlesnake Key. He hooked up on his first cast and reeled in a redfish too small to keep. Julep almost leaped into the water at the sight of the splashing fish. A few more undersized reds convinced Kemper to try another spot, then it was hit or miss for the next dozen casts.

Kemper finally caught one in the slot, but he threw it back. He didn't want any keepers. He just wanted a big fight.

He dropped the trolling motor and navigated to another creek before anchoring thirty feet from a grassy bend with a deep cut. Kemper fixed a chunk of blue crab on a J-hook and pitched it next to the grass above the bend. He looked at his dog, expecting a show of appreciation for such a lovely cast. Julep licked his muzzle.

Kemper jigged the bait once, then twice, and on the fall, the line tightened. He counted to two Suwannee two, then set the hook with a sharp tug. The water exploded as the fish hit the surface and tried to shake the hook free. Julep jumped up on the casting platform, barking his excitement. The fish ran low and tried to get into the grass. Kemper tightened the drag and steered it away. Then it ran under the boat, and Kemper loosened the drag to let out more line. This pattern repeated itself a dozen times before the bull red finally gave out.

He brought the exhausted beast alongside the boat. The fish thrashed its tail one last time and splashed water on both the angler and the dog. Kemper interpreted the action more as a grudging salute rather than as a gesture of defiance. He didn't bother to bring the redfish into the boat. It was forty inches at least. Julep stretched his head over the gunwale, straining for a lick.

Kemper kept a firm grip under its gill plate as he removed the hook, then held it steady so he could catch his breath. He faced the tired fish into the current so it, too, could recuperate. When its tail began to waggle, he released it and watched it disappear in the tannic water.

Exhilaration and exhaustion overwhelmed him. Kemper sat in the boat, stroking Julep's head and breathing deeply. After a few minutes, he poured fresh coffee into his thermos cup and reached into his back pocket for his can of Copenhagen, only to discover less than half a pinch remained. Undeterred, he opened a dry storage box and retrieved a weathered pouch of Beech-Nut chewing tobacco. He sometimes enjoyed a different delivery method for his nicotine.

Kemper stuffed a generous amount of the shredded leaves into his mouth, chewed, and sipped his coffee. A while passed before he exited the creek, then he cut the engine and drifted with the tide.

As he floated further on the flats, he reflected on how he'd spent most of these last several years adrift, even on land. Existing but not living. He needed what his friend Ben would call a 'come to Jesus' moment of brutal honesty. Kemper looked around and took in his surroundings. Clear skies. Calm water. Gentle breeze. He had drifted into the Church of the Cedar Key Flats, and it was time for an altar call.

Kemper scratched the stubble on his chin as he considered the recent decisions of those around him. Ange should not have given him a badge, yet she had. Rylan should not have argued for him to keep it, yet he did. His outburst at the Sheriff's Office and his cynical attitude toward the investigation had relegated him to the sidelines. Yet here he was, still part of the team.

Each attempt at self-sabotage had been met with a turn in his favor. Ben would call that a God thing. Despite this, something was missing, leaving Kemper irritable and frustrated.

His phone vibrated, and he pulled it out of his pocket. Ben's name flashed across the screen. He chuckled and looked heavenward. "Nice touch."

"Hope I'm not interrupting some high-speed pursuit," Ben said after Kemper answered.

"Just pursuing these reds," he replied.

"You're fishing? I thought you were catching bad guys."

"I'm off today. I'm just killing time."

"Killing time is time well spent," Ben said. "We don't do it enough. I'll get to the point of my call: I've been working on that ice box in Horseshoe Beach, and I think I figured something out."

"Go ahead."

"You need a better capacitor. You see, all these parts have their own demands for electricity, and the capacitor distributes it based on what they need. The problem is it's gauged for average loads, but in different conditions, there's different demands that will sometimes exceed the averages."

"I think I'm following."

"Your factory-installed capacitor gives out too little here and too much there, and that's when things break down. Your thermostat goes out one day and your blower the next. If I get a new capacitor, you'll have better storage and distribution."

"And fewer breakdowns," Kemper concluded. "Permission granted."

"Good. Now they ain't cheap. I'll pay for it up front, and we can true-up later."

Kemper smiled. "Tell me, Ben, what's going to happen when all my ice machines work properly, and you have nothing else to do?"

"Poor Martha," Ben said with a chuckle. "But isn't that a question I should be asking you?"

"What do you mean?"

"After you find Jerry's killer."

"Killers. There might be two."

"Really? Interesting. Okay, after you bring the killers to justice, what's going to happen to you? Are you going to be content running back and forth between your ice machines?"

"I reckon so."

"I doubt it. It ain't who you are. You've spent six years acting like ice vending is your job, but it ain't. You're meant for something else."

Kemper turned the conversation back to fishing, and after a few minutes, they said goodbye and hung up.

He returned to his reflecting mood and wasn't careful as he stepped aft and slipped on the wet surface caused by the redfish's thrashing. The jarring action caused him to swallow a mouthful of tobacco juice. He looked painfully at Julep.

"Now I know why you hate the stuff."

With the bitter aftertaste in his mouth, Kemper reached back to that dark day when it all fell apart.

He looked at the back of his hand and remembered the sticky blood on swollen knuckles as a man spat out broken teeth and feebly tried to hold his jaw in place. The crowd on Dock Street, people he knew—shocked and horrified—and a woman's pleading as he wheeled the axe handle and continued beating the man within an inch of his life, a man he had never met and who had committed no crime.

The Cedar Key Town Council had suspended him as the FDLE opened an investigation. His wife left for Alabama. Then, a few weeks later, the investigation abruptly ended. He had not even suffered the indignity of a perp walk. Kemper signed a piece of paper, turned in his badge, and retreated to the margins of society.

In the weeks and months that followed, the town council appointed an interim police chief, Doyle and Kimmy continued working their rounds, and Gladys continued making awful coffee. Pidge showed homes, Tommy sold baits, and Willie steamed clams. The locals went about their business, and visitors came and left.

The world continued to turn on its axis even though Kemper wasn't there to spin it around, leaving him with a harrowing thought that Cedar Key didn't need him. Perhaps it never did.

He sat on the gunwale in silence, understanding at last the source of his discontent. Julep whimpered, then went silent, too. After a solemn period of reflection—Kemper wasn't sure for how long—his phone vibrated with a text message from Rylan: "Mtg sheriff's office 10 sharp. Big announcement."

Kemper stared at the words until he drew the only conclusion that made sense: Killers found. What other big announcement could there be?

Disappointment for not being there to slap on the cuffs flashed in his head, but quickly disappeared, replaced by an inventory of his contributions to the case. Kemper had found the place where Jerry had been killed, and he had figured out Mama Thighs's involvement, which led to Danny, which led to Dewey, and now to this moment of finding the men who had murdered his friend.

He raised his chin as the corners of his mouth lifted under his thick mustache. His efforts had been essential, after all. Cedar Key, by God, still needed Kemper McRae.

He dropped the motor and raced back to the boathouse. After a quick shave and shower, he climbed in his truck and drove to Bronson, the big F-350 Super Duty announcing the hero's return with its distinctive gurgling growl.

 Kemper arrived at the Sheriff's Office with a few minutes to spare. He joined Doyle and Kimmy in the lobby. Rylan waved them over to the conference room. Sheriff Lane stood against the wall and not at the head of the conference table. Her clenched jaw betrayed a tight-lipped smile.

Other officers filed in. They stood against the wall opposite the sheriff and police chief. Bill, looking sallow, entered with a man and woman in dark business suits. Finally, another man entered and walked to the head of the table, his dark hair combed back, resembling a hard plastic shell. He wore a navy suit, a white dress shirt, and a red necktie. A tiny shield, too small for Kemper to make out, was pinned on his lapel.

The man set a manila folder on the table, opened it, and studied its contents. A minute of awkward silence passed.

Angela cleared her throat. "Everyone is here if you want to begin."

"Thank you, Sheriff," the man said without looking up. Another minute passed.

"Greetings, everyone," he said at the precise moment the second hand reached the top of the clock's face on the wall. "Thank you for your prompt attention to this hastily called meeting." He paused long enough to make eye contact with everyone in the room. A broad smile revealed perfect teeth. "My name is Mike Tinsel. I am Acting Special-Agent-In-Charge of the Drug Enforcement Administration, Atlanta Field Division." He paused again to allow the weight of his authority to sink in. "I know that's a mouthful, so let's keep it simple."

A final pause, this time for dramatic effect.

"I'm in charge of this investigation now."

STAGE THREE — STORM

Intensifying winds become more circular,
and an emerging core begins to form

The Captain had flown for six hours since clearing the storm. Both shoulders ached, his stomach growled, and he struggled to keep his wounded eyes open. He needed food. He needed rest.

He scanned the horizon, hoping to see land or at least white foam that might indicate a skittish school of fish, but his right eye had failed him, and his left one showed only blurry blue. Despite a strong sense of smell, he could no longer pick up the scent of land. He couldn't recall a time when he had ventured so far from shore, and the Captain had lived many years.

His energy drained, he could not stay airborne much longer. Not without nourishment and rest. He coasted low and splashed down. For the next hour, he enjoyed the rhythmic lift and fall over gentle swells. He even drifted to sleep, but for how long he didn't know.

The Captain awoke when an errant wave crested and rolled him under its white cap, and it disappointed him to find he was no longer splashing down in the feeding pools of his dreams with a belly full of fish, surrounded by his fellows.

He beat his wings to lift off the swell. A shaft of pain burned in his shoulders, yet he rose out of the water and flew at a low altitude. He could never return to his colony, but he could at least find his old feeding pools. Then he would search for an uninhabited mangrove where he could roost and recover his strength. He turned in a southeasterly direction.

The pelican alternated between gliding and flapping as he climbed to fifty feet. After an hour, he saw a haze of white in the blurry blue. He circled and climbed a dozen more feet. Then he pulled his wings back and dove into the foamy disruption.

He immediately felt small displacements all around him as fingerlings scattered. Some, confused and disoriented, collided with his body. He opened his bill and swept it side to side, but came up with nothing. His natural buoyancy brought him back to the surface. He lifted his wings from the water. Intense pain shot through him, which he ignored, concentrating instead on the darting silver bodies. He ducked his head beneath the surface and kicked furiously, hoping the panicked fry would swim into his open pouch.

His reflexes were too slow. His frustration grew. The Captain used the momentum of the swell to pursue the fish, but they skittered away. He stabbed his bill harder, creating an even greater disturbance. Finally, his bill struck and stunned one, and he scooped it into his pouch.

Instinct alerted him to another displacement lurking below. A large one. It moved rapidly toward him. The Captain beat his wings with a fury he didn't know he possessed and lifted off the surface, reaching twenty feet in the air before the sea exploded beneath him. A spray of water reached him, but the beast didn't. The pelican climbed higher and did not look back.

He flew for another hour on a boost of adrenaline and without concern for direction. Then the pain returned, as did the exhaustion. He glided to take the pressure off his sore muscles, but it wasn't enough. Nor was the one small fish enough to replenish his strength.

The Captain inhaled deeply, hoping for a whiff of land. He smelled only a churning sea of white crests on quickening waves. And rain. The blurry blue soon became gray. A short while later, he felt the distant vibration of thunder.

He had no choice but to return to the water. The pelican glided low and touched down in the restless sea. Hours passed. The waves rose higher and fell harder.

The Captain felt neither fear nor sadness. As the wind and rain intensified, he pulled his wings close, rested his head on aching shoulders, and waited for the storm to take him.

— *Chapter 21* —

I want to welcome you all to Operation Windswept."

Mike Tinsel looked around the crowded conference room, making sure all eyes were on him. He recognized some of the attendees from the dossiers that his team had quickly assembled, compiled from commendation reports, newspaper clippings, social media posts, internal affairs reports, and anything else they could find about the personnel of the Levy County Sheriff's Office and Cedar Key Police Department. These included files on Angela Lane and Rylan McRae.

"First, I want to thank Sheriff Lane and Police Chief McRae for their efforts to apprehend the suspect in the murder of"—he paused and looked down at his one-page executive summary—"the murder of Jerry Whitmore."

Rylan nodded. Angela stared ahead.

"Secondly, your suspect is our suspect in a much larger criminal probe. Operation Windswept is a multi-jurisdictional, multi-state effort, two-and-a-half years in the making, aimed at disrupting and dismantling methamphetamine rings in the southeastern United States. Its targets are drug traffickers, money launderers, gangs, and transnational criminal organizations."

The Acting Special-Agent-In-Charge paused to take note of those who appeared impressed with what they had heard and those who looked like they had wandered into the wrong room. The older man with the thick mustache and cowboy hat belonged in the latter category. Tinsel had a file on him too.

He continued. "I want to thank Sheriff Lane in particular for inviting us down and agreeing to integrate her investigation into our larger operation. Based on the facial composite we received from your office, we are confident in identifying your suspect as Paul Dell Williams." Tinsel cleared his throat. "Paulie, as he's known, is a trafficker for an Atlanta-based gang known as Three Dead Dogs. TDD is an affiliate of a larger DTO called Gangster Disciples."

Rick Delaney nodded knowingly, but everyone else looked either passive or puzzled.

Tinsel's tone became professorial. "Pardon me, we use a lot of acronyms and not everyone is familiar with these terms. The Gangster Disciples is a Drug Trafficking Organization, or DTO, formed originally in the south side of Chicago and currently operating in twenty-five states. Like other DTOs, they receive a high-quality product from Mexican cartels. *Para la Operación Windswept, el objetivo es el Cártel Jalisco Nueva Generación.*"

He even rolled his Rs.

Kemper rolled his eyes.

Tinsel continued. "Placing Paul Dell Williams in the Cedar Key area means TDD, and by extension, Gangster Disciples, has expanded their zone of influence. Consequently, Operation Windswept can now cast a wider net."

He looked at his colleague sitting next to the staff attorney. She subtly shook her head. He sighed. "Ladies and gentlemen, our presentation appears to be at odds with your technology. Let's take a short break, say, ten minutes, and then we'll resume."

Deputies and officers looked around awkwardly before a few shuffled out of the room. One of the sheriff's aides began fumbling with the agent's laptop.

Angela and Rylan exchanged words, then she broke away, murmured something to her staff attorney, then approached Kemper, Kimmy, and Doyle. "My office, now," she said to the group. Rylan trailed behind, a scowl on his face.

"Nice new friend, Sheriff," Rylan quipped as he entered the sheriff's office.

"Knock it off."

"Seriously, what the hell were you thinking, inviting them to take over our investigation? Excuse me, *your* investigation."

"I said knock it off, Chief. I asked you all to come here so I can explain what happened, not to be lectured by you. Or anyone else," she added, eyeing Kemper. She sat in her button-tufted chair. Everyone else stood. Kemper leaned against the wall. "First of all, I did not invite the DEA to come down and take over the investigation."

"That's not what we heard," Rylan snapped.

Angela's tone sharpened. "And if you had more experience in law enforcement, you wouldn't be so gullible."

"Gullible?"

"They invited themselves," Bill said, hoping to de-escalate the tension in the room. "That's how it works. The Atlanta field office called shortly after we had faxed them the facial composite. They said they already had eyes on the suspect, part of an ongoing investigation, yada-yada-yada. They said they'd like to come down and partner with us. That may sound like a request, but believe me, it isn't. When the DEA wants to get involved, the only two acceptable responses are 'yes' and 'yes, pretty please, with a fucking cherry on top.'"

"Bill!" Angela's eyes widened as she reproached him. She turned to the others. "Look, I'm not happy with this either, but I've talked to Special Agent Tinsel—"

"You mean, Acting Special-Agent-In-Charge," Rylan snarked.

The sheriff cleared her throat. "Acting Special-Agent-In-Charge Tinsel has assured me they will not lose sight of what our investigation is about. In fact, he would like some of our team to work on his task force. He was quite emphatic that finding our suspects is critical to the overall success of his operation."

"Bullshit," Kemper said as all eyes turned to him. "The DEA will call the shots now, which means they'll control the calendar. Jerry will be moldering in his goddamn grave before these big shots move on the killers."

"Justice delayed is justice denied," Kimmy added.

Kemper nodded. "Damn straight."

"Quit jumping to conclusions," Angela said. "We are going to stay focused on apprehending Jerry's killers. As for the DEA, look, we are getting overwhelmed with meth in our community, and we don't have the resources to slow it down, much less stop it. It would be irresponsible of me to turn down their assistance, especially since, as Bill so eloquently said, we don't really have a choice."

"This is not about drugs," Kemper growled. "It's about murder!"

"I know what this is about, and—"

"The hell you do!"

Angela slapped a hand on her desk and locked her eyes on him. "That's enough, deputy!"

And Kemper, like a fish that swallowed the bait too deeply, could do nothing as the sheriff yanked the hook free, pulling his guts out along with it.

"You are done here, and you are done, period," she said. "Leave your badge with Bill and go back to your ice machines."

"That was short-lived," Bill muttered, but not softly enough. It drew a look from both Kemper and Angela.

The sheriff stood. "Now, I believe the rest of us are needed back in the conference room."

Kemper watched them file out as he removed the badge from his belt. He could holler an apology to the sheriff, or he could ask Rylan to win another argument on his behalf. But his pride wouldn't allow it.

His chin dropped to his chest, and he cursed himself, convinced that he had just blown his last chance to bring the killers to justice. He ran his thumb over the badge one last time, tossed it on her desk, and left.

— *Chapter 22* —

Bill caught Kemper in the lobby as he headed toward the exit. "Hold up, Kemp! I wanted to apologize for my remark. You deserved better than that."

Kemper turned. "I've had worse."

"Yeah, I figured a grizzled guy like you would shake it off. Look, she's still pissed at you for the outburst in the interrogation room. And now this. She doesn't want an ass-kisser like Delaney, but she does expect people to respect the chain of command and to show a professional demeanor. That's not asking too much. And don't forget, she stuck her neck out for you by bringing you back on."

"You followed me out here to tell me that?"

"No, I followed you out here to tell you to get back inside. I think you should sit in on this meeting."

"I've been fired, Bill."

"Let me work on that. In the meantime—"

"You wily old dog." Kemper raised an eyebrow. "First, you drop the F-bomb in front of Saint Ange, and now you're engaged in what looks like insubordination. You're not just a tad agitated by these DEA folks, are you?"

"Well, like you, I'd prefer they stick to their business, and we stick to ours. This Tinsel guy says they're casting a wide net. I suspect it's more akin to dragging a trawl, and I worry people who have nothing to do with Jerry's murder might get caught up in it."

"So, how's me going back in there going to change that?"

"It won't. But what else are you going to do?"

"Go home. Get drunk. Listen to Bocephus."

"That can wait. Ange won't do anything if you step inside. Wouldn't want to cause a scene, you know. She might take me to the woodshed later, but I'll survive." He winked. "Probably."

Kemper followed Bill to the conference room and stood by the back door. He avoided eye contact with Angela.

Mike Tinsel began his presentation. He pointed a red dot clicker at an organizational chart projected onto a wall screen. "We're going to walk through the leadership structure of Three Dead Dogs to see where your suspect fits in."

The next slide showed a man's mugshot. "TDD was founded by this man, Marvin Lee Johnson, a little over nine years ago. Mr. Johnson had worked his way up from street corner slinger to enforcer in the Lakewood Heights neighborhood. Legend has it there were three dead dogs in an abandoned lot where Gangster Disciples gave Marvin permission to form his own crew. Others say the dogs were alive and that he shot them in an act of cruelty as part of the initiation, but that cannot be confirmed."

A click brought up a new slide, showing a surveillance photo of Marvin wearing a black and red tracksuit. A woman in professional business attire walked alongside him.

"The woman next to him is Sylvia Jackson King. Unlike Mr. Johnson, Sylvia managed to escape her troubled neighborhood and graduate from Spelman College with a degree in computer and information sciences. She began working at FedEx Logistics as a data entry specialist, was promoted to shipping and receiving, and eventually became a warehouse operations manager, making good middle-class money."

Tinsel held both hands in front of him as he spoke, as though holding an invisible flowerpot. He continued. "Unfortunately, Sylvia King could not break old habits. You see, Marvin Johnson was Sylvia's high school flame. She became known to the Fulton County Sheriff's Office when she moved in with Mr. Johnson.

"Then, a little over three years ago, Marvelous Marvin, as he was known, was sentenced to eighteen years in a federal penitentiary for RICO conspiracy and attempted murder in aid of racketeering. Sylvia King became the proxy leader while he ran the gang from a prison cell in Arkansas. His sentence, however, was cut short when three prisoners belonging to a rival gang—soldiers, if you will— shivved him in the back and neck using makeshift weapons. He was thirty-four years old.

"Sylvia King then became the *de facto* leader of TDD. With ruthlessness learned from Marvin and her own talent for logistics, the gang grew from a small crew controlling a few street corners into one with territory outside Atlanta and even outside of Georgia. If Marvelous Marvin is the muscle, then Full Stop Sylvia, as she is known, is the brains of Three Dead Dogs."

Rylan tried to suppress a snicker, but it caught the attention of the Acting Special-Agent-In-Charge. "I know it may seem unusual to some of you that a woman could lead a gang," Tinsel said with a haughty tone. "We live in different times, gentlemen, and we need to check our privilege. We should not feel threatened by powerful women in powerful positions. Your sheriff is a shrewd and savvy leader on the right side of the law. Is it really so hard to believe there are shrewd and savvy female leaders on the other side?"

Rylan tilted his head toward Angela. "I think he just called you a shrew."

Tinsel raised his voice. "Chief McRae, don't you agree?"

"It's the names, that's all," Rylan said defensively. "Three Dead Dogs. Full Stop Sylvia. They sound silly."

"Certainly, the names do not sound like ones you'd hear in a Hollywood movie. Nevertheless, I hope you take them seriously. In addition to drug trafficking, TDD has engaged in armed robbery, carjacking, extortion, and murder. As for Miss King, ask yourself: How many drug arrests are precipitated by careless moving traffic violations? Broken taillights? Speeding on the interstate? Her drivers are paid well to be extra careful, to not roll through stop signs. Thus,

Full Stop Sylvia. It might not sound cutthroat, but do not underestimate this adversary because of name or gender."

Tinsel clicked through to the next slide, and Paulie's face appeared on the screen along with a dozen more photos—some mugshots, some surveillance. "Which brings us to your suspect, Paul Dell Williams. Paulie is one of several drivers for Sylvia King. On screen are her soldiers, slingers, and enforcers who make up the rest of TDD. Sheriff Lane has made me aware of a second suspect in the local murder here. I would wager it is one of these three." He ran the red laser side to side across the faces of the enforcers. Their full names appeared in small type under their photos, but their street names stood out—Bones, C-Dog, and Tank.

Kemper wondered if he could keep a straight face while apprehending someone called C-Dog. Then he remembered that he no longer needed to concern himself with arresting them. He was just an observer, here at Bill's odd invitation.

"This gang is active in your community," Tinsel said. "In other places, it's the Latin Kings, Tri-City Bombers, or some other DTO. These are the gangs spreading Mexican Ice and Chinese fentanyl throughout the southeast, and they are the targets of Operation Windswept."

After a quick glance at Rylan, Tinsel raised a finger for emphasis. "I assure you, Three Dead Dogs is a lethal organization, and Full Stop Sylvia, despite the name, is a smart, strategic, and— yes—ruthless leader. You underestimate her at your own peril."

— *Chapter 23* —

Sylvia was having a good cry.

The cathartic tears helped her keep a toehold in reality. Recent events had threatened both her life and her sanity.

A few minutes before, Sylvia had stepped outside her bedroom. She hadn't left her room much since arriving at the meth house. Tank had arranged it so she didn't have to. Unlike Paulie, Tank's face wasn't known in Cedar Key or Otter Creek or anywhere else in Levy County, so he made food runs and served her meals in the bedroom.

Tank made other efforts to increase her comfort. Walmart's version of purple silky sheets covered a new queen-size Serta mattress. A toilet seat in wood veneer with chrome hinges replaced the stained and cracked plastic one. Glade air fresheners sprang from every electrical outlet except for the one powering an air purifier and another one juicing the seventy-two-inch television. Scented candles covered the nightstand, dresser drawer, and bathroom countertops.

Despite these efforts, the place still had a dingy odor, a damp feel, and the persistent smell of rotting wood. Tank assured her he'd look for a better place. "A palace for my queen," he would say.

Sylvia hated him calling her queen, but he had stepped up, which she appreciated when lucid enough to think about it. She stayed on a steady cocktail of pills—Xanax, Tylenol with codeine, and a muscle relaxer. They helped her sleep for long hours and tolerate her surroundings when she was awake.

Thoughts of the attempt on her life drifted in and out as did memories of high living and deep loving from when she belonged to

Marvelous Marvin Johnson. A decorative sign that read 'The Queen's Palace' had greeted her every time she entered her luxury apartment in Lakewood Heights. She would only ever be Marvin's queen. She would never be Tank's.

Sylvia pushed herself up on the bed and propped a pillow behind her. She called out for Tank, but got no reply. She called out again and, again, nothing. The fog lifted, and she remembered he had left yesterday to drive back to Atlanta to retrieve the small safe from her apartment. Two hundred thousand dollars in cash and jewelry were locked inside.

She began dialing Paulie's number on the burner phone but remembered he had also left, driving north to Apalachicola to pick up product from a different supplier at an alternative drop site. Despite getting muscled out of Atlanta, she still had a business to run.

Sylvia punched Tank's number. A few seconds later, the ringtone blared outside her bedroom door. It went unanswered. He must have returned from Atlanta, which confused her because he normally rushed into her room whenever she summoned him.

Tank loved seeing her propped up in bed, surrounded by the fluffy pillows he had bought for her. His eyes always drifted to her chest and hips. She knew what he wanted, but she would never let that happen.

Sylvia had taken C-Dog into her bed after Marvin's death, but, to her, it was strictly maintenance sex. C-Dog understood the assignment. He never tried to establish an emotional connection. An emotional connection with Tank didn't worry Sylvia, but his reputation for sexual aggression and brutality did. Tank the Enforcer on the street, Tank the Rapist in the sheets.

She got up and walked to the door on unsteady legs. Sylvia called out his name, but got no response. She cracked the door open and called out again. Nothing. She opened the door a little further and saw her safe on the floor in front of the coffee table, and next to it, the decorative sign from her apartment: 'The Queen's Palace.'

Sylvia swung the door open and stepped into the living room. "Tank, why the hell—"

She froze.

Tank lay passed out on a filthy couch, head back, mouth open, a scrawny, decrepit old woman curled around him. Her scarred legs straddled one of Tank's muscular ones, and her thin arms reached around his chest. The old woman's face, pocked with sores, nuzzled under his chin, her matted gray hair tangled with Tank's unkempt beard. She mewled softly and slowly, gyrating on his leg.

Sylvia blinked, her breath caught in her throat. The old woman turned her jaundiced eyes and squinted to make out the figure by the bedroom door. She smiled, revealing yellow nubs of teeth on rotting gums. "You must be Queenie," she said as she continued to gyrate. Her voice sounded like a rusty hinge. "My name's Sweetie. Ain't that somethin'?"

Full Stop Sylvia staggered back into her bedroom. She slammed the door shut. Images flashed in her mind. C-Dog down, blood spilling from his head. Bones running away and then collapsing on the sidewalk. Marvin removing her blindfold to show her their new apartment. A suitcase filled with Hamiltons and Jacksons. Tank beating a street corner slinger with a crowbar. A doctor telling her she would never carry a baby to term. Marvin's rhythmic breathing as she clung to him under mulberry silk sheets.

All replaced with the image of Sweetie dry-humping Tank in her trashy meth palace.

The room swirled. Sylvia fell face-first onto the bed and gathered the pillows around her. And she wailed. Hurt, fear, and sadness poured out of her. She rocked against the pillows, and the harder she rocked, the better she felt. The wailing diminished into what could have been mistaken for whimpering when, in fact, it was just a good cry. Eventually, a sensation she had not had since arriving at the meth house seized her: hunger. Genuine hunger.

Sylvia used her sleeve to dry her eyes. She got out of bed and felt calm, lighter. Her arms and legs felt looser, stronger. She inhaled deeply through her nose, stretched her arms and arched her back. Sturdy on her feet, she stormed out of the bedroom, picked up the Queen's Palace sign, and heaved it at Tank. Sweetie rolled off him just in time.

"Get your junk ass up," Sylvia yelled, "and go get me a motherfuckin' cheeseburger, some motherfuckin' fries, and some motherfuckin' clam chowder. And when you get back, don't you dare come into my room calling me your motherfuckin' queen!"

When Paulie returned from Apalachicola in the late evening, Tank met him underneath the uneven awning with the rusty frame. The enforcer offered no help as Paulie transferred product from his car's trunk to the rain barrels. He just glowered at him, scratching his arms and grinding his teeth.

Paulie recognized the look—the pinkish face and glassy eyes. The short, quick breaths. This was the erratic phase of a meth high, and Paulie did not want to be on the receiving end of Tank's wrath.

"I like your connection, T," he said, hoping flattery would soothe the savage beast. "Good stuff. Cut, weighed, bagged. Ready to go."

Tank blinked. "Yeah, man. It's good shit. Told you I had a good connect. I got connects you don't know nothing about."

"That's why Full Stop needs you."

Tank's reddened eyes narrowed. "She don't know all my connects, man. She thinks she knows, but she don't know. There's going to be change, P. Real soon. You best not cross me." Then, after a flurry of scratching, he changed subjects. "We gotta go."

"I just got here."

"Shut up. We gotta go."

"But—"

"Finish that and let's go."

Paulie saw no point challenging him. Ten minutes later, they pulled onto State Road 24, heading into town. "Hey, T, you're driving the wrong way. I can't go to Cedar Key! Turn around!"

Tank smiled and accelerated the vehicle. He leveled off at the speed limit, which gave the trafficker some reassurance that the enforcer had not fully abandoned his senses. Paulie slouched down in the passenger seat when they reached town. Tank rolled down the driver's side window and propped his elbow on the door. The cool, salty air rushed in.

"Please, T, please!" Paulie yelled as he slid from the seat to the floorboard. "My face is freaking everywhere, man!"

Tank turned up the radio and drove through town. He drove down Dock Street, around the marina, and down what seemed like a dozen side roads. Then Tank parked and turned off the music.

"Are we still in Cedar Key?" Paulie whisper-hissed. He stretched his neck to look over the door, then slouched even lower. "Oh shit!"

Tank seemed more focused than before, and the scratching had stopped. He called out to a pedestrian, "Hey, what time does that place close?"

"You mean the Breeze?" came the friendly reply. "It just closed. Come back tomorrow. Live music starts—"

"Shut up," Tank said, cutting him off. He looked down at Paulie. "Gimme a cigarette."

Paulie handed him the whole pack and his lighter, and Tank passed the time smoking while Paulie sat uncomfortably on the floorboard.

"Sit up," he said to Paulie after he finished his smoke.

"C'mon, T. Someone will recognize me."

"Sit your ass up, or you'll be walking back."

Paulie reluctantly obliged. Dock Street was empty, but activity loomed in The Wayward Breeze. Dark silhouettes moved around the open-air restaurant. They occasionally passed under the light by the entrance.

"Which one is she?" Tank said.

"Who?"

"The bitch you talked to. The one who told the police what you looked like."

Paulie's stomach hollowed out as it became clear why Tank had taken the risk of bringing him into town. "Hey, this ain't necessary. Did Full Stop—"

"Ain't nothing going to happen here. I'm not stupid like you. I'm not going to make a scene where someone can recognize my face. Now tell me which one is her."

Paulie felt trapped. He didn't want to betray the pretty waitress, but he also didn't want to be the target of Tank's wrath. Two women passed under the light. He considered identifying the wrong woman, but then Tank's violence would fall on an innocent victim.

And the pretty waitress was not innocent, he reminded himself. She had given the police his description. She wanted him arrested for something Tank had done.

The two women left the restaurant and paused under a streetlamp where one of them lit a cigarette. They waved back at a man wearing a chef's apron.

"Last fucking time, loser," Tank said. "Which one is your girlfriend?"

With a heavy sigh, Paulie issued the death sentence. "The one with the cigarette."

"Christ, man, I was hoping you'd say that. Why didn't you tell me she looked that good?"

"She's not a threat, T. Not to you or me or Full Stop or anyone. The police here don't know what they're doing. They're just dumb hicks. They even let Danny go 'cause they ain't got nothing."

Tank turned and glared at Paulie. "What do you mean they let Danny go? When did they pick up Danny? When did he talk to the fucking police?"

Paulie's bowels loosened. He had just issued a second death sentence. Before he could talk it back, Tank's attention turned to the waitress who got into a faded black Monte Carlo and drove off. He pulled away from the curb and followed at a safe distance.

"What else haven't you told me, you fucking weasel?" Tank spat out the words as he drove.

Paulie didn't respond. He slouched in his seat and looked out the side window as Tank followed the black car onto State Road 24 and across the bridge, the same bridge where they had dumped the golf cart and the old man's body. They turned onto a county road that forked to the left and drove another two miles before they saw the vehicle's brake lights. It turned right and disappeared. Tank pulled onto the shoulder of the road and turned off the headlights. After a few minutes, he drove cautiously forward.

A lime rock road cut through a stand of pines. Three clustered palm trees on the opposite side of the road were unique enough to remember. He would be back. Tank turned the vehicle around and drove toward the meth house.

Paulie lit a cigarette with a shaking hand.

"Why are you so nervous?" Tank said. "You worried about your girlfriend? I didn't think a shit town like this would have a woman like that. I'm going to have to get to know her better."

"She doesn't know anything that can hurt us," Paulie said, his voice soft and shaky. "And Danny's cool, man. They let him go. Said it was nothing."

Tank ignored him.

"Is Full Stop okay with this?" Paulie asked.

Tank's hand darted across the seat and snatched Paulie by the ear. He twisted it clockwise, then counterclockwise as the trafficker squirmed and yelped before the enforcer released him with a shove.

"Full Stop ain't got nothing to do with this, fool," Tank said. "If you were paying attention, you'd know who's in charge now."

Tank's thoughts turned to Sylvia. After all he had done to get her safely out of Atlanta, the ungrateful bitch had not brought him into her bed. He would fix that. He could see himself on top of her, his forearm pressed across her neck, doing to her what he had done to so many weaker women. But he couldn't do it yet. Not until all the pieces were in place. So, he would keep Sylvia in her drug-addled fog, believing in her authority, at least for a little while longer.

Tank, instead, would release his rage on the waitress.

Then he would kill her.

— *Chapter 24* —

Do you prefer Kemper or McRae? I suppose Chief McRae is still an acceptable honorific, although it might get confusing with—"

"Kemper is fine."

"Then Kemper it is," Tinsel said, slightly mocking Kemper's Southern accent. He lifted his White Claw and sipped. "And in an informal setting like this, you may call me Mike."

Kemper did not call him anything. They sat in the corner of the Way Key Restaurant & Inn on Second and B Street in Cedar Key. The lunchtime crowd had already left, and dinner patrons would not arrive for another few hours. They were alone except for the waitstaff and an elderly woman sitting in the screened porch section by the window. She wore a gown and shawl, oversized sunglasses, and a large sun hat despite being indoors. Her hand rested on a sketch pad, and she stared out at the blue sky as if awaiting inspiration.

Tinsel set his drink on a white cocktail napkin next to a file folder with Kemper's name printed on the tab. "Will you have some lunch?" Tinsel asked.

"No, I came because Chief McRae—"

"Your son?"

"Yes, my son."

Convenient, Tinsel thought. "Interesting," he said instead. "Do you have other family in law enforcement?"

Kemper sipped from his water glass. "Had a great-great who was a Texas Ranger before my folks moved east."

"Is that why you wear a cowboy hat? I mean, I don't see many men wearing cowboy hats here."

"Not many in Cedar Key, I'll grant you. But you'll see a lot of these up and down the Big Bend."

"So, you really are an outsider?" Tinsel said with a raised eyebrow. "Even when you were on the inside."

Kemper looked at the file folder, then back at Tinsel. "My son said you wanted to talk to me. I'm here out of respect for him."

"Out of respect for him," Tinsel repeated. "Sounds like you don't want to be here."

"I'm not sure how I can help you, and I don't want to waste your time."

"I'm the one who asked to meet, so it's not a waste of my time. Is it yours?"

Kemper shrugged. "I've got nothing to do and all day to do it."

Tinsel smiled. "Nothing to do and all day to do it. I like that."

A flash of annoyance crossed Kemper's face. He tapped a finger on the manila folder. "I reckon you can write it down in your file. Is that why we're here? Something in there interests you?"

"To the point. Very good." Tinsel sipped his White Claw and sucked his teeth. "I'll start with what's not in the file. I'm not impressed with the local authorities here. You, however, well, the sheriff's attorney tells me you're the reason we're even on the scent of the suspects. Yet you've been out of this business for quite some time."

No response came from Kemper, his face impassive.

"I'll confess," Tinsel said, "I'm having a tough time reading this community."

"That's what you wanted to talk about—the community? I'm not a historian, and I ain't a tour guide."

Tinsel leaned forward and opened the file. *Time to move some pieces on the chessboard.* "Chief of Police Kemper McRae. Reserve Deputy Kemper McRae. Fishing tournament legend Kemper

McRae. And Kemper McRae, proprietor of Twice the Ice vending machines. You get around. You've been around."

"Your point?"

"I'd like you to join Operation Windswept."

A deep belly laugh erupted, drawing the attention of the woman by the window and a waiter setting silverware at nearby tables.

"Why do you find this funny?" Tinsel asked.

"You talked to Bill. You know I got fired."

Tinsel couldn't disguise his satisfaction. "Actually, you haven't been fired. I had reviewed your file earlier and liked what I saw, so I mentioned bringing you onto the task force. The sheriff shot it down. Said she had dismissed you. Her attorney, however, said he had not followed through on your termination. So, technically, you are still a sworn officer."

"I'll be sure to thank Bill for slow-walking the paperwork."

"It was very odd, their exchange. Anyway, the sheriff dropped her objection. I think she appreciates our ability to interdict drug trafficking in her county. She sees the problem. With your experience, Kemper, you'd be helping… You're laughing again."

"I am because it's funny. You see, I don't want to be part of your task force. I don't even want y'all here." Kemper's face hardened. "We were damn close to finding the killers, then y'all came in and stopped us cold. So, if you're looking for my contribution, here it is: Go back to Atlanta, and let us do our work."

Enough with the pawns. Move a rook. "The murder investigation has not stopped," Tinsel said. "I didn't share this at the briefing, but I actually interviewed your suspect a few years ago. Some rookie cop in Fulton County had botched the intake procedure after an arrest, so Paulie was about to be released from custody. I spoke to him, hoping to develop him as a confidential informant. He wasn't interested."

"Where's this going?"

"Paul Dell Williams is a nervous, weak-minded fool. That was my assessment then, and I'm sure nothing has changed. If we get ahold of him now, I'll break him and roll up the rest of the gang."

Kemper's eyes narrowed. "But you want him for trafficking. I want him for murder."

"We can tag a murder charge on him."

Kemper looked like he needed to spit. "Something about tagging on rubs me the wrong way. Like it's a secondary matter when, to me, it's the only thing that matters."

"There's a practical reason for that, if I may be candid. You see, the appropriate federal agency for murders across jurisdictions is the FBI. If we lead with murder, the FBI would have cause to step in."

Kemper smirked. "Sure would hate to see an outside agency disrupt your investigation."

"Touché," Tinsel said with a tip of his White Claw. "You know, I'm surprised you don't want to help us. You've dedicated your life to protecting this town. Meth, fentanyl, and other opioids are ravaging many communities, especially rural ones."

"I'm not happy about it, but I don't think it's as bad as you do. At least not in Cedar Key."

"The signs are all around you, Kemper. Think of what happened to Jimmy."

"Who the hell is Jimmy?" Kemper snarled.

"I meant Jerry." *Unforced error.* Tinsel took a sip of White Claw. "My point is, meth trafficking is not a victimless crime, and the purpose of Operation Windswept is to remove these bad actors who are bringing in the drugs and creating the conditions where good people like Jerry get killed. The briefing I got on Cedar Key painted the picture of a quaint little fishing village. Off the beaten path. A throwback to Old Florida. Don't you want to protect that?"

Kemper straightened, and pride resonated in his voice. "Cedar Key's different and definitely charming, but what it is not is a town full of meth heads. We got crusty old anglers and clam farmers, burnt out hippies and Southern legacies, too." He nodded toward the lady with the shawl and sunglasses. "Even artsy eccentrics. Then there's people like Jerry, a Yankee snowbird who found paradise by the pier."

"What about you?"

"Me? I reckon I'm just an old saltwater cowboy."

Tinsel raised an eyebrow, then he looked at the file. *Better deploy the knights.* "Ice vending businesses between Crystal River and Steinhatchee. Steen or stine?"

"It's steen," Kemper said. "Steinhatchee."

"Ever heard of Louisa, Kentucky, or Concord, New Hampshire? Small towns, lots of charm, lots of pride. Then meth came in and gutted them. Now they're husks of their former selves."

"Not my problem."

"Is that because the victims are mostly poor whites or blacks across the tracks?"

Kemper abruptly rose from the chair. "You can take that class and race bullshit somewhere else. I'm not interested in solving everyone's problems. My friend got murdered, and I want to bring his killers to justice." He turned to leave.

"You can't do that sitting on the sidelines. With me, you can still hunt the killers. Without me, the termination papers go through."

Tinsel waited until Kemper turned back. "We have new intelligence. At least two members of Sylvia's crew were killed recently in a gang-related shooting, and word is Sylvia King is no longer in Atlanta, that she fled somewhere off the radar. Probably somewhere near here."

"What makes you think that?"

"Sylvia is going to lay low while she plots her revenge. She has other territories, and we're looking at all of them. But this area makes the most sense, and Paulie was spotted here."

Kemper sat back down. "I know. I was at the briefing."

Tinsel swigged his drink. "I'm leaving here today on that pathetic strip of asphalt you call an airport. This storm brewing in the Gulf is supposed to turn into a hurricane, and it's heading toward the panhandle. We have some major figures under surveillance there, and I don't want them slipping through the cracks due to an 'Act of God.'"

Slide the bishop into position. "We're using a rental here as a temporary headquarters, and my agents are staying behind. But they do not know the area like you do. I'm not asking you to take down the whole trafficking apparatus. Just help us find the man who killed—"

"Good lord!" Kemper exploded, slapping a hand on the table, his eyes wide, nostrils flaring above his thick mustache. "That's what we were doing before you people showed up!"

The eccentric artist pushed away from her table and stood, making the effort as noisy as possible to signal her dissatisfaction. She tucked the sketch pad under her arm and marched out of the room. "Knaves," she huffed as she passed the two men.

Tinsel leaned back in his chair. *Position the queen.* "Then it will be easy for you to resume, this time working with my task force. I'll make a deal with you, Kemper. You help us find Paul Dell Williams, and I'll separate him and his accomplice from Operation Windswept once the indictments drop. Your locals can then prosecute them on Murder One."

Kemper raised an eyebrow.

Tinsel shrugged. "I get what I want, which is a big sweep of arrests and contraband. You get what you want—justice for your friend."

"Why do I get the feeling you're trying a little too hard to get me on your team? There's plenty of badges who know the area."

So he's not as dumb as the rest of these rubes, Tinsel thought. *Maneuver and misdirect.* "Because it's not about you, Kemper. It's about me. As a backgrounder, I did my undergrad at UCLA and my Juris Doctorate at Harvard. I'm one of the youngest agents to ever hold this level of authority at the Drug Enforcement Administration, and I want more. I cannot afford to have this go sideways because some gangbangers start a war on the eve of my operation."

Feint and fade. "To be honest, I'd rather not work with you. Your forced retirement, your assault on a tourist, and the subsequent investigation by the Florida Department of Law Enforcement. These are not things I want recruits finding in the footnotes when the history of Operation Windswept is written."

Kemper shifted uncomfortably in his seat.

Tinsel waved a dismissive hand. "Water under the bridge, Kemper. The guy you beat up didn't even press charges, if I read that correctly. And I don't think too highly of the FDLE either. One thing I've learned going up against the cartels is you've got to paint outside the lines sometimes. Still, deputizing you for the task force is problematic, but I'm willing to risk it."

"I'm not sure—"

"I can do that?" The smug look returned to Tinsel's face. "Of course, I can. Look, I'm the decision-maker here, not the sheriff and not your son. I can carve out Murder One for Paul Dell Williams and his accomplice, and I can assign you to the task force."

"I was going to say, I'm still not sure I want to be part of it."

"Work with me, Kemper. Give me a week, and then we'll reassess."

Tinsel waited until he saw a nod, then he pushed a business card across the table. "The address for our temporary HQ is on the back. Come by and we'll sign some papers and bring you up to speed."

Kemper, looking a bit puzzled, took the card and left.

"Checkmate," Tinsel said after Kemper left the room. He tipped the last sip from his White Claw and called to a nearby waiter, "Get me another one of these. Black Cherry."

He pulled out a small notepad from the inside pocket of his jacket and jotted down the day and time, followed by: 'Met with Target.'

Tinsel logged suspicions in the notepad that were too underdeveloped to share with his colleagues for fear of jeopardizing his carefully cultivated image as the brilliant 3D chess master. One way to always appear right is to hide the many times one is wrong. Tinsel's speculations stayed tucked away until they were ready for primetime.

The White Claw arrived, and he drank deeply. In Atlanta, he seldom drank alcohol, but something about the atmosphere of this breezy little town invited careless consumption. Even though he knew better. Even though he was on duty. The alcohol had the added benefit of encouraging his paranoia, where he saw drug dealers and corrupt cops everywhere. With Kemper McRae, Tinsel saw both. The arrogant son of a bitch even referred to himself as a saltwater cowboy!

Years ago as a newly minted agent, Mike Tinsel had practically memorized the case file of Operation Everglades, the 1980s bust of pot smugglers who called themselves saltwater cowboys. That DEA operation netted hundreds of arrests, including some who wore the badge.

Parallels between the small fishing villages of Everglades City and Cedar Key were too tempting to ignore. History was repeating itself, and Tinsel smiled at the thought of Operation Windswept being studied by the next generation of DEA agents who would marvel at how he connected dots no one else could see.

His suspicion began on the drive down from Atlanta when Tinsel read Kemper's file and then spoke to the FDLE investigator who had handled Kemper's case.

"Lost his cool, my ass," said the investigator, now retired and bitter. "No way he just snapped. He knew the guy he beat up."

"How so?" Tinsel asked.

"Start with that big house he's got. The one no one on a police chief's salary could ever afford. It belonged to a rich old lady who moved down from up north and—get this—she leaves it to Kemper in her will."

"She's not related to him?"

"Nope. A gorgeous Gulf view home on exceptional waterfront property given to the local yokel police chief."

"Was he screwing her?"

"It wasn't sexual with her, but it gets us to the juicy part. See, the man Kemper nearly killed was the old lady's son-in-law, which means she had a daughter. But the old lady leaves the house to Kemper, not the daughter. Kemper then goes and beats the hell out of the son-in-law, almost killing him."

"What did the victim say about it?"

"Never got a statement. Ten days after the incident, the son-in-law leaves the hospital, resigns his cushy job at the University of Florida, and returns to his home country. Can you believe that? Left the goddamn country! The wife—that is, the old lady's daughter—she's some fancy professor at UF, or maybe administration. She said it had to do with her husband's cultural machismo—his old-world pride wouldn't allow him to stick around and live in shame. So he left her, left his career, left the country."

"Did you interview her and confirm the affair?"

"Was going to, but I had to close it out before I could."

"Good Ole Boy system?"

"No, something else. We had a major clusterfuck in my jurisdiction that pulled me away from Kemper's crimes. Back in Gainesville, a joint city-county sting had nabbed a bunch of pervs on the internet trying to hook up with underage kids. One of the pervs was the paper's editorial writer who stroked the liberal politicians in town. Bottom line—he didn't get the perp-walk. Well, word leaks as it always does, so we're called in to see how far up the chain the order went to let him go."

"That's why you backed off Kemper?"

"Had to. The locals couldn't investigate themselves. We were short-staffed, and this overshadowed everything else, including what happened in Cedar Key. So I'm told to lock in a deal with McRae and get to work on the newspaper's pedo and his political friends."

Tinsel detected bitterness in the retired investigator's voice. "Kemper deserved jail time for what he did to that man. He'd already put him on the ground, then he starts whaling on him with an axe handle. Right in front of everyone, like he didn't give a damn! My boss said it'd be enough to get his badge, force him into retirement. I didn't like it, but that's what I did. Truth be told, it was made harder to investigate after the victim disappeared back into his shithole country."

"What country is that?" Tinsel asked.

The response came with a mocking Hispanic accent. "Meh-hee-co."

Tinsel scratched his chin. "Lots of drugs come out of Mexico."

"Yep."

"Think there's more to the assault than just lust for the old lady's daughter?"

"Maybe."

"Would you like another shot at Kemper McRae? On my dime this time?"

"Absolutely."

— *Chapter 25* —

Kemper's meeting with the Acting Special-Agent-In-Charge had left him unsettled. As much as he wanted to continue pursuing Jerry's killers, he suspected Tinsel had a hidden motive. He called his friend and sounding board, Ben.

"Let's meet at Pauline's," Ben said.

"In Steinhatchee?"

"There's only one."

Kemper sighed. He wasn't in the mood to be in a good mood.

Pauline's Comfort Foods & Fixin's had that effect on people, and not just because of the delectable dishes. Pauline and her husband, Brad, had been high school sweethearts separated by circumstance for thirty-plus years. When their stars finally realigned, Brad quit his city job and moved back to the small town he grew up in. They opened a restaurant so they could spend all their working hours together.

The couple served up satisfying comfort food along with heaping sides of laughter and cheerful conversation. Seven years on, their playful banter continued as lively as it had been at the grand opening. People who wanted their stomachs filled and spirits lifted knew where to go.

"Can we pick another place?" Kemper asked.

"No, sir. I saw Brad and Pauline a few days ago and told them I'd stop by. Plus, I'm already in Steinhatchee. I'll be working on your ice box for about as long as it'll take you to get here."

"What's wrong with it?"

"Nothing. Just routine maintenance. When that storm in the Gulf starts moving again, I reckon it'll come our way."

"You think it'll turn?"

"It'll turn. Which means there's going to be a run on ice."

"Fine, I'll come."

"Bring your dog. He needs to get out, too."

The dinner hour had not yet arrived when Kemper did, but the restaurant was already a quarter full. He ordered the country fried steak, mashed potatoes and gravy, and a side of butter beans. Ben chose the catfish with fried cauliflower instead of French fries. For his second side, he picked 'Surprise Me' from the menu. This brought Pauline to the table because she loved telling customers about her special fixings.

"I recall inviting you to come here with your bride, not this old feller," she said to Ben. She looked at Kemper. "Don't say a word, I know your face. You're…Kemp. Mc-Something. From Cedar Key. Yes, you went with Bobbie Jean a few years back…uh, oh.… Well, anyways, back to today's Surprise Me. This here is pickled swamp cabbage. Got these from Wendy over in Horseshoe."

"The Shoe!" came Brad's voice from the kitchen. He had been watching his wife work the room.

Pauline continued. "Our hunting camps are side by side, you know, so we get together—oh my gosh, you should see their new camper with those fancy slides. They had to upgrade, of course, with all them crazy grandkids. Um, where was I?"

"Squirrel!" Brad shouted. Losing her train of thought always brought an affectionate tease from her husband. She gave him a hands-on-hips headshake before turning back to Ben. "Anyways, you're going to love it. It is amazing!" She delivered the last line in a sing-songy voice.

Ben grinned and nodded, dropping a hand to his side and retrieving a small bottle of unlabeled hot sauce from a leather case on his belt. He unscrewed the cap and prepared to shake a few splashes on the meal.

"You stop that right now!" Pauline snapped. Then she threw the back of her hand against her forehead and cried out to the kitchen. "Honey, this man is violating my vittles. You must defend my honor!"

Brad stepped out of the kitchen and looked Ben over. "I dunno, Pauline, we should probably steer clear of any man who holsters his hot sauce."

"Very well." She looked at Kemper. "Oh, last thing. Is that your handsome dog in the bed of that truck?"

"Yes'm."

"Would you mind if I gave him a treat? We always have snacks for our furry friends."

"That's mighty kind of you. His name is Julep."

The men dug into their dinner for a few minutes before Kemper got to the point of the meeting. "I think I'm being set up," he said.

Ben, who had drawn his hot sauce again, stopped mid-splash. "By the sheriff?"

"No, by the DEA."

"DEA? What the heck are they doing in Cedar Key?"

"It's been crazy since we last talked. Turns out the suspects in Jerry's death are tied to some drug gang up in Atlanta, so the DEA showed up to throw their weight around."

"They're interfering with the sheriff's investigation?"

"They took over the sheriff's investigation."

Kemper explained the situation, including his recent meeting with the Acting Special-Agent-In-Charge and the background file Tinsel had on him.

"What makes you think he's after you?" Ben asked.

"Dunno. A hunch, I reckon. Something ain't right."

"Does a hunch ever get rusty? Yours has been out of practice."

"That's why I'm running it by you," Kemper said, a touch annoyed.

Ben ate a few bites before responding. "I wonder if it's not so much this Tinsel guy rubbing you wrong as it is the DEA drawing attention away from Jerry and putting it on the problem of drugs in our community."

Kemper repeated Ben's last words with derision. "Drugs in our community."

"Don't dismiss it, Kemp. It's real and it's bad. You remember Red Ferguson? He lived in your neck of the woods but went to my church."

"Yeah, I know him."

"And his wife, Julie or Julia, can't remember which. Everyone called her Sweetie. Pediatric nurse."

"What's your point?"

"They had a good life. Above the below but below the upper, you know. Little place hidden away not far from Otter Creek."

"I know where they live," Kemper said. "I bought a trolling motor from him once. Took us an hour to get it off his boat because the wiring was all screwed up. She kept the sweet tea coming. Yeah, good people."

"Broken people," Ben corrected. "She got into drugs. Started self-medicating in the doctor's office. Got caught. Got fired. Lost her nursing license. She could have gotten it back, but she moved on to meth. Nasty stuff. Red broke down one night after Bible Study and told me all about it."

"That's a shame," Kemper said for lack of anything else to add.

"They split up. Sweetie still lives there, but Red moved down to Sarasota, where he's got a sister and nephews. He hopes she'll hit rock bottom before she kills herself and then maybe she can get some help. He doesn't want to be an enabler, but he still pays the bills so she can keep a roof over her head. They're broken people."

"We're getting sidetracked."

"Maybe that's your problem," Ben said, irritated. "Everything's a sidetrack if it ain't about the life and times of Kemper McRae."

"I didn't mean it like that. It's a sorry mess, I know. I saw plenty of sorry messes when I was police chief. But that's not the issue here."

Ben replied with a heavy sigh. "So back to the DEA. Does this Tinsel fella have any reason to think you're some kind of drug lord?"

"No."

"Other than the big house on the water, the fancy boats, the hoss truck with the vanity plate. All on an ice vendor's salary."

"If you're going to joke about this—"

"I'm being polite, or maybe delicate is a better word. If the DEA is really after you, then you need to look at what they might be seeing. That's going to take you back to the chaos surrounding your departure from law enforcement, and how you landed on your feet afterward."

"What do you mean landed on my feet? My wife left me."

"I didn't say you stuck the landing. Look, Kemp, when you were going through that mess, Martha and I figured the best we could do was offer our prayers and friendship. We didn't ask questions. Keep in mind, Martha was close friends with Bee Bee. It pained her when she left for Alabama."

"We're supposed to be talking about the DEA."

"It's connect-the-dots with them, Kemp. C'mon, you know this. And if you're in their crosshairs—and that's a big if—then they're looking at assets that seem outsized for your financial situation. Your house fits that category, and it was certainly obtained under mysterious circumstances."

"Wasn't no mystery. Everyone knows what happened."

"Yeah, and everyone was scratching their heads about your sudden fall from grace, saying there's gotta be more to the story. It's darn peculiar, Kemp. You were a living legend around here, everything above reproach. Then some old Yankee woman leaves you a fancy house in her will, and you celebrate by beating a man half to death. Then there's the rumors—"

"Rumors?"

"About another woman. The old lady's daughter."

Kemper shifted in his chair.

"Look, I'm not accusing you," Ben said. "I'm not judging. Only the Savior can judge. But I'd like you to be honest with me."

Kemper would rather his friend believe he was a drug-dealing cop than continue with this line of inquiry. "We've drifted off the flats. Let's stick with the DEA."

"Fine. It's never the right time to face your demons, is it?" Ben forked a mouthful of pickled swamp cabbage, leaned back, and scratched his chin. "I know you well enough to know you didn't deal dope or take kickbacks to look the other way. You'd never dishonor the badge like that. So I'm thinking it's something else."

He forked a piece of fried catfish into his mouth and took his time chewing. The surrounding chatter and laughter and Pauline's sing-songy small talk soured Kemper's mood. "Dammit, Ben, are you waiting for dessert? If you're—"

"I'm thinking, and I think better when I'm chewing food." He dabbed the corners of his mouth with a napkin and tossed it on the table. "This guy Tinsel is a wannabe big shot who is trying to keep you on your toes. I've seen that leadership style. Don't like it, but I've seen it. He wants a big drug sweep so he can be a big shot among big shots. To do that, he needs you. But he also knows you have stature in this community."

"Had stature," Kemper said.

Ben smiled. "No, sir. You've still got it. You only pretend you don't. Now, may I continue?"

"You want to clean your plate first?"

"This Tinsel fella wants to knock you down a peg. One strutting peacock cannot tolerate another."

"I ain't no peacock."

"He doesn't know that. Mind you, my assessment is based only on what you've told me. You don't want to explore that other stuff, so maybe I'm missing something. That said, I don't think you have anything to worry about. Wear that badge with pride."

Kemper nodded. "Reckon I will."

Ben grinned. "Good. Now that'll be $99.95."

"How 'bout I pick up the check instead?"

Kemper drove alone with his thoughts back to Cedar Key. He scratched Julep's head, took a pinch of snuff, and turned up the radio, hoping to escape into the music. Ben's words about the problems from six years ago crowded out the noise.

"You wanna hear it again?" he said to Julep.

A blue hair from New England living alone in a big house on the water. A kindly police chief looking in on the newest resident in his community. Too much house for one person, he had told her. Bought it with her husband, she explained, but he died before they could complete their move to Cedar Key.

"What brings you here?" Kemper had asked on that first visit.

The old lady beamed with pride. "Our daughter. She's a professor at the University of Florida. We wanted to be close to her, but not too close. Hopefully, she'll give me grandchildren soon. This will be the perfect place to spoil them."

Kemper soon learned her daughter was their only child, a gift received at an advanced maternal age. She grew up pampered and privileged, attending the best prep schools in Connecticut, vacationing around the world, and receiving an Ivy League education. Professionally ambitious and accomplished, she married another academic who didn't share these same qualities, the old lady quickly added.

Kemper looked in on her at least once a week. He told her of places to see and people to know. He made sure her garbage rolled out on the curb on Mondays and referred her to the right people for yard and home maintenance.

After six months, he shared with her the meeting times of nearby churches. A year later, he brought her an invitation from a women's group that played Bunco once a month. The old lady, however, seemed content with being alone.

Then she might as well learn to fish, he thought. Kemper brought her a rod and reel and showed her where to set up on her dock that extended one hundred and fifty feet on the water.

"As your police chief, I must warn you it's illegal to have a dock this big and not fish it. It's somewhere in the town ordinances." He smiled. She did not. He tried again. "You've got the beginnings here for a mighty fine boathouse. It'd take some work to put in a frame and enclose it, but you could make something special. Then when them grandkids come around—"

"I'm not getting any grandchildren, Chief McRae," she said. "He hurts my daughter."

The professor soon began spending time at the big house on the water, the sprawling estate meant for laughing kids and a happy family instead used as a refuge for an emotionally scarred and battered woman. Kemper sometimes caught a glimpse of her sitting on the dock, staring off into the horizon, but he did not approach her. His concern centered more on the old lady whose health seemed to decline a little more with each visit.

Kemper didn't know when the change came, but a new feeling soon stirred in him. He found himself disappointed if the professor didn't come around, and he became a touch more chivalrous when she did. A few short conversations with her turned curiosity into infatuation. Her porcelain complexion contrasted with the sun-kissed skin of most Cedar Key residents. She had a small nose and sleepy eyes, and she carried herself in an elegant manner that Kemper found attractive, despite her sad countenance. Or perhaps because of it. He told himself his Bee Bee would win a beauty contest between the two, but he did not consider why he had made such a comparison.

One day in the second year of her residency, the old lady said to Kemper, "You must meet with me and my daughter. She will be here tomorrow. I will make us dinner."

"I don't think I can do dinner, but I appreciate the invite."

"Nonsense. I will prepare one of my special dishes. Connecticut comfort food."

"That's mighty nice, but I don't—"

"I am dying, Chief McRae." She looked more disappointed than sad. "I will not leave my daughter unhappy. She needs to divorce this awful man, but she's scared of him, so she won't. I can't make sense of it, and I cannot leave this place to her while she's married to him. She needs sound advice. I need you for reinforcement. You must help me."

Helping her, he could do. A good police chief went above and beyond every now and then to look after the people of his community. *That's why I wear a badge*, he told himself.

Yet Kemper left his badge in the truck before entering the old lady's house the following night, and for the first time in twenty-seven years of marriage, he lied to his wife about where he planned to go. Only later did he wonder why he had done either of those things.

A whimper from Julep brought him back to the present, and Kemper saw the Golden Arches approaching. He flicked the blinker. "McDouble time?"

He would be home soon. His empty home. Ben had Martha, and Brad had Pauline, just as he once had Bee Bee. Although he had felt it before, the longing sensation to win back his estranged wife seemed more intense now. He remembered how he used to arrive home from work and announce with deliberately poor grammar, "Brenda Belinda McRae, I is home!"

She would greet him with a kiss, not deep and passionate, but never just a peck either. As Kemper pulled away from the drive-thru, he thought of how good it would feel to be with her again.

He remembered a lesson from his church-going days of how the Deceiver often places temptation next to good intentions. Kemper, in weakness masquerading as compassion, had taken the bait. Then came the lie and then the broken trust and then the ruin—all stemming from an initial kindness to an old lady from Connecticut.

"Burn in hell," he said and spat into his dip cup.

— *Chapter 26* —

I don't know whether to thank you or cuss you," Kemper said.

"What do you mean?" Bill replied, even though he knew exactly what Kemper meant. "Hey, Kemp, I've got you on speaker. Is that okay? I'm fixing Libby a bite."

"Fine by me."

"Just an old lawyer's habit. Making sure—"

"I said I'm okay with it," Kemper snapped. "What I'm not okay with is this conversation I had with Mike Tinsel. He asked me to join the task force. I'm not sure what to make of it."

Bill set the phone on a dinner tray by the stove. He used a spatula to lift the edge of a grilled cheese sandwich and check its browning. Then he picked up a spoon and stirred the tomato soup that warmed in a saucepan.

"I can tell you what I make of it, Kemp. You're still involved. You've got a role to play. That's a good thing, right?"

"I get that. I'm just trying to figure out what's your stake in all this."

"What do you mean?" Again, Bill already knew the answer to his question.

"For Christ's sake, Bill. A short time ago you were against me coming on as a reserve deputy, and now you're telling this Tinsel fella that I'm the man for his DEA task force. What gives?"

"Hold on a sec." Bill flipped the grilled cheese, stirred the soup again, and walked into his dining room. He retrieved a bowl and plate from the glass cabinet. The Flow Blue China had been in his wife's family for three generations, and he had recently begun using it for all occasions. The delay helped him think of a reply.

"Ange is a good sheriff," he said once back in the kitchen, "but at heart, she's a diplomat who will go along to get along. I don't think she understands how disruptive the DEA can be, and I'm not sure she will be able to protect her prerogatives."

"And I can? I'm a reserve deputy, and one who was on his way out until your slow-walking intervention."

Bill turned off the stove burners and transferred the soup and sandwich to the fine China. He sprinkled some shredded cheddar over the soup. "Look, Kemp, I gotta go."

"Fine, but before you do, tell me what you meant the other day when you said you were worried about the DEA dragging a trawl net and snatching up the wrong people. I got to thinking about that. What did you mean by wrong people?"

The sheriff's staff attorney had begun walking with the dinner tray but flinched at the comment, and some soup spilled over the bowl's rim. "Dammit, Kemp, it's just a figure of speech." He set the tray down and hit the cancel button on the phone, then used a paper towel to tidy up the presentation and added another pinch of cheese to the soup.

Bill stepped toward the family room but stopped again. Kemper's call had soured his mood, and he did not want his wife to see him deflated. She could always read his emotions ever since they had been love-struck college students. He did not want to give her something else to worry about. His job was to lift her spirits, not dampen them.

He closed his eyes, and his mind went back to their dating years when he would keep her laughing by singing her favorite songs intentionally off key or reciting love poems with an Arnold Schwarzenegger accent. A particular memory involving *Monty Python* impersonations provoked a chuckle, and he knew exactly what to do.

Bill set the tray down again. He sucked in his stomach, pulled his pants up as high as they would go, and tightened his belt so that the waistline rested just below his chest. Then he pulled off his necktie and wrapped it around his head like a bandana. A goofy grin spread across his face as he picked up the tray and high-stepped into the family room, announcing his presence with an atrocious British accent.

"And now, made with tender, loving care for me exquisite bride, the Countess of the Cucumber Garden and fairest princess in all the realm, I humbly and beseechingly present thee—Elizabeth Cooke Rogers—a most delightful grilled cheese sandwich and tomato soup ensemble!"

Libby smiled, then chuckled, and then her whole body shook with laughter. "You're so silly."

Reclining on the couch, Libby faced the rear window. A streak of gray ran through the wavy, brown hair that framed a Grecian nose and heavy cheeks. Though currently overweight, she hadn't always been. The extra weight came from inactivity. She used to love long evening walks with her husband, tending to her extensive garden, or running around backyards and playgrounds while keeping up with her grandkids.

"You want anything else with the soup and sammich?" Bill asked in his normal voice. He set the tray over her legs as she shifted into a more upright position.

She squeezed his hand. "No, dear. This is perfect."

Bill smiled as he took off the necktie bandana and readjusted his pants, and she hummed to some musical notes as she ate.

"You think you're up for a walk this evening?" he asked.

She pursed her lips in contemplation and tore off a corner of the sandwich before dipping it in the soup. "Maybe."

"We could watch a movie later or go through some pictures together. I saw a shoebox full of them. We could start adding names and dates."

"No, I want to do that with Candace and the kids when they get here. Which reminds me, we need to straighten up the guest rooms and dust the dollhouse. Clean sheets on all the beds."

"I can do that."

"I'll get up and do the bedsheets after I eat."

Her willingness to move about encouraged Bill. "That would be great."

"Oh, and Bella said she wants my shrimp and grits. Can you check to see if we have any shrimp in the freezer? If we do, you need to move them to the fridge to thaw."

Happy to oblige, Bill walked briskly to the kitchen. He rummaged through the freezer drawer and found a large bag of shrimp. "Gots the shrimps, milady!" he called out in his silly British voice. "Are you sure they wouldn't prefer tea and crumpets?"

He expected to hear her chuckle again. Instead, she responded with the words he had been dreading. "Honey, can you get me my pills?"

His shoulders sagged. He looked at the package in his hand. The image showed a trawler cutting through the waves as a couple of men in yellow slickers strained to pull in a large net. More than shrimp would be in the net, of course—other fish would be in there too, caught for being in the wrong place at the wrong time.

He moved the shrimp to the fridge and walked back into the family room. "Why don't you let me do the beds, honey, and I'll put on a show for you?"

"Did you hear me? I said I need my pills. The pain is really starting to get aggravating." Her smile had vanished, her expression dull and resigned.

Bill asked a question to which he already knew the answer. "Did you take your prescribed meds?"

"Of course, I did," she snapped. "It's not enough. I wish it were, but it's not."

His expression became every bit as resigned as hers. "Okay, honey. I'll be right back."

In the walk-in closet of their bedroom, Bill punched in the combination to his safe. Behind mementos, legal papers, and handgun ammunition, he pulled out a pill bottle of Oxycontin. The names on the label did not belong to either Libby or her doctor. He also grabbed the brochure next to the pill bottle. Maybe this time, he thought. He lightly shook the bottle and estimated around a half-dozen pills remained. Time to call his brother.

Bill's younger brother, Toby, was the black sheep of the Rogers family. Once a dope-smoking high school dropout, Toby had aged into a discreet and reliable marijuana supplier for the upper-income folks who liked to smoke grass every now and then.

This Occasionally High crowd didn't buy pot from pock-faced, seedy-looking kids in the Circle K parking lot. Instead, they called people who knew people, and Toby Rogers was one of those people who people knew. Quite a few business, education, and health care professionals had Toby's number in their phones. Willie Quintus Maximus Get-High-With-Us knew Toby because he enjoyed smoking a big fatty on the balcony of his restaurant after all his happy customers had gone home.

Toby liked to help people enjoy what he considered a harmless habit, but brother Bill had always been embarrassed by it. It dishonored the family name. Yet six months after Libby's hip replacement surgery, Bill called Toby—the first time they had spoken to each other in years.

The drug dealer did not curse his older brother, nor did he gloat. Instead, he hurried over. After all, this was family.

Bill had heard claims about the medicinal benefits of marijuana from legalization advocates, and Libby's pain had made him desperate to find relief. Libby tried it and, indeed, began to feel a little better. But it wasn't strong enough.

He showed Toby the prescription bottle for Oxycontin. "She needs more of these. We've been to her doctor a half-dozen times since the surgery. At first, he increased the dosage, but now he says he won't give her anything else. He only recommends physical therapy. We tried two others, including a pain management specialist, and got the same answer."

Toby took the prescription bottle and looked at Libby. "Big bro thinks I'm a big-time drug dealer, but all I really do is sell a little weed. But I know some people, and they know people, so let me see what I can do."

Two days later, Elizabeth Rogers, wife of the sheriff's chief counsel, began using illegal opioids.

Bill returned to the family room and gave his wife a pill. He saw the relief on her face as she washed it down with water. He presented the brochure he had brought from the safe. "I'm going to try this again, my love, and I want you to be open-minded about—"

"Oh for Heaven's sake, Bill! Put that thing away. I'm not an alcoholic or drug addict. I have pain, and it won't go away."

"And that's what these people specialize in. This is a treatment program—"

"For addicts!"

"It's a treatment program for dependencies of all kinds."

"It would be the most humiliating thing of my life!"

"They're very discreet."

"No way, mister."

"Libby, you can't keep this up."

"I can't help it. It's the pain. It will level off soon, and then this nightmare will be over."

Bill lived in a different kind of nightmare. It had started as soon as the DEA arrived. He did not think his family was exposed, but he also did not think Mike Tinsel would be too discriminating when it came to people using illicit drugs. Nausea had become his constant companion, and he smirked at the irony of knowing what his brother would recommend for treating it.

He called Toby to tell him he was low on Libby's pills. The next morning, little brother stopped by with the refill.

"Hey, let me ask you something," Bill said as they walked back to Toby's truck. "You only dabble in dope, right? You don't, you know, sell other hard drugs, do you?"

Toby laughed. "Well, I've been running an oxy gig for a very special lady."

"I'm serious, Tobe. Stuff like crystal meth."

"I would not recommend that for pain management."

"It's not about Libby. I'm just worried about you. That's a bad business to be in."

"I don't disagree. That's why I stick with the friendly weed. No harm, no foul."

"So you're not involved in the meth business, right?"

Toby looked down and pushed some dirt around with his boot. "Not as a main source of income. That said, I have moved that particular product before. Maybe once. Maybe twice."

Bill's nausea intensified. "You're not tied into anyone in particular for that, are you?"

"Let's just say I know people who know people."

Bill, lightheaded and worried he might topple over, grabbed the tailgate to steady himself.

"You okay, bro?" Toby asked.

After a minute of silence, Bill looked at his brother. "There's something you need to know."

— *Chapter 27* —

Tank smacked a mosquito on his forearm. "I hate this fucking place," he muttered.

He sat in the nondescript Toyota Corolla on the side of the road two hundred feet from the turn-in to the waitress's house. He shifted uncomfortably in the small car.

Tank smacked another mosquito that had alighted on his other arm. Six or seven more flew in the car, their high-pitched whining all around his ears. He lit a cigarette and blew a stream of smoke at the small opening where he had cracked the window. The smoke seemed to discourage others from venturing in, and he liked the idea that he had trapped some and that they would soon die.

Another one bit his neck, the pin-prick sting more annoying than painful. He shooed it away, preferring to kill it once it touched down on his arm. Tank did not want the smear of blood anywhere near his face.

He missed Atlanta, where headlights, cars, and people roamed everywhere at night. Here, not a single headlight had shone for the last twenty minutes. This part of the country seemed devoid of life. Except for the mosquitoes.

After cruising past The Wayward Breeze and seeing the waitress inside, Tank had driven to the fork in the road and then to the turn-in where he remembered the numbers on the mailbox and the cluster of palm trees. He drove cautiously down her driveway as it cut through a stand of pines. He expected to see a lone house in the clearing. Instead, three manufactured homes lay spread out on an upland field, and he had no idea which one belonged to the waitress.

So instead of hiding inside her home for when she returned, Tank would have to creep into her house after she arrived. After he knew which one was hers.

He returned to the road and drove fifty yards further down before backing into a discreet break in the tree line. A dozen more mosquitoes met their demise before a beam of headlights appeared down the road. A vehicle turned onto the waitress's driveway and disappeared into the trees.

Tank used the light on his phone to illuminate a small glass vial in the cup holder. He poured its contents on the back of his hand and shaped the powder into a line. He snorted it, licked the residue from his skin, and rubbed his nose.

Immediately, his face went numb, and a warming sensation swiftly spread to his chest and limbs. A quickening heartbeat thumped in his chest. The euphoria intensified, culminating with a sexual arousal, a wolfish grin, and an eagerness to encounter the waitress. He gripped his hands over and over, anticipating the softness of her skin and the stickiness of her blood.

Tank exited the car, leaving the keys in the ignition. He left his phone, too, but he grabbed a roll of duct tape and stuffed a few cords of rope into his pocket. He felt good. Invincible.

"Post route deep fly," he said to himself as he sprinted down the middle of the road. When he reached the ingress, he planted one foot and made a sharp turn like a wide-open receiver in the endzone. "Touchdown!" he said before slipping on loose gravel and tumbling into the ditch.

He sat up and shook his head. Abrasions burned on his arms. Tank's elation turned to anger, and he welcomed the anger for what he planned to do. Walking down the lime rock driveway, he quickened his pace when he reached the clearing. The clouds, smothering the moon and stars, cooperated with his murderous scheme.

Only the house furthest away had a porch light on. It cast off enough light for Tank to see the outline of the other two. The homes were far enough apart that he did not believe a physical commotion in one would be heard in another, and there would be no screams because duct tape would cover her mouth.

Where was the duct tape?

Tank looked at his empty hands, then back to where the woods met the road. He must have dropped it when he fell. And he realized something else—he had left his crowbar in the car. These careless errors angered him further, but he decided not to go back for them. The cocaine rush made him confident he would overcome any mistakes. Or resistance.

From what he had seen outside the restaurant, the waitress looked about the same size as Full Stop Sylvia, maybe an inch or two taller, maybe a few pounds lighter. Sylvia had a bigger butt. The waitress had bigger boobs. He figured it balanced out. Once he got on top of her, she wouldn't stand a chance.

The comparison left him with an image of Sylvia King. She lay on purple sheets, wearing only an expression of contempt. He would wipe that look off her face, and then he would brutalize her face and inflict more pain than she knew possible.

Tank's anger escalated as he closed in on the nearest home and saw the Monte Carlo. He gingerly climbed the deck stairs, making sure they did not creak under his weight. Light from inside spilled through the windows. He crouched next to a pair of aluminum chairs. Some rusty tools lay scattered under one of them, and he grabbed a flathead screwdriver, figuring he could use it to jimmy the door or disfigure her face or both.

He surveyed the area. No water bowls or pet toys. Tank crept closer, straining to hear inside, listening for a bark or yap or paws on the floor. No sound. No dog. The curtains on the nearby window hung partially open, so he hazarded a closer look inside and saw only an empty living room.

Tank took a deep breath. It had been a good day. He had tied off one loose end earlier when Danny Blabbermouth came by for his weekly pick-up. Now he would tie off another loose end, but in a much more satisfying way.

The metallic-tasting drip in the back of his throat boosted his confidence. He figured he had about twenty minutes left of the high. Tank put the flathead against the latch plate and partially turned the doorknob. To his surprise, the door opened. He shook his head. Of course, these Mayberrys left their doors unlocked. She was making this easy.

Tank took another look through the window and slipped inside, leaving the door cracked in case he needed to make a hasty exit. He crouched behind the couch and looked down the hallway into what was probably the master bedroom. Though not fully concealed, he would be difficult to spot, assuming she was in the bedroom.

Music played. Fucking country music. The waitress sang along. Fucking hillbilly twang. At least he knew where she was now. At least he wouldn't cut short a promising career in Nashville.

The waitress walked into view, and Tank almost gasped. She stood in front of the bedroom doorway, wearing a bra and cut-off jean shorts. She looked down at her phone from where the music played, then tossed it on her bed as the sound transferred to a speaker system. The waitress unzipped her shorts and dropped them to her feet, revealing low-cut cheeky panties. She reached behind her back and unhooked the clasp on her bra, but stepped out of view before exposing her heavy breasts.

"Shit!" Tank blurted and quickly covered his mouth. He hoped his voice had been too low for her to hear over the music. For the next minute, the silence reassured him. No panicked reaction, no scream, and no slam of the door. Then, the sound of pattering water wafted down the hallway. He sighed with relief.

Close call, Tank. No more mistakes.

The waitress passed by the doorway a few seconds later, now wearing a big T-shirt and holding her purse. A lit cigarette dangled from her lips. She disappeared again, probably back into the bathroom. Tank could barely control his excitement. This would be his first redneck girl, and she was damn near perfect, prancing around half-naked, smoking a cigarette, and singing country music. She had no idea the hell she was about to endure.

Tank crept down the hallway and reached the bedroom. He peered in. No waitress. Steam from the shower spilled through the open bathroom door. He crouched down, ready to rush her if she stepped into view. He slowly angled to see more of the bathroom. Her purse lay on the counter by the sink, and he made a mental note to take her tip cash when he finished with her.

Still no waitress. *Just how big do they make the bathrooms in these shitty little trailers?*

A few moments later, a small cart with plastic trays of brushes, aerosols, and a hairdryer rolled into view. It bumped into the door jamb and stopped over the threshold. He stared at it, and a moment passed before he realized the waitress had pushed it there to create an obstacle.

Which meant she knew she had an intruder.

Tank pulled the cords from his pocket, took two steps, and kicked over the vanity cart. With rope in one hand, screwdriver in the other, he presented himself. "My turn, bitch!"

The waitress stood in front of the toilet ten feet away. *It really is a big bathroom!* Her arms extended toward him, but not in the defensive manner he anticipated, and her hands clasped together, the index fingers pointing at him. The whites of her eyes fully surrounded the irises, and her mouth stretched into an unexpected smile.

"Late for supper, jackass!" she shouted.

The fingertips flashed, and pain grazed Tank's neck. The shower's plexiglass behind him shattered, and a deafening bang rattled in his ears. He staggered back, dropping the rope and screwdriver, and raised a hand to his neck as blood seeped through his fingers.

Tank looked at his hand and then at the waitress and saw that it was not her fingers pointing at him. It was steel. "Motherfu—"

The steel flashed again, and his left ear exploded. Tank fell back into the shower, scalding water rushing over him. He yelled in equal parts pain and fear, which summoned his survival instinct. He pushed off the wall, lunged toward the door, caught his foot between the cart trays, then stumbled and fell onto the bedroom floor.

Tank heard a frustrated 'fuck', then the waitress appeared in the doorway. He freed his foot and kicked the vanity cart. It slid into her legs just as she fired a third round that splintered the veneer below his crotch. He rose to his feet, darting out of the bedroom and down the hallway. A sharp turn in the living room, and he bolted out the front door.

He pitched himself over the deck railing and rolled onto the grass. Porch lights came on at the other house. He held a hand to his neck and then to his ear. Adrenalin pumped out blood, but shock masked the pain.

Tank saw the tree line and sprinted for it. The waitress's twangy voice sounded behind him. "That's right, you run or get you some more holes!" Other voices shouted as he reached the driveway, male voices calling out in the darkness. "That's coming from Charlene's!" and "You okay, Charlene?"

Tank made a sharp pivot when he hit the asphalt and covered the fifty yards to his car. He paused long enough to catch his breath, hands on knees, blood dripping on his shoes. The left side of his face, neck, and chest were wet and sticky. He pulled off his shirt, bundled it up, and used the dry side to staunch the flow of blood.

The car started with the first key turn, and Tank raced back to the fork in the road and turned onto State Road 24. No vehicles in sight and no headlights behind him.

Twenty minutes later, Tank sat on a dingy couch in the meth house. His cocaine high had gone. The adrenaline and shock had gone, too. Acute pain throbbed in his ear and neck, his face and arms scorched.

Sweetie tended to his injuries with bandages, gauze pads, and rubbing alcohol from the First Aid kit she had fetched from the trunk of the Corolla.

"Holy shit, what happened to you?" Paulie said as he approached from behind.

"Keep your voice down," Tank growled. "The queen is sleeping." His words dripped with contempt.

Paulie came around the couch and stood in front of him. "Seriously, T, your face is all red and shit. Damn, man, you're missing your ear!"

"Got scratched by a bear," Tank said. "Now shut the fuck up and grab me a beer."

"Are there really bears around here?" Paulie asked. He turned and walked into the kitchen, where the time displayed on the microwave. "Oh damn, I've been asleep for, like, twelve hours!"

"You took those pills I got for Sylvia?" Tank asked.

"You said I could," Paulie answered defensively.

"Then that's why you slept for twelve hours, dumbass."

Paulie returned with the beverage and handed it to Tank, who tilted his head back for a swig. The movement re-opened the neck wound. Sweetie grabbed another bandage. Tank had been surprised when Sweetie informed him she was a nurse. He had only known her as a meth head granny.

"I slept through the pick-ups," Paulie said. "Full Stop's gonna be pissed."

"I took care of them," Tank said.

Paulie pointed at his ear. "Like that?"

"No, shithead. Before." He flinched as Sweetie snipped away some dangling flesh.

"That's my job!" Paulie protested. "I handle pick-ups. Did Full Stop tell you to do that?"

"Now you're getting on my nerves. If you haven't figured this out yet, I'm the one running the show here. I'm the one keeping this crew together. So I suggest you show some goddamn respect, okay?"

"Yeah, T, I didn't mean anything. I just—"

"I took care of your slingers, including your boy, Danny. I took care of him real good."

"Danny? He's supposed to be lying low. He's not doing packages."

"Danny's a fritterhead, and so is his girl. For them, lying low means staying high." Tank lit a cigarette and took a deep drag. He smiled despite the pain. "I gave him some from my Feel-Good stash as a reward for not talking to the police. He won't be picking up packages no more."

"What does that mean?" Paulie asked, but he knew the answer already.

"Now shut the fuck up and listen to me. I'm about to change the game here. I'm tired of this shit. I'm bringing down some heavy hitters who owe me. You got a piece with me, P, and you ain't got shit with her no more. You feel me?"

Paulie retreated outside and lit a cigarette by the blue rain barrels. He dug in his pocket, pulled out his burner phone, and called Danny.

No answer.

Paulie considered walking around and tapping on Full Stop's window to warn her about Tank's plot, but if she responded by confronting Tank—and of course she would—it would not end well for Sylvia. Paulie would rather leave Tank plotting than doing.

In fact, Paulie would rather just leave. Drive north to Cliftondale. A vision fluttered in his head of entering his grandmother's house, smelling her homemade chicken-and-dumplings. Then he had another vision of holding hands with Sylvia and introducing her as his girlfriend.

He chuckled at the absurdity of it, and his bleak, miserable reality returned. Paulie had reached a decision point unlike any before. No more thinking about leaving. He needed to act.

Paulie dialed his grandmother's number and waited for her to answer.

"God's mercy!" she exclaimed upon hearing his voice.

After affectionate greetings, Paulie got to the point. "You know that box on my desk? The one with the baseball cards I used to collect? Um, there's a business card mixed in there. It's from the DEA, you know, the Drug Enforcement Agency. I, uh, installed some computer programs for them once. Can you get that for me?"

A minute later, she came back on the line. "Thanks, Grams," Paulie said. "Can you tell me the number on the back? They liked my work and said they'd give me a job if I ever wanted one." He faked a chuckle as he stored the number in his phone that she read off.

Paulie took a deep breath and felt better. "Yes, Grams, this means I'm coming home. I can't wait to see you. Can you make those chicken-and-dumplings I like?"

It had been years since he had been detained by the police and questioned by the DEA. Then, he had rejected the agent's offer to become a confidential informant. Now, it didn't sound like such a bad idea, especially if it led to his separation from the gang life and, hopefully, to Tank's arrest. Even better, maybe Tank would die in a shootout with the police. He wondered if the agent he had spoken to still worked at the DEA.

Paulie hit the call button and waited to speak to the man who had once promised him a clean break.

— *Chapter 28* —

The next morning, Charlene told her brother Wesley what had happened when he called to check in on her, which he did every few days before starting work as Cedar Key's only veterinarian.

Measured, methodical, and meticulous, Wesley exemplified the exact opposite traits of his big sister. He was calm under pressure and rarely prone to anger. This was one of those rare occasions.

"Why didn't you call the police?" he shouted.

"It was just a prowler," she said. "I'd have called if I had killed him, but he got lucky."

"You still needed to call the police!"

"That fool found Jesus last night. He ain't coming back. I gotta get new shower glass though," she added, almost as an afterthought.

"For God's sake, Char, you discharged a firearm. Someone broke into your home. You've got to report that!"

"Don't 'got' me, baby brother. I'm done with it, and I'm not calling the police. I don't need them up here in my business."

He expected the flippant attitude. For Charlene, a confrontation went only as far as the people directly involved. No need for third-party intervention, even if the third party was the police. She had learned this lesson at seventeen when no one, including the police, had stepped in to stop an abusive father and drug-addled mother. She handled it on her own, driving a thousand miles from Blossom, Texas, to Cedar Key with her younger brother and a few meager possessions in her car.

Wesley called it in. He reached Gladys, hoping she would dispatch Doyle to the scene instead of Rylan. He also called Tommy. He didn't like Tommy, but figured he should know what had happened to his girlfriend.

His two assistants arrived as he headed out the door. He told them he needed to go to his sister's but didn't say why. Telling them to reschedule morning appointments was enough for them to know it was serious.

Wesley made one more call on his drive out to Charlene's. He called Kemper, and not because he knew Kemper was back in law enforcement. Wesley saw in him something close to a father figure. He knew Charlene saw something else, but that didn't bother him. Whenever a problem arose, he wanted Kemper McRae around.

"Oh for shit's sake, turn off those damn lights," Charlene said, scolding Rylan as he exited the F-150 Police Responder. "You're disturbing the peace with those things."

She stood on her redwood deck next to her brother, wearing a flannel shirt with faded jeans. Two other people sat in the aluminum chairs. Rylan stepped back to his truck and turned off the flashing lights.

Tommy pulled in right behind him. He hustled out of his truck, quick-stepped over to the stairs, and stopped at the top to catch his breath. Charlene knew he would want an embrace, so she shot him a look that gave him pause.

"Wes told me what happened," Tommy said. "I came as soon as I heard."

"Figures."

"You alright, honey?"

"I'm fine. I don't know what the fuss is all about."

Rylan spoke as he climbed the deck stairs. "The forensics team from the county is going to come by and collect evidence. We need to go over what happened and get statements. There's a suspect you evidently injured, and we need to find and apprehend him. That's what this is all about. Now, were you injured in any way?"

"No," she replied.

He looked at the older couple seated in the chairs. "Are you the neighbors?"

"Yes, sir," the lady said, pointing to her home.

"I came after I heard the shots," the man added.

Rylan nodded. "I hope you don't mind, but we'll need statements from you both. Doyle will be here soon." He looked toward the third manufactured home. "What about—"

"That's old Dale Bowser," the man said. "He ain't there now. He's at work."

"I know where he works," Tommy said. "I can help with that."

Rylan ignored him. Charlene disappeared into her home. She came back with a Coke in one hand and a cigarette in the other. Her hand trembled as she lit it.

She took a drag on the cigarette. "It's a shame you're going to cause all this trouble just because some dumbass prowler snuck into my home. I don't know what the big deal is."

"It's a big deal anytime someone breaks into a home," Rylan said, "and it's a big deal anytime someone shoots a gun at somebody."

He subtly studied her, the trembling hand, the higher-than-usual pitch of her voice. Rylan had never seen her rattled. He pulled a toothpick from his shirt pocket to chew on.

"That's what I told her," Wesley added. "She's stubborn, but this isn't the time for stubborn, right, Chief? Have there been any reports of people with gunshot wounds going to the hospital or urgent care?"

Rylan ignored Wesley's questions. His eyes remained fixed on Charlene. "Your safety is always a big deal."

"Got something for you, Chief," Doyle said after he parked his truck. He stood in the yard, twirling a roll of duct tape on a pen. "Found this by the road. Wonder if last night's visitor left it behind."

"He didn't have no duct tape when I shot him," Charlene said.

"Bag it," Rylan said to Doyle. He turned to Tommy and Wesley. "Y'all stay out here. I'm going to take a look inside with Charlene." He opened the door and gestured to her. "Now, why don't you show me where you fired the gun?"

In the bedroom, the police chief observed the damaged flooring, the toppled vanity cart, and the shattered plexiglass. He followed the trail of reddish-blackish blood stains. Rylan pointed to the pieces of rope. "Your prowler wasn't here to steal, Charlene. He had other intentions."

She rolled her eyes as if to dismiss the comment, but then she sighed heavily. Her breath caught, and her bottom lip quivered. She shoved her hands in her pockets and looked away.

Rylan also struggled in the moment, his professional demeanor slipping. The thought of what might have happened to her shook him. His phone dinged, and the sheriff's name lit the screen, a bridge back to police work and professional behavior. He turned it to silent mode.

"This is about last night and today, okay?" he said gently. "It's not about what happened in the past between us."

"Nothing happened between us."

"You've survived a serious trauma. It's okay to be upset. It's okay to let it out. I'm here as your police chief. Not as"—he paused, knowing he was about to broach a sensitive subject—"whatever it was we had together."

Anger flashed in her hazel eyes. "We didn't have anything, Rylan. You still don't get it."

Charlene turned and muttered something he couldn't make out. She rubbed her nose and then turned back to him. "Go find the bastard and leave me alone. You think I'm going to cry on your shoulder? You think you're going to ease me into that bed if I let it all out?"

"My God, Charlene, can you back off for a minute? I'm here to help."

"Help? Yeah, like you did at the Quik Stop? You and your helping hands? Send Doyle in. I'd rather him handle this."

Rylan reached out and grabbed her before registering his actions. The police chief was gone, but the broken man who yearned for the woman who despised him was present and ready for duty. His voice cracked. "What's wrong with you? Why do you hurt me like this?"

Her response shocked him.

Charlene threw her arms around him and buried her head in his chest. The tears burst wide open. So did the contradictions. "You need to leave," she said while leaning into him and tightening her grip. "I don't want you in my house."

"I'm not going anywhere."

His phone vibrated. He ignored it.

"You need to get that," Charlene said but pressed harder against him so he couldn't free his hand. "It's probably important."

"Nothing is more important than this."

They stood in the aftermath of the violence that had come to claim her life and embraced in an intimacy of emotional release. Rylan knew not to jeopardize this moment with an attempted kiss or awkward 'I love you.'

Charlene kept her arms around him until the tears dried up, then dabbed her eyes with his shirt. She pulled back, creating a little separation between them. "Every time I see you, you give me that weird look like you might propose. You need to know it ain't gonna happen."

"I wish you'd give us a chance. I don't know why you've made me the bad guy."

Her eyes flashed with a mix of hurt and anger. "You think you're the bad guy? You made me the bad guy. You made me the other woman. I broke up your engagement. I never wanted to be that kind of girl."

"But you're not. We didn't go all the way."

"God, you're a jackass! We didn't need to go all the way to make me into the other woman. You left her. Broke up with her. Y'all had been together for five years, and you threw it all away." The phone vibrated again in his pocket. "For Christ's sake, answer the damn phone."

"What's done is done."

She pushed away. "How about you go back and marry her?"

Rylan pulled her back. "I tried. She said no."

"Smart woman."

"Dammit, there you go." He turned away and began to pace. "You say I should go back to her, but then you say she's smart for not taking me back. It makes no sense. You make no sense!"

"I don't need to make sense to you."

"And you were a willing participant. I remember that night. Oh God, how I remember that night! *You* came over to my table and ran your fingers across the back of my neck. *You* asked if I would stick around until you got off work. And *you* were unbuttoning my shirt as fast as I was unbuttoning yours. I remember, Charlene, and I relive it every goddamn night when I go home to an empty house!"

"What I did doesn't matter. I don't need to explain myself to you."

"I swear to God, you're like that Billy Joel song, you know—casually cruel, laughing as you cut me to the bone. You want me to be miserable, don't you? That's the private hell you put me in."

Charlene didn't have a snappy comeback. She looked away briefly before turning back. "Why are you always chewing on a toothpick?"

"What?"

The phone vibrated again, and he continued to ignore it. Doyle's voice came from the front of the house. "Hey, Chief, looks like Kemper is here."

Rylan sighed. He removed the toothpick from his mouth and offered her one last thought. "I would be good to you."

Kemper stepped into the bedroom. "You ain't answering your phone, son. You off-duty?"

"We're looking over the scene," Rylan said.

Charlene hurried past Kemper, averting her watery eyes.

"What's going on here, son?"

"Not a damn thing. And it's Chief today, not son. Got it?"

Kemper suppressed a smirk. "You look more like a forlorn lover."

"Go to hell." Rylan pulled his phone from his pocket and scrolled through the missed calls.

"Why didn't you answer earlier?"

"Yeah, I see the sheriff called. What's so urgent?"

"You need to get your head right, Chief." Kemper paused long enough to make sure he had Rylan's attention. "Danny Miles is in the hospital. Looks like he and his girlfriend overdosed."

Rylan stared at his father, stunned. Kemper continued. "That's why I called you. I'm sure that's why the sheriff called. You see, when you're the chief of police, you can't be—"

"Wait, wait, back up. Are they?"

"They've been airlifted to Gainesville. The girl's mother found them unresponsive."

Rylan's phone vibrated again. This time, he answered it.

"Are you okay, Chief?" Sheriff Lane said. "I've been trying to reach you."

"I'm fine. Kemper is telling me Danny and Tonya OD'd."

"Tonya died *en route* to the hospital. Danny is still alive but probably not for long. Someone needs to tell Danny's mother. She may already know, but we're not sure. I can send a deputy, but I understand you're close to her."

"I'll go see her."

"Now what happened with the waitress last night?"

Rylan explained what he knew, and he could sense the frustration in Angela's response.

"Two potential witnesses almost died on the same night," she said. "Something tells me Danny's situation may be more than just a careless overdose. I don't know what the Acting Special-Agent-In-

Charge will do once he's made aware, but we're going to step it up on our end right now."

"Count me in, Sheriff."

"We can't afford delays from the DEA. I'm tired of these drugs destroying our people, and I'm tired of not having the resources to fight back. I know you're dealing with the hurricane—"

"Ain't nothing to deal with. It stalled in the Gulf, and its trajectory is still Mississippi."

Charlene walked back into the room. Eyes clear, hair freshly brushed, a touch of mascara on the lashes. She looked ravishing, but she kept her eyes on Kemper. Rylan sighed. "Listen, Sheriff, I'm with the victim now. I'll update you when I'm done here."

"I ain't no victim," Charlene said after Rylan hung up.

"Ben thinks the storm will turn our way when it starts moving again," Kemper said. "Wouldn't surprise me."

Charlene offered a weak smile. "It'd fit right in with all the craziness around here."

Kemper pointed to the damaged floor and looked at Rylan. "You ought to let Doyle handle this while you go see Mama Thighs. That needs to be you."

Rylan opened his mouth to rebuke his father for the unsolicited advice, but before he could come up with a witty insult, Kemper turned to Charlene.

"As for you, you'd be better off with my son."

Rylan and Charlene stared at Kemper as he left. Then, the police chief cleared his throat, his confidence slightly elevated. "There was a spark between us, Charlene, and you're right that the situation was wrong then. But time has passed."

Charlene turned to face him, a sneer at the corner of her mouth. "I ain't..." His hopeful eyes wiped away her disdain, and her voice softened. "I don't want you to feel hurt, Rylan. It's just—"

"We can make this work."

"Maybe," she said in a way that sounded like it had slipped out.

"Hey, Chief," Doyle said, interrupting. He stood over the door threshold. "Kemper sent me in. What do you want me to do?"

Rylan sighed. He was still the police chief. "Yeah, mark the room for evidence and get Charlene's statement. I need to go tell Mama Thighs what happened to her son."

— *Chapter 29* —

I t turned.

The tropical storm lumbering through the Gulf got knocked off its Mississippi trajectory by a high-pressure system sweeping east. The turn was sharp and sudden, and it strengthened into a hurricane as it headed toward the Big Bend of Florida. High winds would reach Cedar Key within twenty-four hours. Landfall in thirty-six.

Kemper's turn was also sharp and sudden. His skepticism toward the investigation diminished, replaced with a growing confidence that he would soon find Jerry's killers.

He wasn't sure where this newfound confidence came from. It wasn't from working with Mike Tinsel and the DEA task force. He had spent the last two days driving agents around, visiting abandoned properties, and contacting people who had past troubles with methamphetamine. The search for the meth house, or what the agents called the stash house, had come up empty.

Today's shift would pair him with Rick, who had been assigned to the task force from the Sheriff's Office. That, too, did not inspire confidence. From the daily briefings, Delaney seemed solely focused on ingratiating himself with the Acting Special-Agent-In-Charge.

Kemper propped a pillow behind him and sat up in bed. Floor-to-ceiling windows offered an exquisite view of the Gulf. The sun sat a thumb's width above the water on the horizon. Those calm waters would soon turn choppy as the hurricane approached. He thought of calling Ben to congratulate him on his prediction about the storm.

Something else Ben had said sprung to mind—that he and Martha were praying for him. It wasn't just a figure of speech. They really were, and probably others were, too. Perhaps that's where his confidence had come from—the power of prayer, even if it came from others. He and Bee Bee used to pray together, and they went to church together. Now she lived in Alabama, and he lived alone in a house he didn't belong in for reasons he didn't want to put before God.

Kemper reached over and grabbed his snuff can from the nightstand. He thumped it a few times before taking a pinch as he watched a pod of pelicans fly over the flats. Below them, the baitfish skittered, speckled trout gathered at grassy points, and redfish rummaged in the creeks. Everything followed a pattern. That was the natural order of things, and he smiled knowing that even after the chaos and destruction of a hurricane, the birds and fish and other creatures of God's creation would simply go back to doing what they were meant to do.

Kemper now had a clarifying sense of what he was meant to do. He was a lawman, a husband, and a father. For the last six years, he had done a piss-poor job at all three. Now he would change that. What his friend Ben called redemption, Kemper viewed as restoration to the way things were. And not a partial restoration, either. He would get it all back. For the first time, he saw the possibility of not only restoring his standing in the community but also of healing the rift with his son and reuniting with his estranged wife.

The spontaneous advice he had given to Charlene—that she would be better off with Rylan—now made sense. He had not planned to say that to her. It had just come out, and now he knew why. It was time to win back Bee Bee. For that to happen, he needed to close the door on Charlene and not leave it cracked open as he selfishly had.

He also needed to end his entanglement with the professor, *entanglement* being a more accurate word than *relationship*. Previous efforts had been too exhausting, with Kemper surrendering to her emotional blackmail and threats of self-harm. But it was different now. It felt different.

Yet Bee Bee would never live in the big house on the water. It wasn't her home.

He picked up his phone on the nightstand and called Pidge. It went straight to voicemail, so he left a message for the Realtor.

"This is Kemper. I want you to reach out to the couple who bought my old house and see if they'd be interested in a cash offer. If they ain't, I want you to get me a list of any houses on the market that are similar in size to the one I used to have."

A longing to hear Bee Bee's voice surprised him, but he no longer had her number. It was too soon anyway, so he did the next best thing.

"Have you talked to your mother recently?" Kemper asked when Rylan answered the phone.

"Yeah, day before last."

"She doing all right?"

"She's doing fine."

"You think she'd take a call from me?"

Rylan paused before answering. "I dunno, Dad. She might."

"When you talk to her next time, let her know I'm getting it together. I'm making everything right again."

"What exactly does that mean?" Rylan asked. "And what do you think she'll do with that information? Come charging into your arms? All forgiven and forgotten? I know Mom still loves you, but you hurt her, and you've spent the last five or six years acting like it wasn't your fault. You never owned up to what you did. Is that what you're ready to do now?"

"I'm trying to make things right. Like with Charlene—"

"Stop right there. I'm glad for what you said to Charlene, but I don't owe you anything for it. As for Mom, until you come clean with her, you don't stand a chance of reconciling."

"Just tell her I want to talk to her. Tell her that, okay?"

"Fine."

Kemper sensed that more than just his phone call had upset his son. "Did I set you off or were you already agitated?"

Rylan sighed. "I'm stuck in this frickin' Gainesville traffic. I just left the hospital. Wasted effort. Danny's a drooling vegetable. We got the lab results back on that meth he and the girl smoked, and it was laced with fentanyl. A lethal amount."

"Think the sheriff will call it homicide?"

"I'm calling it a homicide!" Rylan shot back. "The sheriff's got her own problems."

Kemper paused as he adjusted to the moving parts of the conversation. "What do you mean?"

Rylan's tone rose a notch. "How can you be on the task force and so far out of the loop?"

"What the hell are you talking about?"

"One of her people overheard Rick Delaney talking with one of Tinsel's agents. Apparently, someone in Ange's camp has a side hustle that has drawn the attention of the DEA."

"One of her deputies is dealing? That's bullshit."

"I'm just telling you what was heard. And Tinsel wants to make a big show of it because that's his style. Can't say I'd be too upset if Ange's holier-than-thou reputation got a bit tarnished before the election."

"It's by-the-book, not holier-than-thou," Kemper said, "although the two do blur together sometimes. I haven't heard anything about this."

"Maybe your team didn't fill you in because they think you're the dealer," Rylan said with a chuckle.

Kemper didn't find it funny. "I'm going to call Ange and figure this out."

"You won't get her. She's meeting with Mr. Special-Agent-In-Charge this morning."

"How do you know all this, son?"

"I have my sources. Not everyone over there wants the sheriff re-elected."

"Something's not right," Kemper said, more to himself than to Rylan. "What the hell is Tinsel up to?"

The conversation ended without answers, but Kemper's mind had already supplied them. His suspicion about Tinsel's motives resurfaced despite Ben's earlier assurances.

He got out of bed and readied himself to leave. As he washed his face, he saw in the mirror a man already abandoning the path laid before him to get things right. He would get back to it, he told himself, as soon as he finished talking to the sheriff.

— *Chapter 30* —

Angela's meeting with the Acting Special-Agent-In-Charge had not gone as she had hoped. She had demanded to know who from her office was under investigation, and she had pressed him for an Operation Windswept launch date. Tinsel denied the first, deflected the second, and strutted out of her office knowing he had gotten the best of her.

Her mind had been elsewhere. It still was.

Angela looked at the pictures on the mantle behind her desk, pictures of her husband and two sons and another of her parents in their later years. She reached over and picked up a third frame, propping it next to her coffee mug. A young face with features similar to hers held a smile, school-colored ribbons in her hair, pom-poms in her hands, and one leg cocked behind her.

The expression of joy on the cheerleader's face affected her the most, for her mother had seldom known such happiness in her adult life. Angela dabbed at her eyes with a wadded-up tissue. Today marked the fourth anniversary of her mother's death, and it did not get any easier with each passing year.

A buzzing phone brought her back to the present. Her administrative assistant informed her that Kemper McRae was in the lobby waiting to speak with her.

"Send him in," she said, finding the timing of his visit more than coincidental.

She stood as Kemper entered and waited until he sat before returning to her chair. "Are you going to tell me what's going on with the task force?"

"I was going to ask you the same thing," Kemper replied.

"Really?" Her eyes danced with a mixture of curiosity and concern. "You mean you're not in-the-know with the Acting Special-Agent-In-Charge?"

"I'm not one of his favorites. Word is he and his Atlanta boys got their sights on someone with a badge."

"Rumors, Deputy."

"Maybe so, but it's a distraction from what we're supposed to be doing, and there seems to be no urgency to find this meth house or stash house or whatever the hell they're calling it."

"The DEA has the lead on this, but I've—"

"We've got two dead people, Sheriff, and another one might as well be. Then there's the attempted murder of Charlene, and we don't have that many people around here to begin with."

"Your point?"

"Have you considered that deference to the DEA might have limitations?"

Angela's calm voice contrasted with Kemper's aggressive tone. "What I was saying before you interrupted me, Deputy, is that the DEA has the lead but the Sheriff's Office is pursuing these suspects independently. If we come across them first, I assure you we will take them into custody."

"You're giving up on diplomacy?"

"Interagency cooperation, and I'm not giving up on it, but I'm also not losing sight of my responsibility as sheriff."

"You don't seem too bothered by any of this."

"Oh, I am plenty bothered, but I don't complain to subordinates. You may not like my style, but it's the best way I know to ensure justice is done."

Kemper's anger flared. "Not if we don't catch the killers!"

"What's your alternative?" Angela snapped. "What would you have me do?"

An awkward pause followed before Kemper replied. "Eh, I'm sorry. I appreciate the opportunity you've given me, and I know I haven't handled it right."

Angela shook her head lightly. "You've been a challenge. There's no denying that. I'll admit, I've got a soft spot for you. Do you remember that morning in your boathouse when I made you a reserve deputy?"

"Hard to forget."

"Exactly!" Angela straightened in her chair. "Things that really matter are not easily forgotten. Whether it's a few weeks ago, a few years ago, or even forty years ago." She touched the picture frame on her desk. "Mom died four years ago today."

Kemper lowered his chin. "She did, didn't she?"

Angela turned the picture so Kemper could see the teenage version of her mother. "Tell me about my mom."

Confusion washed over Kemper's face. "Are you serious?"

"Kemper, I can defend your appointment on professional grounds, but that's not why you're still wearing that badge. It's a sentimental reason, which will remain between us."

Kemper nodded.

Angela continued. "You once did something that gave a tired old lady a memory she could turn to whenever times got tough. A momentary escape from a hard life. What happened between you two back then was important to her, so it's important to me. When she was in hospice, she told me about the first time she met you. It stayed with her all those years, seared into her memory. Those awful men and how you showed up like a knight in shining armor."

"You've been reading too many romance novels."

Her gentle eyes bore into him. "A frightened seventeen-year-old girl stuck in a dangerous place. Then you happened to come along."

"It was a popular spot."

"I know, for partying."

"For screwing."

His bluntness did not even cause her to blink. He sighed. "You wanna do this, Ange? Fine. I remember that night. I remember it because it was so damn unusual. I had gone there with a young lady"—he offered a wry smile—"to enjoy the moon over the water. But then I saw your mom standing by the river's edge. Looking terrified. That's something you don't easily forget."

Kemper lifted his chin. "Then I saw them boys and, yeah, they were a rotten bunch. Sipping whiskey, passing the bottle between them. Toying with your mom, suggesting she do certain things to get a ride out of there. I couldn't for the life of me figure out how she ended up there with them boys. It made no sense. Anyway, they tried to run me off, but I got the best of them."

"Mom said they were men, not boys. Each in their twenties. And you didn't just run them off. You knocked them all out. Three grown men."

"Something like that. Well, anyway, your mother got in my truck and we left."

"She didn't mention you had another girl with you."

"The other girl didn't stay with us long. She didn't like the change in plans and, frankly, she said some prejudicial things about your mom. So I dropped her off at the gas station and told her to get another ride."

"And you took my mom safely home, virtue intact."

"I didn't take her straight home. Don't give me that look. It was her nerves. That's another thing I'll never forget. When we got on the main road, she broke down. Grabbed my arm, put her head on my shoulder, and started crying. I asked her where she lived, and her sobbing got worse. She started shaking. So I figured I needed to keep driving until she felt better. Burned half a tank of gas on that prescription. Then I took her home and watched her sneak back inside."

Angela smiled. "Kinda makes you a decent guy."

"I have my moments."

"She hinted that there was more to the story between you two."

Kemper stayed silent.

Angela pressed on. "Look, Daddy was tough. Cruel, sometimes. I love the guy but, Lord knows, he put my mother through a lot. If she had memories she could retreat to—escape to, really—then I'm fine with that."

Kemper stroked his mustache, still silent.

"Mom took her faith seriously, Kemp. You should have seen the relief on her face when I told her it wasn't cheating on Daddy to enjoy those memories of you. Lying there on that hospice bed, she looked like I'd relayed words straight from the mouth of the Savior."

"If she didn't give you details, Ange, then I don't think I'm at liberty—"

"Oh c'mon! I'm a big girl. Tell me."

"Well," Kemper said as the wry smile returned, "she got better at sneaking out of her house."

Angela slapped a hand on the desk. "I knew it! You two had a secret romance."

"For about three months. It was over the summer, and it was secret because that's how she wanted it. The race thing was kind of taboo back then, and she feared her parents finding out."

"So showing up at her funeral was not to support me but to say goodbye to a long-lost love."

"You're back in your romance novels, Ange."

"Did you two… Wait, I don't want to know." She stood and circled the desk as Kemper pushed up from the chair. Her wistful tone vanished. "Thank you for sharing that with me. Things happen for a reason, Kemp, and as challenging as you've been, I don't regret appointing you reserve deputy. I'm glad you're on the task force. My meeting with the Acting Special-Agent-In-Charge was, frankly, disappointing. He seems to be working at his own pace."

"I recall making that very point."

"Don't ruin the moment, Kemp. We have an active threat in our community, and we need to apprehend the suspects before there's another attempt on someone's life. In your position with the task force, you may come across actionable intelligence—"

"Which I can give to you before Mike Tinsel gets his pieces in place." Kemper smiled. "Not exactly by-the-book, now, is it?"

"Don't give me that look, deputy. This is about protecting our community."

"I'm riding with Rick Delaney later today. He's been with you a lot longer than I have. I'm surprised you're not leaning on him."

Something close to a scowl formed on Angela's face. "Delaney's auditioning for a job with the DEA. I wouldn't trust him to tell me anything useful."

"You know, he's where this rumor started about an impending arrest within your ranks."

"Look, I know I was dismissive of your concern earlier. The truth is, I can't imagine anyone under my supervision being a target for arrest."

"That's because you see the DEA as an honest partner in this."

Her eyes narrowed. "Because they are. We have a disagreement about the timeline, Kemper. Not the end goal."

"And what is the end goal?"

"Fewer drugs in our community, fewer addicts, fewer overdoses."

He shook his head in disgust. "And here I am, thinking this was about justice for Jerry."

"Of course, it's about justice for Jerry. Don't question my commitment to that."

"I'm curious, Sheriff. What will you do when you learn the DEA's goals are not the same as yours? What are you prepared to do?"

Angela offered no response. Kemper turned to leave but stopped at the door. "You know it'll eat you up if I don't answer your earlier question."

"What question?"

"About your mother and me, and whether…you know."

Angela's eyes widened. "Oh God, Kemper, I don't want to hear that my mom was just another notch on your belt."

"Well, she wasn't. We did what a lot of teenagers did—kissing, necking, that sort of thing. But no matter how hard I tried, she wouldn't go all the way. Thought you'd feel better knowing that."

Angela tried to say thank you, but the words caught in her throat. She approached him and scanned his face for any hint of deception. "There's something more, isn't there?"

Kemper held her gaze until she blinked. "Skinny dipping."

"What?"

"She didn't go all the way, but I got her swimming nekkid in the Suwannee River."

Angela gaped and a moment passed before she recovered. "That's a level of detail I didn't need to know." She punched him softly on his shoulder. "Now get out of my office, you dirty old man."

The sheriff watched him walk down the corridor before closing the door. She turned and leaned against it. Then she laughed as hard as she cried.

— *Chapter 31* —

ill Rogers was a dinosaur. And a monster truck. He reared back and shook his shoulders. Then he dipped forward and growled, "Vroom-roar," and resumed his crawl of terror across the yard.

His grandchildren squealed with delight.

Bill struggled to catch his breath and was grateful that only a few more minutes of playtime remained before dinner. A spread of clouds floated in the distance, the yard smelled like green crayons, and the sound of laughter surrounded him. He continued lurching around on all fours with the grands awkwardly balanced on his back.

He roared again, this time sincerely, as a sandspur buried itself into the heel of his hand. Bill fell to one elbow and flicked the spur off. William dropped off his back and ran over to a castle playset. Bella tightened her grip around her grandfather's neck.

The green turtle sandbox lay dead ahead. "Aha! The pit of endless tickles awaits ye!"

"No, Popsie, no!"

Bella's fate was sealed. There was no stopping the beast.

Just then, William sortied from the castle, Batman action figure in hand, and crashed into Popsie's side. He had not anticipated a flanking attack from the young squire. The dinosaur-monster truck moaned and toppled over. Bella and William squealed with glee as they tickled their grandfather before all three laughed in exhausted delight.

A police siren's double-burst—*bwoop-bwoop*—interrupted the yard play. Bill waved a hand in the air without looking. Deputies often drove by his house, which was situated near a main road leading to Williston. The short double-burst was a friendly hello.

Another double-burst made him sit up. He trapped a grandchild under each arm so they couldn't squirm away. Instead of a deputy's cruiser, he saw a black SUV pulling into the yard, its red and blue lights pulsating from the top of its tinted windshield. Two more black SUVs followed.

Bill's grandson imitated the siren sound. "Bwoop-bwoop!"

"Well, this is a curious bug," Bill said.

Curiosity turned to horror when Acting Special-Agent-In-Charge Mike Tinsel exited the first vehicle, wearing reflective sunglasses, a black bulletproof vest, and a smug look on his face.

"Oh, God," Bill whispered.

"Bwoop-bwoop!" William repeated.

Bill hugged his grandchildren tight and kissed each on the top of their heads. "Now, now, little June bugs, run inside to Mommy and Memaw. Popsie needs to talk to these gentlemen for a few minutes."

"No, Popsie, no!" Bella protested.

"Please, kids. Now!" His tone was sharp but not angry, and the grandchildren obeyed. William trotted toward the porch. Bella skipped.

Three additional DEA agents and two officers from the U.S. Marshals Service accompanied Tinsel. Two of the agents had their service weapons drawn but pointed toward the ground.

Already sweating and breathing heavily from yard play, heat rushed to Bill's face, and his heart raced. He wiped his brow.

"Bill Rogers, I recently had the pleasure of making your brother's acquaintance," Tinsel said. "After hearing nothing but how much of a straight arrow your sheriff is, you can imagine how surprised I was to discover the illicit drug trade reached all the way up to her executive team."

Bill wanted to say Ange knew nothing of Libby's opioid addiction, but he knew to remain silent since any effort to explain, rationalize, or plead would undoubtedly be used against him. Still, he could not keep his mouth from opening because nausea overtook him. As the marshals prepared to take him into custody, Bill vomited in the grass.

"We're on it," Delaney said into his phone. "Be there in ten."

Kemper raised an eyebrow. "You're taking dispatch on your phone instead of CAD?"

"It works like that sometimes," Rick replied. He hit the siren and lights and pressed down on the accelerator. The cruiser raced onto Alt 27.

"Location on the meth house?" Kemper asked.

"Nope. Something else." Delaney tried unsuccessfully to suppress a grin.

"What's so important it takes priority over finding the meth house?"

"Stash house."

"Stash house, meth house, whatever. This is the last shift before we're shut down by the hurricane, and it'll be days before we can get back to it. Doesn't Tinsel want to launch Operation Windswept soon?"

"It will launch when it's ready. We got that under control."

Kemper's irritation rose. "Listen, sport, I'm part of the task force, too. Perhaps you can enlighten me?"

Delaney smirked. "If you're not in the know, then it's because you're not supposed to know."

They rode in silence. A twist in his stomach added to Kemper's uneasiness. He recalled Ben Matthews assuring him he had nothing to fear from Mike Tinsel. As far as he was concerned, his friend had lied to him.

"Almost there," Delaney whispered as if to himself.

Kemper took it as a taunt. He wanted to turn the tables and get under Delaney's skin. Then maybe he would let something useful to the sheriff slip. He pulled a can of Copenhagen from his back pocket.

"I don't like you dipping in my car," Delaney said.

"Too bad," Kemper replied as he put a pinch between his bottom lip and gum. He stuffed a napkin into a Styrofoam cup, making it suitable for spittle. "Doesn't seem the DEA knows what the hell it's doing. We're running from place to place without a plan, but you're too far up Tinsel's ass to notice."

Delaney smirked again. "You don't know what you're talking about. Operation Windswept is proceeding according to plan."

Kemper raised an eyebrow. "I just noticed, you sound a lot like your daddy."

"Really? You knew my daddy?"

"Yeah, he was a grade A piece of shit too."

"Th—that was uncalled for," Delaney stammered.

"I knew your mom, too, back in my younger days. Come to think of it, a lot of us boys did."

"You're such an asshole!"

Kemper chuckled. Delaney tried to keep his composure. "I'm reporting this," he said. "This is harassment as far as I'm concerned."

"I'm trying to figure out how we got so far off target from a simple murder investigation."

"Nothing's off target, Kemper. You don't know what you're talking about because you don't know what I know. You're not in a position to know what off target is."

Kemper spat a stream of tobacco juice deliberately over his Styrofoam cup. It splattered on the dash. "There, shithead. That's off target."

Rick slammed his hand on top of the steering wheel. "That's enough, damn you! That is enough!"

Kemper was certain that a few more minutes of agitation would cause Delaney to reveal something important just to demonstrate his superior inside knowledge. Instead, Delaney flicked the blinker and decelerated the vehicle. The opportunity had passed.

They entered a residential neighborhood off the main road. Red and blue lights pulsated from the black SUVs parked in front of a tidy middle-class home. Delaney parked and hurried into the yard. Kemper also exited the vehicle but stood frozen as he tried to absorb the scene in front of him.

Bill Rogers, the sheriff's staff attorney, knelt in the grass, sobbing, hands cuffed behind him, his face red and sweaty. Two small children clung to a young twenty-something, presumably their mother, making the sight even worse. She, too, cried, but the children devastated Kemper the most as they wailed and screamed and pleaded for their Popsie.

One agent wearing a bulletproof vest stamped with DEA insignia stood between Bill and his family. A man with a U.S. Marshal's emblem on his jacket stood behind Bill, and another talked on his phone next to Mike Tinsel, who looked triumphant.

A nosy neighbor peered from her porch, soon followed by another. A car slowed down on the connecting street so its driver could gawk at the pathetic figure cuffed and crying on his knees.

Kemper clenched his jaw so hard, he thought he might break his teeth. He sensed a great wrong playing out in front of him, an excessive show of force intended to humiliate a man in front of his family.

"What the hell is going on here?" Kemper shouted as he stormed across the yard.

A DEA agent stepped between Kemper and Tinsel, raising a cautionary hand.

"Deputy McRae, glad you could join us," Tinsel said with a smirk.

"Answer me, damn you. What the hell—"

"That's not how this works," Tinsel replied. "If you continue with this hostile bearing, I will have you physically restrained."

Kemper didn't want to end up on the grass next to Bill. "I want to know the cause for his arrest," he said as mildly as he could muster.

Another DEA agent exited the house and approached Tinsel. "Sir, the female person of interest—"

"Person of what?" Kemper growled.

The DEA agent continued. "The person of interest is conscious and resting, and she has no visible injuries from her fall. She does not want paramedics called."

"Are you sure?" Bill shouted, panic in his voice. "Are you sure she's not hurt?"

"What happened to his wife?" Kemper asked.

"Fainting spell."

The children continued crying hysterically and calling for Popsie. Their mother spoke up. "May we go inside now so they can see their Memaw? It would be a great comfort to her and would also help calm the children."

"Can I see my Libby?" Bill pleaded.

Tinsel gave a lordly nod. "Agent Crenshaw, please escort this woman and her children into the house so they can be with their grandmother. Agent Williams, you may resume your search of the premises. Take Dodd with you. The situation out here is under control."

Three DEA agents followed the woman and children into the house. The fourth one stayed near Delaney and Tinsel. A marshal stood next to Bill.

"I want to see the arrest warrant," Kemper said.

"No, you may not see it."

"Where's the sheriff? Does she know you've gone after her attorney?"

"We will contact her shortly. For reasons of operational integrity, it was important to make the arrest before notifying her office."

Heat rushed to Kemper's face. "This is bullshit! What happened to your Atlanta gang and your big sweep of all the meth dealers?"

"It's not wise to launch an interdiction plan with a partner agency that has its own drug problem," Tinsel said. "It will be interesting to see how deep the rot is in the Sheriff's Office. Or who else might be involved."

Kemper wanted to argue. He wanted to yell. He wanted to beat the hell out of Rick Delaney and Mike Tinsel, but he could only stand there, angry and impotent. He spat in disgust.

The U.S. Marshal put his phone away, approached Tinsel, and spoke softly. Tinsel nodded and turned to the man guarding Bill. "You may take Mr. Rogers for processing. I will have Agent Dodd accompany you."

Tinsel furrowed his brow as if a troubling thought had struck him. "Oh my, with first appearances suspended because of the pending hurricane, I don't think he will be released for at least four or five days. Maybe longer."

"Hell no," Kemper vented.

"Please, sir, can I please see my Libby?" Bill sobbed.

"No, you may not," Tinsel replied.

Bill turned to Kemper. "Do something, Kemp. Please!"

Kemper turned away. He could not bear to look at the broken man. "I'm sorry, Bill. There's not a goddamn thing I can do."

— Chapter 32 —

The sheriff arrived at Bill's home after the U.S. Marshals had taken him away. Angela Lane and Mike Tinsel exchanged words—angry words from her, arrogant ones from him. Kemper stayed silent, not trusting himself to speak or act. After a few minutes of private conversation with Bill's family, Angela offered Kemper a ride back to Bronson.

"Are you going to let Bill sit in jail for the next four or five days?" Kemper said.

"I don't know."

"What are you going to do? You can't—"

"I told you I don't know, Kemper. I just don't know."

Kemper remained in his thoughts for the rest of the drive. Tinsel's claim of drug trafficking in the Sheriff's Office struck him as absurd. Angela had built her reputation by rooting out bad actors and corrupt practices, with Bill serving as her right-hand man as well as a decent family man.

Angela broke the silence as she pulled into the parking lot of the Sheriff's Office. "I'm still trying to get my arms around this."

"Well, don't take too long. You've only got until November to figure it out."

She hazarded a confused glance in his direction. Kemper filled in the blanks. "Having your staff attorney arrested for drugs probably won't sit well with the voters."

"I haven't even thought about that, and, frankly, I couldn't care less right now."

"That's the first encouraging thing I've heard from you yet. Did Tinsel show you the arrest warrant?"

"He did."

"Well? I can't imagine it's legit."

"I think there are problems with it, but I'm not prepared to discuss it with you."

"What the hell does that mean, Ange?"

"It means, Kemp, that I need to make some phone calls and find out what options I have. I don't know if I can get Bill released without—"

"Breaking rules?" Kemper said with a sneer. "You're still trying to figure out how to do this by the book, aren't you? Meanwhile, a good man is sitting behind bars, no one knows where the goddamn meth house is, and Jerry's killers are getting away with murder! This ain't justice, Sheriff. This is far from justice."

He waited for the rebuke. Instead, sounding defeated, Angela muttered, "I know."

Kemper got out of the vehicle and watched the sheriff drive away under a heavy overcast sky. The wind picked up, and drops of rain fell. In the distance, he saw nothing but gray clouds.

Kemper climbed into his truck and stared out the windshield. He sat in silence, but for how long he wasn't sure. The wind picked up, and the rain strengthened into a drizzle. Soon, it fell in sheets across the parking lot. He took a pinch of snuff and waited until the tobacco worked its way into his bloodstream before starting up the F-350 Super Duty.

He pulled onto the road and accelerated. The familiarity of the crankshaft's irregular vibrations and the engine's gurgling growl eased some of his frustration, and he had half a mind to take his truck into the Florida scrub and run it hard despite the weather conditions. A ping from inside the center console deflated his mood; he didn't need to look at his Tracfone to know he had missed a call from the professor. And Katty Langer knew how to sap the joy from a man in his truck.

Kemper recalled how the professor had chided him with her left-wing academic analysis of truck ownership. "Men only buy big trucks to compensate for what they lack elsewhere," she had said breezily during one of their early wine and whiskey retreats.

"And you think that applies to me?" he said with a rakish grin.

Katty blushed. "Well, in your case, no. You're the exception, Kemper, but it doesn't disprove feminist theory. The pickup truck is an extension of the male ego. It's overcompensation for feelings of inadequacy and insecurity."

She planned to add more, but Kemper began tickling her sides until she spilled her wine and rolled into his arms. After a few more drunken retreats, she presented him with a vanity plate with his name stenciled inside the silhouette of a redfish. She meant it as an ironic insult and wasn't amused when he fastened it to the front of his truck.

"You're such an uncouth redneck," she said when they returned to the hotel room.

"You say that like it's a bad thing," Kemper replied before unbuttoning her blouse.

Kemper shook his head. Despite the professor's sanctimony, he wished his truck could extend manly power to him. His confidence shattered, he had reached a low point with no good options. Similar conditions had set the stage for his initial involvement with her, which was the beginning of all that had gone wrong and a reminder of all he had lost.

He pressed harder on the accelerator. The muscles around his neck tightened, and he lifted his chin. "No, by God," he said aloud. "I'll get at least one thing right today."

He retrieved the Tracfone and called the one number programmed into its memory. To his surprise, she answered on the first ring.

"I've got something to tell you," Kemper said.

He heard a dismissive *pfft* before Katty spoke. "People who begin conversations like that seldom say what they really mean."

"What?"

"Carry on, Kemper. I can only anticipate—"

"We're done. We're not going to see each other again."

A brief pause followed, as if she were waiting for him to get it out of his system. "See what I mean?" Katty said. "You don't really mean that."

"The hell I don't!"

She sighed. "Are you canceling our rendezvous again?"

"You're not listening to me."

"Oh, I hear you. But you know that's impossible. Not with all we've been through." The consonants were less crisp, her words slightly slurred. "If you're feeling the urge to screw that slutty young waitress or that tramp from the marina, then—"

"Jesus Christ, Katty, you're drunk, and it ain't even dark yet."

"Don't you talk to me about being drunk!" A few ragged breaths turned into a sob. Her voice cracked. "I won't take your abuse."

Kemper wanted to hang up, but they had been through a lot together. He waited. She changed subjects.

"Will the hurricane damage the house?" she asked after recovering her composure.

"The house will be fine," he said.

"And the boathouse?" she said in a voice tinged with worry. "Will the, uh… What are those things called?"

"Pilings."

"Yes, pilings. Will they stay in place?"

"They're steel. They ain't coming up, if that's your worry. Your secret is safe."

"Our secret, Kemper. Our secret of what lies beneath."

Kemper spat into his dip cup. *Our secret.* A second fight, worse than the first, when the professor's husband arrived at the big house on the water after his release from the hospital. Kemper was with Katty, and desperate measures followed.

A minute passed in silence. Kemper saw a familiar fork in the road and flicked the blinker. Katty sniffed a few times, then broke the silence. "This is why we're bonded. Forever."

Kemper had slowed the vehicle as he veered onto the new route, but now he stepped hard on the gas to press out his frustration. The passenger side wheels threw up a spray of standing water by the road's edge.

"This thing we have ain't good," Kemper said. "We don't fit together. We never did. It was a fucked-up situation that put—"

"Is that what you call what we've been through? How dare you!" She spoke like an offended aristocrat, one prone to repeating dramatic expressions. "How dare you!"

Kemper slowed the vehicle and turned onto a sandy ingress. "I'm going to make one good decision for the both of us, and that's to end this thing. I can sign the house over to you, or I can put it up for sale. But either way, I'm out in thirty days."

"You cannot do that. That's my mother's house."

"For Christ's sake, Katty, it's not like you grew up there. You went there to hide."

"You must stay there! The house is—"

"A goddamn anchor around my neck!" Kemper hit the brakes, stunned by his outburst.

The professor spoke without anger. Just crisp, callous consonants. "It's not your neck the anchor is around." A short silence followed before she spoke again. "I'm coming to you. And our cursed home."

The line went dead before he could object. He pushed the redial button, but the call went to voicemail. "Sonofabitch," he said through gritted teeth.

Kemper stroked his mustache as he got his bearings, surprised to find he wasn't sitting in his driveway, as if his truck had taken over the navigation while he was preoccupied with the phone call. The windshield wipers cleared the view, revealing sago palm, saw palmetto, and an old familiar trail.

He shifted the vehicle into four-wheel drive and dropped the hammer. The F-350 Super Duty surged forward, and Kemper spent the next ten minutes rumbling over the uneven ground of the Cedar Key Scrub State Reserve. He even let out a holler as he escaped into The Zone.

Kemper straightened the wheels and increased speed as he approached his destination. Oaks, cypress, and slash pine closed in around him, and it took several seconds before he spotted the opening for the clearing ahead.

As he had done many times before, he closed his eyes. "One Suwannee one, two Suwannee two, three Suw—"

A loud bang and sudden jolt, and he pitched sideways in the cab. He opened his eyes to sparks coming from the glancing blow. Kemper cut the wheel in time to avoid another tree, regained control of the vehicle, and made it through.

"Dammit," he growled as he stopped the truck on the edge of the bluff. He looked out the passenger window. The side mirror was missing. Kemper stepped out of the truck and into the rain and walked to the passenger side where the dangling mirror held on only by a pair of wires. He cut it free with his pocketknife and tossed it into the truck bed, then stepped back to survey the damage.

Severe dents and stripped paint ran along the front and rear door panels. Kemper kneeled and looked under the truck, relieved to see the tire and axle free of damage. He spat in the sand. Rain pelted his body.

He got back in the truck, pulling a towel from the backseat and a bottle of Jim Beam from under the seat. He glugged a mouthful. It warmed his throat. Another glug warmed the rest of his body. He found a channel on the radio that updated him on the weather.

The hurricane was approaching at eight miles per hour. At its current pace, the good people of Cedar Key would wake up tomorrow to eighty-mile-per-hour winds with gusts topping one hundred.

Kemper looked out and saw the effects of a blowout tide—the water had receded from a reverse storm surge coinciding with low tide. The wiregrass that concealed the creeks lay flattened by stiff winds. An oyster bar in the center of the bay stood alone. Abandoned.

"You and me both."

Kemper looked at the contents in the bottle. There was enough bourbon to get him over the edge. He took a sip and considered staying right where he was to welcome the hurricane ashore.

A pinch of snuff followed another swig, and the cab filled with the aromas of his favorite vices. He found some Outlaw Country on the radio and turned it up. Wind and rain accompanied fiddle and guitar, and somewhere between Waylon Jennings and Johnny Cash, Kemper McRae settled into a sipping mood.

— *Chapter 33* —

You know we're closing in a half-hour," the waitress said as Mike Tinsel entered The Wayward Breeze.

"I just need a quick bite," he replied.

"You're not from here, are you?" she asked with a quizzical look. "I think I would remember a face like yours."

Tinsel smiled. "I'm visiting."

She tilted her head. "I thought visitors were supposed to head inland. We got a hurricane coming, you know."

"I'm not your ordinary visitor."

He expected more curiosity from her, but all he got was, "We're still closing in thirty. By order of the police chief or something."

Clear vinyl tarp covered the window frames of the open-air restaurant, and plywood equal to the size of the frames leaned against the walls. Tinsel looked around until he spotted his target. "I want her to serve me," he said, pointing to the busty waitress with long dark hair. "Where should I sit?"

"Sit anywhere. Hey, Charlene, you've got a fanboy."

"Did you call me a femboy?" Tinsel sputtered indignantly.

She tilted her head again. "A what?"

"Never mind."

Tinsel sat at a small table. He straightened his back against the chair. Not a wrinkle on his powder blue button-down nor on his perfectly creased khakis. He placed a manila folder on the table.

Charlene greeted Tinsel with a plastic cup of water. "You want anything else to drink?"

"I'll have a White Claw."

Charlene stopped smacking her chewing gum. "Seriously?"

"Black cherry, *por favor.*"

She turned to leave.

"I'll need a menu," he said.

She turned back, hand on hip. "No menu today. You can have grouper or flounder. Bunky's frying up the last of the fish so it don't go bad."

"That's it?"

"You get fries too. There's a hurricane coming, in case you haven't heard, and we still got to board up the windows."

"Flounder will be fine."

She returned with the White Claw and a small Styrofoam cup, steam rising from its contents. "Here's some clam chowder. On us. Hurricane special."

Tinsel would have preferred a fancy meal at a classy restaurant to celebrate the arrest of the sheriff's staff attorney, but this was not a victory dinner. The turn of the hurricane had compressed his timetable, and he had contingencies to manage.

One such contingency was the unexpected phone call from Paul Dell Williams. The drug trafficker, whom Tinsel had once tried to recruit as a confidential informant, now wanted to get out of the gangster life. He said he could help the DEA round up the rest of Three Dead Dogs as well as other gangbangers in Atlanta and Apalachicola. But only if he got immunity.

Granting immunity to suspected killers was not unknown to the DEA, but it was easier to justify when the victims were other 'soldiers' fighting turf wars. It's a tougher sell when the victim is a local hometown favorite. Still, the Acting Special-Agent-In-Charge did not want to miss the opportunity to pad his numbers for Operation Windswept.

Charlene interrupted his train of thought when she set a basket of food on the table. "Anything else?"

"Yes," Tinsel replied. He flashed his badge. "Your undivided attention."

Charlene, unimpressed, smacked her chewing gum. "Make it fast, mister, 'cause there's a lot to do before I can close."

"I'm Mike Tinsel, Acting Special-Agent-In-Charge of the Drug Enforcement Administration, Atlanta Field Division."

"Oh Lordy, what did you call yourself?"

He began to repeat his title before realizing she was just sassing him. "I have some questions for you," he said instead.

"Am I in trouble? 'Cause I don't smoke dope if that's what you're wondering."

"Not at all, but I understand you were recently a victim of—"

"Victim? No, sir, you've got the wrong person. I ain't nobody's victim."

She's going to be a tough one, Tinsel thought. He pushed the chair back and crossed a leg over his knee. "Yes, Charlene, I read the police report about your case, and I am aware you were not a victim in that you were not injured or killed. You brandished a weapon, and—"

"Is that a fancy word for 'shot him'?"

Patience, he told himself. "I was coming to that. Yes, it was your good fortune that you happened to have a firearm nearby at the time of the assault. Not everyone would be so lucky."

"Mister, we've all got guns around here."

"You know, statistically, there's a greater—" Tinsel paused and sucked his teeth. She had sassed him again. He pulled a mugshot from inside the manila folder. "I'd like you to take a look at this photo and tell me if this was the man who broke into your home and tried to assault you."

Charlene arched up on her toes and looked over her server tray as if it were some kind of barrier between them. "Hmm, hard to tell. Maybe you should ask him to pose again."

Tinsel muted his frustration. He understood her. The dismissive attitude was a form of defensiveness, a manifestation of her insecurity. Women of her class and background were often intimidated by men of authority and superior intellect. He needed to be patient.

"I know the incident was disturbing," he said, "and you handled it bravely. But I must insist on your assistance. To be clear, I have the authority to compel your cooperation, but it shouldn't come to that. Just sit with me and answer some of my questions."

She stopped smacking the gum long enough to blow a bubble. It popped. "Fine. Let me set this down." She exaggerated the shift of her hips when she spun around and walked to the kitchen.

Charlene returned a minute later with another White Claw and a Miller Lite. She turned a chair around and straddled the seat, her big bosom bulging over the top of the chair.

"I don't know why this is necessary," she said. She lifted a cigarette to her lips. "I've already talked to the police, but if this is how you get your thrills, have at it."

Tinsel pointed again to the photo of the enforcer known as Tank. "Is this the man who broke into your house?"

"I reckon that could be him," she said after a drag.

"You reckon as in you're pretty sure? Or you reckon as in maybe?"

She blew a stream of smoke past his ear. "I reckon both."

"Aren't there laws about smoking in restaurants?" he said with a pinched face.

She looked around the room. "The restaurant's closed. This is now a shelter for stray cats."

Tinsel had to check himself. Her poor, white-trash qualities—each one contemptible on its own—combined to make her perversely appealing, which was ironic since he wasn't normally attracted to women like her. Or to women in general. He needed to maintain his professional distance.

The Acting Special-Agent-In-Charge asked if she had been drinking that night or if she took any other substances that might have altered her ability to identify the suspect.

"No substances for me," she said, then chugged her beer. "You're looking at a woman untouched by the sins of the world."

"You need to take this seriously."

"Fine. Then that's him. Go pick him up."

"Do you recall seeing him with the first suspect—the one you described for the facial composite?"

"No, I don't. But he'll be easy to identify. He's the feller missing part of his face."

"The problem is we don't know when we will come into contact with him, and the police report does not specify where on his face you shot him. A wound affecting bone structure leaves him disfigured, but a grazing wound might heal before he's apprehended. Do you recall specifically where you shot him?"

"He held a hand to the side of his face, then ran off like a scared rabbit."

"Of course, there's the possibility your shot was fatal, and he died of his wounds after fleeing from your dwelling."

"Fine by me. Can we be done? This hurricane is supposed to make landfall tomorrow, and I've got a lot to do before then."

Tinsel sipped the White Claw. He felt good. A little buzzed. Although he had not anticipated it, Charlene's style—he would not call it charm—had eroded his professional distance. Or maybe it was the White Claw. Regardless, it was her lucky day. He uncrossed his legs.

"Tell me, Charlene, where are you planning to ride out this storm?" He tapped the folder. "Says here you live in a manufactured home. That's not a safe place to be in a hurricane."

"Aw, that's so sweet. Are you worried the whittle waitress might get hurt by this big, bad storm?"

"I'm concerned for your safety. I want to make sure important witnesses are protected. You've now identified two individuals, at least one of whom is the main suspect in the murder of Jerry Whitmore, and both are known to us as members of a criminal organization that we've been tracking. So I don't want anything to happen to you. If you need a safe place to stay—"

"Does the DEA have a witness protection program for weather events? You know, like the FBI has for the mafia."

"Well, technically, the FBI—" He stopped, then flashed a smile. "I'm just saying, I could arrange—"

"Mister, are you making a pass at me?"

He sipped his White Claw and cleared his throat. *Keep it smooth, Tinsel.* "We have rules against bringing civilians into our mobile headquarters, but—"

"There's a DEA headquarters in Cedar Key?"

"Temporary. It's a rental house." He took another sip of White Claw. "I'm running a big operation here, and I want to be close to the action."

"Ooh, what kind of action?"

"I can't say exactly, but we had a significant arrest earlier. A high value target. My team is driving back to Atlanta to wait out the storm, but I'm staying behind to plan the next phase."

She flicked her beer bottle with a fingernail. "Stuck in a vacation rental all by yourself. Too bad you got them rules about visitors."

His confidence swelled. He leaned forward. "I'm the Acting Special-Agent-In-Charge, which means I can waive the rules."

She looked him up and down and arched an eyebrow. "So you're the Big Dog. Does that mean you tell the police chief and sheriff what to do?"

Big Dog. Tinsel liked that. He could see new recruits calling him Big Dog Tinsel as they marveled at the success of Operation Windswept. He could even see a nameplate on his desk: Mike 'Big Dog' Tinsel.

He drank from the White Claw again. "Technically, your sheriff and police chief are independent, but I provide oversight, especially when it comes to life and death situations. They may not like it, but, yeah, I'm calling the shots."

Charlene's eyes narrowed. "Is that because they don't like you calling the shots, or because they don't like the shots you're calling?"

Nicely dissected, he thought. *Maybe she's not as dumb as she acts.* He tipped his can of White Claw and drank.

"I don't get it," she said. "I can't imagine you doing something they wouldn't like."

He sighed. "We often have to make morally complex decisions. I wish it were otherwise, I really do. Your sheriff and chief are playing a game of checkers, but at my level the game is more like chess."

She giggled. "I never understood chess, but I do like those horsey pieces."

Tinsel smiled. She was obviously dazzled by his authority. Time to make his move. "Why don't we go back to my headquarters? I've got a chess set there, and I'd love to show you some of my better moves."

Charlene bit the edge of her lip, as though weighing his offer. Then she stood. "I need another beer and you need another fizzy drink."

She pranced off to the kitchen. Tinsel took a moment to consider his performance. He had already breached protocol by divulging both the existence of a DEA operation and an arrest of a high-value target. Just mentioning a mobile headquarters was problematic. Yet he was dealing with a simple waitress with simple needs and simple desires. Otherwise, he thought, she might be pumping him for information.

Close the deal, he told himself, *and don't disclose any more sensitive information.*

"Was I too forward?" he asked when she returned.

Charlene sat down and leaned toward him, bulging in all the right places. "It's a very tempting offer. I would need to go to my place first and get some things." She looked at him with doe-eyed innocence. "Unless you'd want me to leave after showing me your chess moves. You wouldn't do that, would you? Not with the hurricane coming and all."

Tinsel had not thought that far ahead. Of course, he would want her to leave. He could not risk the professional and reputational damage if agents returned to find a floozy in the mobile headquarters. And he damn sure didn't want the place smelling like menthol cigarettes.

"Of course not," he lied.

She looked relieved. Then she looked hungry. "Tell me, Mr. Big-Dog-In-Charge, what's so morally complex that it would piss off the sheriff and police chief?"

Tinsel sipped his White Claw. "I cannot go into details, you understand. Just know the decision-making for an operation like this is at a much higher level than they're used to. Chess master level, you might say. A chess master, you see, must stay several moves ahead of his adversary, and the best move is not always the nearest kill shot, although it's important to move some pieces off the board like I did today."

"You mean the high-value target?"

"Exactly. And sometimes you give a pass to lower value targets like pawns so you can spring a trap on higher value pieces like rooks and bishops." He winked. "Then you capture them with the horsey piece, which is called a knight, by the way."

Charlene put a finger to the side of her mouth. "But pawns can still kill your pieces, right?"

Tinsel smiled. "Not if they're working for me."

A look of awe spread across her face. "Big Dog level, definitely. So the weirdo I served that night—the one with the bad ankle—he's one of those pawns. And what about the jackass I shot? Is he also one of your pawns?"

"He's a maybe. Either way, it's my decision to make. Thus, the morally complex dilemma I grapple with."

She reached out and squeezed his hand. "You poor thing." Then she tilted her head. "But how do they end up working for you? I mean, they're still bad, right?" A quick intake of breath, and she snapped her fingers. "Wait, I've seen this on TV! You make a deal with them. If they help you get the important bad guys, you let them off the hook. There's a word for this. What do they call it?"

He took a swig of White Claw and leaned back in his chair. "I believe the word you're looking for is immunity."

"For the guys who killed Jerry."

A warning shot fired off in his brain. Too late. "I, uh, meant I might. It's possible, you know, because I have the authority."

Her smile vanished. No innocence in her eyes. No awe on her face. The look Tinsel saw, instead, mirrored the one he normally reserved for himself whenever he called checkmate on a foe.

Charlene stood. "Well, Mr. Shithead-In-Charge, you can go straight to hell." The waitress grabbed the cup of clam chowder and dumped it on Tinsel's crotch, then she tore the ticket off her server pad, bunched it up, and tossed it in his face. "Now, pay your bill, jackass."

She stormed away but paused by the kitchen long enough to grab an umbrella. "Hey, Bunky," she called to the cook.

A big burly man stepped into view. "Yeah?"

"Make sure this creep pays. I'm going home."

Charlene reached her car and lit a cigarette before starting the engine. Her face burned hot at the thought of Jerry's killers escaping justice because of this little turd Tinsel. She could tell Rylan or the sheriff, but it wouldn't matter since the DEA man outranked them, or so it seemed. Even if they could do something, nothing would happen until after the hurricane passed.

Get your mind off this mess, she told herself. *You've got an important appointment to keep.* She needed to get home, pack her overnight bag, and get to her destination before the weather conditions made it too dangerous to drive.

— *Chapter 34* —

Paulie closed his eyes and held the smoke in his lungs, and for a moment, the *tink-tink-tink* of rain falling on his grandmother's tin roof filled his head. With it came a comforting memory of spooning mouthfuls of homemade chicken and dumplings into his adolescent body as he reclined on her couch, wrapped in one of her handmade quilts while hickory crackled in the fireplace.

He exhaled and was back in the meth house, standing in front of the wide window, watching the rain fall on the open field. The stench of armpits, cat piss, and moldering furniture surrounded him. He looked around at the pathetic crew of a dying gang gathered to ride out a hurricane they didn't even know was coming until the Apalachicola gangbangers arrived.

An annoying *plunk-plunk-plunk* sounded from the kitchen where a five-gallon bucket caught dripping water from a leaking roof. He closed his eyes again and inhaled the smoke for another momentary escape.

Sylvia called out, "Hey, P, where'd Tank go?"

"I think he's crashed out in his room," he replied.

She stood in the doorway to her bedroom, her purple bathrobe tied snugly around her waist, the legs of her jumpsuit showing through the slit in the robe. Her laced-up sneakers also drew his attention. *Wouldn't it be funny*, he thought, *if she sprinted out of the house and ran away?* But she wouldn't do that. After all, Full Stop Sylvia was the leader of the gang.

Yet Paulie's chance to escape had finally arrived. The phone number his grandmother retrieved earlier had connected him to the DEA office in Atlanta. After a few transfers, he spoke to the same man who had tried to recruit him years before as a confidential informant.

Mike Tinsel had not seemed interested in helping him this time until Paulie mentioned his new supplier for his meth product. The proffer came quickly: Help the DEA get this new network in addition to Three Dead Dogs, and Tinsel would grant Paulie immunity from prosecution.

"I'm out of my pills," Sylvia said. "I don't want to deal with this hurricane."

"You want me to get Tank up?" he asked warily, dreading her answer.

She hesitated. "No, I'll get them later." She closed the door.

Paulie weighed the resignation in her voice. She now understood what Paulie already knew: Full Stop Sylvia was no longer in charge.

Tank had steadily increased control over the crew, bringing in enforcers from Apalachicola who were in his debt for freelancing a few killings for them. He told Sylvia they were muscle for their return to Atlanta, and she had not challenged him. Paulie wondered if Sylvia had come to terms with an even darker reality. A gang's leader didn't get demoted to a lower rank. He—or in this case, she—got eliminated. It was inevitable.

Unless there's a hero, Paulie thought. He pulled the smoke deep into his lungs, and he went to an alternative world where Sylvia received immunity with him. A package deal. Then she'd accompany him to his grandmother's house, and in their retreat, Sylvia would develop a love for him like he had for her.

He exhaled and chuckled at the absurdity. No way would Sylvia go for him. No way would the DEA give her immunity. Only he would get it.

Paulie's pulse quickened. The offer from the DEA man had been only verbal, nothing written. Without Tinsel's signature on a document, he would be as vulnerable to arrest as everyone else. He looked out the wide window again. Winds pushed the rain across the field.

He hurried down the hallway to the laundry room, where hundreds of baggies of meth had been moved from the blue rain barrels into the dryer drum. He approached Tank's bedroom, where the enforcer kept the knock-out pills he fed Sylvia. Paulie needed her passed out like Tank. Then he could leave and return. He would take his chances that the rest of the crew wouldn't care enough to say anything.

Paulie entered the bedroom, and the smell of cinnamon overwhelmed him. Red candles flickered on the dresser drawer. The hum and rattle of the air conditioning window unit drowned out other noises.

A small figure sat up in the bed. "You need some Feel Good?" Sweetie asked in her rusty voice. She turned on a lamp.

Paulie winced and waited for the lump covered in blankets to move. It didn't. Sweetie, as if reading his mind, looked at the lump. "He's just purring like a tiger. Ain't that somethin'?"

The lamplight illuminated pill bottles and a brown wooden box. Paulie reached for the bottles. "Full Stop needs her sleeps."

"Come sit. You look nervous."

Paulie was nervous, and he didn't want to sit.

"You should take the Feel Good," Sweetie said. She opened the box and began prepping a needle. Clear crystals resembling small ice cubes lay in a cup coaster. "It's a special batch, but he won't mind if you take a bump. He gave some to your friend."

His mind elsewhere, Paulie missed the reference. "Knock yourself out, Sweetie. I've got something to do."

She smiled, revealing rotting gums and yellow-nubbed teeth. "You sure, hun? A little sting, and you'll forget all about that silly ol' hurricane."

Knock-out pills in hand, Paulie turned and left, unaware that Tank had not been asleep.

Mike Tinsel felt the sting of defeat as he walked out of The Wayward Breeze. He ducked his head in the falling rain and trotted to his vehicle. As he drove to his temporary headquarters, he replayed the scene frame by frame and concluded that he had not been outwitted by the hick waitress but rather had made an unforced error with the unfortunate assistance of the White Claw.

A simple mistake. Even Bobby Fischer made mistakes, and Bobby Fischer had been a chess grandmaster.

That someone like Charlene would get the last laugh at his expense added anger to his frustration, and in a small town full of gossips, he knew the sheriff and police chief would soon hear about the encounter.

The best way to overcome a setback was to put a checkmark in the win column, and that opportunity presented itself when his phone chimed as he entered his dwelling. He shut the door as he answered, not bothering to lock it.

"Are you here or back in Atlanta?" the nervous man said.

"I'm in Cedar Key," Tinsel replied.

"That's good. Because I need something from you. Tonight!"

Tinsel took control of the conversation. After a few minutes, the Acting Special-Agent-In-Charge had arranged a hasty meeting, laughing after he ended the call.

He had been only half serious about offering immunity when he first spoke to Paulie. Although the extra arrests and additional contraband were tempting, Operation Windswept would yield impressive numbers, even without Paulie's contribution. Given the circumstances, an immunity deal might not be worth the inevitable pushback from the Justice Department or the blowback from the locals.

If he backed away now, however, these low-grade rednecks would believe he had been bested by the waitress. Unacceptable.

Tinsel stepped into the kitchen for another White Claw as he weighed the rules he was about to break. He had no armed agents with him. No assistant U.S. attorney to draft the terms. Tinsel was tipsy and did not care. He needed a bold move. A Bobby Fischer move.

He returned to the dining room, turned on his laptop, and began editing an immunity agreement that had been drafted for another drug thug in another jurisdiction. Tinsel swapped in the name Paul Dell Williams. Then he changed some words, making the agreement vaguer and more tentative. His mind worked fast. Bobby Fischer fast.

And if something went wrong? Tinsel removed a stack of files from the table and lifted his briefcase from the chair. He opened it and pulled a Glock 26 Gen5 pistol from its holster. He checked the magazine. Fully loaded, just in case.

He finished the White Claw, feeling ballsy and bold. The alcohol gave him grandiose thoughts. He opened another, and then opened the file on Kemper McRae as he waited.

Tinsel saw pieces on a chessboard. A small-town police chief involved in some way with a wealthy, elderly matriarch. An assault that almost killed her son-in-law. Was it just about an affair with the daughter? Kemper was forced to resign, losing his modest salary but ending up with an exceptional house on exquisite waterfront property.

Almost like a reward, Tinsel thought. But why? For what purpose? For beating up a guy…or for replacing him?

The victim of Kemper's fury came from Mexico. Lots of drugs poured into America's rural towns from Mexico. Was he a middleman for a cartel? Is that what Kemper found out and then, instead of arresting him, replaced him?

Other pieces fit the narrative he had constructed in his mind. An isolated asphalt landing strip for pick-up and delivery. Kemper's son serving as the current police chief, and a sheriff who owed Kemper for helping her get her start.

Tinsel saw his opponent's chess pieces arrayed across the board in a defensive position. Like a protection racket.

He took another sip of White Claw and considered Operation Everglades, the case he had studied when he first joined the DEA, where corrupt local officials facilitated, rather than prevented, the illicit drug trade. With every sip, Tinsel became more certain that Cedar Key suffered from the same corruption. The agents who took down the Saltwater Cowboys, corrupt cops, and crooked politicians became legends inside the DEA.

It was Tinsel's time to become a legend.

The narrative came together nicely, except for the problem of evidence, of which none existed. He needed to connect the local officials to the drug trafficking operation. The arrest of the sheriff's staff attorney helped, but Tinsel needed something more.

He needed a masterstroke.

Fortunately, he had a known trafficker desperate to make a deal. Tinsel smirked, knowing Paul Dell Williams would say and sign anything in exchange for immunity. He pulled a small notepad from his jacket pocket, where he scribbled his speculations, and added this latest twist. Then he typed in new language to the immunity document on his laptop.

"Black Queen to B-6," Tinsel said, thinking of a particularly brilliant Bobby Fischer masterstroke.

It would not be the first time the DEA did something like this, and he had learned from D.C.'s other alphabet agencies that there was little downside to pushing a false narrative. He would be rewarded for the claim and chaos that followed, and Mike 'Big Dog' Tinsel would be comfortably ensconced in a higher position of authority by the time he was proven wrong. In the federal government, people in power failed upward. Only the little people got burned.

Tinsel tucked the notepad back in his jacket and took a sip of White Claw. He ran his fingers through his wet, disheveled hair. Only then did he feel the dampness of his shirt. He looked down at the clam chowder crotch stain. The Acting Special-Agent-In-Charge couldn't host a meeting looking like this, even if it was an unconventional, off-the-record meeting.

He hurried to the bedroom to change his clothes and comb his hair, but before he could remove his jacket, the front door opened and shut.

His guest had arrived.

— *Chapter 35* —

Charlene blinked when she caught a glance of her trailer in the rearview mirror just before she passed through the tree line. She reached the road and looked over her shoulder, confirming her luggage sat in the back seat. Her free foot tapped repetitively on the floorboard. She white-knuckled the steering wheel as she turned on the blacktop and accelerated. The rain came down harder, so she eased off at forty miles per hour and chewed on her bottom lip.

The weather didn't worry her. Tommy's daughters did. She was finally going to meet them.

Since the break-in, Tommy had surprised her with frequent phone calls and visits to The Wayward Breeze to check on her. He even bought new locks to put on her doors, but agreed to return them after Charlene reminded him she had left her door unlocked on that fateful night.

He called when the hurricane changed course. "Are you staying at your brother's?"

"Oh, hell no," she had replied, not needing to explain that her brother's house doubled as an overflow shelter for the pets his veterinary clinic couldn't accommodate.

"Why don't you come over here? I'll have my girls, and I reckon it's time for an introduction."

The girls' mother also lived in the path of the hurricane, but further inland. Tommy had a generator to keep the lights on should the storm knock out the power. Given the choice, the girls wanted to stay closer to the action with their dad. Hunkering down in a hurricane is a rite of passage for Floridians.

That alone was reason enough for Charlene to like them. But would they like her?

She figured that was the reason for her anxiety. Or perhaps meeting them meant her relationship with Tommy had entered a new phase. She didn't know if she was ready for that.

Charlene reached the fork in the road and stopped at the yield sign. She rummaged in her purse and found a pack of near-empty menthols beneath the four bags of Jolly Ranchers that would serve as a substitute for cigarettes. No smoking around the girls.

How would she greet them? Maybe tell them how pretty they are and how much their daddy talks about them. Or maybe let Tommy handle it. And how would she greet him? A hug or a peck on the cheek?

She lit the cigarette and cracked the window enough to keep rain from coming in. Charlene did not believe her relationship with Tommy would ever get serious. She did her thing, he did his, and sometimes they did things together. He was normally nice, occasionally generous, and usually fun.

But he was not Kemper McRae.

She scolded herself for letting Kemper intrude on her thoughts, especially while on her way to stay with her boyfriend. Especially since Kemper told her she would be better off with another man. *Keep it between the ditches*, she told herself as she eased onto State Road 24, *and keep Kemper off your mind*.

Then, the other man entered the picture, and Charlene found herself comparing the affections of Tommy, Kemper, and Rylan. Tommy acted the way a boyfriend should, Kemper had shown nothing but indifference, and Rylan was hopelessly in love with her.

She had believed Rylan's infatuation was just the lustful craving of a lonely man. Now she knew better. His gentle behavior and confessed devotion the day after the break-in had surprised her. He had shown a kindness and honesty she had not asked for and did not expect. And it felt good to be held in his arms.

Charlene wanted to hear his voice. She scrolled for his number and pressed the call button. Rylan answered on the first ring.

"Is everything okay?" he asked, surprised.

"There's something you need to know."

"I'm listening," he said, hopeful.

Too hopeful. Charlene changed her mind. "Never mind. I forgot."

"Oh," he said, deflated.

She knew Rylan deserved better than that. After an awkward pause, she thought of something to talk about. "That DEA jackass came by to see me at the Breeze."

"Really?"

"So are y'all still trying to find Jerry's killers or is that something they're doing now?"

"The suspects in Jerry's death are also targets of the DEA. That's where our efforts intersect. We have received intelligence that they're probably hiding out in the area. Can I ask what your interest in this is?"

"Catching Jerry's killers, Sherlock."

"Of course. I meant—"

"Well, they're getting immunity, or at least one of them is."

"I'm sorry, what?" came the startled response.

"Thought you should know."

"Mike Tinsel told you this?" Rylan asked after a short pause. "He just came out and told you?"

His tone annoyed her. "You think I'm lying to you?"

"Sonofabitch."

"Anyhoo, I wanted to pass it along."

"I'll get with the sheriff to see how she wants to handle it." Rylan cleared his throat. "About this hurricane, are you going to be okay?"

"Why wouldn't I be?"

"It's just, uh, you know, where you live and all?"

"What's wrong with where I live?"

"Nothing. I mean, I wanted you to know that if you needed to stay somewhere else, you know, somewhere safer, that—"

"I'm staying at my brother's," she said and ended the call. Charlene found nothing attractive about men who hemmed and hawed. She cracked the window a little further and flicked out the cigarette, then reached into her purse and shook the pack. One left.

Her car slipped a little to the right, and in her frustration, she had sped up to sixty miles-per-hour. She eased off the gas. A minute later, her phone chimed. Tommy's name appeared on the display. She tapped the speaker button.

"Just checking on you," he said, upbeat and chipper. "Making sure you're on the way."

"I'm on the way."

"The way you zip along in that car gives me heartburn, especially on a wet road. I should probably get you some new tires."

"My tires work fine. I should be there in a few minutes." She fumbled in her purse for a Jolly Rancher.

"Listen, I want to go over a few things before you get here. I've set up the guest room for you. I'm going to put your things in there. I told the girls you're a good friend but that you live in a little trailer that might not make it through the storm. That's why you're staying over."

"A friend?"

"C'mon, Char. You know what I mean. It's only until the girls go to sleep. Then you can come to my room?"

"So I'm your girlfriend only when your girls go to sleep? What the hell, Tommy?"

"I don't want to overwhelm them. They're already keyed up about this hurricane. I think it's better if I tell them I'm helping you out."

Charlene mimicked a little girl's voice. "I can't possibly be your daddy's girlfriend because I'm a poor waitress who lives in a shitty trailer. Poor whittle me. May I play with your Barbies now?"

"Now don't be like that, Char."

"This is bullshit." She ground the Jolly Rancher in her teeth.

"Listen, I'm worried if we start off telling them we're a couple, it might be too confusing for them, especially with our age difference. But if everything goes well tonight, maybe we can tell them tomorrow. I don't wanna move too fast with them."

"I've been your so-called girlfriend for how many years now? And I still haven't met your daughters. Every time they're in town, you shoo me away."

"C'mon, Char. Don't be like that. I'm just trying to protect my girls."

"Protect your girls? Protect them from who?"

"I didn't mean—"

"You can go lick a wet turd, Tommy! I'm staying at my brother's house."

Charlene hung up and slammed a hand on the steering wheel. Then she lit her last cigarette. The faded Monte Carlo sped up as it passed the turn to Tommy's house. She figured she would loop through town and then head to her brother's and crowd in with all the extra animals.

She would need more cigarettes. The Quik Stop appeared up ahead and, to her surprise, the lights inside were on. Charlene pulled up and honked until Mama Thighs cracked the door open, then she darted inside.

"Dang, girl, don't you know you're supposed to be locked down for this hurricane?" Charlene said. She grabbed a fistful of napkins at the coffee station and began patting herself dry.

"I needed to bring some things back to the house," Mama Thighs said. "I've got to get it ready for Danny. I fried up a batch of chicken to take with me. Do you want some?"

"Honeychile, please," Charlene said as she teased her hair with her fingers. She turned and presented herself. "There. All better."

Mama Thighs chuckled. "You so silly."

"I need some cigs." Charlene pulled cash from her pocket and scribbled on a notepad by the register. "I'm leaving these for Rache," she said and slipped three twenties under the notepad. Then she walked behind the counter and grabbed a carton of menthol cigarettes from the shelf.

She looked at Mama Thighs. "What's that you said about Danny?"

"He's coming home. They're going to release him from the hospital as soon as this hurricane passes."

"That's great news! So he's doing better?"

"A little better," Mama Thighs said as her expression closed up. "He'll never get back to normal, at least that's what the doctors say. He can't walk because his brain doesn't send the right messages to his legs, and the overdose messed up his speech, too. He only says a few words. I'm getting better at understanding him."

"I'm so sorry."

"They say rehab will help, but he don't want to go."

"Really?"

"Cause it's at the nursing home. Whenever I bring it up, he starts to panic, shaking and shouting, 'No nursing home, no nursing home.' Poor thing. He got so scared yesterday, he peed on himself. But that's where his rehab is, so I just don't know."

"Maybe he thinks you'll leave him there."

"I would never do that. I'm going to take good care of my boy."

A short silence followed before Charlene figured out a way to change the subject. "Why don't we work out together sometime? You know, after the hurricane passes. You can be real pretty if you want to."

Mama Thighs waved a dismissive hand. "You so silly."

Charlene replied with a sympathetic smile. "You need me to help you get back to your house?"

"No, I can handle it. I don't mind getting a little wet."

Charlene said goodbye and darted out the door. She idled her car in the parking lot. Her phone beeped, indicating missed calls.

Tommy and Rylan had both left voice messages, but she wasn't in the mood to check them. She sat in her car, wet and miserable. A feeling of emptiness took hold, and she wasn't sure what she needed to do to shake it off.

She lit a cigarette and pulled onto the road, unsure of where to go.

— *Chapter 36* —

Kemper wasn't drunk, but he was damn close. He sat in his truck enjoying his resentments. There was no sunset to watch, swirling gray clouds having hidden the sinking orange ball. To his left and right, trees swayed under persistent winds. The small bay in front of him started to fill with the incoming tide. A storm surge would soon bring a lot more water.

The hurricane neared.

His phone brightened, illuminating Ben's name. Kemper considered ignoring the call, but he had a few things he wanted to get off his chest. He answered with an accusation. "You lied to me."

A chuckle preceded Ben's reply. "How did I do that?"

"You said I didn't need to worry about the DEA."

"You do?"

"They picked up Bill Rogers on some bullshit drug charges."

"Ain't he the sheriff's attorney? What's that got to do with you?"

"I got this feeling."

"Listen, you ain't him, and he ain't you, and you ain't making sense." Ben paused. "Are you drunk?"

"Working on it."

"Well, before you take another sip, why don't you fill me in on what's going on, and then I'll tell you why I called."

Kemper took another sip. Then he rambled through all that had happened since their lunch together in Steinhatchee, finishing with, "They humiliated him in front of his family and hauled him off to jail!"

Ben spoke, but only after a long pause. "You may not want to hear this, but there may be some basis for the arrest. Let's say the DEA overdid it to embarrass him and the sheriff. That sounds like something this strutting peacock would do. But the arrest may still be legitimate. We don't know what's going on in his personal life."

"He ain't a druggie!"

"People can keep up appearances long before they pass the point of no return. I'm thinking about Sweetie, ole Red's wife. She kept up appearances for more than a year as she got deeper and deeper into her addiction. She was the perfect little nurse until she wasn't. Maybe—"

"I ain't interested in some damn nurse. Hell, I ain't interested in this conversation. Why'd you call?"

"I called to tell you I've locked down your ice machines for the hurricane, but I can see you're not interested in that. What aren't you telling me?"

"What do you mean?"

"Oh, cut the crap, Kemp. Let's assume you ain't paranoid and this DEA bigshot is after you next. Why do you think that is? Did the FDLE miss something when they investigated you?"

"Nothing to do with drugs."

"Then tell me about the nothing part."

Kemper didn't. Instead, he hung up on his friend and spat into his dip cup. He frowned and brooded through a few songs. When he seemed back on track for a good drunk, he was interrupted again. This time it was Rylan.

"You ready for the hurricane?"

"Didn't know I had to report to you," Kemper said.

"We might lose cell service soon, so I wanted to check in. I don't think it's going to make a Cat Two. In fact, it's weakening as we speak."

Kemper said nothing, so Rylan continued, his mood upbeat. "Thought you'd like to know we followed your original protocols to prepare the town. Cedar Key is ready. Dock Street still worries me, though."

"It'll flood," Kemper said in a dour tone.

"I went by your place, and poor old Julep looked nervous."

"I ain't leaving my dog out in a hurricane," Kemper snapped, but he silently cursed himself for almost doing just that.

"I was going to put him in your house, but it was locked up. You also had some things lying in the yard that could become flying objects in these winds, so I moved them into the boathouse. A roll of chain link fence, some post hole diggers—"

"They go in the shed."

"Your shed was locked, too."

"Why'd you come by the house?"

"I came by to tell you I spoke to Mom. Told her you were wearing the badge again and updated her on what was going on. She seemed happy. She said she wanted to talk to you. I think that's a good sign."

"She wants to talk to me?"

"Yeah. I'll text you her number, and since we might lose phone service when the hurricane hits—"

"I'll call her."

"Well, one last thing before I let you go. You're one of my designated calls tomorrow when the hurricane eye passes over, assuming we still have phone service. Part of your Four Corners protocols you put in place years ago. I'll be checking in with Wesley too. He's another designated call, and that's where Charlene said she'll be staying. You know, I appreciate you putting some distance between you and her. Maybe she'll start to come around. Who knows? Maybe we'll both get second chances with these women— you with Mom and me with Charlene."

If he was waiting for Kemper's approval, he didn't get it.

"I've got more calls to make," Rylan said. "I'll see you on the other side of the storm."

Kemper turned off the radio and sat listening to the howling wind. His phone dinged, and he looked at the number from Rylan's text message. Bee Bee's number.

He wished now that he had either drunk none of the whiskey or all of it. He wasn't prepared to talk to her, but he knew he had to. With everything else going wrong, maybe this one thing would go right. He was due for a good turn. He tapped the number. She answered after the first ring, as though waiting for him.

"Looks like you're in for a little rain," she said instead of a greeting.

"And wind," Kemper replied, savoring her delicate voice and habit of understatement.

"I imagine you'll be okay. You're good at weathering storms, aren't you?"

"I try."

"And that house on the water, do you think it'll get flooded?"

"It can blow into the Gulf as far as I'm concerned."

"Now, why would you say a silly thing like that?"

Kemper recognized an opening, but he wasn't ready. He wasn't sure he could put the right words together. "How's Mint?"

"She's a good ol' girl."

"Think she misses Julep?"

"I don't rightly know. She hasn't said anything to me about it, but I'm not fluent in dog."

Kemper smiled. She sounded like the same Brenda Belinda Chastain he had known before she became Bee Bee McRae. Might as well jump in and go for it. "There's a lot that's happened, and not much of it good. Actually, none of it good."

"Rylan told me about your troubles. Are you going to catch the men who killed your friend?"

"At this point, I'm not sure."

"Have faith, Kemper. Faith will get you through."

"Here's the thing. All the stuff that's been going wrong, well, it's shaken me up, but in a good way."

"That's encouraging."

"I'm setting everything straight, Bee Bee. Right and true. You used to use that phrase, remember? Right and true."

"I remember. And I still use it. But—"

"So that's what I'm doing. Making things right and true. I'm getting rid of this house, and I think I might be able to get our old one back." A lump rose in his throat. "And I want you back. Do you hear me? I need you back. I know I made mistakes, and I did you wrong, and I want you to know how deeply sorry I am for that."

The wind howled outside as Kemper waited for her reply. It came like a soft breeze. "Thank you for that. I often wondered why you couldn't say those simple words."

His confidence rose. "We belong together. We should have never separated, and that's my fault, but I'll never make that mistake again. I promise you, Bee Bee, everything will be right and true from now on. Everything is going—"

"Kemper, I need to—"

"—to be perfect. I promise you—"

"No, stop it!" she shouted, her voice breaking. "You must know something."

Kemper, startled by the interruption, stared at the phone. Then came her voice.

"I'm seeing someone else. I've moved on."

STAGE FOUR — HURRICANE

*A pronounced rotation of fierce wind and rain,
organized around a calm central core*

The Captain rolled under a crashing wave, its force pushing him a dozen feet below the surface. Natural buoyancy, more than effort, lifted him back to the top. Stinging darts of rain peppered his body as he raised his head and inhaled the wet air. He no longer heard the roll of thunder or crack of lightning, those sounds drowned out by the exploding waves.

The hurricane pushed in every direction. The pelican rose on a white-topped swell only for it to collide with another. Down beneath the surface he went again, his body rolling, his feet kicking, his wings twisting.

The Captain reached the surface and gasped for air, then stretched and beat his wings. He lifted off the water, but only for a moment before a wave broke across his body. It spun and rolled him, pushing him beneath the water again. He kicked his webbed feet, this time to dive deeper, not wanting to surface. The water churned all around him, and he spun rapidly as a vortex pulled him further down.

He descended until he reached a relative calm. Surrounded by blackness, he wanted to stay in the peaceful zone, but he couldn't breathe. The pelican lifted his bill and kicked upward, and when he broke the surface, he sucked in all the air his lungs could hold.

Dizzy and exhausted, he rolled in the turbulent sea, white foam surrounding him. The furious wind and ferocious waves wouldn't give him rest. He rose on another wave, flapped his wings as he neared its crest, and gained separation, but flew directly into a massive breaker.

Another large swell lifted him again, and he stretched his wings as he reached its peak. With a triplet of flaps, he separated from the angry sea. This time, he stayed airborne. He beat his wings with all the strength he could muster, ignoring the shafts of pain hammering his body.

The Captain flew downwind, climbing higher and picking up speed. He accelerated rapidly, flying faster than he had ever known. He stretched his wings and glided, tilting left and right to maintain his balance in the wind force of the hurricane.

For what seemed like hours, the pelican raced on winds within the circular wall. Vibrations reverberated all around him. A distant howl turned into a piercing scream. He became dazed and disoriented.

Then, there was calm. He had broken through the inner wall of the hurricane and reached the eye of the storm. Out of energy, he tumbled from the sky and crashed into the sea where the waves were not as violent as before. Their lift and fall soothed his aching body. He drifted to sleep.

The Captain awoke sometime later to the howl of wind that grew louder as the back end of the hurricane approached. Waves white-capped. Then came the chaos of torrential rains and violent winds.

He rode a swell to its peak and flapped hard, but he didn't fly as much as hop over its foamy top. The pelican eased down the backside of the wave before sliding onto a new swell. He cleared two dozen waves in this manner, but with each small victory, his body weakened.

The hurricane intensified, waves colliding and exploding, sucking him into the maelstrom and throwing him out again where ferocious winds and blinding rain assailed his battered body.

At last, the Captain understood what was happening. He neared Forever Rest. The slow fade came as darkness edged around his *blurry vision. He longed for the calm shoals near the mangroves of Cayo Avalos, and he wondered if he would find his way back there, this time as a gentle breeze.*

Then one last spark of defiance fired within him.

The Captain summoned a final reserve of strength and burst through a white-topped crest with a frenetic beat of his wings. He lifted free of the sea. He flew high. He flew fast. And he joined the fury of the hurricane.

— *Chapter 37* —

Kemper stared ahead, seeing nothing. Like hammers on an anvil, *I'm seeing someone else* and *I've moved on* pounded in his head.

The outer band of the approaching hurricane had arrived, bringing heavy winds and rain from the Gulf. He stroked his mustache, then he ran a finger under his lip, opened the truck door, and flicked out the snuff tobacco. His senses returned, and he shook his head. Buzzed but not drunk—yet another failure to add to his growing list.

Bee Bee would not return to him. He would not find the meth house, and he would not apprehend the killers. He had even failed to end the toxic entanglement with the professor. She was probably at his house.

His pulse quickened. Mike Tinsel might also be at his house, waiting to do to him what he had done to Bill Rogers. If Tinsel found a drunk and vulnerable Katty Langer blabbing about the boathouse, then Kemper would face more than just a humiliating arrest.

Ben Matthews would dismiss it as paranoia, but Jim Beam reinforced all his worries.

He started up the truck. The F-350 Super Duty rumbled through the hammock and entered the scrub. He struggled to see through the pounding rain, but he soon found the blacktop and headed toward home. Kemper had enough alcohol in his system to make high-quality bad decisions, and his route would take him within a block of the DEA's temporary headquarters. Maybe he would go there and give Tinsel a piece of his mind. Or maybe ram his truck into any black SUVs parked nearby.

Then reality set in. Everyone would be hunkered down for the hurricane, including the professor and the Acting Special-Agent-In-Charge. Kemper would return to an empty house and continue with his empty life.

When he reached home, he turned onto his driveway. Darkness hid his house except where light spilled out from the windows. An outdoor flood lamp illuminated an empty parking area in front of the porch.

Julep bounded into view, his barking muted by wind and rain. The sight of his dog brought some relief to his troubled mind even as the rest of his world had fallen apart. Julep continued to bounce and bark in front of the truck, so Kemper cut the engine fifty feet from the porch, pulled his cowboy hat down over his ears, and jogged the distance home.

He reached the porch, his clothes heavy and soaked by the rain. Julep had his paws all over him, and Kemper returned the affection by stroking his head. He even laughed when Julep shook the water loose from his furry coat.

"Wish I could do the same," he said, removing his hat. "Reckon it's just you and me for a little hurricane party."

A noise from inside, like the legs of a chair scraping across the wooden floor, suggested otherwise.

Kemper stared at the double doors and recalled Rylan saying they had been locked. He looked back to the yard, but he couldn't see beyond the spill of the flood lamp. Any vehicle further back would be cloaked in darkness. He began to question if he had even heard a noise inside when another one came, this time a creak on the floorboards.

Worst case scenarios flashed in his whiskey-wet mind, and he tried to guess which version of trouble had come to collect its debt.

The doors opened, and Charlene stepped into view.

"How'd you—"

"You never asked for your key back," she said, interrupting, "from when we were together."

"And you kept it?"

"All this time."

Kemper took her in as she stood in the doorway, her hourglass figure framed perfectly by the light. She had her dark hair pinned up in a causally twisted mess above scallop shell earrings and a string necklace of small seashells, a long-sleeve fishing shirt, turquoise and snug, tucked into black yoga pants. Everything about her seemed perfectly put together. A stunning woman. A ravishing beauty. She could easily be a mermaid in a lonely sailor's dream.

Her startling presence made Kemper consider his own. Soggy and pathetic. He looked down at his wet shirt and jeans, embarrassed. She didn't seem to care.

Julep, unimpressed with either, scurried past Charlene into the warmth of the house.

"He was barking when I got here," she said, "but he wouldn't come in with just me."

"You been here long?" Kemper asked.

"A while. I parked behind the shed where the ground's a little higher."

Kemper tried to make sense of things, one of which was her voice. It seemed tentative. Apprehensive. Full of twang, devoid of sass.

"Was there—"

"Were you expecting someone else?" she asked.

"I'm not sure."

"Maybe a tall, leggy woman? Likes to wear fancy dresses in the rain?"

He looked back to the yard but didn't see the professor's vehicle. "Where is she?"

Charlene waited until he turned back to her. "We had words."

"Words?"

"Maybe a little more," Charlene said, revealing a hint of a smile. "She decided to leave."

"She left?"

"That's what I said, ain't it?" Her sharp tone quickly tapered off. "That was like an hour ago, and the rain wasn't nearly as bad as it is now, if that's what you're worried about."

"It's not that."

"Are you really seeing someone who drives a Volvo?"

"I'm not seeing her."

"Who is she?"

"Nobody important."

"You got that right, cowboy." Some sass had returned.

"Figured you'd be at Tommy's," Kemper said.

"You figured wrong. He and I are done."

"And what about Rylan?"

"Shut up."

"I just think—"

"Shut up, Kemp. I've made my choice."

He stared at her, knowing only a damn fool would send her away, and only a damn fool would stand there saying nothing.

Charlene titled her head to indicate the living room, where a mixed drink and a bottle of Jim Beam stood on the table. "I got your brand."

Kemper nodded.

She bit her bottom lip and fixed her hazel eyes on his. "I am your brand."

"I know."

"Then don't just stand there looking dumb and handsome. Come kiss me."

Kemper stepped forward, wrapping his arms around her as his hands slid from her back to her waist. She leaned back, her mouth parted, his lips finding hers. He kissed her, soft at first, then firm.

Charlene's hands worked up from his arms to his shoulders and found his face, and she returned the kiss with one so deep that it chased away all of Kemper's worries.

— *Chapter 38* —

Checking this fucker off my bucket list."

Charlene propped a hand under her head as she raised herself up on an elbow. She rested at the foot of the bed. "I knew I'd get another one out of you," she added. "Old man, my ass."

Kemper sat up against the headboard, a curious smile on his face. "I was on your bucket list? Darlin', this ain't our first time."

"Don't flatter yourself, Einstein." She waved a hand at the windows overlooking the Gulf, where wind and rain continued their assault. "This! This is my first time staying through a hurricane, and I always had a particular notion for how I'd like to ride one out." Her naughty eyes sparkled. "Okay, I reckon you're part of it, too, but only like a backup singer is to the band."

Kemper tossed a pillow at her.

All through the night, the hurricane had battered the big house on the water as Kemper and Charlene rediscovered each other. A high-pitched whistling noise lifted and faded according to its own mysterious tempo. The howling wind intensified, accompanied by windows that rattled, a roof that creaked, and a bed that shook.

Kemper had nodded off shortly before morning with Charlene resting her head on his chest. She roused him as gray introduced the dawn. Above her rhythmic humming, the whistling outside became shrill before reaching a climax. Then it faded. The eyewall of the hurricane had passed.

The winds diminished, and more light spilled through the windows. Thoughts Kemper had kept at bay began swirling in his head once again, like the swirling clouds outside, reflecting the disorganized chaos of his mind. He was, at once, satisfied and frustrated, happy and miserable, exhilarated and exhausted.

A tug on his toe drew his attention to Charlene. "What's the matter?" she asked with a pouty face. "You don't look very pleased. So much for my best effort."

"It's not you, darlin'. Everything is fine."

"You got that right, cowboy." She rolled on her back, pulled the corner of the bedsheet across her waist, and watched the calming storm pass through the skylight above.

A few minutes later, she slid off the bed and slipped on her panties. She walked over to one of the four large windows that stretched from floor to ceiling. Her long, dark hair bounced against her bare back. His eyes followed her. She pressed her palms and forehead against the glass. "You worried these windows might break?"

"Hurricane-rated."

She turned to face him, instantly improving Kemper's view of the Gulf. "The eye is next, right?" she asked.

"Yeah, the eye is passing over. It'll be calmer for an hour or so. Then the back-end hits, and there's real danger there."

She walked from window to window. "Your boathouse is holding up."

"It should. Built it myself."

Charlene detoured to the nightstand for a cigarette. Kemper had also been craving tobacco. He reached down and pulled his Copenhagen can from the damp jeans that lay crumpled by the bed. It caught her attention when he thumped it a few times, and she turned on him. "Oh, hell no, you don't!"

"What?"

She blew out a stream of smoke, then flicked the ash in an empty water glass. "You ain't kissin' on me if you keep dipping that nasty stuff."

Kemper chuckled and pinched the ground tobacco between thumb and finger. Then he saw her disapproving glare. He opened his mouth to protest, but decided the irony was endearing as she took another drag on her cigarette. He shook his head. "Then get me a beer. I think a hurricane is a mighty fine reason to drink beer for breakfast."

"I like the way you think," she said as she left the bedroom.

He tossed the snuff can on the nightstand. "And let Julep out," he shouted. "He needs to do his business."

The winds weakened. No howl. No whistle. The eye of the hurricane had arrived, and it was calmer outside those windows than inside his head. What Charlene had chased away during the night now returned, clustered into its own kind of storm.

Let it go, he told himself. Let go of the foolish notion that he could repair the past, that he could regain his stature in the community and return to the days when he wore the badge with pride. Let go of the desire to bring his estranged wife back from Alabama. Let go of the hope that he would find the men who had murdered his friend.

Let fate take the win and accept the present circumstances, which were pretty damn good. Charlene was sexy and sassy and a sight to behold. A gift. It made no sense that she liked him or maybe even loved him, but she had given herself to him unconditionally and without restraint. All he had to do was let go of the past and accept the present.

Charlene returned, wearing one of his flannel shirts, unbuttoned with the sleeves rolled up, holding a beer in each hand. "How come we still got power? I even have phone service. You know, I'm beginning to get a little disappointed in this hurricane."

Kemper sipped the beer, ran his tongue over his teeth, then took a deeper draft. "The second half is coming. There's a good chance we'll still lose power if that's what you want."

Charlene nodded at his beer. "When you finish that, you're going downstairs and cooking me some steak and eggs. I seen them ribeyes in the fridge."

Kemper was about to answer in the affirmative when his phone vibrated on the nightstand. He glanced at it. "I need to get this."

She raised an eyebrow. "Fine. I need to powder my nose anyway."

Kemper waited until she disappeared into the bathroom before answering.

"Checking in like I said I would," Rylan said, sounding upbeat. "Still got cell coverage, I see."

"Obviously."

"How's your power situation?"

"Still got it, and the generator's ready just in case."

"Okay, good. Best guess for now is we've lost power in about a hundred homes. The rest of Cedar Key is holding up, and the hurricane's weakening. It'll probably drop below a Cat One before long. Wind damage is minimal. We got one call about a waterspout. Now we're just worried about a second-half storm surge."

Kemper could sense Rylan fishing for a compliment. He lowered his voice. "You've done a good job, son. I'm proud of you."

"Thanks. I'm following the example you set."

"Yeah, well, I reckon I'll let you go."

"Wait, one more thing. You talked to Tinsel?"

Kemper frowned. "Why?"

"Do you know anything about a possible immunity deal?"

"Immunity?"

"I figured with you on the inside—"

"What the hell are you talking about?" Kemper insisted.

"Tinsel might give our suspects immunity in exchange for helping with Operation Windswept."

Kemper's breath caught in his throat. His muscles tightened. "The ones who killed Jerry?"

"Yeah. At least one of them."

Though he didn't think it possible, Kemper's frustration and sense of hopelessness worsened. He stayed silent until Rylan prompted him.

"You still there?"

"I haven't heard a goddamn thing about immunity. Who told you this?"

A note of triumph rang in Rylan's reply. "Charlene. I figured she might have called you, but I reckon not. Tinsel met with her yesterday, and that's what he told her."

Kemper looked to the bathroom. The door hung ajar. Water ran in the sink as Charlene brushed her teeth in the mirror's reflection.

"I'm not taking this lightly," Rylan said. "I'm going to get the sheriff involved, and maybe there's something we can do about it."

Kemper said nothing. The sudden awareness that his friend's killers might escape justice with the help of the DEA turned his stomach. The realization that he was so unimportant to the matter that Charlene had not even bothered to tell him made the bile more bitter.

Rylan continued. "I'm calling Wesley after I get off the phone with you, assuming he still has phone service. He's one of my strategic check-in calls from your four-corners approach, and Charlene said she's staying there until the storm blows over. I want to tell her I'm going to push back on this immunity plan, but I don't want to give her false hope, you know, in case it's a done deal. What do you think?"

Kemper dropped the phone to his side, gut-punched by the words.

Rylan's voice came faintly through the receiver. "Dad? You still there?"

Charlene stepped out of the bathroom. Planting one hand on her hip, she wagged the toothbrush at him and spoke with her distinctive twang. "Listen here, old man, you need to get some pineapple in your diet."

Rylan's voice rose from the phone. "What the? Is that—"

Kemper thumbed the button to end the call.

"Was that your girlfriend with the Volvo?" Charlene asked, her tone playful. The phone buzzed again. She approached the bed. "If that's her calling back, you can put her on speaker and let me have a few words with her."

Kemper held up the phone so she could see the name on display. "Oh shit."

"Maybe you should have a few words with me instead," he snarled. "A few words about an immunity deal you didn't want to tell me about."

"What?"

"Immunity!" he yelled as he flung the phone to the corner of the room. It skipped and banged off the wall. He swung his legs off the bed. His eyes narrowed. "You told Rylan, but you didn't tell me. You don't think I needed to know?"

"It didn't come up," she shot back. "And don't yell at me. I'm not keeping it from you. We've been busy doing other things, unless you forgot already, you senile old jackass."

Charlene crossed the room and lit a cigarette. She stared out the window as he opened a dresser drawer and pulled out some clothes. Her voice quivered. "You didn't deserve to hear from me after your stupid advice from the other day, but I was going to call and tell you anyway. Then I got the idea to come over instead. I thought you were glad to see me."

Kemper finished dressing. What she said made sense. He looked at her and couldn't tell if she was hurt or pissed. "Would you accept some steak and eggs as an apology?"

She turned and faced him. "You better be nice to me, or I'll put you in the nursing home."

He chuckled. "Nursing home?"

"That's right. You can be roommates with Danny Miles."

Kemper started toward the door, but stopped. "What'd you say?"

"I'm teasing you. I don't care how old and decrepit you get. I'd push you around in a wheelchair before I put you in one of those. I'll be the naughty nurse, and you'll be my only patient."

"I meant what you said about Danny."

"Oh, it's nothing. I saw Mama Thighs when I got my cigs yesterday, and she said Danny is coming home from the hospital. She said he was scared he might be sent to a nursing home. I found it funny. I guess it kinda stuck in my head."

Kemper stroked his mustache. "I didn't know he was talking. I thought the overdose left his brain scrambled."

"That's what I thought, too, but Mama Thighs says he can say a handful of words. It's all slurred and garbled, but she understands him, I guess."

"Did he say anything about where he got the drugs or where the dealers hang out? That's the key. If I knew where they were hiding."

"We didn't talk about that. She's happy to be getting her boy back, and he's happy he ain't going to a nursing home."

"Why'd you find it funny?"

"Find what funny?"

"That he's scared of a nursing home."

"I dunno. I guess because no one told him he was going to one. He just kinda invented it and then went on and on about it."

"Is that a fact?" Kemper said absently.

"I reckon that's what happens when your brain gets fried. Does this make me a shithead for finding it funny?"

Kemper didn't answer. His police instincts had kicked in. Similar yet different words echoed in his head, one of which came from an earlier conversation with Ben. His eyes fixed on Charlene, but he looked through her, not at her. "Nurse, huh?" he muttered, loud enough that she heard him. And misread him.

Charlene turned her shoulders, and the flannel shirt shifted to reveal a generous portion of her body. She started toward him. "Correction, old man. Naughty nurse. Breakfast can wait if you'd like this naughty nurse to check your vitals."

"Stop." His voice was cold and distant.

"Excuse me?"

Kemper didn't notice the offended look on Charlene's face, and he wouldn't have cared if he had. He spoke aloud, but the words were intended more for him than her. "You think Danny may have been saying something different, and Mama Thighs heard it wrong? Like maybe he's saying *nurse's home* instead of *nursing home*. He didn't want to go back to the nurse's home."

"I guess, but why would it matter?"

"It matters, by God. It damn sure matters!"

Goosebumps spread across his arms, and a tingling sensation raced up his spine as the revelation became clear.

Kemper knew where the killers were hiding.

— *Chapter 39* —

Don't forget the grits," Charlene said as Kemper left the bedroom.

The expression on his face concerned her, but not enough to question him about it. She chewed her lip and wondered if he would invite her to stay after the hurricane had passed. She knew what her answer would be.

Charlene returned to the window. Small waves capped with white foam rolled over the dock that led to the boathouse. Broken tree limbs lay on the ground. Standing water in the backyard looked only a few inches deep. Charlene shook her head, disappointed.

She opened the music app on her phone and found Reba McEntire on her playlist. Charlene sang the first few lines to a song that had been a hit when she was a kid, and she laughed because it was still too modern for Kemper's tastes. He really was significantly older than her, and she really didn't care. Let the biddies gossip. Wasn't it always older men chasing after younger women? Yet here she was, the pursuer.

Reba's voice faded away, but before the next song began, another sound came from outside—the gurgling growl of Kemper's truck.

"Oh, hell no, you don't!" she shouted. She ran out of the room, down the stairs, and through the living room, then passed the kitchen before reaching the front doors.

Kemper's truck pulled around the driveway, its wheels sending tiny waves rippling through the standing water. Julep splashed alongside the truck.

"What the hell are you doing?" she yelled.

The truck didn't stop, the window didn't roll down, and Kemper didn't answer.

She shouted again and watched as the vehicle accelerated, rooster tails spraying higher as it gathered speed. Julep stopped, his tail wagging, a look of anticipation on his face. He knew his master would return.

Charlene wasn't so sure. She ran back into the house, to the kitchen counter, where she had left her purse and keys. The purse was still there, but the keys were not.

"Bastard," she said, then cursed herself for not reading him better. A gust of wind pushed through the open doors. She called for Julep, and in the time it took to get him inside, she wondered what would cause Kemper to leave the security of his home in a hurricane.

Charlene ran upstairs and snatched her phone from the bed. She called Kemper's number, unsure whether she wanted to cuss at him or plead with him. Instead, she screamed when his phone vibrated in the corner of the room.

The second half of the hurricane neared. Anger and anguish, fear and frustration—each took a turn before numbness settled in as she resigned herself to the possibility that she might never see Kemper again.

The numbness Kemper had felt since that moment of revelation abruptly wore off when his F-350 Super Duty slid sideways on the water-clogged road. He corrected the wheel and eased down on the brake, and the truck halted just before leaving the asphalt.

Kemper felt disconnected from what was happening, like an out-of-body experience where he observed himself sitting in his truck. He didn't remember leaving his house, but he knew he had.

He had first experienced this incoherent haze years earlier when he had spotted the professor's husband by the boat ramp, talking to one of the locals. A burst of rage followed, and he remembered the detached feeling of watching himself beat the man with an axe handle. Unable to control his actions. Unable to stop.

The sensation returned when the husband, recently released from the hospital, showed up at the big house on the water while Kemper visited the professor. Another out-of-body feeling. Another episode of blinding rage.

Kemper looked at a lime rock driveway that cut into a thick stand of trees amidst a thicker undergrowth of vegetation. It looked a lot different since the last time he had visited, but he was certain of the place. No serious angler ever forgets where he bought a boat motor. That goes for trolling motors, too.

He remembered Red Ferguson fumbling with his tools and stumbling over his words, trying to justify the convoluted, jerry-rigged wiring on an otherwise perfectly good Minn Kota trolling motor. Kemper eventually took over and untangled, untied, pulled, and snipped the colored cords that ran from bow to stern.

It took an hour to liberate the trolling motor, the passage of time made more pleasant by Red's wife, Sweetie, who brought the men a tray of iced teas, smoked mullet dip, and crackers. A plain, pudgy woman in nurse's scrubs, she talked about the upcoming Cedar Key Seafood Festival while the men worked.

Kemper recalled Ben's comments about Sweetie's decline into addiction and Red moving out but paying the bills because he couldn't bear the thought of Sweetie being homeless. That would explain why her house didn't appear on the list of abandoned properties the task force used to search for the stash house or meth house or whatever the hell it was called.

Danny hadn't mumbled his fear of returning to the nursing home but rather the *nurse's home.* Sweetie's home. He was afraid of the nurse's home because bad people were there—people responsible for his overdose and for his girlfriend's death.

People who had murdered Jerry.

The F-350 Super Duty gurgled and growled and began its approach. Kemper crossed over a cattle guard by a gate that lay rusted and bent along the fence line. The muddy, ungraded lime rock road deteriorated into a worn path that zig-zagged for fifty yards through a thick hammock of trees and underbrush. He braked before the path opened to a large field.

Across the field and partially covered by oak boughs stood Sweetie's house, filthy and neglected. The metal awning, under which Kemper and Red had worked on the trolling motor, had collapsed. Several cars, some of which appeared inoperable, lay scattered in a front yard comprised mostly of dirt and weeds.

Kemper leaned forward and stroked his mustache. He had no plan or ability to apprehend the killers. He couldn't just mosey up there and place them under arrest. These were gangsters, after all. They would not be inclined to go along peacefully.

The wind howled its fury as a ring of cumulus clouds scurried across the gray sky. A deafening crack to his right signaled a slash pine snapping and falling. A sheet of rain swept across the field, blurring his vision of the nurse's home. The back end of the hurricane had arrived.

It was too dangerous to stay. It was too dangerous to go.

He frowned at his predicament and grabbed the bottle of Jim Beam on the passenger seat. A little bourbon remained from last night, so he took a swig. He opened the console and found a can of Copenhagen, and he tucked a generous pinch of the smokeless tobacco between his bottom lip and gum.

Kemper spent the next few minutes revisiting everything that had gone wrong since losing his badge, losing his wife, and losing his standing in the community. His anger swelled, and he welcomed it. He needed it.

He thought about Jerry's final moments: a metal tool splitting his skin, breaking his bones, cracking his skull. He thought about the terror his friend must have felt before blackness took him. The howling wind became a roar. Anger descended into rage.

A jagged bolt of lightning flashed, and thunder reverberated all around him. Somewhere from behind came a shrill whistling noise, then the snapping of trees, echoing like gunshots. He white-knuckled the steering wheel as the numbness returned.

Kemper's Smith & Wesson Magnum .44 hung in the magnetic gun mount beneath the steering wheel. His axe handle lay across the backseat. The F-350 Super Duty, already in four-wheel drive, growled in anticipation.

Then, briefly, the wind and rain died down, as if the hurricane had paused to catch its breath. And in the deadly calm, Kemper lifted his boot off the brake and slammed the accelerator to the floor.

— *Chapter 40* —

Paulie stood in front of the wide window. The rain and wind had intensified. The distant tree line looked like a smudge. He shifted his weight from one foot to the other and mumbled to himself, "He shouldn't have done that, man. He shouldn't have done that."

He repeated the motion and the mumble a minute later, and an empty beer can passed over his shoulder and bounced off the window, followed by, "Shut the fuck up, man. I'm tired of you acting all weird and shit."

Paulie didn't want to shut up. Sad and depressed, his meth high was rapidly burning off. "He shouldn't have done that."

He, of course, was Tank, who had followed Paulie to Tinsel's temporary headquarters, ruining his chance for immunity. And it was Tank who callously dumped Sweetie's body on the floor of the laundry room, claiming she had overdosed on his Feel-Good stash when, instead, it looked like she had been strangled.

And it was Tank who forced his way into Sylvia's bedroom. Paulie could still hear her screams—defiant at first, then desperate. It lasted all through the night, and then she went silent.

"He shouldn't have done that."

Sylvia's voice—weak and pathetic—now wafted through the house. She had not suffered the same fate as Sweetie. At least, not yet. She pleaded for anyone who could hear her outside the bedroom. Creeper and Charlie, the enforcers from Apalachicola, snickered from the couch.

"Man, I wish he'd shut her up."

"Damn straight. And he said we'd get a taste when he's done, but she's starting to piss me off."

Paulie wondered if anyone would help her. Big D, Chris, and Kenny were in the kitchen. Chris was a driver like Paulie and didn't carry, but Big D and Kenny were armed. Yet no one moved. Paulie stared at them for a few seconds before turning back to the window. He wondered what it would be like to be a hero. To grab the gun on the coffee table and kill Creeper and Charlie, and then Tank. To rescue Full Stop Sylvia. To receive her love.

A break in the rain gave Paulie a better view of the field. He saw movement by the tree line. He squinted. A truck threw up rooster tails of water and turf, speeding toward the house, leaving black ruts in the soggy grass. It was surreal. He wondered if he had imagined it, the effect of one last chemical disruption in his brain.

Then he heard over his shoulder, "What the hell is that?"

Kemper covered the distance in mere seconds. The F-350 Super Duty bounced up and down as the tread on its tires sought purchase. Kemper struggled to maintain control as swirling winds returned and threatened to flip the truck on its side. He jostled left and right, forward and back, but he kept the accelerator pressed firmly to the floor.

Behind him, the hurricane roared like a freight train. The front tires lifted over a slight rise and splashed down in the muddy front yard. The back tires popped up and lost contact with the ground.

Just as a mighty windblast caught the undercarriage of the truck and hurled it into the meth house.

A flash, an earsplitting explosion, and blackness.

Kemper opened his eyes and lifted his head off the passenger seat. His upper body lay twisted across the center console. He wasn't sure if he had been unconscious for thirty seconds or thirty minutes. The cloud of dust surrounding the cab suggested the shorter option.

A coppery metallic odor mingled with the smell of diesel. He lifted his fingers to a warm, sticky residue on the side of his face, then he touched a deep gash above his ear and eye. The touchscreen display panel was smashed and blood-smeared.

Commotion outside the cab caught his attention, but the dust cloud prevented him from seeing beyond the spider-webbed windshield. His senses sharpened, and, to his surprise, he recognized another sound. The F-350 Super Duty sputtered and coughed rather than gurgled and growled, but it still ran.

A ferocious howl smothered the other noises. The truck began to shudder. It continued for several minutes. Then the squall passed. Kemper pushed up from the seat but almost collapsed as his arm struggled to support his weight. Blood covered his face and neck, and sharp pains in his ribs and shoulder matched the throbbing ache in his head.

Kemper cleared his mind of the pain. He had work to do.

The stinging rain convinced Paulie he was still alive when his initial thought after the explosion was that he had entered some kind of spiritual realm. He remembered watching the truck as it got closer. When he realized it was not a meth-induced hallucination, he dove toward the hallway with a shout of 'God's mercy!' escaping his lips as the truck smashed through the wide window and part of the wall.

Confused and dazed, he propped himself up on his elbows. His eyes, throat, and nostrils burned, and he choked on the dust from pulverized drywall and cinder block. More of the exterior wall crumbled, a section of roof collapsed, and wires dangled from the ceiling, their ends sparking in the rain. A truck idled in the living room among the overturned furniture.

"God's mercy," he said again through labored breaths, and Paulie realized he channeled his grandmother's faith with those words. He used to mock her silly expression, but now, in desperation, it slipped out of him as naturally as a sigh.

Pellets of rain slashed sideways between the truck and wall, and he raised an arm in front of his face for protection. Groans behind him were followed by voices.

"What the hell happened?"

"Was that a tornado?"

"Oh, God! Look at Chris, yo! He's done."

A fierce blast of wind knocked Paulie on his back and swooped the dust cloud upward through a hole in the ceiling. For several minutes, the walls and floor shook, and objects crashed and collided while rain sprayed in every direction. He covered his face with his arms, repeating 'God's mercy' over and over until the roar died down.

Paulie wondered if any shelter would remain to protect him before it was over. His grandmother's expression came to mind once more. This time, he closed his eyes and asked for it in the form of prayer. When he opened them, to his horror, he knew he had failed to invoke God's mercy.

For the devil stood next to the pickup truck, his face red and glistening, his profile stern, with a gun in one hand and an axe handle in the other.

— *Chapter 41* —

The thunder clapped so loud and sharp that Paulie thought lightning had struck inside the house, but the acrid odor of gunpowder did not belong to Mother Nature. Something tumbled, and he strained to look over the broken chair he had cowered behind. Sneakers and bent legs above an overturned coffee table meant there was one less enforcer among the living.

A new rainband arrived with a howl, and the deluge sprayed through the gaping holes in the roof and wall. Paulie crawled on his elbows toward the back door, hoping the blurring rain would conceal his movement. He could sense the devil's presence moving across the room, stepping over obstacles, pushing them aside. Getting closer.

Paulie reached the overturned coffee table, but a deafening bang paralyzed him. He wasn't sure if it was another gunshot or the clanging of falling objects. He flattened himself on the soggy carpet. His body convulsed from a combination of fear and wind force. He lifted his head enough to see a dark stain spreading in the middle of Creeper's shirt. Lifeless eyes stared back at him.

The squall passed, followed by a terrifying silence, then a shout. "Light that motherfucker up!"

Gunfire exploded all around him. Paulie pulled his arms over his head and curled into a fetal position. He did not count the rounds, but at least a dozen—maybe twenty—had fired before there was a pause. The sound of ticks and tinks came from the truck as the engine smoked, and popping and buzzing sounds echoed from inside the broken wall. Dangling wires sparked as they swayed in the wind. The gunfire resumed.

Three handguns fired indiscriminately in the direction of the truck. For once, Paulie appreciated the violent nature of his gang. Charlie, Big D, and Kenny fought back, although Paulie couldn't tell who was who because he saw only their hands holding pistols above the objects they hid behind.

Another pause, then shouts.

"I think I got him, man."

"Where is he?"

"I need another clip, yo. I'm out."

The gangsters hesitantly stood, guns pointing toward the vehicle. Paulie crouched and prepared to sprint for the back door. His arms and legs still shook, and his teeth chattered so hard, he felt a sharp pinch on his tongue and tasted blood.

They must have shot him, he thought. They wouldn't be standing unless it was safe. He looked at the gangsters for encouragement as he worked up the nerve to run.

Then Charlie's head snapped back violently in sync with a loud, sharp thunderclap. Blood, brain, and shards of skull sprayed across the room before his body hit the floor.

The two other gunmen stared in horror at their fallen comrade, but before they could move another thunderclap struck and another gangster got knocked back several feet before collapsing to the ground.

Big D dove behind a couch. A moment of silence passed before a shaking hand raised a pistol in the air. "Hey, man, don't shoot! You hear me? You a fed, right? You five-oh? Don't shoot me!" He waved the gun a few times like a white flag, then he tossed it toward the truck. "You see that? I'm giving up, yo. I ain't got no clip, man. I ain't got no gun!"

An old man stepped into view. Red rivulets ran down his face, giving him a ruddy sheen. Blood, rain, and sweat dripped from his thick mustache. A dark spot on his jeans above the knee, his shirt blood-soaked, he winced and breathed heavily through his mouth as he staggered forward. He pointed his revolver at Big D and flicked the barrel upward as he issued a command. "Up."

Slowly, the gangster stood, his hands out in front of him, his head turned slightly to avoid direct eye contact. The old man looked him over and flicked the barrel again. "Turn."

Big D complied and showed the other side of his face. The old man sighed, disappointed. The muzzle flashed, and Big D tumbled backward.

The concussive blast thumped in Paulie's chest like a subwoofer. Nausea rose in his stomach, and he sank against a broken chair. The room swirled. "I want Grams," he whimpered. "I want my Grams."

"Grams ain't here," came the reply in a deep, gravelly voice.

Paulie looked up to see the man standing in front of him, gun in one hand, axe handle in the other. More terrifying were his black, hollow eyes that reminded Paulie of the merciless killers he used to see when he vegged out watching *Shark Week* on TV.

Immobilized by fear, he began to tremble. Then he vomited.

Kemper looked down at the pathetic creature with puke on his shirt, but his mind's eye saw something else—the sketch rendering of the suspect in Jerry's murder. He used the end of the axe handle to lift Paulie's chin for a better look. "Where's your partner?" he said.

Paulie's eyes fixed on the axe handle, which unexpectedly separated from Kemper's hand and seemed to levitate because, in a blur, Tank had crashed into him.

The two men somersaulted across the room, grunting, wheezing, and growling. The axe handle and revolver fell at Paulie's feet. When the tumbling stopped, Tank was on top of Kemper, his elbows pumping like pistons as his fists pounded into face and chest. A sickening thwack accompanied each solid blow as Kemper struggled to deflect Tank's punches. Tank slammed his massive forearm down on Kemper's neck. Next came elbows hammering on chin and chest.

"Ground and pound, baby," he sputtered as he alternated between fists, forearms, and elbows.

Kemper flailed his arms weakly, unable to stop the assault. Tank leaned back on his haunches, catching his breath and looking satisfied. He spotted a broken cinder block within arm's reach and pulled it near, then he hoisted it with two hands above his head. "Now you know, motherfucker. Now you know."

But a ferocious windblast knocked Tank off balance, and Kemper shoved with all his might. Tank fell to the side, the death blow undelivered.

Kemper pushed himself up, dizzy, lightheaded, and coughing blood, but alert enough to swing his steel-toed boot into Tank's mouth. The kick broke several teeth and bought Kemper time to get out of Tank's reach. He took only two steps before the wind knocked him to the floor. He rolled in the direction of an upturned couch and crawled around to its underside as a spray of rain provided gray cover.

The respite would not last long, and Kemper was fading. His breathing grew shallow and raspy. He inhaled for a deep breath, but the pain was too severe, and he coughed up more blood. He figured his sternum was broken. Maybe his collarbone, too.

And he was tired. Bone tired. His whole upper body felt bludgeoned, his neck burned, and bruised and torn tissue swelled around his mouth, nose, and eyes. Worst of all, he knew this monster of a man would be on him again as soon as the squall passed. He closed his eyes and thought how nice it would be if he could simply fall asleep and drift away.

Then, Kemper sensed a presence about him, and in the howling wind and pounding rain, a familiar voice spoke. "Well, Kemp, you sure got yourself into a pickle."

He opened his eyes but saw nothing in the gray rain, yet he knew he had heard it and who had said it. He shook his head. "I'm getting too old for this, Jerry."

"Yes, you are," came the reply, as clearly as if they sat together on the pier. "And from what I see, you're pretty screwed."

Kemper managed a feeble smile. "Thanks for the vote of confidence."

"You don't need confidence. You just need to stay awake."

"And then what do I do?"

"I'd say you either fish or catch bait."

Kemper chuckled, causing his ribs to ache even more. "It's 'cut bait,' Jerry. 'Fish or cut bait.' You never could get that right."

A coughing spasm ended the conversation. Kemper hacked up bloody phlegm mixed with tobacco juice. The wind intensified, even as the rain died down, and some objects were cast about.

Including Kemper's axe handle.

It cartwheeled across the room and thumped into the upturned couch, landing an arm's reach away. Then the winds calmed. With his adrenaline pumping, Kemper grabbed the axe handle and stood. He turned as Tank charged at him, closing fast.

"There you are!" the big man screamed. "I got you, motherfu—"

Kemper smashed the hard hickory into Tank's face. Blood sprayed as his nose flattened, and the big man staggered a few feet before toppling over the television. Kemper stepped closer and slammed the axe handle across Tank's back, then he repositioned himself, trying to get a better angle. He wanted to end the fight with one blow.

But he hesitated. A gauze pad dangled from a bloody raw wound where there should have been an ear. Kemper had not noticed it while being pummeled, but he saw it now, and he realized he was fighting Charlene's attacker, the other suspect in Jerry's death.

The hesitation was costly. Tank sprang up and rammed his shoulder into Kemper's stomach, driving him backward. Kemper hammered the butt of the axe handle on Tank's back and struggled to keep his feet under him, for he knew if he got pinned down again, he would never get up.

They crashed into the wall by the bedroom. Kemper pushed away and swung at the mangled flesh on the side of Tank's face. Tank ducked the blow and grabbed Kemper's arm, spun him around, and slung him back to the center of the room. Kemper tumbled hard, felt a crack in his right shoulder, followed by stinging pain.

He pushed up and readied himself for the next attack. To his surprise, Tank kept his distance. Then Kemper heard a woman's voice, "Shoot him, P! Shoot him now!"

A distinct click sounded behind him, and he recognized it as the cylinder turning in his Smith & Wesson Magnum .44. His gun was in the hands of the punk with puke on his shirt and was most likely pointed at his back.

The woman shouted again. "Shoot him now!"

Kemper expected darkness. Time seemed to freeze as he chewed on the notion that he was about to be killed with his own gun, and he found it strange that images of significant past events or the faces of family and friends didn't flash before his eyes in some kind of instant life review. Instead, he thought about honor and reputation. If it was his time to die, so be it. But, by God, he did not want to get shot in the back like a coward.

He turned to face his killer only to see the gun aimed at Tank, who—with arms out and palms up—took a hesitant half-step toward a woman standing in the doorway of the bedroom a few feet away.

Kemper recognized her from the pictures he had seen at that initial DEA briefing. And he recognized something else. In his many years as Cedar Key Police Chief, he had only once been at the scene of a violent rape, but he had never forgotten the look on the victim's face. He saw it again as he stared at Full Stop Sylvia—the shattered look, the defeated eyes. Her purple bathrobe hung torn and stained around her with what looked like dried blood.

She swayed as she pleaded, "Kill him now, P. Please!"

Paulie pulled the trigger. And missed.

A chunk of drywall exploded between Sylvia and Tank as the thunderclap echoed around the room. Tank had thrown his arms over his head and hunched down, but now he stood erect and took another half-step toward Sylvia.

Kemper understood why. The Magnum .44 packed a powerful kick, but Paulie held the weapon with a shaky hand and trembling arm. It was too risky for Tank to charge across the room, but he could force Paulie to drop the weapon if he could use Sylvia as a shield. He was almost within reach of her. Then he lunged.

Paulie fired again, and Tank collapsed on top of Sylvia.

Kemper looked for an exit wound but saw none as the big man pushed himself up.

"Oh, God, no!"

The anguished cry came from Paulie. He dropped the gun and ran to where Sylvia King lay motionless in the doorway. "Please, Jesus, don't let this be happening!"

Kemper looked at the gun. So did Tank. The old man was closer, but the big man sprinted to the prize before Kemper could get his broken body there.

Tank snatched the weapon and spun around. He smiled and raised the barrel to Kemper's face. "I'm gonna watch your head explode, old man."

Kemper tightened his grip on the axe handle. "Better be sure."

Tank squeezed the trigger but heard only a click as the empty cylinder turned. He tried it again and got another click. He looked at the revolver, but he should have been looking at Kemper, who had widened his stance and put his waning strength into a slugger's swing.

Thirty-six inches of hard hickory, curved to concentrate its load force at the point of impact, connected with Tank's head. His skull cracked, and the big man collapsed at Kemper's feet.

Kemper heaved a sigh of relief, which triggered another coughing spasm, bringing up more bloody phlegm. He limped over to Paulie, who sat against the door jamb, cradling Sylvia in his arms. He had pulled her torn bathrobe across her front to protect her dignity and hide the bullet hole between her breasts. Blood stained the purple fabric and spread across the carpet.

Paulie sobbed as he stroked her hair, softly repeating, "God's mercy, God's mercy, God's mercy." He stopped when a pair of boots appeared in front of him. He wiped his eyes with the cuff of his shirt and looked up. "This isn't real," he said. "I'm not a killer."

"Maybe not," Kemper replied as he raised the axe handle above his head. "But I am."

— *Chapter 42* —

Kemper managed to drag Paulie and Tank through the debris field of the meth house despite nearly passing out in the process. He bound their hands with zip ties from his truck's toolbox. The deadlifts almost killed him, but after several attempts, he got them into the bed of his truck. His reward was five minutes of retching and a kaleidoscope of starbursts for vision.

Buzzing and popping sounds came from inside the broken wall, and a whoosh of flame flashed as he climbed into the cab. He rested his forehead on the steering wheel. Intense pain racked his body, but his face had stopped bleeding, and he began to believe he might make it home.

The truck suffered almost as much damage as he had. Its engine rattled and clanged, and smoke spilled out from under the hood. It had defaulted into park at the moment of impact, so he shifted it into reverse. The gears caught with a jolt, and the F-350 Super Duty rumbled over the rubble of broken roof and wall.

Kemper took one last look at what remained of the nurse's home. Smoke poured out of the ceiling vents, only to be whisked away by the wind. He put the truck in gear and drove away. It slipped and shuddered as it passed through standing water and high winds. Its front tires wobbled, and the steering wheel shook violently, but it stayed on the road until Kemper reached his driveway.

Little waves rippled toward the house as the truck cut through a foot of standing water. He caught a glimpse of Charlene and Julep as they rushed out of the house and sloshed after him. She yelled, and the dog barked, but he ignored them and continued toward the dock. He misjudged the distance, and the front tires rolled over the edge of the bank. The hood disappeared underwater, the back end teetered up, and—after one last gurgling growl—the F-350 Super Duty died.

"What the hell's going on?" Charlene shouted as she pulled at the truck door while Kemper pushed from the other side. It opened, and water rushed in. She grabbed his arm and tugged, and the two fell onto the dock. Julep joined the pile with anxious paws and worried licks.

"Lemme up," Kemper grumbled. He grabbed Julep's muzzle and shoved him away.

"You're hurt," Charlene said. "What happened?"

"Got in a fight, darlin'."

She helped Kemper stand as Julep reluctantly retreated. Two men sat slumped over in the back of the truck, face down, hands zip-tied behind their backs. Cinder blocks and broken drywall surrounded them.

"What have you done?"

Kemper didn't answer. He was on the move, limping toward the boathouse. The rain returned and slashed across the water. A stiff wind unsteadied him. She ran forward, threw an arm around his waist, and helped him stagger inside. He flipped the light switch, but the room remained dark.

"Yeah, the power went out a little while ago," Charlene said.

"Bet you were thrilled," Kemper replied. He limped over to the generator, primed it, and pulled the recoil cord. It rumbled to life on the third attempt. After plugging in an extension cord, the lights flickered and stayed on.

Charlene's eyes widened. The interior of the boathouse was dry, the hurricane affecting nothing inside.

Kemper sensed her surprise. "Floaters underneath and rollers on the beams keep her above the rising water. I built it myself," he added with a touch of pride.

Two boats—a bay and a flats—hung in their harnesses. The only things out of place were a shovel, post hole diggers, and a roll of chain link fence just inside the door. A picture frame fallen to the floor was another blemish. She resisted the urge to re-hang it.

Kemper disrupted her distraction. He had limped to his workstation and pointed to a coil of anchor rope atop a high shelf. "Grab that, Charlene."

"You need to tell me what happened," she said as she balanced on a bench stool and retrieved the rope. He headed toward the door. "Dammit, Kemp, answer me! I don't know where you went, and I don't know what you're trying to do now, but you need medical attention."

"No time," he said over his shoulder.

"You need a doctor!"

"No doctor."

They reached the truck, and Kemper held out one end of the rope. "Climb in there and tie this around their chests."

Charlene planted fists on hips. "No, sir. Not until you tell me what the hell is going on."

The rain had calmed to a drizzle as if Mother Nature had given Kemper a chance to explain himself. He pointed to the bed of the truck. "Them boys are the ones who killed Jerry."

"Oh, God," she gasped.

"And I'm taking them to justice."

"Taking them to justice? Kemp, you ain't taking them anywhere. You're hurt, and we're still in a hurricane."

"I got 'em this far, didn't I?"

"And this is as far as they need to go! Let's hold them for the sheriff. We still got cell coverage, and my phone is—"

"No sheriff. Just help me get…." A coughing fit kicked in.

"Okay, we'll tie them down in the boathouse, but then we're waiting for the sheriff, agreed? And I'm calling you a doctor."

Kemper's eyes narrowed, and he spat blood in the water.

"Fine," Charlene said, "then I'll call my brother. You won't be the first mangy dog he's patched up."

Charlene climbed into the truck bed as Paulie twisted onto his side. "Can you call my Grams?" he said politely. His words were slurred, and his ears and nose were caked with dried blood, the result of a concussion. "She'll come get me. Hey, I know you."

"Yeah, I know you, too, you piece of shit."

Tank managed to turn over, revealing the mangled flesh where Charlene had shot him when he had come to rape and kill.

And she lost it.

"Hallelujah, motherfucker!" Charlene stomped her boot down, grinding the heel into his raw ear hole. Tank screamed and flopped around like a landed fish. She kept stomping his face until a gash opened on his cheek, and she lost her balance. Kemper reached out to steady her. "Leave me alone," she snapped. "I'm fine."

She pulled the rope under Tank's arms and tied it off. "Yeah, this is Florida," she taunted, "and we fry bastards like you!" Charlene finished the knots and lowered the tailgate. She looked at Kemper. "Do we still do the chair here, or is it the injection thingy?"

Kemper pulled the rope, Charlene pushed with her boots, and the two men toppled into the water. Julep barked excitedly and nuzzled up to his master's leg. Kemper bent down, nose to nose, and stroked his dog's head. "You need to stay here and be a good boy."

The exchange startled Charlene, and it took her a moment to figure out why. This was Kemper's first show of emotion since returning. It was a fleeting moment.

"Grab those blocks," he said, turning his attention to Charlene. She toted a pair of cinder blocks as Kemper dragged the men through the water. He tied the rope to a dock cleat and headed inside the boathouse. Charlene set the blocks down and followed him.

Kemper flipped a couple of switches on the support beam between the boat slips. An aluminum door retracted upward, and his bay boat eased down into the water. Wind, rain, and waves raced through the opening. Water sprayed everywhere.

Kemper pointed to a metal contraption leaning in the corner of his workstation—an L-frame, two-by-two, with a pulley and winch, and a downrigger mount. "Take that to the boat," he said, followed by a broken cough.

She picked it up. "What is it?"

"It's a hoist to lift crab traps out of the water." He added a wry smile. "Wouldn't want to hurt my back, now, would I?"

Kemper dragged the roll of chain link fence to the boat and pushed it in.

"What's that for?" she asked.

He didn't answer. He eased himself into the boat and mounted the hoist in a rod holder. "Meet you back on the dock."

Kemper backed the boat out of the slip with a push pole and steered it to where Tank and Paulie bobbed in the choppy water like popping corks. He snatched Paulie's rope with a gaff and snapped the winch hook to the knot behind his back. The hoist clickety-clicked as Kemper cranked the handle, and the skinny man slowly rose out of the water. Kemper swung him into the boat.

Tank kicked his legs furiously as he tried to push away. "You ain't getting me, motherfucker."

Kemper leaned over and whacked him on his swollen head with the gaff's wooden shaft, then he hooked him in the waist, the sharp point penetrating flesh. Tank yelped like an injured dog as the clickety-click began again.

The L-frame bent under the strain of Tank's weight. Cracks opened at the base of the rod holder, and more cracks spread across the gunwale, but the hoist managed to lift the big man above the waterline. Kemper pulled the gaff, and Tank screamed as he swung into the boat. He fell hard on the deck, squirming and cursing. Kemper kicked his swollen head, and the big man went limp.

Charlene noted the casual cruelty on display. Kemper showed no more emotion than if he had gaffed a fish. She watched as he bound the two men's feet with anchor rope, then he pulled the cinder blocks off the dock. They fell, chipping his boat's fiberglass deck. Kemper didn't give it a second look.

But Charlene did. The cracked gunwale and chipped deck would cost thousands of dollars in repairs, and Kemper didn't seem to care. An $80,000 truck lay partially submerged in the water, but he wasn't bothered in the least. She figured his entire house could blow into the Gulf, and Kemper would not so much as blink. He had driven through a hurricane and suffered great injury to bring back the men who had killed Jerry. For what? To hold them for the sheriff? To keep them secure so they could get immunity from the DEA?

As Kemper's intentions became clear, Charlene's face flushed, her stomach hollowed, and she wobbled on unsteady feet. "Bastard," she said absentmindedly.

Kemper staggered toward the helm. "Both of 'em."

Her jaw tightened. "I'm not talking about them."

No one would ever accuse Charlene of being meek. She had inflicted her share of pain on people who had deserved it, and she had even thrown the first punch a time or two. But she had never aided and abetted what she now knew was happening. Although she was not a regular churchgoer, she knew a Judge of the Universe held everyone to account, and long ago He had declared, "Thou shalt not murder."

Kemper turned the key and faced her as the boat engine roared to life. His expression could have been chiseled in granite. "This is about Justice. That's where these boys belong."

Julep barked from the bank and raced up the dock. Too late. The boat had drifted out of jumping distance. Kemper turned the bow toward the horizon and pushed down on the throttle.

Charlene watched him disappear behind the boathouse, then she ran inside and over to the four-poster bed to peer through the window. Julep jumped on the bed, and they both watched as the bay boat got smaller in the choppy waves. Then it disappeared into the blurry mist.

Julep whimpered his confusion. Charlene rested a hand on his head. There was nothing else she could do.

She turned and saw the fallen picture frame, the least important thing that had happened. Yet she felt compelled to pick it up and place it back on the wall. That's when she noticed its title: The Cedar Key Mystery Fishing Tournament. And she remembered that the challenge of the tournament was to find Kemper's most elusive fishing hole.

A place he called Justice.

— *Chapter 43* —

Justice is hard to find, or so it's been said. Yet in the year represented on the framed map in the boathouse, Kemper had found such a place.

High tides came in higher than they had in a decade, allowing him access to new areas along the coastline. Kemper had spotted a narrow creek guarded by long rows of oyster bars stretching parallel to the shore. After a hundred yards of twists and turns, the shallow creek opened into deeper water. Alligator holes, actually. The big toothy reptiles had dug out deep depressions in the peat muck with their claws and snouts, and dozens of these holes combined to create one wide area rich in aquatic life and concealed by tall stands of sawgrass.

Baitfish like mullet and menhaden feasted on a buffet of algae and insects, apple snails, and grass shrimp, while blue crabs scurried over bivalves. Into this came the trophy fish anglers dream of—fat flounder, gator trout, bull reds, and black drum.

The Gulf swell wouldn't last, and this place would become unapproachable again, but in that particular year, the tide charts promised plenty of water for the weekend of his fishing tournament, so Kemper gave it his highest designation. He named it Justice.

Stabbing pain, more intense than he had ever felt, shot through his body every time the vessel lifted over a wave and slammed down on the water. Kemper gritted his teeth and pressed on, pushing down and pulling back on the throttle, jerking the wheel left and right to avoid the side-on waves that threatened to capsize his boat.

Paulie and Tank tossed violently against the boat's sides and each other, their screams drowned out by wind and water. They pissed and vomited on themselves, but the waves breaking over the bow carried their waste into the bilge.

More than half an hour passed before Kemper spotted a spread of seafoam a hundred feet from where the shoreline should have been. He had reached an area with a hard-shell bottom and submerged rocks known to be tricky, even in normal conditions. Kemper eased up on the throttle and raised the trim. He angled the boat parallel to the break, then zigged and zagged through a series of runs. Only once did shell scrape on the fiberglass hull when he veered too close to an oyster bed lurking beneath the surface.

The last turn brought him into the mouth of the creek. Rocks and mussels broke the waves, but enough of a cut existed to allow Kemper and his quarry to coast in on relatively calm waters. The tall stands of sawgrass weakened dying winds, and the rain diminished to a light drizzle.

Kemper reached in his back pocket for a can of Copenhagen that wasn't there. His frustration lasted only a moment before he opened his dry storage box and pulled a heaping portion of Beech-Nut chewing tobacco from its pouch. He stuffed it in his mouth. His cut gums burned as the tobacco released its juices.

"You gotta take us in!" Tank shouted. "You hear me? You can't do this!"

Paulie's concussion had left him slack-jawed. His voice faltered. "I didn't kill anyone, mister. I was just there. It was Tank—"

"Shut the fuck up!" Tank yelled. "You don't say shit to him. He's a cop or FBI or something, and he can't be doing no vigilante shit. He's trying to scare us. You hear that, old man? I done figured you out! You gotta take us in!"

"Are you the DEA?" Paulie asked politely. "Because I was supposed to meet this nice man, but Tank wouldn't let me."

"Shut up, dammit. I told you to shut the fuck up!"

"Maybe I could call him."

"He's no longer interested in you," Kemper said.

"Oh, that's too bad."

Kemper idled the engine and dropped the anchor. Ten feet of rope pulled over the side before it slackened. He tied it off and lifted the bent L-frame hoist from the damaged rod holder and placed it in another one on the port side.

"Fuck you, old man. You ain't doing shit to—ow!"

A thick stream of tobacco juice splattered in Tank's eye. Kemper wiped his mouth with the back of his hand, but he couldn't wipe the grin from his face.

Tank screamed and kicked his feet. Kemper caught his legs under his good arm and twisted them as Tank's center of gravity shifted, flipping him on his stomach. He snapped the hook in place and began cranking the handle. The gunwale cracked as it had on the other side.

Tank lifted off the deck, and Kemper swung him out of the boat, where he dangled above the murky water. "You can't do this!" he protested.

Kemper released the lock, and Tank splashed into the water. He thrashed desperately and furiously. Then came Paulie's turn. He seemed confused as the strap tightened, and he spoke calmly as he swung over the gunwale. "Sir, I didn't do the killing."

Kemper spat in the water. "Maybe not, but that don't change a thing."

Paulie splashed down. When he bobbed back up, his eyes were tightly closed, and he mouthed something Kemper couldn't quite hear.

Kemper pulled up the anchor and repositioned the boat in front of the men. He cut two short cords of rope and used one piece to tie a cinder block to the chain link fence. Then he dropped it over the side and watched a third of the fence unroll into the water.

Tank screamed more threats and curses, but Paulie remained silent. The chain link fence stretched over their heads as Kemper pushed the boat past them. He tied the last cinder block to the remaining section of fence and dropped it into the water.

The fence exerted slow, downward pressure and was too cumbersome for the two men to swim out from under, especially with their hands and feet bound. Tank sucked in mouthfuls of water as he screamed his final curses. Then he held his breath, hoping to stay buoyant. His effort failed. With fury in his eyes, Tank descended to his watery grave.

Paulie arched his head back until only his nose peaked above the surface. He inhaled one last time, but it was not briny marsh water he smelled. It was the rich aroma of his grandmother's chicken and dumplings, ready to come off the stove.

— *Chapter 44* —

A force more destructive than the hurricane had been unleashed, and Sheriff Lane did not need a bulletin from the National Weather Service to know its name. She idled her vehicle at the entrance to Kemper's property. Eight to ten inches of water covered the driveway, but that wasn't why she stopped. The storm surge wasn't an obstacle. Coming to terms with what had happened was.

The emergency call had come in from county fire rescue immediately after the hurricane passed. Dark smoke between Cedar Key and Otter Creek had drawn a fire engine to the site of a burning house. Once it was under control, firefighters entered and found bodies—dead not from fire or smoke inhalation, but from gunshot wounds.

Angela had been alerted by the call center at the Sheriff's Office. She raced to the scene, and as she walked through the wrecked meth house, it became clear what had happened. The death and destruction had a distinct signature. A large caliber weapon, larger than a standard service handgun or any of those found at the scene, had made the wounds. She knew whose gun fit the description. She knew because she had permitted him to carry it.

Her face flushed, and she clenched her fists as adrenaline pumped through her body. Angela sped away from the house, not bothering to tell subordinates her destination. Standing water in certain places on the main road forced her to slow down, and that forced her to consider her role in what had happened. By the time she reached Kemper's place, Angela was as mad at herself as she was with him.

She had given him a badge because she had been one-upped by Rylan. Then she kept Kemper on despite his anger, erratic behavior, and insubordination. If wounded pride triggered her initial bad decision, her ongoing poor judgment was due to weak sentimentality.

The FDLE would have her badge if the voters of Levy County didn't take it from her first. She felt sick and angry and strangely confused about what to do. Call for backup, of course, was what she *should* do, yet doubt clouded her mind as if an inner voice told her to find another way to resolve the problem.

Julep barked when the green and white Chevy Tahoe with 'Sheriff' emblazoned on its side pulled up. Kemper and Charlene sat on the porch with a deck of cards and a bottle of Jim Beam on the table between them.

Angela waited until the little wavelets had rippled across the yard before she exited the vehicle. She looked around the property, partly as a threat assessment but mostly out of curiosity. Kemper's truck lay tipped over on the bank's edge, the front end submerged in deeper water. His bay boat also rested on the bank, leaning on its port side. It looked like it had run aground.

She sloshed through the water until she stood a few feet from the porch. Kemper's cowboy hat shaded his face, but not enough to conceal bruises and black eyes. His left arm hung in a makeshift sling, a bloodstained cloth wrapped around a leg, and he slouched rather than reclined in the cast aluminum patio chair.

A lit cigarette dangled from Charlene's mouth as she noisily smacked on bubblegum. The sleeves of her flannel shirt were rolled up, and her tousled hair hung over her shoulders. She leaned forward and placed a card on top of the pile. Then she took a shot of whiskey.

Kemper sluggishly leaned forward and played one of his cards on top of hers. He grimaced as he leaned back, then looked at the sheriff. "You want in? We're playing Nines."

Irritated by their indifference, Angela pulled a pair of handcuffs from her gun belt and lobbed them through the air. They landed on the table and scattered the cards.

"Now, what the hell'd you do that for?" Charlene snapped, her words slightly slurred.

"Put them on," Angela said to Kemper. "You're coming with me."

Charlene stood. "Hey, I'm talking to you."

Angela rested a hand on her sidearm. "I'll ask you to stand aside, ma'am. My business here is with my deputy."

"The hell it is. Can't you see he's hurt?"

"How'd you get those injuries, Kemper?"

Kemper leaned forward again and filled the shot glass. He threw his head back and tossed the whiskey down. Angela caught a glimpse of a bandage under the brim of his cowboy hat. His glassy eyes suggested that he had consumed much of the bottle already.

Charlene answered for him. "He got hurt in the hurricane. My brother's coming over to patch him up."

"Your brother's a doctor?"

"Veterinarian."

"Why haven't you called for paramedics or taken him to emergency care?"

Charlene put a hand on her hip. "Because we're playing Nines."

Angela found Charlene's defiance and hostility unsettling. Ridiculous, even. "I don't have time for games. I know what happened." She looked at Kemper. "I saw the bodies."

"Well, why don't you fill us in, Sheriff?" Charlene said. "We've been here the whole time."

Angela's anger rose. "Kemper, this doesn't have to be difficult. You need to—"

"I said we were here the whole time," Charlene said, her tone sharp. "His boat broke loose, and he got hurt trying to rescue it, to answer your question about injuries."

"And the truck?"

"I did that. Woman driver, you know."

Enough of this, the sheriff thought. *Time to put her on notice.* "You need to watch what you say because there are serious consequences for lying to a law enforcement officer. I will hold you accountable for any falsehoods."

Charlene blew a stream of cigarette smoke in her direction. "Did I stutter?"

A tingling sensation ran down Angela's neck. She did a quick threat assessment. Charlene, like Kemper, was likely under the influence of alcohol. She possessed no apparent weapon, other than brightly painted fingernails. Taller than the average woman, she stood probably around five-foot-eight and appeared to be in good physical condition, her arms and legs toned if not muscular.

The threat assessment gave way to a catty one. Charlene was built for the tastes of vulgar men and the fantasies of adolescent boys. Cowboy boots under cut-off jeans were as tacky as chewing bubblegum while smoking a cigarette. A single button on her flannel shirt restrained her large bosom, and a rhinestone belly button ring sparkled on her flat, tanned stomach. Angela could only imagine what the lower back tattoo looked like.

An inner voice spoke, scolding her for judging the young woman so harshly. The sheriff took a deep breath and tried to remain calm. She had a job to do as the chief law enforcement officer in a county where bodies were stacking up. Kemper's actions were not only a reflection of her poor judgment. They were illegal vigilante killings.

Angela climbed onto the porch steps. Charlene moved in front of her. They stared at each other, and in that moment, the sheriff recalled a training workshop from long ago on how the eyes can reveal someone's state of mind. Eyes usually dilate when a person is under stress or threat, yet Charlene's were golden brown with greenish hues surrounded by bright whites, visible both above and below her irises. The Japanese call this condition *sanpaku*, but the workshop trainer had used another term: the psychopathic stare.

Charlene, a smirk on her face, flicked her cigarette into the standing water and calmly tied her hair up in a knot.

And for the first time in her professional career, Angela flinched.

She had a handgun, taser, baton, and self-defense training. The sheriff had taken down drunken men much bigger than Charlene. Yet in this surreal, untethered moment, she saw bullets bouncing off boobs and her taser simply supercharging this Redneck Queen of the Shitkicker Parade.

Angela backtracked into the standing water, dumbfounded. The inner voice spoke again, telling her a confrontation wasn't necessary. She turned and walked to her vehicle, searching for a way to save face.

"Been here this whole time, huh?" she said, more as a statement than a question.

The sheriff opened the liftgate and grabbed the vanity plate with Kemper's name stenciled inside the silhouette of a redfish. She tossed it in his direction. It splashed in the water.

"Found this at the meth house, Kemp. There will be hell to pay."

— *Chapter 45* —

"Tinsel is dead!"

"What?"

"Dead!" Rylan shouted through the phone's speaker. "I'm at his temp headquarters and he's—"

"Wait, slow down. You're telling me—"

"Mike Tinsel is dead, Sheriff, and all hell is about to come down on us. I mean, the entire freakin' Atlanta DEA and half of Washington will be here by this time tomorrow."

"Calm down, Chief. Tell me what happened."

Angela had returned to her office still in a state of shock from the encounter at Kemper's. She listened in stunned silence as Rylan told her about receiving a report of gunshots last night, and how he had checked the dwelling once the hurricane had passed, found it unlocked, and then found the Acting Special-Agent-In-Charge on the floor—not shot, but bludgeoned to death.

"Who could have done that?" she asked absently.

"How the hell would I know? I just got here and called you. I need Doyle—"

"Keep your cool," Angela said, interrupting. She was surprised at how emotional and irrational Rylan sounded, and she was equally surprised at how calm and clinical she felt. "Tell me what you see. What evidence is there?"

"What do I see? There's blood! Fuckin' blood everywhere!" A pause. An audible sigh. Then Rylan continued. "I dunno, Sheriff, there's his service weapon, couple cans of White Claw, laptop and notepad… Oh wait, there's something else."

"What?"

"Okay, I got a call yesterday. From a source. Said Tinsel was considering immunity for one or both of the guys we're looking for."

"The suspects in Jerry's death?"

"Yes, and now I'm looking at a draft agreement on his laptop with the name Paul Dell Williams on it."

Angela's shock turned to anger. She needed to stay on top of her emotions. She took a deep breath. "Do you think either of these suspects might have killed Tinsel?"

"Why would they? They're getting immunity."

"Think, Chief. Let's say one or both came over but found the terms of the agreement not to their liking. Or maybe Tinsel changed his mind."

"Jesus Christ, I'm standing in the middle of a goddamn murder scene, and you're spit-balling motives. I need Doyle here, and I need your forensics people. I need everyone you can spare!"

"No, not yet," Angela said, surprised that those words had slipped from her mouth.

So was Rylan. "Not yet? What does that mean?"

After a brief pause, the sheriff answered. "I want to look it over myself before we involve anyone else."

"Anyone else? What the hell, Ange?"

"Don't call anyone, at least not yet," she said firmly. "I just came from your father's place, and there are some things you need to know that I can only tell you in person."

"What's going on?"

"I'll brief you when I get there. Secure the laptop and any paperwork lying around, and check to see if there are any security cameras in the house or around the perimeter."

Angela ended the call. Mike Tinsel's smug mug flashed in her head, as did that initial DEA briefing with the photos of the gang members. None of the bodies in the meth house looked like Paul Dell

Williams or the enforcer they called Tank. They were either still at large or in someone else's custody. Or disposed of.

She thought of her oath of office and her commitment to keeping her community safe. Oddly, she no longer saw the two as inextricably connected. She looked at the picture frame on her desk. "Make it make sense, Mom."

As sheriff, she would have operational control over both crime scenes, at least until tomorrow when the DEA and FBI would arrive in force, searching for those responsible for the death of Acting Special-Agent-In-Charge, Mike Tinsel.

Then, weeks or months later, they would leave, and crystal meth, fentanyl, and other deadly drugs would continue to ravage her community, destroying the people she swore to protect. Neither the outside agencies nor her by-the-book approach had reduced, much less removed, the threat.

But Kemper had.

A scenario played out in her head, and she frowned because she found it appealing. She searched for a better justification for what she intended to do before accepting the simple truth that she wanted to protect a man who had wrongly done something right.

Angela was in uncharted waters, yet she felt confident she could manage the events of the next twenty-four hours. Perhaps for the next week. Maybe for the next ten years.

She met with Rylan and explained the situation. They settled on a strategy. Then, she put in the necessary calls to get Bill Rogers released from jail. She would need her staff attorney's skills in the coming days, and he would need her help untangling himself from his legal issues.

The sheriff had never leveraged her reputation and authority in this manner, and she was alarmed by the thrill it gave her.

Angela closed her eyes and began to take these troubles to the Lord as she always did when overwhelmed by circumstance. This time, she stopped. She could not ask forgiveness for sins planned but not yet committed.

— *Chapter 46* —

The hurricane had not been as devastating as initially feared, although it left Cedar Key with considerable property damage. Regional news coverage aired footage of a dock floating down Dock Street while the mayor proudly announced that most of the town would be up and running within days.

Ground-level businesses near the pier were hit hardest. The storm surge wrecked the flooring inside The Wayward Breeze. The owner called his employees, including Charlene, to let them know it would be at least a month before the open-air restaurant would reopen.

Over at Pinner's Tackle & Gear Store, Tommy's daughters sloshed across the concrete slab in their pink rubber boots. One of his live wells had collapsed, releasing a thousand shrimp into the four inches of standing water. The girls giggled as they scooped up the crustaceans in their kiddie fishing nets. Tommy kept an eye on them as he rearranged displaced shelving and contemplated another phone call to Charlene.

The Holey Moley Cafe had already opened for business. Pidge sat on the wooden deck above the soggy ground, smearing cream cheese on a bagel and fussing on the phone with one of the Hammond brothers about getting roof damage repaired on a property. She pressed the phone to her blouse and shouted a compliment to Gladys, who walked toward the police department, styling a pair of blue rubber boots dotted with yellow dandelions.

Willie Quinn, or Quintus Relaxus Gratitudinus, propped his feet up on one of the outdoor patio tables of his second-floor restaurant. His business would open tomorrow, and he and his cook had just finished a review of inventory. Off in the distance, a familiar liveaboard trawler motored into the channel that cut through the flats. Quinn took a toke of a fat doobie and passed it over to Scotty.

"Looks like Mac's bringing the lady in for supplies," Scotty observed.

"Getting ready for his Fanny," Quinn said. "Luckiest ugly Irishman I ever met."

"What's bothering you, honey?" Martha asked.

"I don't know," Ben replied. "Something don't feel right."

With no damage to their home and power out only briefly, Ben and Martha considered themselves fortunate. Blessed, even. Their phone service had been temporarily disabled, but when it returned, the two of them checked on family and friends and were relieved to find all of them safe and sound.

Martha brought her husband a cup of coffee and sat next to him at the kitchen table. "You haven't called Kemper yet. Is that what's concerning you?"

"Nah, he's a sturdy old goat. I'll call him after I have a look at his ice machines. That way, I can give him a proper update."

Martha stirred French vanilla creamer in her cup. His furrowed brown and sad eyes concerned her. "Then what is it, dear?"

"I thought I had Red Ferguson's number saved in my phone. You remember him, right? From my bible study? Moved away after his wife got into…you know."

"I remember. Such a sad situation."

"Well, I just had this urge to call him. See if he'd like me to go by his old place and look in on Sweetie. I doubt she was prepared for the hurricane, and I'm mad at myself for not thinking about it before the dang thing arrived."

Martha patted his hand. "I'm sure his number is here somewhere. Probably on a sticky note in your old King James."

Mama Thighs fingered the wrapper for another cracker. Only crumbs remained. She sighed and pushed the button on her chair to lift her up, then walked into the kitchen and retrieved an unopened box of Lance crackers from the counter—Captain's Wafers, her favorite. She brought two packets back into the room just as Dr. Phil delivered one of his signature lines: "How's that working for you?"

After settling into a comfortable recline, a grunt drew her attention. It came from the chair next to hers. Same model, but in pine green. Her son grunted a second time. She was getting better at interpreting them. Perhaps this one meant he enjoyed the program. Or maybe he had crapped in his pants again.

Since the overdose, the few words he spoke were all garbled except for when he fell into one of his fits and started babbling about the nursing home. He would shake, and she would pat his head with a cool washcloth until the panic attack ended. Then she would wipe the drool from his mouth and return to her chair, and they would watch another one of her programs.

The nursing home was the place for his physical and speech therapy. Mama Thighs knew how important therapy was for her son's recovery, but she could not bear the thought of further traumatizing him by keeping his appointments. All he really needed, she told herself, was the love and care she could provide right there in her little home by the Quik Stop, his green power recliner next to her red one.

The colors made her think of Christmastime. Her son was, indeed, a precious gift. She opened the new packet of crackers and turned up the volume as applause erupted from the television.

Rylan returned home after an interview with a news reporter covering a story about the area's only hurricane-related fatality—a retired pediatric nurse who died in an electrical fire after her house partially collapsed due to high winds.

He pulled a beer from the fridge and retreated to his back porch to watch the clam boats motoring up the channel. His self-loathing reached a new dimension as he reflected on how easily he had been outmaneuvered by his political rival.

"Let him burn," had been Rylan's initial response when the sheriff told him what Kemper had done at the meth house and possibly at Tinsel's temporary headquarters. He was indignant when the sheriff outlined what she planned to do about it. Rylan changed his tune, however, when she let him know that Charlene would be implicated in these serious crimes if Kemper was arrested.

In hindsight, a different outcome was easy to see had he been wiser. He could have recorded Angela's conspiracy on his phone and used it to force her out of the sheriff's race. Then he would have been the only candidate on the ballot, inevitably becoming the county's top law enforcement officer. And he could have used the recording against Kemper in exchange for another shot at Charlene's affection.

He could have gone even bigger by going public and bringing Ange down along with Kemper. The police chief would be seen as a man so committed to the rule of law that he had turned in his own father while exposing a corrupt sheriff. No telling where that kind of narrative would take him. State Senator? U.S. Representative? Maybe even Governor eventually.

Coulda-woulda-shoulda. That ship had sailed.

Instead, Rylan had gone along with the sheriff's plan, thus implicating himself in the cover-up. Worst of all, protecting himself from exposure meant protecting the man he once again hated—his own father.

Tinsel's laptop disappeared into the Gulf waters eight miles west of Corrigan Reef. The small notepad, however, remained in Rylan's possession. He thumbed through it—for the twentieth time—and wondered what he could do with the curious information scribbled on its pages.

A clam farmer shouted his hello. The police chief wished he could change places with him. He sighed and thought about the badge on his dresser in the bedroom where he slept alone. Next to it was his service weapon, holstered but loaded.

He thought about that, too.

The lady at the bar sipped her wine and glanced at the football game on the television screen. She didn't know what the players were doing, and she reflected on the irony of living in a Southern college town and not knowing the first thing about the sport. Fish out of water, she had once been told.

Although Gainesville was not in the direct path of the hurricane, much of the city had shut down. Some places had not reopened, including her preferred bar, which did not have television screens.

She looked around the near-empty room. An older man, lumpy and balding, sat at the bar a few stools down. Two men half her age drank at a nearby table. The one with the man bun and neatly trimmed beard noticed her looking at them. A minute later, he stood at her side.

"I think I know you," he said.

She didn't hide her contempt or her slurred words. "Oh God, is that the best you can do?"

"Excuse me?"

"That's not much of a pick-up line."

"Oh, I wasn't…I mean, that wasn't a pick-up line. I really do recognize you. You're Katherine Langer, aren't you? Associate Dean, College of Liberal Arts and Sciences?"

"That's only a part of who I am. You left out Professor of Linguistics, author of four monographs and thirty-seven articles published in peer-reviewed journals. Do you know how insulting it is to be diminished in a place like this?"

The bartender stood within earshot. He shook his head as he polished a glass with a hand towel.

"I wasn't trying to insult you," the young man said. "I'm a big admirer. I heard your remarks at the welcoming reception last fall. I'm in the graduate program."

Katty rolled her eyes, dreading the academic banter sure to follow. Paradigm this, modalities that. She wasn't in the mood for man-bun boy. "Run along, child. It's not safe to approach me in the wild. I am a cursed woman."

"Jeez, lady, I was—"

"Lady? Oh, you don't know me at all." She looked him up and down as though appraising his value. "I bet your hands are soft."

The young man opened his mouth to speak but changed his mind. Katty watched him retreat to his table. She turned and took another sip of wine.

"I'd have told you to go fuck yourself," came a voice down the bar.

Katty turned to see the lumpy, balding man smiling at her. She raised an eyebrow. "Excuse me?"

"You heard me." He took a sip from his drink, stood, and moved to the stool next to hers. "Then I would have bought you another drink." He looked at the bartender. "How about another one for the professor here?"

The bartender obliged, pouring her a fourth glass.

"You laid it on thick to that poor boy," the man said. "Almost as thick as your makeup."

Katty lit a cigarette. "Oh, you're a real charmer."

"What are you trying to cover up?" he asked. Her eyes widened. His didn't. "The makeup around your eye. Looks like you're covering up a shiner. Did someone give you a black eye?"

"No one gave me a black eye." She blew a stream of smoke. "I earned it."

They drank in silence until a news update interrupted the game with a comment on the hurricane.

"Cedar Key sure dodged a bullet," the lumpy man said. He turned and looked at Katty. "What do you think, Professor?"

"Why do you bring up Cedar Key? What's so special about that little clam town with its fisher people and smelly bait? I wish it would have drowned in the hurricane."

"That's not a nice thing to say. A lot of good people live there."

"Some good people. And one awful man."

"Is that so?"

"An awful man in an awful house with awful secrets."

"Secrets? Well, that sounds interesting." The lumpy, balding man—a retired FDLE investigator—downed the last of his gin and tonic. He raised the glass for another before turning his attention back to the professor. "And you said something about being cursed. I would love to hear all about it."

In the days that followed, no one in the DEA raised the issue of a proposed immunity agreement when discussing the suspects, leaving Sheriff Lane and Police Chief McRae to conclude that Mike Tinsel had not shared his plans with his inner circle. More than one agent vented their frustration that Tinsel often kept colleagues in the dark until the last minute. If only they had his laptop, which should have been, but wasn't, networked to the regional DEA headquarters.

Soon, the strongest lead pointed back to Atlanta, where the DEA and FBI believed Tank and Paulie had returned after killing the Acting Special-Agent-In-Charge and the rest of the Three Dead Dogs gang, including its leader, Sylvia King. It was a plausible theory, especially since there was no trace of them in or around Cedar Key.

A week later, Angela sat in her office when the call came in that the remaining federal agents had left for Atlanta. There would be follow-up reports and maybe another site visit, but nothing new was expected. The Cedar Key portion of the investigations into Mike Tinsel's murder and the massacre at the meth house were effectively closed.

She closed her eyes. A turn in her favor normally warranted a prayer of gratitude, but she couldn't follow through. Such an act now would be obscene. Grotesque. Like making the Redeemer complicit in the cover-up.

Sheriff Lane opened her eyes. Awards, citations, and certificates hung on the walls around her, attesting to her professionalism and integrity. To her ethical leadership. She drew a heavy sigh, then cursed the name of Kemper McRae.

— *Chapter 47* —

Wesley drove down the driveway to Kemper's house. Only an inch or two of water remained on the ground. He frowned when he saw the whiskey bottle on the table between Kemper and his sister, just as it had been for the last two days.

He assumed Kemper drank to numb the pain of his injuries. On his first visit, Wesley gave him antibiotics and pain relievers clinically approved for both animals and humans. Kemper was more lucid the following day and refused veterinary medicine, opting instead for standard Ibuprofen and some leftover amoxicillin he had in his medicine cabinet.

If Kemper drank to dull the pain, Wesley wondered, what was Charlene's excuse? She seemed like her normal self, talkative and sassy, but she mixed a bourbon and Coke as he exited his vehicle. It wasn't even noon, and he suspected this wasn't her first drink of the day.

In unguarded moments during his earlier visits, Charlene revealed a kind of pain different from Kemper's. Wesley could see it in her eyes. It reminded him of the unfixable sadness children experience when they're told a favorite pet must be put down.

It flashed again as he climbed the porch steps. "You okay, sis?"

"I'm fine and dandy, bro. Shouldn't you be asking this old man that question?"

"I'm getting to it." He paused to pet Julep, who tried to lick an object in his other hand. The dog gave up, scrambled down the steps, and splashed across the yard.

Wesley presented the object. "This here is a Figure 8 Splint, and it'll help immobilize your broken collarbone and relieve pressure on your sternum, which I suspect is also fractured."

Kemper raised an eyebrow. "This hasn't been on any animals, has it?"

Wesley raised his right hand like a good Boy Scout. "Nary a horse, goat, or pig." He winked at his sister. "Just a mangy ole possum or two."

"Looks like a Japanese slingshot," Kemper said by way of consent. Off in the distance, Julep barked.

Wesley slipped the loops around Kemper's shoulders. "I still recommend you go to emergency care or see your doctor. You're not out of the woods. You need X-rays on your chest, and I'm worried about your leg. I can understand not wanting to bring attention to a gunshot wound, and I've not asked any—"

"Stop right there, baby brother," Charlene warned.

Kemper nodded sympathetically. "I appreciate your concern, Wes. A buddy of mine is friends with the physician at the Cross City prison, and they're coming over here later today."

Julep's persistent barking caught Charlene's attention. She sauntered to the end of the porch and leaned on the rail. "What the heck's wrong with your dog? Looks like he's… I dunno… I think he's got something out there."

"Then go see what it is," Kemper said, wincing as Wesley tightened the straps on the splint.

"Don't be a jackass. I'm barefoot."

Wesley turned from his patient to assess the commotion. The dog barked a challenge at something within a cluster of sago palms near the fence line.

Kemper rubbed his shoulder. "Go on out there, Wes, and see what that dang dog is after."

"Then you try to get comfortable with this. I can adjust it when I get back."

Kemper waited for Wesley to leave before he turned his attention to Charlene. "Come on over here, girl."

Charlene sashayed over to him, expecting a kiss on the lips, a peck on the cheek, or at least a pinch on the rear. She got neither.

"Your brother asked if you were okay."

"And I answered him."

"With a lie."

She broke eye contact and sipped her drink. "Nothing's wrong with me. I beat you in cards, didn't I?"

Kemper grabbed her hand. "Darlin', you've drunk more bourbon than I have these last few days. Good thing I buy it by the case. What's wrong?"

She pulled away as she gathered her thoughts, then turned to face him. "I don't like what happened, Kemp. It wasn't right."

"Them boys—"

"I ain't talking about them boys. I'm talking about me. What I did. What you made me do."

"Charlene, look at me. What happened to them boys is on me, not you."

"Those are just words, Kemp. Just words. I wanted to help you because you were hurt, and the next thing I know I'm...." Her voice trailed off. She lit a cigarette. "I was caught up in it, and it was like I couldn't stop. You had no right to involve me that way, and it can't be taken back. Not ever."

"They killed Jerry."

"That's not the point, dammit!" Her voice broke. "You could not have done what you did had I not helped, which means I killed them just as surely as you did, and I never wanted to kill anyone, and I can't forgive you for that, Kemper. I don't think I'll ever forgive you for that."

Kemper's face hardened. "So you're like everyone else. You want justice, but not if you have to get your hands dirty. Or bloody.

Fine. I reckon that's what I'm supposed to do—handle the things delicate people can't."

She looked away. "I ain't delicate."

A moment passed before Kemper spoke again. "So why don't you leave?"

"I dunno. Reckon I'm supposed to go down with the ship, too."

"It's a pelican. He's badly injured."

Wesley climbed the porch steps, cradling the wounded animal in his jacket. Charlene's mood instantly changed. She flicked the cigarette away and cleared the table. Her brother gently set the bird down, its long bill sheathed in a jacket sleeve. What was visible resembled a fleshy ball of mangled feathers.

The veterinarian gripped its webbed feet with one hand and placed his other hand on its chest. He closed his eyes and concentrated. "Weak, very weak."

Julep raised himself up for a closer look, his front paws on the table's edge. He whimpered his concern. Kemper rubbed his dog's head while Charlene stroked the pelican's feathers.

"I don't think his vision is any good," Wesley said as he wiped reddish-yellowish pus from its eye. He pulled the bird's bill from the jacket sleeve and turned its head. "Now be alert. If he jabs you with that bill, it'll leave a mark."

"I don't think it can lift its head, much less get in a jab," Kemper said, but as a precaution he placed a hand over its bill.

The pelican convulsed when Wesley lifted its wing, and its bill slipped free from Kemper's grip. He got a hand on both upper and lower mandibles, and the bird collapsed with its mouth open.

Kemper squinted. "I'll be damned. It's got a treble hook lodged in its pouch."

"That's the least of his troubles." Wesley continued his examination, prodding his fingers around its belly and running his hand across its other wing. He shook his head. "Both wings are broken. Injuries on its torso. Internal bleeding, no doubt. Malnourished. Poor thing is not long for this world."

"What do you mean?" Kemper growled.

"The bird isn't going to make it. He's in pain. He's in shock. Best thing to do is put it down. I got some Pentobarbital in my kit in the truck. It'll just go to sleep. Very humane."

Kemper glared at the veterinarian. "You ain't putting this bird down."

"I'm with Kemp," Charlene said. "You're a vet, baby bro. You need to fix him."

"He can't be fixed. Believe me, I'd love to. But I've seen birds in similar shape, and it never ends well. Even if he doesn't succumb to his injuries, he'll never fly again. He can't forage for food."

"I'll catch him all the dang fish he can eat." Kemper's raised voice triggered a coughing spasm that bent him over. When he recovered, Wesley saw a different man than the one he had treated for injuries. Tall and erect, his jaw firmly set, Kemper fixed piercing and resolute eyes on the veterinarian. "This bird ain't dying. Now, you got anything in that kit that can help?"

"Sure," Wesley replied, warming to the challenge.

"Then go get it." Kemper turned to Charlene. "And you, I got some needle nose pliers in the kitchen drawer, the one with all the ketchup packets. I'll get that hook out, by God."

"I'm on it," Charlene said and quick-stepped into the house.

Kemper turned back to Wesley. "Don't just stand there. Go get that bag and let's get to work."

A smile crossed Wesley's face. "He'll need a lot of attention."

"I've got nothing to do and all day to do it."

Wesley left the porch. Kemper called after him, "And leave that pepto-barbasol crap in your truck. I don't want it nowhere near this bird."

Charlene returned with the pliers and handed them to Kemper. "What are we gonna call him?"

Kemper leaned closer as he maneuvered the tool. "Call him?"

"If he's gonna stay here, he'll need a name. Ain't that right, Julep?"

Kemper twisted his wrist, the pelican flinched, and the hook pulled free. Julep offered a sympathetic lick.

"He's a tough old bird," Charlene said. "Handsome, too, even if he is all beaten up. Reminds me of a certain retired police chief I know."

"You want to call him Chief?"

Charlene rested a finger on pursed lips. "Might get confusing with two chiefs around here. I'm thinking something more nautical, you know, like Captain."

"Captain," Kemper said with his first smile in days. He reached out with his good arm and pulled Charlene close. "I like that. And the Captain is right where he belongs."

THE END

AUTHOR'S NOTE

THANK YOU!
I hope you enjoyed the story! If you did, please share your thoughts with friends and neighbors, on social media posts, and consider posting an honest review on sites like *Amazon* and *Goodreads*.

Stay in touch!

*Your feedback is important to me,
and we'll let you know when Kemper McRae rides again!*

ABOUT THE AUTHOR
Edward Braddy was born in Fort Lauderdale, Florida, and grew up in Dixie County, where the Suwannee River meets the Gulf. He attended Santa Fe College, the University of Florida, and earned a master's degree in history at James Madison University in Harrisonburg, Virginia.

He has worked in higher education for over twenty-five years and has served in elective office, first as a city commissioner and later as mayor in Gainesville, Florida. He and his wife, Pauline, are avid anglers and enjoy the outdoors. They live in Old Town, Florida.

Until next time …